Anne of Ingleside

Anne paused by the Dryad's Bubble on her way back. She loved that old brook so. Every trill of her childhood's laughter that it had ever caught it had held and now seemed to give out again to her listening ears. Her old dreams . . . she could see them reflected in the clear Bubble . . . old vows . . . old whispers . . . the brook kept them all and murmured of them; but there was no one to listen save the wise old spruces in the Haunted Wood that had been listening so long.

L. M. MONTGOMERY

Anne of Ingleside

PUFFIN CLASSICS

PUFFIN BOOKS

UK | USA | Canada | Ireland | Australia
India | New Zealand | South Africa

Puffin Books is part of the Penguin Random House group of companies
whose addresses can be found at global.penguinrandomhouse.com.

puffinbooks.com

Penguin
Random House
UK

First published in Great Britain by George C. Harrap & Co. Ltd 1939
Published in Puffin Books 1983
Reissued in this edition 2015

005

Copyright © L. M. Montgomery, 1939
All rights reserved

Set in 11.5/15pt Minion Pro
Typeset by Palimpsest Book Production Ltd, Falkirk, Stirlingshire
Printed in Great Britain by Clays Ltd, Elcograf S.p.A.

British Library Cataloguing in Publication Data
A CIP catalogue record for this book is available from the British Library

ISBN: 978-0-141-36008-9

www.greenpenguin.co.uk

To W. G. P.

1

'How white the moonlight is tonight,' said Anne Blythe to herself, as she went up the walk of the Wright garden to Diana Wright's front door, where little cherry blossom petals were coming down on the salty, breeze-stirred air.

She paused for a moment to look about her on hills and woods she had loved in olden days and still loved. Dear Avonlea! Glen St Mary was home to her now and had been home for many years, but Avonlea had something that Glen St Mary could never have. Ghosts of herself met her at every turn . . . the fields she had roamed in welcomed her . . . unfading echoes of the old sweet life were all about her; every spot she looked upon had some lovely memory. There were haunted gardens here and there where bloomed all the roses of yesteryear. Anne always loved to come home to Avonlea even when, as now, the reason for her visit had been a sad one. She and Gilbert had stayed for a week. Marilla and Mrs Lynde could not bear to have her go away too soon. Her old porch gable room was always kept for her, and when Anne had gone to it the night of her arrival she found that Mrs Lynde had put a big, homely bouquet of spring flowers in it for her, a bouquet that, when Anne buried her face in it, seemed to hold all the fragrance of unforgotten years. The Anne-who-used-to-be was waiting there for her. Deep, dear old gladnesses stirred in her heart. The gable room was putting its arms around her, enclosing her, enveloping her. She looked lovingly at her old bed with the apple-leaf spread Mrs Lynde had knitted and the spotless pillows trimmed with deep lace Mrs Lynde had crocheted . . . at Marilla's braided rugs on the floor . . . at the mirror that had reflected the face of the little orphan, with her unwritten child's forehead, who had cried herself to sleep there that first night so long ago. Anne forgot that she was the joyful mother of five children . . . with Susan Baker again knitting mysterious bootees at Ingleside . . . and was Anne of Green Gables once more. Mrs Lynde found her still staring dreamily in the mirror when she came in, bringing clean towels.

'It's real good to have you home again, Anne, that's what. It's nine years since you went away, but Marilla and I can't seem to get over missing you. It's not so lonesome since Davy got married. Millie is a real nice little thing . . . such pies! . . . though she's curious as a chipmunk about everything. But I've always said and always will say that there's nobody like you.'

'Ah, but this mirror can't be tricked, Mrs Lynde. It's telling me plainly, "You're not as young as you once were,"' said Anne whimsically.

'You've kept your complexion very well,' said Mrs Lynde consolingly. 'Of course you never had much colour to lose.'

'At any rate I've never a hint of a second chin yet,' said Anne gaily, 'and my old room remembers me, Mrs Lynde. I'm glad. It would hurt me so if I ever came back and found it had forgotten me. And it's wonderful to see the moon rising over the Haunted Wood again.'

'It looks like a great big piece of gold in the sky, doesn't it?' said Mrs Lynde, feeling that she was taking a wild, poetical flight and thankful that Marilla wasn't there to hear.

'Look at those pointed firs coming out against it . . . and the birches in the hollow still holding their arms up to the silver sky. They're big trees now . . . they were just baby things when I came here; that *does* make me feel a bit old.'

'Trees are like children,' said Mrs Lynde. 'It's dreadful the way they grow up the minute you turn your back on them. Look at Fred Wright. He's only thirteen, but he's nearly as tall as his father. There's a hot chicken pie for supper and I made some of my lemon biscuits for you. You needn't be a mite afraid to sleep in that bed. I aired the sheets today, and Marilla didn't know I did it and gave them another airing . . . and Millie didn't know either of us did and gave them a third. I hope Mary Maria Blythe will get out tomorrow, she always enjoys a funeral so.'

'Aunt Mary Maria – Gilbert always calls her that although she was only his father's cousin – always calls me "Annie",' shuddered Anne. 'And the first time she saw me after I was married she said, "It's so strange Gilbert picked you. He could have had so many nice girls." Perhaps that's why I've never liked her, and I know Gilbert doesn't either, though he's too clannish to admit it.'

'Will Gilbert be staying up long?'

'No. He has to go back tomorrow night. He left a patient in a very critical condition.'

'Oh, well, I suppose there isn't much to keep him in Avonlea now, since his mother went last year. Old Mr Blythe never held up his head after her death . . . just hadn't anything left to live for. The Blythes were always like that . . . always set their affections too much on earthly things. It's real sad to think there are none of them left in Avonlea. They were a fine old stock. But then, there's any amount of Sloanes. The Sloanes are still Sloanes, Anne, and will be for ever and ever, world without end. Amen.'

'Let there be as many Sloanes as there will, I'm going out after supper to walk all over the old orchard by moonlight. I suppose I'll have to go to bed finally, though I've always thought sleeping on moonlight nights a waste of time . . . but I'm going to wake early to see the first faint morning light over the Haunted Wood. The sky will turn to coral and the robins will be strutting around . . . perhaps a little grey sparrow will alight on the windowsill, and there'll be gold and purple pansies to look at . . .'

'But the rabbits has et up all the June lily bed,' said Mrs Lynde sadly, as she waddled downstairs, feeling secretly relieved that there need be no more talk about the moon. Anne had always been a bit queer that way. And there did not any longer seem to be much use in hoping she would outgrow it.

Diana came down the walk to meet Anne. Even in the moonlight you saw that her hair was still black and her cheeks rosy and her eyes bright. But the moonlight could not hide that she was something stouter than in years agone . . . and Diana had never been what Avonlea folks called 'skinny'.

'Don't worry, darling, I haven't come to stay . . .'

'As if I'd worry over *that*,' said Diana reproachfully. 'You know I'd far rather spend the evening with you than go to the reception. I feel I haven't seen half enough of you and now you're going back the day after tomorrow. But Fred's brother, you know . . . we've just got to go.'

'Of course you have. And I just ran up for a moment. I came the old way, Di . . . past the Dryad's Bubble . . . through the Haunted Wood . . . past your bowery old garden . . . and along by Willowmere. I even stopped to watch the willows upside down in the water as we always used to do. They've grown so.'

'Everything has,' said Diana with a sigh. 'When I look at young Fred! We've all changed so, except you. You never change, Anne. How *do* you keep so slim? Look at me!'

'A bit matronish, of course,' laughed Anne. 'But you've escaped the middle-aged spread so far, Di. As for my not changing . . . well, Mrs H. B. Donnell agrees with you. She told me at the funeral that I didn't look a day older. But Mrs Harmon Andrews doesn't. *She* said, "Dear me, Anne, how you've failed!" It's all in the beholder's eye – or conscience. The only time I feel I'm getting along a bit is when I look at the pictures in the magazines. The heroes and heroines in them are beginning to look *too young* to me. But never mind, Di, we're going to be girls again tomorrow. That's what I've come up to tell you. We're going to take an afternoon and evening off and visit all our old haunts . . . every one of them. We'll walk over the spring fields and through those ferny old woods. We'll see all the old familiar things we loved and hills where we'll see our youth again. Nothing ever seems impossible in spring, you know. We'll stop feeling parental and responsible and be as giddy as Mrs Lynde really thinks me still in her heart of hearts. There's really no fun in being sensible *all* the time, Diana.'

'My, how like you that sounds! And I'd love to. But . . .'

'There aren't any buts. I know you're thinking, "Who'll get the men's supper" –'

'Not exactly. Anne Cordelia can get the men's supper

as well as I can, if she is only eleven,' said Diana proudly. 'She was going to anyway. I was going to the Ladies' Aid. But I won't. I'll go with you. It will be like having a dream come true. You know, Anne, lots of evenings I sit down and just pretend we're little girls again. We'll take our supper with us . . .'

'And we'll eat it back in Hester Gray's garden . . . I suppose Hester Gray's garden is still there?'

'I suppose so,' said Diana doubtfully. 'I've never been there since I was married. Anne Cordelia explores a lot, but I always tell her she mustn't go too far from home. She loves prowling about the woods, and one day when I scolded her for talking to herself in the garden she said she wasn't talking to herself, she was talking to the spirit of the flowers. You know that dolls' tea-set with the tiny pink rosebuds you sent her for her ninth birthday, there isn't a piece broken . . . she's been so careful. She only uses it when the Three Green People come to tea with her. I can't get out of her who she thinks *they* are. I declare in some ways, Anne, she's far more like you than she is like me.'

'Perhaps there's more in a name than Shakespeare allowed. Don't grudge Anne Cordelia her fancies, Diana. I'm always sorry for children who don't spend a few years in fairyland.'

'Olivia Sloane is our teacher now,' said Diana doubtfully. 'She's a B.A., you know, and just took the school for a year to be near her mother. *She* says children should be made to face realities.'

'Have I lived to hear *you* taking up with Sloanishness, Diana Wright?'

'No . . . no . . . *no*! I don't like her a bit. She has such round, staring blue eyes, like all that clan. And I don't mind Anne Cordelia's fancies. They're pretty, just like yours used to be. I guess she'll get enough "reality" as life goes on.'

'Well, it's settled then. Come down to Green Gables about two and we'll have a drink of Marilla's redcurrant wine . . . she makes it now and then in spite of the minister and Mrs Lynde, just to make us feel real devilish.'

'Do you remember the day you set me drunk on it?' giggled Diana, who did not mind 'devilish' as she would if anybody but Anne used it. Everybody knew Anne didn't really mean things like that. It was just her way.

'We'll have a real do-you-remember day tomorrow, Diana. I won't keep you any longer . . . there's Fred coming with the buggy. Your dress is lovely.'

'Fred made me get a new one for the wedding. I didn't feel we could afford it since we built the new barn, but he said he wasn't going to have *his* wife looking like someone that was sent for and couldn't go when everybody else would be dressed within an inch of her life. Wasn't that like a man?'

'Oh, you sound just like Mrs Elliott at the Glen,' said

Anne severely. 'You want to watch that tendency. Would you like to live in a world where there were no men?'

'It would be horrible,' admitted Diana. 'Yes, yes, Fred, I'm coming. Oh, *all* right! Till tomorrow then, Anne.'

Anne paused by the Dryad's Bubble on her way back. She loved that old brook so. Every trill of her childhood's laughter that it had ever caught it had held and now seemed to give out again to her listening ears. Her old dreams . . . she could see them reflected in the clear Bubble . . . old vows . . . old whispers . . . the brook kept them all and murmured of them; but there was no one to listen save the wise old spruces in the Haunted Wood that had been listening so long.

2

'Such a lovely day . . . made for us,' said Diana. 'I'm afraid it's a pet day though . . . there'll be rain tomorrow.'

'Never mind. We'll drink its beauty today, even if its sunshine is gone tomorrow. We'll enjoy each other's friendship today even if we are to be parted tomorrow. Look at those long, golden-green hills . . . those mist-blue valleys. They're *ours*, Diana. I don't care if that farthest hill is registered in Abner Sloane's name . . . it's *ours* today. There's a west wind blowing. I always feel adventurous when a west wind blows; and we're going to have a perfect ramble.'

They had. All the old dear spots were revisited . . . Lover's Lane, the Haunted Wood, Idlewild, Violet Vale, the Birch Path, Crystal Lake. There were some changes. The little ring of birch saplings in Idlewild, where they had had a playhouse long ago, had grown into big trees; the Birch Path, long untrodden, was matted with bracken, the Crystal Lake had entirely disappeared, leaving only a damp, mossy hollow. But Violet Vale was purple with violets, and the seedling apple tree Gilbert had once found far back in the woods was a huge tree peppered over with tiny, crimson-tipped blossom-buds.

They walked bareheaded. Anne's hair still gleamed like polished mahogany in the sunlight and Diana's was still glossy black. They exchanged gay and understanding, warm and friendly glances. Sometimes they walked in silence . . . Anne always maintained that two people as sympathetic as she and Diana could *feel* each other's thoughts. Sometimes they sprinkled their conversation with do-you-remembers. 'Do you remember the day you fell through the Cobb duckhouse on the Tory Road?' 'Do you remember when we jumped on Aunt Josephine?' 'Do you remember our Story Club?' 'Do you remember Mrs Morgan's visit when you stained your nose red?' 'Do you remember how we signalled to each other from our windows with candles?' 'Do you remember the fun we had at Miss Lavendar's wedding, and Charlotta's blue bows?' 'Do you remember the old Improvement Society?' It almost seemed to them they could hear their old peals of laughter echoing down the years.

The A.V.I.S. was, it seemed, dead. It had petered out soon after Anne's marriage.

'They just couldn't keep it up, Anne. The young people in Avonlea now are not what they were in *our* day.'

'Don't talk as if "our day" were ended, Diana. We're

only fifteen years old and kindred spirits. The air isn't just full of light . . . it *is* light. I'm not sure that I haven't sprouted wings.'

'I feel just that way, too,' said Diana, forgetting that she had tipped the scale at one hundred and fifty-five that morning. 'I often feel that I'd love to be turned into a bird for a little while. It must be wonderful to fly.'

Beauty was all around them. Unsuspected tintings glimmered in the dark demesnes of the woods and glowed in their alluring byways. The spring sunshine sifted through the young green leaves. Gay trills of song were everywhere. There were little hollows where you felt as if you were bathing in a pool of liquid gold. At every turn some fresh spring scent struck their faces . . . spice ferns . . . fir balsam . . . the wholesome odour of newly ploughed fields. There was a lane curtained with wild cherry blossoms; a grassy old field full of tiny spruce trees just starting in life and looking like elvish things that had squatted down among the grasses; brooks not yet 'too broad for leaping'; starflowers under the firs . . . sheets of curly young ferns . . . and a birch tree whence some vandal hand had torn away the white skin wrapper in several places, exposing the tints of the bark below. Anne looked at it so long that Diana wondered. She did not see what Anne did . . . tints ranging from purest creamy white, through exquisite golden tones, growing deeper and deeper until the inmost layer revealed the deepest, richest brown as if to tell that all birches so maiden-like and cool exteriorly, had yet warm-hued feelings.

'The primeval fire of earth at their hearts,' murmured Anne.

And finally, after traversing a little wood glen full of toadstools, they found Hester Gray's garden. Not so much changed. It was still very sweet with dear flowers. There were still plenty of June lilies, as Diana called the narcissi. The row of cherry trees had grown older, but was a drift of snowy bloom. You could still find the central rose walk, and the old dyke was white with strawberry blossoms and blue with violets and green with baby fern. They ate their picnic supper in a corner of it, sitting on some old mossy stones, with a lilac tree behind them flinging purple banners against a low-hanging sun. Both were hungry and both did justice to their own good cooking.

'How nice things taste out of doors,' sighed Diana comfortably. 'That chocolate cake of yours, Anne . . . well, words fail me, but I must get the recipe. Fred would adore it. *He* can eat anything and stay thin. I'm always saying I'm *not* going to eat any more cake, because I'm getting fatter every year. I've such a horror of getting like Great-aunt Sarah, she was so fat she always had to be pulled up when she sat down. But when I see a cake like that, and last night at the reception . . . well, they would all have been so offended if I didn't eat.'

'Did you have a nice time?'

'Oh, yes, in a way. But I fell into Fred's Cousin Henrietta's clutches and it's such a delight to her to tell all about her operations and her sensations while going through them, and how soon her appendix would have burst if she hadn't had it out. "I had fifteen stitches put in it. Oh, Diana, the agony I suffered!" Well, she enjoyed it if I didn't. And she *has* suffered so why shouldn't she have the fun of talking about it now? Jim was so funny. I don't know if Mary Alice liked it altogether . . . well, just one teeny piece . . . may as well be hung for a sheep as a lamb I suppose . . . a mere sliver can't make much difference; one thing he said, that the very night before the wedding he was so scared he felt he'd have to take the boat-train. He said all grooms felt just the same, if they'd be honest about it. You don't suppose Gilbert and Fred felt like that, do you, Anne?'

'I'm sure they didn't.'

'That's what Fred said when I asked him. He said all he was scared of was that I'd change my mind at the last moment like Rose Spencer. But you can never really tell what a man may be thinking. Well, there's no use worrying over it now. What a lovely time we've had this afternoon! We seem to have lived so many old happinesses over. I wish you didn't have to go tomorrow, Anne.'

'Can't you come down to a visit to Ingleside sometime this summer, Diana? . . . before – well, before I'll not be wanting visitors for a while.'

'I'd love to. But it seems impossible to get away from home in the summer. There's always so much to do.'

'Rebecca Dew is coming at long last, of which I'm glad, and I'm afraid Aunt Mary Maria is, too. She hinted as much to Gilbert. He doesn't want her any more than I do . . . but she is "a relation", and so his latch-string must be always out for her.'

'Perhaps I'll get down in the winter. I'd love to see Ingleside again. You have a lovely home, Anne, and a lovely family.'

'Ingleside *is* nice . . . and I do love it now. I once thought I would never love it. I hated it when we went there first . . . hated it for its very virtues. They were an insult to my dear House of Dreams. I remember saying piteously to Gilbert when we left it, "We've been so happy here. We'll never be so happy anywhere else." I revelled in a luxury of homesickness for a while. Then . . . I found little rootlets of affection for Ingleside beginning to sprout out. I fought against it, I really did, but at last I had to give in and admit I loved it. And I've loved it better every year since. It isn't too old a house . . . too old houses are sad. And it isn't too young . . . too young houses are crude. It's just mellow. I love every room in it. Everyone has some fault, but also some virtue – something that distinguishes it from all the others, gives it a personality. I love all those magnificent trees on the lawn. I don't know who planted them, but every time I go upstairs I stop on the landing . . . you know that quaint window on the landing with the broad, deep seat . . . and sit there looking out for a moment and say, "God bless the man who planted those trees, whoever he was." We've really too many trees about the house, but we wouldn't give up one.'

'That's just like Fred. He worships that big willow south of the house. It spoils the view from the parlour windows, as I've told him again and again, but he only says, "Would you cut a lovely thing like that down even if it does shut out the view?" So the willow stays, and it *is* lovely. That's why we've called our place Lone Willow Farm. I love the name Ingleside. It's such a nice, homey name.'

'That's what Gilbert said. We had quite a time deciding on a name. We tried out several, but they didn't seem to *belong*. But when we thought of Ingleside we knew it was the right one. I'm glad we have a nice big roomy house . . . we need it with our family. The children love it, too, small as they are.'

'They're such darlings.' Diana slyly cut herself another 'sliver' of the chocolate cake. 'I think my own are pretty nice, but there's really something about yours . . . and your twins! *That* I do envy you. I've always wanted twins.'

'Oh, I couldn't get away from twins, they're my destiny. But I'm disappointed mine don't look alike, not one bit alike. Nan's pretty, though, with her brown hair and eyes and her lovely complexion. Di is her father's favourite, because she has green eyes and red hair . . . red hair with a swirl to it. Shirley is the apple of Susan's eye. I was ill so long after he was born, and she looked after him till I really believe she thinks he is her own; she calls him her "little brown boy" and spoils him shamefully.'

'And he's still so small you can creep in to find if he has kicked off the clothes and tuck him in again,' said Diana enviously. 'Jack's nine, you know, and he doesn't want me to do that now. He says he's too big. And I loved so to do it! Oh, I wish children didn't grow up so soon.'

'None of mine have got to that stage yet . . . though I've noticed that since Jem began to go to school he doesn't want to hold my hand any more when we walk through the village,' said Anne with a sigh. 'But he and Walter and Shirley all want me to tuck them in yet. Walter sometimes makes quite a ritual of it.'

'And you don't have to worry yet over what they're going to be. Now, Jack is crazy to be a soldier when he grows up . . . a soldier. Just fancy!'

'I wouldn't worry over that. He'll forget about it when another fancy seizes him. War is a thing of the past. Jem imagines he is going to be a sailor, like Captain Jim, and Walter is by way of being a poet. He isn't like any of the others. But they all love trees and they all love playing in "the Hollow", as it's called. A little valley just below Ingleside, with fairy paths and a brook. A very ordinary place . . . just "the Hollow" to others but to them fairy-land. They've all got their faults, but they're not such a bad little gang . . . and luckily there's always enough love to go round. Oh, I'm glad to think that this time tomorrow night I'll be back at Ingleside, telling my babies stories at bedtime and giving Susan's calceolarias and ferns their meed of praise. Susan has "luck" with ferns. No one can grow them like her. I can praise her ferns honestly . . . but the calceolarias, Diana! They don't look like flowers to me at all. But I never hurt Susan's feeling by telling her so . . . I always get around it somehow. Providence has never failed me yet. Susan is such a duck, I can't imagine what I'd do without her. And I remember once calling her "an outsider". Yes, it's lovely to think of going home and yet I'm sad to leave Green Gables too. It's so beautiful here . . . with Marilla . . . and *you*. Our friendship has always been a very lovely thing, Diana.'

'Yes . . . and we've always . . . I mean . . . I never could say things like you, Anne . . . but we *have* kept our old "solemn vow and promise", haven't we?'

'Always, and always will.'

Anne's hand found its way into Diana's. They sat for a long time in a silence too sweet for words. Long, still evening shadows fell over the grasses and the flowers and the green reaches of the meadows beyond. The sun went down, grey-pink shades of sky deepened and paled behind the pensive trees . . . the spring twilight took possession of Hester Gray's garden where nobody ever walked now. Robins were sprinkling the evening air with flute-like whistles. A great star came out over the white cherry trees.

'The first star is always a miracle,' said Anne dreamily.

'I could sit here for ever,' said Diana. 'I hate the thought of leaving it.'

'So do I, but after all we've only been pretending to be fifteen. We've got to remember our family cares. How those lilacs smell! Has it ever occurred to you, Diana, that there is something not quite . . . chaste . . . in the scent of lilac blossoms? Gilbert laughs at such a notion; he loves them, but to me they always seem to be remembering some secret, *too*-sweet thing.'

'They're too heavy for the house, I always think,' said Diana. She picked up the plate which held the remainder of the chocolate cake . . . looked at it longingly . . . shook her head, and packed it in the basket with an expression of great nobility and self-denial on her face.

'Wouldn't it be fun, Diana, if now, as we went home, we were to meet our old selves running along Lover's Lane?'

Diana gave a little shiver.

'No-o-o, I don't think that would be funny, Anne. I hadn't noticed it was getting so dark. It's all right to fancy things in daylight, but . . .'

They went quietly, silently, lovingly home together, with the sunset glory burning on the old hills behind them and their old unforgotten love burning in their hearts.

3

Anne ended a week that had been full of pleasant days by taking flowers to Matthew's grave the next morning, and in the afternoon she took the train from Carmody home. For a time she thought of all the old beloved things behind her and then her thoughts ran ahead of her to the beloved things before her. Her heart sang all the way because she was going home to a joyous house, a house where everyone who crossed its threshold knew it was a *home*, a house that was filled all the time with laughter and silver mugs and snapshots and babies . . . precious things with curls and chubby knees . . . and rooms that would welcome her . . . where the chairs waited patiently and the dresses in her closet were expecting her . . . where little anniversaries were always being celebrated and little secrets were always being whispered.

'It's lovely to feel you like going home,' thought Anne, fishing out of her purse a certain letter from a small son over which she had laughed gaily the night before, reading it proudly to the Green Gables folks, the first letter she had ever received from any of her children. It was quite a nice little letter for a seven-year-old who had been going to school only a year to write, even though Jem's spelling was a bit uncertain and there was a big blob of ink in one corner.

'Di cryed and cryed all night because Tommy Drew told her he was going to burn her doll at the steak. Susan tells us nice tails at night but she isn't you, Mummy . . . she let me help her sow the beats last night . . .'

'*How* could I have been happy for a whole week away from them all?' thought the chatelaine of Ingleside self-reproachfully.

'How nice to have someone meet you at the end of a journey!' she cried, as she stepped off the train at Glen St Mary into Gilbert's waiting arms. She could never be sure Gilbert would meet her, somebody was always dying or being born; but no homecoming ever seemed just right to Anne unless he did. And he had on such a nice new light-grey suit! (*How glad I am I put on this frilly eggshell blouse with my brown suit, even if Mrs Lynde thought I was crazy to wear it travelling. If I hadn't I wouldn't have looked so nice for Gilbert.*)

Ingleside was all lighted up, with gay Japanese lanterns hanging on the veranda. Anne ran gaily along the walk bordered by daffodils.

'Ingleside, I'm here,' she called.

They were all around her . . . laughing, exclaiming, jesting, with Susan Baker smiling properly in the background. Every one of the children had a bouquet picked specially for her, even the two-year-old Shirley.

'Oh, this *is* a nice welcome home! Everything about Ingleside looks so happy. It's splendid to think my family are so glad to see me.'

'If you ever go away from home again, Mummy,' said Jem solemnly, 'I'll go and take appensitis.'

'How do you go about taking it?' asked Walter.

'S . . . s . . . sh.' Jem nudged Walter secretly and whispered, 'There's a pain somewhere, I know, but I just want to scare Mummy so she *won't* go away.'

Anne wanted to do a hundred things first, hug everybody, run out in the twilight and gather some of her pansies . . . you found pansies everywhere at Ingleside . . . pick up the little well-worn doll lying on the rug, hear all the juicy titbits of gossip and news, everyone contributing something. How Nan had got the top off a tube of vaseline up her nose when the doctor was out on a case and Susan had all but gone distracted. 'I assure you it was an anxious time, Mrs Doctor dear' . . . how Mrs Jud Palmer's cow had eaten fifty-seven wire nails and had to have a vet from Charlottetown; how absent-minded Mrs Fenner Douglas had gone to church *bareheaded*; how Dad had dug all the dandelions out of the lawn . . . 'between babies, Mrs Doctor dear . . . he's had eight while you are away'; how

Mr Tom Flagg had dyed his moustache . . . 'and his wife only dead two years'; how Rose Maxwell of the Harbour Head had jilted Jim Hudson of the Upper Glen, and he had sent her a bill for all he had spent on her . . . what a splendid turnout there had been at Mrs Amasa Warren's funeral; how Carter Flagg's cat had had a piece bitten right out of the root of its tail; how Shirley had been found in the stable standing right under one of the horses . . . 'Mrs Doctor dear, never shall I be the same woman again'; how there was sadly too much reason to fear that the blue plum trees were developing black knot; how Di had gone about the whole day singing, 'Mummy's coming home today, home today, home today' to the tune of 'Merrily We Roll Along'; how the Joe Reeses had a kitten that was cross-eyed because it had been born with its eyes open; how Jem had inadvertently sat on some flypaper before he had put his little trousers on . . . and how the Shrimp had fallen into the soft-water puncheon in the barn. 'He was nearly drowned, Mrs Doctor dear, but luckily the doctor heard his howls in the nick of time and pulled him out by his hindlegs.' (What is the nick of time, Mummy?)

'He seems to have recovered nicely from it,' said Anne, stroking the glossy black and white curves of a contented pussy with huge jowls, purring on a chair in the firelight. It was never quite safe to sit down on a chair at Ingleside without first making sure there wasn't a cat in it. Susan, who had not cared much for cats to begin with, vowed she had to learn to like them in self-defence. As for the Shrimp, Gilbert had called him that a year ago when Nan had brought the miserable, scrawny kitten home from the village where some boys had been tormenting it, and the name clung, though it was very inappropriate now.

'But . . . Susan! What has become of Gog and Magog? Oh . . . they haven't been broken, have they?'

'No, no, Mrs Doctor dear,' exclaimed Susan, turning a deep brick-red from shame and dashing out of the room. She returned shortly with the two china dogs which always presided at the hearth of Ingleside. 'I do not see how I could have forgotten to put them back before you came. You see, Mrs Doctor dear, Mrs Charles Day from Charlottetown called here the day after you left . . . and you know how very precise and proper she is. Walter thought he ought to entertain her and he started in by pointing out the dogs to her. "This one is God and this is My God," he said, poor innocent child. I was horrified, though I thought that die I would to see Mrs Day's face. I explained as best I could, for I did not want her to think us a profane family, but I decided I would just put the dogs away in the china closet, out of sight, till you got back.'

'Mummy, can't we have supper soon?' said Jem pathetically. 'I've got a gnawful feeling in the pit of my stomach. And oh, Mummy, we've made everybody's favourite dish.'

'We, as the flea said to the elephant, have done that

very thing,' said Susan with a grin. 'We thought that your return should be suitably celebrated, Mrs Doctor dear. And now where is Walter? It is his week to ring the gong for meals, bless his heart.'

Supper was a gala meal . . . and putting all the babies to bed afterwards was a delight. Susan even allowed her to put Shirley to bed, seeing what a very special occasion it was.

'This is no common day, Mrs Doctor dear,' she said solemnly.

'Oh, Susan, there is no such thing as a common day. *Every* day has something about it no other day has. Haven't you noticed?'

'How true that is, Mrs Doctor dear. Even last Friday now, when it rained all day, and was so dull, my big pink geranium showed buds at last after refusing to bloom for three long years. And have you noticed the calceolarias, Mrs Doctor dear?'

'Noticed them! I never saw such calceolarias in my life, Susan. How *do* you manage it?' (*There, I've made Susan happy and haven't told a fib. I never did see such calceolarias . . . thank heaven!*)

'It is the result of constant care and attention, Mrs Doctor dear, but there is something I think I ought to speak of. I think Walter *suspects something*. No doubt some of the Glen children have said things to him. So many children nowadays know so much more than is fitting. Walter said to me the other day, very thoughtful-like, "Susan," he said, "are babies *very* expensive?" I was a bit dumbfounded, Mrs Doctor dear, but I kept my head. "Some folks think they are luxuries," I said, "but at Ingleside we think they are necessities." And I reproached myself with having complained aloud about the shameful price of things in all the Glen stores. I am afraid it worried the child. But if he says anything to you, Mrs Doctor dear, you will be prepared.'

'I'm sure you handled the situation beautifully, Susan,' said Anne gravely. 'And I think it is time they all knew what we are hoping for.'

But the best of all was when Gilbert came to her, as she stood at her window, watching a fog creeping in from the sea, over the moonlit dunes and the harbour, right into the long narrow valley upon which Ingleside looked down and in which nestled the village of Glen St Mary.

'To come back at the end of a hard day and find you! Are you happy, Annest of Annes?'

'Happy!' Anne bent to sniff a vaseful of apple blossoms Jem had set on her dressing table. She felt surrounded and encompassed by love. 'Gilbert, dear, it's been lovely to be Anne of Green Gables again for a week, but it's a hundred times lovelier to come back and be Anne of Ingleside.'

4

'Absolutely not,' said Dr Blythe, in a tone Jem understood.

Jem knew there was no hope of Dad's changing his mind or that Mother would try to change it for him. It was plain to be seen that on this point Mother and Dad were as one. Jem's hazel eyes darkened with anger and disappointment as he looked at his cruel parents, *glared* at them, all the more glaringly that they were so maddening indifferent to his glares and went on eating their suppers as if nothing at all were wrong and out of joint. Of course, Aunt Mary Maria noticed his glares . . . nothing ever escaped Aunt Mary Maria's mournful, pale-blue eyes . . . but she only seemed amused at them.

Bertie Shakespeare Drew had been up playing with Jem all the afternoon, Walter having gone down to the old House of Dreams to play with Kenneth and Persis Ford; and Bertie Shakespeare had told Jem that all the Glen boys were going down to the Harbour Mouth that evening to see Captain

Bill Taylor tattoo a snake on his cousin Joe Drew's arm. He, Bertie Shakespeare, was going and wouldn't Jem come too? It would be such fun. Jem was at once crazy to go; and now he had been told that it was utterly out of the question.

'For one reason among many,' said Dad, 'it's much too far for you to go down to the Harbour Mouth with those boys. They won't get back till late, and your bedtime is supposed to be at eight, son.'

'*I* was sent to bed at seven every night of my life when I was a child,' said Aunt Mary Maria.

'You must wait till you are older, Jem, before you go so far away in the evenings,' said Mother.

'You said that last week,' cried Jem indignantly, 'and I *am* older now. You'd think I was a baby! Bertie's going, and I'm just as old as him.'

'There's measles around,' said Aunt Mary Maria darkly. 'You might catch measles, James.'

Jem hated to be called James. And she always did it.

'I *want* to catch measles –' he muttered rebelliously. Then, catching Dad's eye instead, subsided. Dad would never let anyone 'talk back' to Aunt Mary Maria. Jem hated Aunt Mary Maria. Aunt Diana and Aunt Marilla were such ducks of aunts, but an aunt like Aunt Mary Maria was something wholly new in Jem's experience.

'All right,' he said defiantly, looking at Mother, so that nobody could suppose he was talking to Aunt Mary

Maria, 'if you don't *want* to love me you don't *have* to. But will you like it if I just go away 'n' shoot tigers in Africa?'

'There are no tigers in Africa, dear,' said Mother gently.

'Lions, then!' shouted Jem. They were determined to put him in the wrong, were they? They were bound to laugh at him, were they? He'd show them! 'You can't say there's no lions in Africa. There's *millions* of lions in Africa. Africa's just *full* of lions!'

Mother and Father only smiled again, much to Aunt Mary Maria's disapproval. Impertinence in children should never be condoned.

'Meanwhile,' said Susan, torn between her love for, and sympathy with, Little Jem and her conviction that Dr and Mrs Doctor were perfectly right in refusing to let him go away down to the Harbour Mouth with that village gang to that disreputable, drunken old Captain Bill Taylor's place, 'here is your gingerbread and whipped cream, Jem, dear.'

Gingerbread and whipped cream was Jem's favourite dessert. But tonight it had no charm to soothe his stormy soul.

'I don't want any,' he said sulkily. He got up and marched away from the table, turning at the door to hurl a final defiance.

'I ain't going to bed till nine o'clock anyhow. And when I'm grown up I'm *never* going to bed. I'm going to stay up all night, every night, and get tattooed *all over*. I'm just going to be as bad as bad can be. You'll see.'

'"I'm not" would be so much better than "ain't", dear,' said Mother.

Could *nothing* make them feel?

'I suppose nobody wants *my* opinion, Annie, but if I had talked to my parents like that when I was a child I would have been whipped within an inch of my life,' said Aunt Mary Maria. 'I think it is a great pity the birch rod is so neglected now in some homes.'

'Little Jem is not to blame,' snapped Susan, seeing that Dr and Mrs Doctor were not going to say anything. But if Mary Maria Blythe was going to get away with that, she, Susan, would know the reason why. 'Bertie Shakespeare Drew put him up to it, filling him up with what fun it would be to see Joe Drew tattooed. He was here all the afternoon and sneaked into the kitchen and took the best aluminium saucepan to use as a helmet. Said they were playing soldiers. Then they made boats out of shingles and got soaked to the bone sailing them in the Hollow brook. And after that they went hopping about the yard for a solid hour, making the weirdest noises, pretending they were frogs. Frogs! No wonder Little Jem is tired out and not himself. He is the best-behaved child that ever lived when he is not worn to a frazzle and that you may tie to.'

Aunt Mary Maria said nothing aggravatingly. She never talked to Susan Baker at mealtimes, thus expressing her disapproval over Susan being allowed to 'sit with the family' at all.

Anne and Susan had thrashed that out before Aunt Mary Maria had come. Susan, who 'knew her place', never sat or expected to sit with the family when there was company at Ingleside.

'But Aunt Mary Maria isn't company,' said Anne. 'She's just one of the family, and so are you, Susan.'

In the end Susan gave in, not without a secret satisfaction that Mary Maria Blythe would see that she was no common hired girl. Susan had never met Aunt Mary Maria, but a niece of Susan's, the daughter of her sister Matilda, had worked for her in Charlottetown and had told Susan all about her.

'I am not going to pretend to you, Susan, that I'm overjoyed at the prospect of a visit from Aunt Mary Maria, especially just now,' said Anne frankly. 'But she has written Gilbert asking if she may come for a few weeks . . . and you know how the doctor is about such things . . .'

'As he has a perfect right to be,' said Susan staunchly. 'What's a man to do but stand by his own flesh and blood? But as for a few weeks . . . well, Mrs Doctor dear, I don't want to look on the dark side of things . . . but my sister Matilda's sister-in-law come to visit *her* for a few weeks and stayed for twenty years.'

'I don't think we need dread anything like that, Susan,' smiled Anne. 'Aunt Mary Maria has a very nice home of her own in Charlottetown. But she is finding it very big and lonely. Her mother died two years ago, you know . . . she was eighty-five, and Aunt Mary Maria was very good to her and misses her very much. Let's make her visit as pleasant as we can, Susan.'

'I'll do what in me lies, Mrs Doctor dear. Of course, we must put another board in the table, but after all is said and done it's better to be lengthening the table than shortening it down.'

'We mustn't have flowers on the table, Susan, because I understand they give her asthma. And pepper makes her sneeze, so we'd better not have it. She is subject to frequent bad headaches, too, so we must really try not to be noisy.'

'Good grief! Well, I've never noticed you and the doctor making much noise. And if I want to yell I can go to the middle of the maple bush; but if our poor children have to keep quiet *all* the time because of Mary Maria Blythe's headaches . . . you'll excuse me for saying I think it's going a little too far, Mrs Doctor dear.'

'It's just for a few weeks, Susan.'

'Let us hope so. Oh, well, Mrs Doctor dear, we just have to take the lean streaks with the fat in this world,' was Susan's final word.

So Aunt Mary Maria came, demanding immediately upon her arrival if they had had the chimneys cleaned recently. She had, it appeared, a great dread of fire. 'And I've always said that the chimneys of this house aren't nearly tall enough. I hope my bed has been well aired, Annie. Damp bed linen is terrible.'

She took possession of the Ingleside guest room . . . and incidentally of all the other rooms in the house except Susan's. Nobody hailed her arrival with frantic delight. Jem, after one look at her, slipped out to the kitchen and whispered to Susan, 'Can we laugh while she's here, Susan?' Walter's eyes brimmed with tears at sight of her and he had to be hustled ignominiously out of the room. The twins did not wait to be hustled, but ran of their own accord. Even the Shrimp, Susan averred, went and had a fit in the backyard. Only Shirley stood his ground, gazing fearlessly at her out of his round brown eyes from the safe anchorage of Susan's lap and arm. Aunt Mary Maria thought the Ingleside children had very bad manners. But what could you expect when they had a mother who 'wrote for the papers' and a father who thought they were perfection just because they were *his* children and a hired girl like Susan Baker who never knew her place. But she, Mary Maria Blythe, would do her best for poor Cousin John's grandchildren as long as she was at Ingleside.

'Your grace is much too short, Gilbert,' she said disapprovingly at her first meal. 'Would you like me to say grace for you while I am here? It will be a better example to your family.'

Much to Susan's horror Gilbert said he would, and Aunt Mary Maria said grace at supper. 'More like a prayer than a grace,' Susan sniffed over her dishes. Susan privately agreed with her niece's description of Mary Maria Blythe. 'She always seems to be smelling a bad smell, Aunt Susan. Not an unpleasant odour . . . just a bad smell.' Gladys had a way of putting things, Susan reflected. And yet, to anyone less prejudiced than Susan, Miss Mary Maria Blythe was not ill-looking for a lady of fifty-five. She had what she believed were 'aristocratic features', framed by always sleek grey crimps which seemed to insult Susan's spiky little knob of grey hair. She dressed very nicely, wore long jet earrings in her ears and fashionably high-boned net collars on her lean throat.

'At least, we don't need to be ashamed of her appearance,' reflected Susan. But what Aunt Mary Maria would have thought if she had known Susan was consoling herself on such grounds must be left to the imagination.

5

Anne was cutting a vaseful of June lilies for her room and another of Susan's peonies for Gilbert's desk in the library . . . the milky-white peonies with the blood-red neck at their hearts, like a god's kiss. The air was coming alive after the unusually hot June day and one could hardly tell whether the harbour were silver or gold.

'There's going to be a wonderful sunset tonight, Susan,' she said, looking in at the kitchen window as she passed it.

'I cannot admire the sunset until I have got my dishes washed, Mrs Doctor dear,' protested Susan.

'It will be gone by that time, Susan. Look at that enormous white cloud towering up over the Hollow, with its rosy pink top. Wouldn't you like to fly up and light on it?'

Susan had a vision of herself flying up over the glen, dishcloth in hand, to that cloud. It did not appeal to her. But allowances must be made for Mrs Doctor just now.

'There's a new, vicious kind of bug eating the rose-bushes,' went on Anne. 'I must spray them tomorrow. I'd like to do it tonight . . . this is just the kind of evening I love to work in the garden. Things are growing tonight. I hope there'll be gardens in heaven, Susan . . . gardens we can work in, I mean, and help things to grow.'

'But not bugs, surely,' protested Susan.

'No-o-o, I suppose not. But a *completed* garden wouldn't really be any fun, Susan. You have to work in a garden yourself or you miss its meaning. I want to weed and dig and transplant and change and prune. And I want the flowers I love in heaven . . . I'd rather my own pansies than the asphodel, Susan.'

'Why can't you put in the evening as you want to?' broke in Susan, who thought Mrs Doctor was really getting a little wild.

'Because the doctor wants me to go for a drive with him. He is going to see poor old Mrs John Paxton. She is dying . . . he can't do her any good . . . he has done everything he can . . . but she does like to have him drop in.'

'Oh, well, Mrs Doctor dear, we all know that nobody can die or be born without him hereabouts, and it is a nice evening for a drive. I think I'll take a walk down to the village myself and replenish our pantry after I put the twins and Shirley to bed and manure Mrs Aaron Ward. She isn't blooming as she ought to. Miss Blythe has just gone upstairs, sighing at every step, saying one of her headaches is coming on, so there'll be a little peace and quiet for the evening at least.'

'See that Jem goes to bed in good time, will you, Susan?'

said Anne, as she went away through the evening that was like a cup of fragrance that had spilled over. 'He's really much tireder than he thinks he is. And he never wants to go to bed. Walter is not coming home tonight; Leslie asked if he might stay there.'

Jem was sitting on the steps of the side door, one bare foot hooked over his knee, scowling viciously at things in general and at an enormous moon behind the Glen church spire in particular. Jem didn't like such big moons.

'Take care your face doesn't freeze like that,' Aunt Mary Maria had said as she passed him on her way into the house.

Jem scowled more blackly than ever. He didn't care if his face did freeze like that. He hoped it would. 'Go 'way and don't come tagging after me all the time,' he told Nan, who had crept out to him after Father and Mother had driven away.

'Crosspatch!' said Nan. But before she trotted off she laid down on the step beside him the red candy lion she had brought out to him.

Jem ignored it. He felt more abused than ever. He wasn't being used right. Everybody picked on him. Hadn't Nan that very morning said, '*You* weren't born at Ingleside like the rest of us.' Di had et his chocolate rabbit that forenoon, though she *knew* it was his rabbit. Even Walter had deserted him, going away to dig wells in the sand with Ken and Persis Ford. Great fun that! And he wanted so much to go with Bertie to see the tattooing. Jem was sure he had never wanted anything so much in his life before. He wanted to see the wonderful, full-rigged ship that Bertie said was always on Captain Bill's mantelpiece. It was a mean shame, that's what it was.

Susan brought him out a big slice of cake covered with maple frosting and nuts, but . . . 'No, thank you,' said Jem stonily. Why hadn't she saved some of the gingerbread and cream for him? S'pose the rest of them had et it all. Pigs! He plunged into a deeper gulf of gloom. The gang would be on their way to the Harbour Mouth by now. He just couldn't bear the thought. He'd *got* to do something to get square with folks. S'posin' he sliced Di's sawdust giraffe open on the living-room rug? That would make old Susan mad . . . Susan with her nuts, when she knew he hated nuts in frosting. S'posin' he went and drew a moustache on that picture of the cherub on the calendar in her room? He had always hated that fat, pink, smiling cherub because it looked just like Sissy Flagg, who had told round school that Jem Blythe was her beau. Hers! Sissy Flagg! But Susan thought that cherub lovely.

S'posin' he scalped Nan's doll? S'posin' he whacked the nose off Gog or Magog . . . or both of them? Maybe that would make Mother see he wasn't a boy any longer. Just wait till next spring. He had brought her mayflowers for years and years and years, ever since he was four, but he wouldn't do it next spring. No, sir! S'posin' he et a lot of the little green apples on the early tree and got nice and sick? Maybe *that* would scare them. S'posin' he never washed behind his ears again? S'posin' he made faces at everybody in church next Sunday? S'posin' he put a caterpillar on Aunt Mary Maria . . . a big, striped, woolly caterpillar? S'posin' he ran away to the harbour and hid in Captain David Reese's ship and sailed out of the harbour in the morning on his way to South America? Would they be sorry *then*? S'posin' he never came back? S'posin' he went hunting jaggers in Brazil? Would they be sorry *then*? No, he bet they wouldn't. Nobody loved him. There was a hole in his pants pocket. Nobody had mended it. Well, *he* didn't care. He'd just show that hole to everybody in the Glen and let people see how neglected he was. His wrongs surged up and overwhelmed him.

Tick-tack . . . tick-tack . . . tick-tack . . . went the old grandfather clock in the hall that had been brought to Ingleside after Grandfather Blythe's death . . . a deliberate old clock dating from the days when there was such a thing as time. Generally Jem loved it, now he hated it. It seemed to be laughing at him. 'Ha, ha, bedtime is coming. The other fellows can go to the Harbour Mouth, but you go to bed. Ha, ha . . . ha, ha . . . ha, ha!'

Why did he have to go to bed every night? Yes, why?

Susan came out on her way to the Glen and looked tenderly at the small, rebellious figure.

'You needn't go to bed till I get back, Little Jem,' she said indulgently.

'I ain't going to bed tonight,' said Jem fiercely. '*I'm* going to run away, that's what I'm going to do, old Susan Baker. I'm going to go and jump into the pond, old Susan Baker.'

Susan did not enjoy being called old, even by Little Jem. She stalked away in a grim silence. He *did* need a bit of disciplining. The Shrimp, who had followed her out, feeling a yearning for companionship, squatted down on his black haunches before Jem, but got only a glare for his pains. 'Clear out! Sitting there on your bottom, staring like Aunt Mary Maria! Scat! Oh, you won't, won't you! Then take that.'

Jem shied Shirley's little tin wheelbarrow that was lying handily near at the Shrimp, who fled with a plaintive yowl to the sanctuary of the sweetbriar hedge. Look at that! Even the family cat hated him! What was the use of going on living?

He picked up the candy lion. Nan had eaten the tail and most of the hindquarters, but it was still quite a lion. Might as well eat it. It might be the last lion he'd ever eat. By the time Jem had finished the lion and licked his fingers he had made up his mind what he was going to do. It was the only thing a fellow *could* do when a fellow wasn't allowed to do *anything*.

6

'Why in the world is the house lighted up like that?' exclaimed Anne, when she and Gilbert turned in at the gate at eleven o'clock. 'Company must have come.'

But there was no company visible when Anne hurried into the house. Nor was anyone else visible. There was a light in the kitchen . . . in the living room . . . in the dining room . . . in Susan's room and the upstairs hall . . . but no sign of an occupant.

'What do you suppose –' began Anne, but she was interrupted by the ringing of the telephone. Gilbert answered, listened for a moment, uttered an ejaculation of horror, and tore out without even a glance at Anne. Evidently something dreadful had happened and there was no time to be wasted in explanations.

Anne was used to this . . . as the wife of a man who waits on life and death must be. With a philosophical shrug she removed her hat and coat. She felt a trifle annoyed with Susan, who really shouldn't have gone out and left all the lights blazing and all the doors wide open.

'Mrs . . . Doctor . . . dear,' said a voice that could not possibly be Susan's . . . but was.

Anne stared at Susan. Such a Susan . . . hatless . . . her grey hair full of bits of hay . . . her print dress shockingly stained and discoloured. And her face!

'Susan . . . what has happened? Susan!'

'Little Jem has disappeared.'

'Disappeared?' Anne stared stupidly. 'What do you mean? He can't have disappeared!'

'He has,' gasped Susan, wringing her hands. 'He was on the side steps when I went to the Glen. I was back before dark . . . and he was not there. At first . . . I wasn't scared, but I could not find him anywhere. I have searched every room in the house . . . he said he was going to run away . . .'

'Nonsense! He wouldn't do that, Susan. You have worked yourself up unnecessarily. He must be somewhere about . . . he has fallen asleep . . . he *must* be somewhere around.'

'I've looked everywhere . . . everywhere. I've combed the grounds and the outhouses. Look at my dress. I remembered he always said it would be such fun to sleep in the hay loft. So I went there, and fell through that hole in the corner into one of the mangers in the stable . . . and lit on a nest of eggs. It is a mercy I did not break a leg . . . if anything can be a mercy when Little Jem is lost.'

Anne still refused to feel perturbed.

'Do you think he could have gone to the Harbour Mouth with the boys after all, Susan? He has never disobeyed a command before, but . . .'

'No, he did not, Mrs Doctor dear . . . the blessed lamb did not disobey. I rushed down to Drews' after I had searched everywhere and Bertie Shakespeare had just got home. He said Jem had not gone with them. The pit seemed to drop out of my stomach. You had trusted him to me and . . . I phoned Paxtons' and they said you had been there and gone they did not know where.'

'We drove to Lowbridge to call on the Parkers . . .'

'I phoned everywhere I thought you could be. Then I went back to the village . . . the men have started out to search . . .'

'Oh, Susan, was that necessary?'

'Mrs Doctor dear, I had looked everywhere . . . everywhere that child could be. Oh, what I have gone through this night! . . . and he *said* he was going to jump into the pond . . .'

In spite of herself a queer little shiver ran over Anne. Of course, Jem wouldn't jump into the pond . . . that was nonsense . . . but there was an old dory on it which Carter Flagg used for trouting, and Jem might, in his defiant mood of the earlier evening, have tried to row about the pond in it; he had often wanted to, he might even have fallen into the pond trying to untie the dory. All at once her fear took terrible shape.

'And I haven't the slightest idea where Gilbert has gone,' she thought wildly.

'What's all this fuss about?' demanded Aunt Mary Maria, suddenly appearing on the stairs, her head surrounded by a halo of crimpers and her body encased in a dragon-embroidered dressing gown. 'Can't a body *ever* get a quiet night's sleep in this house?'

'Little Jem has disappeared,' said Susan again, too much in the grip of terror to resent Miss Blythe's tone. 'His mother trusted me . . .'

Anne had gone to search the house for herself. Jem must be somewhere! He was not in his room . . . the bed was undisturbed . . . he was not in the twins' room . . . in hers . . . he was . . . he was nowhere in the house. Anne, after a pilgrimage from garret to cellar, returned to the living room in a condition that was suddenly akin to panic.

'I don't want to make you nervous, Annie,' said Aunt Mary Maria, lowering her voice creepily, 'but have you looked in the rainwater hogshead? Little Jack MacGregor was drowned in a rainwater hogshead in town last year.'

'I . . . I looked there,' said Susan, with another wring of her hands. 'I . . . I took a stick . . . and poked . . .'

Anne's heart, which had stood still at Aunt Mary Maria's question, resumed operations. Susan gathered herself together and stopped wringing her hands. She had remembered too late that Mrs Doctor dear should not be upset.

'Let us calm down and pull together,' she said in a trembling voice. 'As you say, Mrs Doctor dear, he *must* be somewhere about. He *cannot* have dissolved into thin air.'

'Have you looked in the coal bin? And the clock?' asked Aunt Mary Maria.

Susan *had* looked in the coal bin, but nobody had thought of the clock. It *was* quite big enough for a small boy to hide in. Anne, not considering the absurdity of supposing that Jem would crouch there for four hours, rushed to it. But Jem was not in the clock.

'I had a *feeling* that something was going to happen when I went to bed tonight,' said Aunt Mary Maria, pressing both hands to her temples. 'When I read my nightly chapter in the Bible the words, "Ye know not what a day may bring forth", seemed to stand out from the page, as it were. It was a sign. You'd better nerve yourself to bear the worst, Annie. He may have wandered into the marsh. It's a pity we haven't a few bloodhounds.'

With a dreadful effort Anne managed a laugh.

'I'm afraid there aren't any on the island, Auntie. If we had Gilbert's old setter Rex, who got poisoned, he would soon find Jem. I feel sure we are all alarming ourselves for nothing . . .'

'Tommy Spencer in Carmody disappeared mysteriously forty years ago and was never found . . . or was he? Well, if he was, it was only his skeleton. This is no laughing matter, Annie. I don't know how you can take it so calmly.'

The telephone rang. Anne and Susan looked at each other.

'I can't . . . I *can't* go to the phone, Susan,' said Anne in a whisper.

'I can't either,' said Susan flatly. She was to hate herself all her days for showing such weakness before Mary Maria Blythe, but she could not help it. Two hours of terrified searching and distorted imaginations had made Susan a wreck.

Aunt Mary Maria stalked to the telephone and took down the receiver, her crimpers making a horned silhouette on the wall which Susan reflected, in spite of her anguish, looked like the old Nick himself.

'Carter Flagg says they have searched everywhere but found no sign of him yet,' reported Aunt Mary Maria coolly. 'But he says the dory is out in the middle of the pond with no one in it as far as they can ascertain. They are going to drag the pond.'

Susan caught Anne just in time.

'No . . . no . . . I'm not going to faint, Susan,' said Anne through white lips. 'Help me to a chair . . . thanks . . . we *must* find Gilbert . . .'

'If James is drowned, Annie, you must remind yourself that he has been spared a lot of trouble in this wretched world,' said Aunt Mary Maria by way of administering further consolation.

'I'm going to get the lantern and search the grounds

again,' said Anne, as soon as she could stand up. 'Yes, I know you did, Susan, but let me . . . let me. I *cannot* sit still and wait.'

'You must put on a sweater then, Mrs Doctor dear. There's a heavy dew and the air is damp. I will get your red one, it is hanging on a chair in the boys' room. Wait you here till I bring it.'

Susan hurried upstairs. A few moments later something that could only be described as a shriek echoed through Ingleside. Anne and Aunt Mary Maria rushed upstairs, where they found Susan laughing and crying in the hall, nearer to hysterics than Susan Baker had ever been in her life or ever would be again.

'Mrs Doctor dear . . . he's there. Little Jem is there . . . asleep on the window seat behind the door. I never looked there . . . the door hid it . . . and when he wasn't in his bed . . .'

Anne, weak with relief and joy, got herself into the room and dropped on her knees by the window seat. In a little while she and Susan would be laughing over their own foolishness, but now there could be only tears of thankfulness. Little Jem was sound asleep on the window seat, with an afghan pulled over him, his battered Teddy Bear in his little sunburned hands, and a forgiving Shrimp stretched across his legs. His red curls fell over the cushion. He seemed to be having a pleasant dream and Anne did not mean to waken him.

But suddenly he opened eyes that were like hazel stars and looked at her.

'Jem, darling, why aren't you in your bed? We've . . . we've been a little alarmed . . . we couldn't find you . . . and we never thought of looking here . . .'

'I wanted to lie here 'cause I could see you and Daddy drive in at the gate when you got home. It was so lonesome I just had to go to bed.'

Mother was lifting him up in her arms, carrying him to his own bed. It was so nice to be kissed . . . to feel her tucking the sheets about him with those caressing little pats that gave him such a sense of being loved. Who cared about seeing an old snake tattooed anyhow? Mother was so nice, the nicest mother anybody ever had. Everybody in the Glen called Bertie Shakespeare's mother 'Mrs Second Skimmings' because she was so mean, and he knew . . . for he'd seen it . . . that she slapped Bertie's face for every little thing.

'Mummy,' he said sleepily, 'of course I'll bring you mayflowers next spring . . . every spring. You can depend on me.'

'Of course I can, darling,' said Mother.

'Well, since everyone is over their fit of the fidgets, I suppose we can draw a peaceful breath and go back to our beds,' said Aunt Mary Maria. But there was some shrewish relief in her tone.

'It was very silly of me not to remember the window

seat,' said Anne. 'The joke is on us and the doctor will not let us forget it, you may be certain. Susan, please phone Mr Flagg that we've found Jem.'

'And a nice laugh he will have on me,' said Susan happily. 'Not that I care . . . he can laugh all he likes since Little Jem is safe.'

'I could do with a cup of tea,' sighed Aunt Mary Maria plaintively, gathering her dragons about her spare form.

'I will get it in a jiffy,' said Susan briskly. 'We'll all feel the sprightlier for one. Mrs Doctor dear, when Carter Flagg heard Little Jem was safe he said, "Thank God." I shall never say a word against that man again, no matter what his prices are. And don't you think we might have a chicken dinner tomorrow, Mrs Doctor dear? Just by way of a little celebration, so to speak. And Little Jem shall have his favourite muffins for breakfast.'

There was another telephone call . . . this time from Gilbert to say that he was taking a badly burned baby from the Harbour Head to the hospital in town, and not to look for him till morning.

Anne bent from her window for a thankful goodnight look at the world before going to bed. A cool wind was blowing in from the sea. A sort of moonlit rapture was running through the trees in the Hollow. Anne could even laugh . . . with a quiver behind the laughter . . . over their panic of an hour ago and Aunt Mary Maria's absurd suggestions and ghoulish memories. Her child was safe.

Gilbert was somewhere battling to save another child's life . . . *Dear God, help him and help the mother . . . help all mothers everywhere. We need so much help, with the little sensitive, loving hearts and minds that look to us for guidance and love and understanding.*

The friendly enfolding night took possession of Ingleside, and everybody, even Susan . . . who rather felt that she would like to crawl into some nice quiet hole and pull it in after her . . . fell asleep under its sheltering roof.

7

'He'll have plenty of company . . . he won't be lonesome . . . our four . . . and my niece and nephew from Montreal are visiting us. What one doesn't think of the others do.'

Big, sonsy, jolly Mrs Doctor Parker smiled expansively at Walter . . . who returned the smile somewhat aloofly. He wasn't altogether sure he liked Mrs Parker in spite of her smiles and jollity. There was too much of her, somehow. Dr Parker he did like; as for 'our four' and the niece and nephew from Montreal, Walter had never seen any of them. Lowbridge, where the Parkers lived, was six miles from the Glen and Walter had never been there, though Dr and Mrs Parker and Dr and Mrs Blythe visited back and forth frequently. Dr Parker and Dad were great friends, though Walter had a feeling now and again that Mother could have got along very well without Mrs Parker. Even at six, Walter, as Anne realized, could see things that other children could not.

Walter was not sure, either, that he really wanted to go

to Lowbridge. Some visits were splendid. A trip to Avonlea now . . . ah, there was fun for you. And a night spent with Kenneth Ford at the old House of Dreams was *more* fun still . . . though *that* couldn't really be called visiting, for the House of Dreams always seemed like a second home to the small fry of Ingleside. But to go to Lowbridge for two whole weeks, among strangers, was a very different matter. However, it seemed to be a settled thing. For some reason which Walter felt but could not understand Dad and Mummy were pleased over the arrangement. Did they want to get rid of *all* their children Walter wondered, rather sadly and uneasily. Jem was away, having been taken to Avonlea two days ago, and he had heard Susan making mysterious remarks about 'sending the twins to Mrs Marshall Elliott when the time came'. What time? Aunt Mary Maria seemed very gloomy over something and had been known to say that she 'wished it was all well over'. Walter had no idea. But there was something strange in the air at Ingleside.

'I'll take him over tomorrow,' said Gilbert.

'The youngsters will be looking forward to it,' said Mrs Parker.

'It's very kind of you, I'm sure,' said Anne.

'It's all for the best, no doubt,' Susan told the Shrimp darkly in the kitchen.

'It is very obliging of Mrs Parker to take Walter off our hands, Annie,' said Aunt Mary Maria, when the Parkers had gone. 'She told me she had taken quite a fancy to him. People *do* take such odd fancies, don't they? Well, perhaps now for at least two weeks I'll be able to go into the bathroom without trampling on a dead fish.'

'A dead fish, Ay! You don't mean –'

'I mean exactly what I say, Annie. I always do. A dead fish! Did *you* ever step on a dead fish with your bare feet?'

'No – o . . . but how . . .'

'Walter caught a trout last night and put it in the bathtub to keep it alive, Mrs Doctor dear,' said Susan airily. 'If it had stayed there it would have been all right, but somehow it got out and died in the night. Of course, if people *will* go about on bare feet . . .'

'*I* make it a rule never to quarrel with anyone,' said Aunt Mary Maria, getting up and leaving the room.

'*I* am determined she shall not vex *me*, Mrs Doctor dear,' said Susan.

'Oh, Susan, she *is* getting on my nerves a bit . . . but of course I won't mind so much when all this is over, and it *must* be nasty to tramp on a dead fish . . .'

'Isn't a dead fish better than a live one, Mummy? A dead fish wouldn't squirm,' said Di.

Since the truth must be told at all costs it must be admitted that the mistress and maid of Ingleside both giggled.

So that was that. But Anne wondered to Gilbert that night if Walter would be quite happy at Lowbridge.

'He's so very sensitive and imaginative,' she said wistfully.

'Too much so,' said Gilbert, who was tired, after having had . . . to quote Susan . . . three babies that day. 'Why, Anne, I believe that child is afraid to go upstairs in the dark. It will do him worlds of good to give and take with the Parker fry for a few days. He'll come home a different child.'

Anne said nothing more. No doubt Gilbert was quite right. Walter was lonesome without Jem; and in view of what had happened when Shirley was born it would be just as well for Susan to have as little on her hands as possible beyond running the house and enduring Aunt Mary Maria . . . whose two weeks had already stretched to four.

Walter was lying awake in his bed trying to escape from the haunting thought that he was to go away next day by giving free rein to fancy. Walter had a very vivid imagination. It was to him a great white charger, like the one in the picture on the wall, on which he could gallop backward or forward in time and space. The Night was coming down . . . Night, like a tall, dark, bat-winged angel who lived in Mr Andrew Taylor's woods on the south hill. Sometimes Walter welcomed her, sometimes he pictured her so vividly that he grew afraid of her. Walter dramatized and personified in his small world . . . the Wind who told him stories at night . . . the Frost that nipped the flowers in the garden ... the Dew that fell so silverly and silently ... the Moon which he felt sure he could catch if he could only go to the top of that far-away purple hill ... the Mist that came in from the sea ... the great Sea itself that was always changing and never changed ... the dark, mysterious Tide. They were all entities to Walter. Ingleside and the Hollow and the maple grove and the Marsh and the harbour shore were full of elves and kelpies and dryads and mermaids and goblins. The black plaster-of-paris cat on the library mantelpiece was a fairy witch. It came alive at night and prowled about the house, grown to enormous size. Walter ducked his head under the bedclothes and shivered. He was always scaring himself with his own fancies. Perhaps Aunt Mary Maria was right when she said he was 'far too nervous and high-strung', though Susan would never forgive her for it. Perhaps Aunt Kitty MacGregor of the Upper Glen, who was reported to have 'the second sight', was right when, having once taken a deep look into Walter's long-lashed, smoky grey eyes, she said he 'did be having an old soul in a young body'. It might be that the old soul knew too much for the young brain to understand always.

Walter was told in the morning that Dad would take him to Lowbridge after dinner. He said nothing, but during dinner a choky sensation came over him and he dropped his eyes quickly to hide a sudden mist of tears. Not quickly enough, however.

'You're not going to *cry*, Walter?' said Aunt Mary Maria, as if a six-year-old mite would be disgraced for ever if he cried. 'If there's anything I *do* despise it's a cry-baby. And you haven't eaten your meat.'

'All but the fat,' said Walter, blinking valiantly, but not yet daring to look up. 'I don't like fat.'

'When *I* was a child,' said Aunt Mary Maria, 'I was not allowed to have likes and dislikes. Well, Mrs Doctor Parker will probably cure you of some of your notions. She was a Winter, I think . . . or was she a Clark? . . . no, she must have been a Campbell. But the Winters and Campbells are all tarred with the same brush, and they don't put up with any nonsense.'

'Oh, please, Aunt Mary Maria, don't frighten Walter about his visit to Lowbridge,' said Anne, a little spark kindling far down in her eyes.

'I'm sorry, Annie,' said Aunt Mary Maria with great humility. 'I should of course have remembered that *I* have no right to try to teach your children *anything*.'

'Drat her hide,' muttered Susan as she went out for the dessert . . . Walter's favourite Queen pudding.

Anne felt miserably guilty. Gilbert had shot her a slightly reproachful glance as if to imply she might have been more patient with a poor lonely old lady.

Gilbert himself was feeling a bit seedy. The truth, as everyone knew, was that he had been terribly overworked all summer: and perhaps Aunt Mary Maria was more of a strain than he would admit. Anne made up her mind that in the autumn, if all was well, she would pack him off willy-nilly for a month's snipe shooting in Nova Scotia.

'How is your tea?' she asked Aunt Mary Maria repentantly.

Aunt Mary Maria pursed her lips.

'Too weak. But it doesn't matter. Who cares whether a poor old woman gets her tea to her liking or not? Some folks, however, think I'm real good company.'

Whatever the connection between Aunt Mary Maria's two sentences was Anne felt she was beyond ferreting it out just then. She had turned very pale.

'I think I'll go upstairs and lie down,' she said a trifle faintly as she rose from the table. 'And I think, Gilbert . . . perhaps you'd better not stay long in Lowbridge . . . and suppose you give Miss Carson a ring.'

She kissed Walter goodbye rather casually and hurriedly, very much as if she were not thinking about him at all. Walter *would not* cry. Aunt Mary Maria kissed him on the forehead – Walter hated to be moistly kissed on the forehead – and said:

'Mind your table manners at Lowbridge, Walter. Mind you ain't greedy. If you are, a Big Black Man will come along with a big black bag to pop naughty children into.'

It was perhaps as well that Gilbert had gone out to harness Grey Tom and did not hear this. He and Anne had always made a point of never frightening their children with such ideas or allowing anyone else to do it. Susan did hear it as she cleared the table, and Aunt Mary Maria never knew what a narrow escape she had of having the gravy boat and its contents flung at her head.

8

Generally Walter enjoyed a drive with Dad. He loved beauty, and the roads around Glen St Mary were beautiful. The road to Lowbridge was a double ribbon of dancing buttercups, with here and there the ferny green rim of an inviting grove. But today Dad didn't seem to want to talk much and he drove Grey Tom as Walter never remembered seeing him driven before. When they reached Lowbridge he said a few hurried words aside to Mrs Parker and rushed out without bidding Walter goodbye. Walter had again hard work to keep from crying. It was only too plain that nobody loved him. Mother and Father used to, but they didn't any longer.

The big, untidy Parker house at Lowbridge did not seem friendly to Walter. But perhaps no house would have seemed that just then. Mrs Parker took him out to the backyard, where shrieks of noisy mirth were resounding, and introduced him to the children, who seemed to fill it. Then she promptly went back to her sewing, leaving them to 'get acquainted by themselves' . . . a proceeding that worked very well in nine cases out of ten. Perhaps she could not be blamed for failing to see that little Walter Blythe was the tenth. She liked him . . . her own children were jolly little lads . . . Fred and Opal were inclined to put on Montreal airs, but she felt quite sure they wouldn't be unkind to anyone. Everything would go swimmingly. She was so glad she could help 'poor Anne Blythe' out, even if it was only by taking one of her children off her hands. Mrs Parker hoped 'all would go well'. Anne's friends were a good deal more worried over her than she was over herself, reminding each other of Shirley's birth.

A sudden hush had fallen over the backyard, a yard which ran off into a big, bowery apple orchard. Walter stood looking gravely and shyly at the Parker children and their Johnson cousins from Montreal. Bill Parker was ten, a ruddy, round-faced urchin who 'took after' his mother and seemed very old and big in Walter's eyes. Andy Parker was nine, and Lowbridge children could have told you that he was 'the nasty Parker one' and was nicknamed 'Pig' for reasons good. Walter did not like his looks from the first . . . his short-cropped fair bristles, his impish freckled face, his bulging blue eyes. Fred Johnson was Bill's age, and Walter didn't like him either, though he was a good-looking chap with tawny curls and black eyes. His nine-year-old sister, Opal, had curls and black eyes, too . . . snapping black eyes. She stood with her arm about tow-headed, eight-year-old Cora Parker and they both looked Walter over condescendingly. If it had not been for Alice Parker Walter might very conceivably have turned and fled.

Alice was seven; Alice had the loveliest little ripples of golden curls all over her head: Alice had eyes as blue and soft as the violets in the Hollow: Alice had pink, dimpled cheeks: Alice wore a little frilled yellow dress in which she looked like a dancing buttercup: Alice smiled at him as if she had known him all her life; Alice was a friend.

Fred opened the conversation.

'Hello, sonny,' he said condescendingly.

Walter felt the condescension at once and retreated into himself.

'My name is Walter,' he said distinctly.

Fred turned to the others with a well-done air of amazement. *He'd* show this country lad!

'He says his name is *Walter*,' he told Bill with a comical twist of his mouth.

'He says his name is *Walter*,' Bill told Opal in turn.

'He says his name is *Walter*,' Opal told the delighted Andy.

'He says his name is *Walter*,' Andy told Cora.

'He says his name is *Walter*,' Cora giggled to Alice.

Alice said nothing. She just looked admiringly at Walter, and her look enabled him to bear up when all the rest chanted together. 'He says his name is *Walter*,' and then burst into shrieks of derisive laughter.

'What fun the dear little folks are having,' thought Mrs Parker complacently over her shirring.

'I heard Mom say you believed in fairies,' Andy said, leering impudently.

Walter gazed levelly at him. He was not going to be downed before Alice.

'There *are* fairies,' he said stoutly.

'There ain't,' said Andy.

'There *are*,' said Walter.

'He says there are *fairies*,' Andy told Fred.

'He says there are *fairies*,' Fred told Bill . . . and they went through the whole performance again.

It was torture to Walter, who had never been made fun of before and couldn't take it. He bit his lips to keep the tears back. He must not cry before Alice.

'How would you like to be pinched black and blue?' demanded Andy, who had made up his mind that Walter was a sissy and that it would be good fun to tease him.

'Pig, hush!' ordered Alice terribly . . . very terribly, although very quietly and sweetly and gently. There was something in her tone that even Andy dared not flout.

'Course I didn't meant it,' he muttered, shamefacedly.

The wind veered a bit in Walter's favour and they had a fairly amiable game of tag in the orchard. But when they trooped noisily into supper Walter was again overwhelmed with homesickness. It was so terrible that for one awful moment he was afraid he was going to cry before them all . . . even Alice, who, however, gave his arm such a friendly little nudge as they sat down that it helped him. But he could not eat anything . . . he simply could not. Mrs Parker, for whose methods there was certainly something to be said, did not worry him about it, comfortably concluding that his appetite would be better in the morning, and the others were too much occupied in eating and talking to take much notice of him. Walter wondered why the whole family shouted so at each other, ignorant of the fact that they had not yet had time to get out of the habit since the recent death of a very deaf and sensitive old grandmother. The noise made his head ache. Oh, at home now they would be eating supper too. Mother would be smiling from the head of the table, Father would be joking with the twins, Susan would be pouring cream into Shirley's mug of milk, Nan would be sneaking titbits to the Shrimp. Even Aunt Mary Maria, as part of the home circle, seemed suddenly invested with a soft, tender radiance. Who would have rung the Chinese gong for supper? It was his week to do it and Jem was away. If he could only find a place to cry in! But there seemed to be no place where you could indulge in tears at Lowbridge. Besides . . . there was Alice . . . Walter gulped down a whole glassful of ice water and found that it helped.

'Our cat takes fits,' Andy said suddenly, kicking him under the table.

'So does ours,' said Walter. The Shrimp had had two

fits. And he wasn't going to have the Lowbridge cats rated higher than the Ingleside cats.

'I'll bet our cat takes fittier fits than yours,' taunted Andy.

'I'll bet she doesn't,' retorted Walter.

'Now, now, don't let's have any arguments over your cats,' said Mrs Parker, who wanted a quiet evening to write her Institute paper on 'Misunderstood Children'. 'Run out and play. It won't be long before your bedtime.'

Bedtime! Walter suddenly realized that he had to stay here all night . . . many nights . . . two weeks of nights. It was dreadful. He went out to the orchard with clenched fists, to find Bill and Andy in a furious clinch on the grass, kicking, clawing, yelling.

'You gave me the wormy apple, Bill Parker,' Andy was howling. 'I'll teach you to give me wormy apples! I'll bite off your ears!'

Fights of this sort were an everyday occurrence with the Parkers. Mrs Parker held that it didn't hurt boys to fight. She said they got a lot of devilment out of their systems that way and were as good friends afterwards. But Walter had never seen anyone fighting before and was aghast.

Fred was cheering them on, Opal and Cora were laughing, but there were tears in Alice's eyes. Walter could not endure that. He hurled himself between the combatants, who had drawn apart for a moment to snatch breath before joining battle again.

'You stop fighting,' said Walter. 'You're scaring Alice.'

Bill and Andy stared at him in amazement for a moment until the funny side of this baby interfering in their fight struck them. Both burst into laughter, and Bill slapped him on the back.

'It's got spunk, kids,' he said. 'It's going to be a real boy some time if you let it grow up. Here's an apple for it . . . and no worms either.'

Alice wiped the tears away from her soft pink cheeks and looked so adoringly at Walter that Fred didn't like it. Of course Alice was only a baby, but even babies had no business to be looking adoringly at other boys when he, Fred Johnson of Montreal, was around. This must be dealt with. Fred had been into the house and had heard Aunt Jen, who had been talking over the telephone, say something to Uncle Dick.

'Your mother's awful sick,' he told Walter.

'She . . . she isn't,' cried Walter.

'She is, too. I heard Aunt Jen telling Uncle Dick . . .' Fred had heard his aunt say, 'Anne Blythe is sick,' and it was fun to crack in the 'awful'. 'She'll likely be dead before you get home.'

Walter looked around with tormented eyes. Again Alice ranged herself by him . . . and again the rest gathered around the standard of Fred. They felt something alien about this dark, handsome child . . . they felt an urge to tease him.

'If she is sick,' said Walter, 'Father will cure her.'

He would . . . he must!

'I'm afraid that will be impossible,' said Fred, pulling a long face, but winking at Andy.

'Nothing is impossible for Father,' insisted Walter loyally.

'Why, Russ Carter went to Charlottetown just for a day last summer and when he came home his mother was dead as a doornail,' said Bill.

'*And* buried,' said Andy, thinking to add an extra dramatic touch, whether a fact or not didn't matter. 'Russ was awful mad he'd missed the funeral, funerals are so jolly.'

'And I've never seen a single funeral,' said Opal sadly.

'Well, there'll be lots of chances for you yet,' said Andy. 'But you see even Dad couldn't keep Mrs Carter alive, and he's a lot better doctor than *your* father.'

'He isn't . . .'

'Yes, he is, and a lot better-looking, too . . .'

'He isn't . . .'

'Something *always* happens when you go away from home,' said Opal. 'What will you feel like if you find Ingleside burned down when you go home?'

'If your mother dies likely you children will all be separated,' said Cora cheerfully. 'Maybe you'll come and live here.'

'Yes . . . do,' said Alice sweetly.

'Oh, his father would want to keep them,' said Bill. 'He'd soon be marrying again. But maybe his father will die too. I heard Dad say Dr Blythe was working himself to death. Look at him staring. You've got girl's eyes, sonny . . . girl's eyes . . . girl's eyes.'

'Aw, shut up,' said Opal, suddenly tiring of the sport. 'You ain't fooling him. He knows you're only teasing. Let's go down to the park and watch the baseball game. Walter and Alice can stay here. We can't have kids tagging after us everywhere.'

Walter was not sorry to see them go. Neither apparently was Alice. They sat down on an apple log and looked shyly and contentedly at each other. 'I'll show you how to play jackstones,' said Alice, 'and lend you my plush kangaroo.'

When bedtime came Walter found himself put into the little hall bedroom alone. Mrs Parker considerately left a candle with him and a warm puff, for the July night was unreasonably cold as even a summer night in the Maritimes sometimes is. It almost seemed as if there might be a frost.

But Walter could not sleep, even with Alice's plush kangaroo cuddled to his cheek. Oh, if he were only home in his own room where the big window looked out on the Glen and the little window, with a tiny roof all its own, looked out into the Scotch pine. Mother would come in and read poetry to him in her lovely voice.

'I'm a big boy . . . I won't cry . . . I wo-o-o-n't . . .' The tears came in spite of himself. What good were plush kangaroos? It seemed years since he had left home.

Presently the other children came back from the park and crowded amiably into the room to sit on the bed and eat apples.

'You've been crying, baby,' jeered Andy. 'You're nothing but a sweet little girl. Momma's Pet!'

'Have a bit, kid,' said Bill, proffering a half-gnawed apple. 'And cheer up. I wouldn't be surprised if your mother got better . . . if she's got a constitution, that is. Dad says Mrs Stephen Flagg would-a died years ago if she hadn't a constitution. Has your mother got one?'

'Of course she has,' said Walter. He had no idea what a constitution was, but if Mrs Stephen Flagg had one, Mother must.

'Mrs Ab Sawyer died last week and Sam Clark's mother died the week before,' said Andy.

'They died in the night,' said Cora. 'Mother says people mostly die in the night. I hope *I* won't! Fancy going to heaven in your nightdress!'

'Children! Children! Get off to your beds,' called Mrs Parker.

The boys went, after pretending to smother Walter with a towel. After all, they rather liked the kid. Walter caught Opal's hand as she turned away.

'Opal, it isn't true mother's sick, is it?' he whispered imploringly. He could not face being left alone with his fear.

Opal was 'not a bad-hearted child', as Mrs Parker said, but she could not resist the thrill one got out of telling bad news.

'She *is* sick. Aunt Jen says so . . . she said I wasn't to tell you. But I think you ought to know. Maybe she has a cancer.'

'Does *everybody* have to die, Opal?' This was a new and dreadful idea to Walter, who had never thought about death before.

'Of course, silly. Only they don't die really . . . they go to heaven,' said Opal cheerfully.

'Not all of them,' said Andy, who was listening outside the door, in a pig's whisper.

'Is . . . is heaven farther away than Charlottetown?' asked Walter.

Opal shrilled with laughter.

'Well, you *are* queer! Heaven's millions of miles away. But I'll tell you what to do. You pray. Praying's good. I lost a dime once and I prayed and I found a quarter. That's how I know.'

'Opal Johnson, did you hear what I said? And put out that candle in Walter's room. I'm afraid of fire,' called Mrs Parker from her room. 'He should have been asleep long ago.'

Opal blew out the candle and flew. Aunt Jen was easy-going, but when she *did* get riled! Andy stuck his head in at the door for a goodnight benediction.

'Likely them birds in the wallpaper will come alive and pick your eyes out,' he hissed.

After which everybody did really go to bed, feeling that it was the end of a perfect day and Walt Blythe wasn't a bad little kid and they'd have some more fun teasing him tomorrow.

'Dear little souls,' thought Mrs Parker sentimentally.

An unwonted quiet descended upon the Parker house, and six miles away at Ingleside little Bertha Marilla Blythe was blinking round hazel eyes at the happy faces around her and the world into which she had been ushered on the coldest July night the Maritimes had experienced in eighty-seven years!

9

Walter, alone in the darkness, still found it impossible to sleep. He had never slept alone before in his short life. Always Jem or Ken near him, warm and comforting. The little room became dimly visible as the pale moonlight crept into it, but it was almost worse than darkness. A picture on the wall at the foot of his bed seemed to leer at him . . . pictures always looked so *different* by moonlight. You saw things in them you never suspected by daylight. The long lace curtains looked like tall thin women, one on each side of the window, weeping. There were noises about the house . . . creaks, sighs, whisperings. Suppose the birds in the wallpaper *were* coming to life and getting ready to pick out his eyes? A creepy fear suddenly possessed Walter . . . and then one great fear banished all the others. *Mother was sick*. He had to believe it since Opal had said it was true. Perhaps Mother was dying! *Perhaps Mother was dead!* There would be no mother to go home to. Walter saw Ingleside without Mother!

Suddenly Walter knew he could not bear it. He must go home. Right away at once. He must see Mother before she . . . she . . . *died*. *This* was what Aunt Mary Maria had meant. *She* had known Mother was going to die. It was no use to think of waking anyone and asking to be taken home. They wouldn't take him . . . they would only laugh at him. It was an awful long road home, but he would walk all night.

Very quietly he slipped out of bed and put on his clothes. He took his shoes in his hand. He did not know where Mrs Parker had put his cap, but that did not matter. He must not make any noise . . . he must just escape and get to Mother. He was sorry he could not say goodbye to Alice . . . she would have understood. Through the dark hall . . . down the stairs . . . step by step . . . hold your breath . . . was there no end to the steps? . . . the very furniture was listening . . . oh, oh!

Walter had dropped one of his shoes! Down the stairs it clattered, bumping from step to step, shot across the hall and brought up against the front door with what seemed to Walter a deafening crash.

Walter huddled in despair against the rail. *Everybody* must have heard that noise . . . they would come rushing out . . . he wouldn't be let go home . . . a sob of despair choked in his throat.

It seemed hours before he dared believe that nobody had wakened up, before he dare resume his careful passage down the stairs. But it was accomplished at last; he found his shoe and cautiously turned the handle of the front door . . . doors were never locked at the Parker place. Mrs Parker said they hadn't anything worth stealing except children, and nobody wanted *them*.

Walter was out, the door closed behind him. He slipped on his shoes and stole down the street: the house was on the edge of the village and he was soon on the open road. A moment of panic overwhelmed him. The fear of being caught and prevented was past, and all his old fears of darkness and solitude returned. He had never been out *alone* in the night before. He was afraid of the *world*. It was such a huge world and he was so terribly small in it. Even the cold raw wind that was coming up from the east seemed blowing in his face as if to push him back.

Mother was going to die! Walter took a gulp and set his face towards home. On and on he went, fighting fear gallantly. It was moonlight, but the moonlight let you *see* things . . . and nothing looked familiar. Once when he had been out with Dad he had thought he had never seen anything so pretty as a moonlit road crossed by tree shadows. But now the shadows were so black and sharp they might fly up at you. The fields had put on a strangeness. The trees were no longer friendly. They seemed to be watching him, crowding in before and behind him. Two blazing eyes looked out at him from the ditch and a black cat of unbelievable size ran across the road. *Was it a cat?* Or . . .? The night was cold: he shivered in his thin blouse, but he would not mind the cold if he could only stop being afraid of everything . . . of the shadows and the furtive sounds and the nameless things that might be prowling in the strips of woodland he passed through. He wondered what it would be like not to be afraid of anything . . . like Jem.

'I'll . . . I'll just pretend I'm not afraid,' he said aloud . . . and then shuddered with terror over the *lost* sound of his own voice in the great night.

But he went on, one had to go on when Mother was going to die. Once he fell and bruised and skinned his knee badly on a stone. Once he heard a buggy coming along behind him and hid behind a tree till it passed, terrified lest Dr Parker had discovered he had gone and was coming after him. Once he stopped in sheer terror of something black and furry sitting on the side of the road. He could not pass it . . . he could *not* . . . but he did. It was a big black dog . . . *was* it a dog? . . . but he was past it. He dared not run lest it chase him . . . he stole a desperate glance over his shoulder . . . it had got up and was loping away in the opposite direction. Walter put his little brown hand up to his face and found it wet with sweat.

A star fell in the sky before him, scattering sparks of flame. Walter remembered hearing old Aunt Kitty say that when a star fell someone died. *Was it Mother?* He had just been feeling that his legs would not carry him another step, but at the thought he marched on again. He was so cold now that he had almost ceased to feel afraid. Would he never get home? It must be hours and hours since he had left Lowbridge.

It *was* three hours. He had stolen out of the Parker house at eleven and it was now two. When Walter found himself on the road that dipped down into the Glen he gave a sob of relief. But as he stumbled through the village the sleeping houses seemed remote and far away. They had forgotten him. A cow suddenly bawled at him over a fence and Walter remembered that Mr Alec Reese kept a savage bull. He broke into a run of sheer panic that carried him up the hill to the gate of Ingleside. He was home . . . oh, he was home!

Then he stopped short, trembling, overcome by a dreadful feeling of desolation. He had been expecting to see the warm, friendly lights of home. And there was not a light at Ingleside!

There really was a light if he could have seen it, in a back bedroom where the nurse slept with the baby's basket beside her bed. But to all intents and purposes it was as dark as a deserted house and it broke Walter's spirit. He had never seen, never imagined, Ingleside dark at night.

It meant that Mother was dead!

Walter stumbled up the drive, across the grim black shadow of the house on the lawn, to the front door. It was locked. He gave a feeble knock . . . he could not reach to the knocker . . . but there was no response, nor did he expect any. He listened . . . there was not a sound of *living* in the house. He knew Mother was dead and everybody had gone away.

He was by now too chilled and exhausted to cry; but he crept around the barn and climbed the ladder to the hay-mow. He was past being frightened: he only wanted to get somewhere out of that wind and lie down till morning. Perhaps somebody would come back then after they had buried Mother.

A sleek little tiger kitten someone had given the doctor purred up to him, smelling nicely of clover hay. Walter clutched it gladly, it was warm and *alive*. But it heard the little mice scampering over the floor and would not stay. The moon looked at him through the cobwebby window, but there was no comfort in that far, cold, unsympathetic moon. A light burning in a house down in the Glen was more like a friend. As long as that light shone he could bear up.

He could not sleep. His knee hurt too much and he was cold . . . with such a funny feeling in his stomach. Perhaps he was dying, too. He hoped he was, since everyone else was dead or gone away. Did nights ever end? Other nights had always ended, but maybe this one wouldn't. He remembered a dreadful story he had heard to the effect that Captain Jack Flagg at the Harbour Mouth had said he wouldn't let the sun come up some morning when he got real mad. Suppose Captain Jack had got real mad at last.

Then the Glen light went out . . . and he couldn't bear it. But as the little cry of despair left his lips he realized that it was day.

10

Walter climbed down the ladder and went out. Ingleside lay in the strange, timeless light of first dawn. The sky over the birches in the Hollow was showing a faint, silvery-pink radiance. Perhaps he could get in at the side door. Susan sometimes left it open for Dad.

The side door was unlocked. With a sob of thankfulness Walter slipped into the hall. It was still dark in the house and he began stealing softly upstairs. He would go to bed, his own bed, and if nobody ever came back he could die there and go to heaven and find Mother. Only . . . Walter remembered what Opal had said . . . heaven was millions of miles away. In the fresh wave of desolation that swept over him Walter forgot to step carefully and set his foot down heavily on the tail of the Shrimp, who was sleeping at the curve of the stairs. The Shrimp's yowl of anguish resounded through the house.

Susan, just dropping off to sleep, was dragged back from slumber by the horrible sound. Susan had gone to bed at twelve, somewhat exhausted after her strenuous afternoon and evening, to which Mary Maria Blythe had contributed by taking 'a stitch in her side' just when the tension was greatest. She had to have a hot-water bottle and a rub with liniment, and finished up with a wet cloth over her eyes because 'one of her headaches' had come on.

Susan had wakened at three with a very strange feeling that somebody wanted her very badly. She had risen and tiptoed down the hall to the door of Mrs Doctor's room. All was silence there . . . she could hear Anne's soft, regular breathing. Susan made the rounds of the house and returned to her bed, convinced that that strange feeling was only the hangover of a nightmare. But for the rest of her life Susan believed she had what she had always scoffed at and what Abby Flagg, who 'went in' for spiritualism, called 'a physic experience'.

'Walter was calling me and I heard him,' she averred.

Susan got up and went out again, thinking that Ingleside was really possessed that night. She was attired only in a flannel nightdress which had shrunk in repeated washings till it was well above her bony ankles: but she seemed the most beautiful thing in the world to the white-faced, trembling creature whose frantic grey eyes stared up at her from the landing.

'Walter Blythe!'

In two steps Susan had him in her arms . . . her strong, tender arms.

'Susan . . . is Mother dead?' said Walter.

In a very brief time everything had changed. Walter was in bed, warm, fed, comforted. Susan had whisked on a fire, got him a hot cup of milk, a slice of golden-brown toast, and a big plateful of his favourite 'monkey face' cookies, and then tucked him away with a hot-water bottle at his feet. She had kissed and anointed his little bruised knee. It was such a nice feeling to know that someone was looking after you . . . that someone wanted you . . . that you were important to someone.

'And you're *sure*, Susan, that Mother isn't dead?'

'Your mother is sound asleep and well and happy, my lamb.'

'And wasn't she sick at all? Opal said . . .'

'Well, lamb, she didn't feel very well for a while yesterday, but that's all over, and she was never in any danger of dying this time. You just wait till you've had a sleep and you'll see her . . . and something else. If I had hold of those young Satans at Lowbridge! I just can't believe that you walked all the way home from Lowbridge. Six miles! On such a night!'

'I suffered awful agony of mind, Susan,' said Walter gravely. But it was all over; he was safe and happy; he was . . . home . . . he was . . .

He was asleep.

It was nearly midday before he woke, to see sunshine billowing in through his own windows, and limped in to see Mother. He had begun to think he had been very foolish and maybe Mother would not be pleased with him for running away from Lowbridge. But Mother only put an arm around him and drew him close to her. She had heard the whole story from Susan and had thought of a few things she intended to say to Jen Parker.

'Oh, Mummy, you're not going to die . . . and you still love me, don't you?'

'Darling, I've no notion of dying, and I love you so much it hurts. To think that you walked all the way from Lowbridge in the night!'

'And on an empty stomach,' shuddered Susan. 'The wonder is he's alive to tell it. The days of miracles are not yet over and that you may tie to.'

'A spunky little lad,' laughed Dad, who had come in with Shirley on his shoulder. He patted Walter's head and Walter caught his hand and hugged it. There was no one like Dad in the world. But nobody must ever know how scared he had really been.

'I needn't ever go away from home again, need I, Mummy?'

'Not till you want to,' promised Mother.

'I'll never . . .' began Walter . . . and then stopped. After all, he wouldn't mind seeing Alice again.

'Look you here, lamb,' said Susan, ushering in a rosy young lady in a white apron and cap who carried a basket.

Walter looked. A baby! A plump, roly-poly baby, with

silky damp curls all over her head and such tiny, cunning hands.

'Is she not a beauty?' said Susan proudly. 'Look at her eyelashes . . . never did I see such long eyelashes on a baby. And her pretty little ears. I always look at their ears first.'

Walter hesitated.

'She's sweet, Susan . . . oh, look at her darling little curly toes! But . . . isn't she rather small?'

Susan laughed.

'Eight pounds isn't small, lamb. And she has begun to take notice already. That child wasn't an hour old when she raised her head and *looked* at the doctor. I have never seen the like of it in all my life.'

'She's going to have red hair,' said the doctor in a tone of satisfaction. 'Lovely red-gold hair like her mother's.'

'And hazel eyes like her father's,' said the doctor's wife jubilantly.

'I don't see why one of us can't have yellow hair,' said Walter dreamily, thinking of Alice.

'Yellow hair! Like the Drews!' said Susan in measureless contempt.

'She looks so cunning when she is asleep,' crooned the nurse. 'I never saw a baby that crinkled its eyes like that when it went to sleep.'

'She is a miracle. All our babies were sweet, Gilbert, but she is the sweetest of them all.'

'Lord love you,' said Aunt Mary Maria with a sniff, 'there's been a few babies in the world before, you know, Annie.'

'*Our* baby has never been in the world before, Aunt Mary Maria,' said Walter proudly. 'Susan, may I kiss her . . . just once . . . please?'

'That you may,' said Susan, glaring after Aunt Mary Maria's retreating back. 'And now I'm going down to make a cherry pie for dinner. Mary Maria Blythe made one yesterday afternoon . . . I wish you could see it, Mrs Doctor dear. It looks like something the cat dragged in. I shall eat as much of it myself as I can rather than waste it, but such a pie shall never be set before the doctor as long as I have my health and strength and that you may tie to.'

'It isn't everybody that has your knack with pastry, you know,' said Anne.

'Mummy,' said Walter, as the door closed behind a gratified Susan, 'I think we are a very nice family, don't you?'

A very nice family, Anne reflected happily as she lay in her bed, with the baby beside her. Soon she would be about with them again, light-footed as of yore, loving them, teaching them, comforting them. They would be coming to her with their little joys and sorrows, their budding hopes, their new fears, their little problems that seemed so big to them, and their little heartbreaks that seemed so bitter. She would hold all the threads of the Ingleside life in her hands again to weave into a tapestry of beauty. And Aunt Mary Maria should have no cause to say, as Anne had heard her say two days ago, 'You look dreadful tired, Gilbert. Does *anybody* ever look after you?'

Downstairs Aunt Mary Maria was shaking her head despondently.

'All newborn infants' legs are crooked, I know, but, Susan, that child's legs are much *too* crooked. Of course, we must not say so to poor Annie. Be sure you don't mention it to Annie, Susan.'

Susan, for once, was beyond speech.

11

By the end of August Anne was herself again, looking forward to a happy autumn. Small Bertha Marilla grew in beauty day by day and was a centre of worship to adoring brothers and sisters.

'I thought a baby would be something that yelled all the time,' said Jem, rapturously letting the tiny fingers cling around his. 'Bertie Shakespeare Drew told me so.'

'I am not doubting that the Drew babies yell all the time, Jem, dear,' said Susan. 'Yell at the thought of having to be Drews, I presume. But Bertha Marilla is an *Ingleside* baby, Jem, dear.'

'I wish I had been born at Ingleside, Susan,' said Jem wistfully. He always felt sorry he hadn't been. Di cast it up to him at times.

'Don't you find life here rather dull?' an old Queen's classmate from Charlottetown had asked Anne rather patronizingly one day.

Dull! Anne almost laughed in her caller's face. Ingleside dull! With a delicious baby bringing new wonders every day . . . with visits from Diana and Little Elizabeth and Rebecca Dew to be planned for . . . with Mrs Sam Ellison of the Upper Glen on Gilbert's hands with a disease only three people in the world had ever been known to have before . . . with Walter starting to school . . . with Nan drinking a whole bottle of perfume from Mother's dressing table . . . they thought it would kill her, but she was never a whit the worse; with a strange black cat having the unheard-of number of ten kittens in the back porch . . . with Shirley locking himself in the bathroom and forgetting how to unlock it . . . with the Shrimp getting rolled up in a sheet of fly paper . . . with Aunt Mary Maria setting the curtains of her room on fire in the dead of night while prowling with a candle and rousing the household with appalling screams. Life dull!

For Aunt Mary Maria was still at Ingleside. Occasionally she would say pathetically, 'Whenever you are tired of me just let me know . . . I'm used to looking after myself.' There was only one thing to say to that, and of course Dr Gilbert always said it. Though he did not say it quite as heartily as at first. Even Gilbert's 'clannishness' was beginning to wear a little thin; he was realizing rather helplessly . . . 'manlike', as Miss Cornelia sniffed . . . that Aunt Mary Maria was by way of becoming a problem in his household. He *had* ventured one day to give a slight hint as to how houses suffered if left too long without inhabitants; and Aunt Mary Maria agreed with him, calmly remarking that she was thinking of selling her Charlottetown house.

'Not a bad idea,' encouraged Gilbert. 'And I know a very nice little cottage in town for sale . . . a friend of mine is going to California . . . it's very like that one you admired so much where Mrs Sarah Newman lives . . .'

'But lives *alone*,' sighed Aunt Mary Maria.

'She likes it,' said Anne hopefully.

'There's something wrong with anyone who likes living alone, Annie,' said Aunt Mary Maria.

Susan repressed a groan with difficulty.

Diana came for a week in September. Then Little Elizabeth came . . . Little Elizabeth no longer . . . tall, slender, beautiful Elizabeth now. But still with the golden hair and wistful smile. Her father was returning to his office in Paris and Elizabeth was going with him to keep his house. She and Anne took long walks around the storied shores of the old harbour, coming home beneath silent, watchful autumn stars. They relived the old Windy Willows life and retraced their steps in the map of fairyland which Elizabeth still had and meant to keep for ever.

'Hanging on the wall of my room wherever I go,' she said.

One day a wind blew through the Ingleside garden, the first wind of autumn. That night the rose of the sunset was a trifle austere. All at once the summer had grown old. The turn of the season had come.

'It's early for fall,' said Aunt Mary Maria in a tone that implied that the fall had insulted her.

But the fall was beautiful, too. There was the joy of winds blowing in from a darkly blue gulf and the splendour of harvest moons. There were lyric asters in the Hollow and children laughing in an apple-laden orchard, clear serene evenings on the high hill pastures of the Upper Glen and silvery mackerel skies with dark birds flying across them; and, as the days shortened, little grey mists stealing over the dunes and up the harbour.

With the falling leaves Rebecca Dew came to Ingleside to make a visit promised for years. She came for a week but was prevailed upon to stay two, none being so urgent as Susan. Susan and Rebecca Dew seemed to discover at first sight that they were kindred spirits . . . perhaps because they both loved Anne, perhaps because they both hated Aunt Mary Maria.

There came an evening in the kitchen when, as the rain dripped down on the dead leaves outside and the wind cried around the eaves and corners of Ingleside, Susan poured out all her woes to sympathetic Rebecca Dew. The doctor and his wife had gone out to make a call, the small fry were all cosy in their beds, and Aunt Mary Maria fortunately out of the way with a headache . . . 'just like a band of iron round my brain,' she had moaned.

'Anyone,' remarked Rebecca Dew, opening the oven door and depositing her feet comfortably in the oven, 'who eats as much fried mackerel as that woman did for supper *deserves* to have a headache. I do not deny I ate my share . . . for I will say, Miss Baker, I never knew anyone who could fry mackerel like you . . . but I did *not* eat four pieces.'

'Miss Dew, dear,' said Susan earnestly, laying down her knitting and gazing imploringly into Rebecca's little black eyes. 'You have seen something of what Mary Maria Blythe is like in the time you have been here. But you do not know the half . . . no, nor yet the quarter. Miss Dew, dear, I feel that I can trust you. May I open my heart to you in strict confidence?'

'You may, Miss Baker.'

'That woman came here in June and it is my opinion she means to stay here the rest of her life. Everyone in this house detests her . . . even the doctor has no use for her now, hide it as he will and does. But he is clannish and says his father's cousin must not be made to feel unwelcome in his house. I have begged,' said Susan, in a tone which seemed to imply she had done it on her knees, 'I have begged Mrs Doctor to put her foot down and say Mary Maria Blythe must go. But Mrs Doctor is too soft-hearted . . . and so we are helpless, Miss Dew . . . completely helpless.'

'I wish *I* had the handling of her,' said Rebecca Dew, who had smarted considerably herself under some of Aunt Mary Maria's remarks. 'I know as well as anyone, Miss Baker, that we must not violate the sacred proprieties of hospitality, but I assure you, Miss Baker, that I would let her have it straight.'

'*I* could handle her if I did not know my place, Miss Dew. I never forget that I am not mistress here. Sometimes, Miss Dew, I say solemnly to myself, "Susan Baker, are you or are you not a doormat?" But you know how my hands are tied. I *cannot* desert Mrs Doctor and I *must not* add to her troubles by fighting with Mary Maria Blythe. I shall continue to endeavour to do my duty. Because, Miss Dew, dear,' said Susan solemnly, 'I could cheerfully die for either the doctor or his wife. We were such a happy family before she came here, Miss Dew. But she is making our lives miserable, and what is to be the outcome I cannot tell, being no prophetess, Miss Dew. Or, rather, I *can* tell. We will all be driven into lunatic asylums. It is not any one thing, Miss Dew . . . it is scores of them, Miss Dew . . . hundreds of them, Miss Dew. You can endure one mosquito, Miss Dew . . . but think of millions of them!'

Rebecca Dew thought of them with a mournful shake of her head.

'She is always telling Mrs Doctor how to run her house and what clothes she should wear. She is always watching me . . . and she says she never saw such quarrelsome children. Miss Dew, dear, you have seen for yourself that our children *never* quarrel . . . well, hardly ever . . .'

'They are among the most admirable children I have ever seen, Miss Baker.'

'She snoops and pries . . .'

'I have caught her at it myself, Miss Baker.'

'She's always getting offended and heartbroken over something, but never offended enough to up and leave. She just sits around looking lonely and neglected until poor Mrs Doctor is almost distracted. Nothing suits her. If a window is open she complains of draughts. If they are all shut she says she *does* like a little fresh air once in a while. She can't bear onions . . . she can't ever bear the smell of them. She says they make her sick. So Mrs Doctor says we must not use any. Now,' said Susan grandly, 'it may be a common taste to like onions Miss Dew, dear, but we all plead guilty to it at Ingleside.'

'I am very partial to onions myself,' admitted Rebecca Dew.

'She cannot bear cats. She says cats give her the creeps. It does not make any difference whether she sees them or not. Just to know there is one about the place is enough for her. So that poor Shrimp hardly dare show his face in the house. I have never altogether liked cats myself, Miss Dew, but I maintain they have a right to wave their own tails. And it is, "Susan, never forget that I cannot eat eggs, please," or, "Susan, how often must I tell you that I cannot eat cold toast?" or, "Susan, some people may be able to drink stewed tea, but I am not in that fortunate class." Stewed tea, Miss Dew. As if I ever offered anyone stewed tea!'

'Nobody could ever suppose it of you, Miss Baker.'

'If there is a question that should not be asked she will ask it. She is jealous because the doctor tells things to his wife before he tells them to her . . . and she is always trying to pick news out of him about his patients. Nothing aggravates him so much, Miss Dew. A doctor must know how to hold his tongue, as you are well aware. And her tantrums about fire! "Susan Baker," says she to me, "I hope you never light a fire with coal oil. Or leave oily rags lying around, Susan. They have been known to cause spontaneous combustion in less than an hour. How would you like to stand and watch this house burn down, Susan, knowing it was your fault?" Well, Miss Dew, dear, I had my laugh on her over *that*. It was that very night she set her curtains on fire and the yells of her are ringing in my ears yet. And just when the poor doctor had got to sleep after having been up for two nights! What infuriates me most, Miss Dew, is that before she goes anywhere she goes into my pantry and *counts the eggs*. It takes all my philosophy to refrain from saying, "Why not count the spoons, too?" Of course, the children hate her. Mrs Doctor is just about worn out keeping them from showing it. She actually slapped Nan one day when the doctor and Mrs Doctor were both away . . . *slapped* her . . . just because Nan called her "Mrs Mefusaleh" . . . having heard that imp of Ken Ford saying it.'

'I'd have slapped *her*,' said Rebecca Dew viciously.

'I told her if she ever did the like again I *would* slap her. "An occasional spanking we do have at Ingleside," I told her, "but slapping never, so put that in pickle." She was sulky and offended for a week, but at least she has never dared to lay a finger on one of them since. She loves it when their parents punish them, though. "If *I* was your mother," she says to Little Jem one evening. "Oh, ho, you won't ever be anybody's mother," said the poor child . . . driven to it, Miss Dew, absolutely driven to it. The doctor sent him to bed without his supper, but who would you suppose, Miss Dew, saw that some was smuggled up to him later on?'

'Ah, now, *who*?' chortled Rebecca Dew, entering into the spirit of the tale.

'It would have broken your heart, Miss Dew, to hear the prayer he put up afterwards . . . all off his own bat, "O God, please forgive me for being impertinent to Aunt Mary Maria. And, O God, please help me to be always very polite to Aunt Mary Maria." It brought the tears into my eyes, the poor lamb. I do *not* hold with irreverence or impertinence from youth to age, Miss Dew, dear, but I must admit that when Bertie Shakespeare Drew threw a spit-ball at her one day – it just missed her by an inch, Miss Dew – I waylaid him at the gate on his way home and gave him a bag of doughnuts. Of course I did not tell him why. He was tickled over it, for doughnuts do not grow on trees, Miss Dew, and Mrs Second Skimmings never makes them. Nan and Di . . . I would not breathe this to a soul but you, Miss Dew . . . the doctor and his wife never dream of it or they would put a stop to it . . . Nan and Di have named their old china doll with the split head after Aunt Mary Maria, and whenever she scolds them they go out and drown her . . . the doll, I mean . . . in the rainwater hogshead. Many's the jolly drowning we have had, I can assure you. But you could not believe what that woman did the other night, Miss Dew.'

'I'd believe anything of her, Miss Baker.'

'She would not eat a bite of supper because her feelings had been hurt over something, but she went into the pantry before she went to bed and *ate up a lunch I had left for the poor doctor* . . . every crumb, Miss Dew, dear. I hope you will not think me an infidel, Miss Dew, but I cannot understand why the Good Lord does not get tired of some people.'

'You must not allow yourself to lose your sense of humour, Miss Baker,' said Rebecca Dew firmly.

'Oh, I am very well aware that there is a comical side to a toad under a harrow, Miss Dew. But the question is, does the toad see it? I am sorry to have bothered you with all this, Miss Dew, dear, but it has been a great relief. I cannot say these things to Mrs Doctor and I have been feeling lately that if I did not find an outlet I would *burst*.'

'How well I know that feeling, Miss Baker.'

'And now, Miss Dew, dear,' said Susan, getting up briskly, 'what do you say to a cup of tea before bed? And a cold chicken leg, Miss Dew?'

'I have never denied,' said Rebecca Dew, taking her well-baked feet out of the oven, 'that while we should not forget the Higher Things of Life good food is a pleasant thing in moderation.'

12

Gilbert had his two weeks' snipe shooting in Nova Scotia . . . not even Anne could persuade him to take a month . . . and November closed in on Ingleside. The dark hills, with the darker spruces marching over them, looked grim on early falling nights, but Ingleside bloomed with firelight and laughter, though the winds came in from the Atlantic singing of mournful things.

'Why isn't the wind happy, Mummy?' asked Walter one night.

'Because it is remembering all the sorrow of the world since time began,' answered Anne.

'It is moaning just because there is so much dampness in the air,' sniffed Aunt Mary Maria, 'and my back is killing me.'

But some days even the wind blew cheerfully through the silvery-grey maple wood, and some days there was no wind at all, only mellow Indian summer sunshine and the quiet shadows of the bare trees all over the lawn and frosty stillness at sunset.

'Look at that white evening star over the Lombardy in the corner,' said Anne. 'Whenever I see anything like that I am minded to be just glad I am alive.'

'You do say such funny things, Annie. Stars are quite common in P. E. Island,' said Aunt Mary Maria.

(*Stars, indeed! As if no one ever saw a star before. Didn't Annie know of the terrible waste that was going on in the kitchen every day? Didn't she know of the reckless way Susan Baker threw eggs about and used lard where dripping would do quite as well? Or didn't she care? Poor Gilbert! No wonder he had to keep his nose to the grindstone!*)

November went out in greys and browns: but by morning the snow had woven its old white spell and all the children shouted with delight as they rushed down to breakfast.

'Oh, Mummy, it will soon be Christmas now and Santa Claus will be coming.'

'You surely don't believe in Santa Claus *still*?' said Aunt Mary Maria.

Anne shot a glance of alarm at Gilbert, who said gravely:

'We want the children to possess their heritage of fairyland as long as they can, Auntie.'

Luckily Jem had paid no attention to Aunt Mary Maria. He and Walter were too eager to get out into the new wonderful world to which winter had brought its own loveliness. Anne always hated to see the beauty of the untrodden snow marred by footprints; but that could not be helped, and there was still beauty and to spare at eventide when the west was aflame over all the whitened hollows in the violet hills and Anne was sitting in the living room before a fire of rock maple. Firelight, she thought, was always so lovely. It did such tricksy, unexpected things. Parts of the room flashed into being and then out again. Pictures came and went. Shadows lurked and sprang. Outside, through the big unshaded window, the whole scene was elvishly reflected on the lawn with Aunt Mary Maria apparently sitting stark upright . . . Aunt Mary Maria never allowed herself to 'loll' . . . under the Scotch pine.

Gilbert was 'lolling' on the couch, trying to forget that he had lost a patient from pneumonia that day. Small Rilla was trying to eat her pink fists in her basket: even the Shrimp, with his white paws curled in under his breast, was daring to purr on the hearthrug, much to Aunt Mary Maria's disapproval.

'Speaking of cats,' said Aunt Mary Maria pathetically . . . though nobody *had* been speaking of them . . . 'do *all* the cats in the Glen visit us at night? How anyone could have slept through the caterwauling last night *I* really am at a loss to understand. Of course, my room being at the back I suppose I get the full benefit of the free concert.'

Before anyone had time to reply Susan entered, saying she had seen Mrs Marshall Elliott in Carter Flagg's store and she was coming up when she had finished her shopping. Susan did not add that Mrs Elliott had said anxiously, '*What* is the matter with Mrs Blythe, Susan? I thought last Sunday in church she looked so tired and worried. I never saw her look like that before.'

'*I* can tell you what is the matter with Mrs Blythe,' Susan had answered grimly. 'She has got a bad attack of Aunt Mary Maria. And the doctor cannot seem to see it, even though he does worship the ground she walks on.'

'Isn't that like a man?' said Mrs Elliott.

'I am glad,' said Anne, springing up to light a lamp. 'I haven't seen Miss Cornelia for so long. Now we'll catch up with the news.'

'Won't we!' said Gilbert drily.

'That woman is an evil-minded gossip,' said Aunt Mary Maria severely.

For the first time in her life perhaps Susan bristled up in defence of Miss Cornelia.

'That she is not, Miss Blythe, and Susan Baker will never stand by and hear her so miscalled. Evil-minded, indeed! Did you ever hear, Miss Blythe, of the pot calling the kettle black?'

'Susan . . . Susan,' said Anne imploringly.

'I beg your pardon, Mrs Doctor dear. I admit I have forgotten my place. But there are *some* things not to be endured.'

Whereupon a door was banged as doors were seldom banged at Ingleside.

'You see, Annie?' said Aunt Mary Maria significantly. 'But I suppose as long as you are willing to overlook that sort of thing in a servant there is nothing anyone can do.'

Gilbert got up and went to the library where a tired man might count on some peace. And Aunt Mary Maria, who didn't like Miss Cornelia, betook herself to bed. So that when Miss Cornelia came in she found Anne alone, drooping rather limply over the baby's basket. Miss Cornelia did not, as usual, start in unloading a budget of gossip. Instead, when she had laid aside her wraps, she sat down beside Anne and took her hand.

'Anne, dearie, what is the matter? I know there's something. Is that jolly old soul of a Mary Maria just tormenting you to death?'

Anne tried to smile.

'Oh, Miss Cornelia . . . I know I'm foolish to mind it so much . . . but this has been one of the days when it seems I just *cannot* go on enduring her. She . . . she's simply poisoning our life here . . .'

'Why don't you just tell her to go?'

'Oh, we can't do that, Miss Cornelia. At least, *I* can't, and Gilbert won't. He says he could never look himself in the face again if he turned his own flesh and blood out of doors.'

'Cat's hindfoot!' said Miss Cornelia eloquently. 'She's got plenty of money and a good home of her own. How would it be turning her out of doors to tell her she'd better go and live in it?'

'I know . . . but Gilbert . . . I don't think he quite realizes everything. He's away so much . . . and really . . . everything is so little in itself . . . I'm ashamed . . .'

'I know, dearie. Just those little things that are horribly big. Of course, a *man* wouldn't understand. I know a woman in Charlottetown who knows her well. She says Mary Maria Blythe never had a friend in her life. She says her name should be Blight, not Blythe. What you need, dearie, is just enough backbone to say you won't put up with it any longer.'

'I feel as you do in dreams when you're trying to run and can only drag your feet,' said Anne drearily. 'If it were only now and then . . . but it's every day. Mealtimes are perfect horrors now. Gilbert says he can't carve roasts any more.'

'He'd notice *that*,' sniffed Miss Cornelia.

'We can never have any real conversation at meals because she is sure to say something disagreeable every time anyone speaks. She corrects the children for their manners continually and always calls attention to their faults before company. We used to have such pleasant meals . . . and now! She resents laughter, and you know what we are for laughing. Somebody is always seeing a joke, or used to be. She can't let anything pass. Today she said, "Gilbert, don't sulk. Have you and Annie quarrelled?"

Just because we were quiet. You know Gilbert is always a little depressed when he loses a patient he thinks ought to have lived. And then she lectured us on our folly, and warned us not to let the sun go down on our wrath. Oh, we laughed at it afterwards . . . but just at the time! She and Susan don't get along. And we *can't* keep Susan from muttering asides that are the reverse of polite. She more than muttered when Aunt Mary Maria told her she had never seen such a liar as Walter . . . because she heard him telling Di a long tale about meeting the man in the moon and what they said to each other. She said he should have his mouth scrubbed out with soap and water. She and Susan had a battle royal that time. And she is filling the children's minds with all sorts of gruesome ideas. She told Nan about a child who was naughty and died in its sleep, and Nan is afraid to sleep now. She told Di that if she were always a good girl her parents would come to love her as well as they loved Nan, even if she did have red hair. Gilbert really was very angry when he heard that and spoke to her sharply. I couldn't help hoping she'd take offence and go . . . even though I would hate to have anyone leave my home because she was offended. But she just let those big blue eyes of hers fill with tears and said she didn't mean any harm. She'd always heard that twins were never loved equally, and she'd been thinking we favoured Nan and that poor Di felt it! She cried all night about it and Gilbert felt that he had been a brute . . . and *apologized*.'

'He would!' said Miss Cornelia.

'Oh, I shouldn't be talking like this, Miss Cornelia. When I "count my mercies" I feel it's very petty of me to mind these things, even if they do rub a little bloom off life. And she isn't always hateful . . . she is quite nice by spells . . .'

'Do you tell me so?' said Miss Cornelia sarcastically.

'Yes . . . and kind. She heard me say I wanted an afternoon tea set, and she sent to Toronto and got me one . . . by mail order! And, oh, Miss Cornelia, it's so ugly!'

Anne gave a laugh that ended in a sob. Then she laughed again.

'Now we won't talk of her any more . . . it doesn't seem so bad now that I've blurted this all out, like a baby. Look at wee Rilla, Miss Cornelia. Aren't her lashes darling when she is asleep? Now let's have a good gab-fest.'

Anne was herself again by the time Miss Cornelia had gone. Nevertheless, she sat thoughtfully before her fire for some time. She had not told Miss Cornelia all of it. She had never told Gilbert any of it. There were so many little things . . .

'So little I can't complain of them,' thought Anne. 'And yet . . . it's the little things that fret the holes in life . . . like moths . . . and ruin it.'

Aunt Mary Maria with her trick of acting hostess . . . Aunt Mary Maria inviting guests and never saying a word about it till they came. *She makes me feel as if I didn't belong in my own home* . . . Aunt Mary Maria moving the furniture around when Anne was out . . . 'I hope you didn't mind, Annie. I thought we need the table so much more here than in the library' . . . Aunt Mary Maria's insatiable childish curiosity about everything . . . her point-blank questions about intimate matters . . . *always coming into my room without knocking . . . always smelling smoke . . . always plumping up the cushions I've crushed . . . always implying that I gossip too much with Susan . . . always picking at the children . . . we have to be at them all the time to make them behave and then we can't manage it always.*

'Ugly old Aunt Maywia,' Shirley had said distinctly one dreadful day. Gilbert had been going to spank him for it, but Susan had risen up in outraged majesty and forbade it.

'We're cowed,' thought Anne. 'This household is beginning to revolve around the question, "Will Aunt Mary Maria like it?" We won't admit it, but it's true. Anything rather than have her wiping tears nobly away. It just can't go on.'

Then Anne remembered what Miss Cornelia had said . . . that Mary Maria Blythe had never had a friend. How terrible! Out of her own richness of friendships Anne felt a sudden rush of compassion for this woman who had never had a friend . . . who had nothing before her but a lonely, restless old age, with no one coming to her for shelter or healing, for hope and help, for warmth and love. Surely they could have patience with her. These annoyances were only superficial after all. They could not poison the deep springs of life.

'I've just had a terrible spasm of being sorry for myself, that's all,' said Anne, picking Rilla out of her basket and thrilling to the little round satin cheek against hers. 'It's over now and I'm wholeheartedly ashamed of it.'

13

'We never seem to have old-fashioned winters nowadays, do we, Mummy?' said Walter gloomily.

For the November snow had gone long ago, and all through December Glen St Mary had been a black and sombre land, rimmed in by a grey gulf dotted with curling crests of ice-white foam. There had been only a few sunny days, when the harbour sparkled in the golden arms of the hills: the rest had been dour and hard-bitten. In vain had the Ingleside folk hoped for snow for Christmas: but preparations went steadily on and as the last week drew to a close Ingleside was full of mystery and secrets and whispers and delicious smells. Now, on the very day before Christmas everything was ready. The fir tree Walter and Jem had brought up from the Hollow was in the corner of the living room, the doors and windows were hung with big green wreaths tied with huge bows of red ribbon. The banisters were twined with creeping spruce, and Susan's pantry was crammed to overflowing. Then, late in the afternoon, when everyone had resigned themselves to a dingy 'green' Christmas somebody looked out of a window and saw white flakes as big as feathers falling thickly.

'Snow! Snow!! Snow!!!' shouted Jem. 'A white Christmas after all, Mummy.'

The Ingleside children went to bed happy. It was so nice to snuggle down warm and cosy and listen to the storm howling outside through the grey, snowy night. Anne and Susan went to work to deck the Christmas tree . . . 'acting like two children themselves,' thought Aunt Mary Maria scornfully. She did not approve of candles on a tree . . . 'suppose the house caught fire from them' . . . she did not approve of coloured balls . . . 'suppose the twins ate them'. But nobody paid any attention to her. They had learned that that was the only condition on which life with Aunt Mary Maria was livable.

'Finished!' cried Anne, as she fastened the great silver star to the top of the proud little fir. 'And oh, Susan, doesn't it look pretty? Isn't it nice we can all be children again at Christmas without being ashamed of it? I'm so glad the snow came . . . but I hope the storm won't outlast the night.'

'It's going to storm all day tomorrow,' said Aunt Mary Maria positively. 'I can tell by my poor back.'

Anne went through the hall, opened the big front door and peered out. The world was lost in a white passion of snowstorm. The windowpanes were grey with drifted snow. The Scotch pine was an enormous sheeted ghost.

'It doesn't look very promising,' Anne admitted ruefully.

'God manages the weather yet, Mrs Doctor dear, and not Miss Mary Maria Blythe,' said Susan over her shoulder.

'I hope there won't be a sick call tonight at least,' said Anne as she turned away. Susan took one parting look into the gloom before she locked out the stormy night.

'Don't *you* go and have a baby tonight,' she warned darkly in the direction of the Upper Glen, where Mrs George Drew was expecting her fourth.

In spite of Aunt Mary Maria's back, the storm spent itself in the night and morning filled the secret hollows of snow among the hills with the red wine of winter sunrise. All the small fry were up early, looking starry and expectant.

'*Did* Santa get through the storm, Mummy?'

'No. He was sick and didn't dare try,' said Aunt Mary Maria, who was in a good humour . . . for her . . . and felt joky.

'Santa Claus got here all right,' said Susan before their eyes had time to blue, 'and after you've had your breakfast you'll see what he did to your tree.'

After breakfast Dad mysteriously disappeared, but nobody missed him because they were so taken up with the tree . . . the lovely tree, all gold and silver bubbles and lighted candles in the still dark room, with parcels in all colours and tied with the loveliest ribbon, piled about it. Then Santa appeared, a gorgeous Santa, all crimson and white fur, with a long white beard and *such* a jolly big stomach . . . Susan had stuffed three cushions into the red velveteen cassock Anne had made for Gilbert. Shirley screamed with terror at first, but refused to be taken out for all that. Santa distributed all the gifts with a funny little speech for every one in a voice that sounded oddly familiar even through the mask; and then, just at the end, his beard caught fire from a candle, and Aunt Mary Maria had some slight satisfaction out of the incident though not enough to prevent her from sighing mournfully.

'Ah me, Christmas isn't what it was when I was a child.' She looked with disapproval at the present Little Elizabeth had sent Anne from Paris . . . a beautiful little bronze reproduction of Artemis of the Silver Bow.

'What shameless hussy is that?' she inquired sternly.

'The goddess Diana,' said Anne, exchanging a grin with Gilbert.

'Oh, a heathen! Well, that's different, I suppose. But if I were you, Annie, I wouldn't leave it where the children can see it. Sometimes I am beginning to think there is no such thing as modesty left in the world. My grandmother,' concluded Aunt Mary Maria, with the delightful incon-sequence that characterized so many of her remarks, 'never wore less than three petticoats, winter and summer.'

Aunt Mary Maria had knitted 'wristers' for all the chil-dren out of a dreadful shade of magenta yarn, also a sweater for Anne, Gilbert received a bilious necktie; and Susan got a red flannel petticoat. Even Susan considered

red flannel petticoats out of date, but she thanked Aunt Mary Maria gallantly.

'Some poor home missionary may be the better of it,' she thought. 'Three petticoats, indeed! I flatter myself I am a decent woman, and I like that Silver Bow person. She may not have much in the way of clothes on, but if I had a figure like that I do not know that I would want to hide it. But now to see about the turkey stuffing . . . not that it will amount to much with no onion in it.'

Ingleside was full of happiness that day, just plain, old-fashioned happiness, in spite of Aunt Mary Maria, who certainly did not like to see people too happy.

'White meat only, please. (James, eat your soup quietly.) Ah, you are not the carver your father was, Gilbert. *He* could give everyone the bit she liked best. (Twins, older people would like a chance now and then to get a word in edgewise. *I* was brought up by the rule that children should be seen and not heard.) No, thank you, Gilbert, no salad for me. I don't eat raw food. Yes, Annie, I'll take a *little* pudding. Mince pies are entirely too indigestible.'

'Susan's mince pies are poems, just as her apple pies are lyrics,' said the doctor. 'Give *me* a piece of both, Anne-girl.'

'Do you really like to be called "girl" at your age, Annie? (Walter, you haven't eaten all your bread and butter. Plenty of poor children would be glad to have it. James, dear, blow your nose and have it over with, I *cannot* endure sniffling.)'

But it was a gay and lovely Christmas. Even Aunt Mary Maria thawed out a little after dinner, said almost graciously that the presents given her had been quite nice, and endured the Shrimp with an air of patient martyrdom that made them all feel a little ashamed of loving him.

'I think our little folk have had a nice time,' said Anne happily that night, as she looked at the pattern of trees woven against the white hills and sunset sky, and the children out on the lawn busily scattering crumbs for birds over the snow. The wind was sighing softly in the boughs, sending flurries over the lawn and promising more storm for the morrow, but Ingleside had had its day.

'I suppose they had,' agreed Aunt Mary Maria. 'I'm sure they did enough squealing anyhow. As for what they have eaten . . . ah, well, you're only young once, and I suppose you have plenty of castor oil in the house.'

14

It was what Susan called a streaky winter . . . all thaws and freezes that kept Ingleside decorated with fantastic fringes of icicles. The children fed seven blue jays who came regularly to the orchard for their rations and let Jem pick them up, though they flew from everybody else. Anne sat up o' nights to pore over seed catalogues in January and February. Then the winds of March swirled over the dunes and up the harbour and over the hills. Rabbits, said Susan, were laying Easter eggs.

'Isn't March an *in*citing month, Mummy?' cried Jem, who was a little brother to all the winds that blew.

They could have spared the 'incitement' of Jem scratching his hand on a rusty nail and having a nasty time of it for some days, while Aunt Mary Maria told all the stories of blood-poisoning she had ever heard. But that, Anne reflected when the danger was over, was what you must expect with a small son who was always trying experiments.

And lo, it was April! With the laughter of April rain . . .

the whisper of April rain . . . the trickle, the sweep, the drive, the lash, the dance, the splash of April rain. 'Oh, Mummy, hasn't the world got its face washed nice and clean?' cried Di, on the morning sunshine returned.

There were pale spring stars shining over the fields of mist, there were pussy willows in the marsh. Even the little twigs on the trees seemed all at once to have lost their clear, cold quality and to have become soft and languorous. The first robin was an event; the Hollow was once more a place full of wild free delights; Jem brought his mother the first mayflowers . . . rather to Aunt Mary Maria's offence, since she thought they should have been offered to *her;* Susan began sorting over the attic shelves, and Anne, who had hardly had a minute to herself all winter, put on spring gladness as a garment and literally lived in her garden, while the Shrimp showed his spring raptures by writhing all over the paths.

'You care more for the garden than you do for your husband, Annie,' said Aunt Mary Maria.

'My garden is so kind to me,' answered Anne dreamily . . . then, realizing the implications that might be taken out of her remark, began to laugh.

'You do say the most extraordinary things, Annie. Of course *I* know you don't mean that Gilbert isn't kind . . . but what if a stranger heard you say such a thing?'

'Dear Aunt Mary Maria,' said Anne gaily, 'I'm really not responsible for the things I say this time of the year.

Everybody around here knows that. I'm always a little mad in spring. But it's such a divine madness. Do you notice those mists over the dune like dancing witches? And the daffodils? We've never had such a show of daffodils at Ingleside before.'

'I don't care much for daffodils. They are such flaunting things,' said Aunt Mary Maria, drawing her shawl around her and going indoors to protect her back.

'Do you know, Mrs Doctor dear,' said Susan ominously, 'what has become of those new irises you wanted to plant in that shady corner? *She* planted them this afternoon, when you were out, right in the sunniest part of the backyard.'

'Oh, Susan! And we can't move them because she'd be so hurt!'

'If you will just give *me* the word, Mrs Doctor dear . . .'

'No, no, Susan, we'll leave them there for the time being. She cried, you remember, when I hinted that she shouldn't have pruned the spirea *before* blooming.'

'But sneering at our daffodils, Mrs Doctor dear . . . and them famous all around the harbour . . .'

'And deserve to be. Look at them laughing at you for minding Aunt Mary Maria. Susan, the nasturtiums are coming up in this corner after all. It's such fun when you've given up hope of a thing to find it has suddenly popped up. I'm going to have a little rose garden made in the south-west corner. The very name of rose garden thrills me to my toes. Did you ever see such a *blue* blueness of the sky before, Susan? And if you listen very carefully now at night you can hear all the little brooks of the countryside gossiping. I've half a notion to sleep in the Hollow tonight with a pillow of wild violets.'

'You would find it very damp,' said Susan patiently. Mrs Doctor was always like this in the spring. She knew it would pass.

'Susan,' said Anne coaxingly, 'I want to have a birthday party next week.'

'Well, and why should you not?' asked Susan. To be sure, none of the family had a birthday the last week in May, but if Mrs Doctor wanted a birthday party why boggle over that?

'For Aunt Mary Maria,' went on Anne, as one determined to get the worst over. 'Her birthday is next week. Gilbert says she is fifty-five, and I've been thinking . . .'

'Mrs Doctor dear, do you really mean to get up a party for that . . .'

'Count a hundred, Susan . . . count a hundred, Susan, dear. It would please her so. What has she in life after all?'

'That is her own fault . . .'

'Perhaps so. But, Susan, I really want to do this for her.'

'Mrs Doctor dear,' said Susan ominously, 'you have always been kind enough to give me a week's vacation whenever I felt I needed it. Perhaps I had better take it next week! I will ask my niece Gladys to come and help you out. And then Miss Mary Maria Blythe can have a dozen birthday parties for all of me.'

'If you feel like that about it, Susan, I'll give up the idea, of course,' said Anne slowly.

'Mrs Doctor dear, that woman has foisted herself upon you and means to stay here for ever. She has worried you . . . and henpecked the doctor . . . and made the children's lives miserable. I say nothing about myself, for who am I? She has scolded and nagged and insinuated and whined . . . and now you want to get up a birthday party for her! Well, all I can say is, if you want to do that . . . we'll just have to go ahead and have it!'

'Susan, you old duck!'

Plotting and planning followed. Susan, having yielded, was determined that for the honour of Ingleside the party must be something that even Mary Maria Blythe could not find fault with.

'I think we'll have a luncheon, Susan. Then they'll be away early enough for me to go to the concert at Lowbridge with the doctor. We'll keep it a secret and surprise her. She shan't know a thing about it till the last minute. I'll invite all the people in the Glen she likes . . .'

'And who may *they* be, Mrs Doctor dear?'

'Well, tolerates, then. And her cousin, Adella Carey from Lowbridge, and some people from town. We'll have a big plump birthday cake with fifty-five candles on it . . .'

'Which *I* am to make, of course . . .'

'Susan, you *know* you make the best fruitcake in P.E. Island . . .'

'I know that I am as wax in your hands, Mrs Doctor dear.'

A mysterious week followed. An air of hush-hush pervaded Ingleside. Everybody was sworn not to give the secret away to Aunt Mary Maria. But Anne and Susan had reckoned without gossip. The night before the party Aunt Mary Maria came home from a call in the Glen to find them sitting rather wearily in the unlighted sun room.

'All in the dark, Annie? It beats me how anyone can like sitting in the dark. It gives me the blues.'

'It isn't dark . . . it's twilight . . . there had been a love-match between light and dark, and beautiful exceedingly is the offspring thereof,' said Anne, more to herself than anybody else.

'I suppose you know what you mean yourself, Annie. And so you're having a party tomorrow?'

Anne suddenly sat bolt upright. Susan, already sitting so, could not sit any uprighter.

'Why . . . why . . . Auntie . . .'

'You always leave me to hear things from outsiders,' said Aunt Mary Maria, but seemingly more in sorrow than in anger.

'We . . . we meant it for a surprise, Auntie . . .'

'I don't know what you want of a party this time of year when you can't depend on the weather, Annie.'

Anne drew a breath of relief. Evidently Aunt Mary Maria knew only that there was to be a party, not that it had any connection with her.

'. . . I wanted to have it before the spring flowers were done, Auntie.'

'I shall wear my garnet taffeta. I suppose, Annie, if I had not heard of this in the village I should have been caught by all your fine friends tomorrow in a cotton dress.'

'Oh, no, Auntie. We meant to tell you in time to dress, of course . . .'

'Well, if my advice means anything to you, Annie . . . and sometimes I am almost compelled to think it does not . . . I would say that in future it would be better for you not to be *quite so secretive* about things. By the way, are you aware that they are saying in the village that it was Jem who threw the stone through the window of the Methodist church?'

'He did not,' said Anne quietly. 'He told me he did not.'

'Are you sure, Annie, dear, that he was not fibbing?'

'Annie dear' still spoke quietly.

'Quite sure, Aunt Mary Maria. Jem has never told me an untruth in his life.'

'Well, I thought you ought to know what was being said.'

Aunt Mary Maria stalked off in her usual gracious manner, ostentatiously avoiding the Shrimp, who was lying on his back on the floor entreating someone to tickle his stomach.

Susan and Anne drew a long breath.

'I think I'll go to bed, Susan. And I do hope it is going to be fine tomorrow. I don't like the look of that dark cloud over the harbour.'

'It will be fine, Mrs Doctor dear,' reassured Susan. 'The almanac says so.'

Susan had an almanac that foretold the whole year's weather and was right often enough to keep up its credit.

'Leave the side door unlocked for the doctor, Susan. He may be late getting home from town. He went in for the roses . . . fifty-five golden roses, Susan . . . I've heard Aunt Mary Maria say that yellow roses were the only flowers she liked.'

Half an hour later, Susan, reading her nightly chapter in her Bible, came across the verse, 'Withdraw thy foot from thy neighbour's house lest he weary of thee and hate thee.' She put a sprig of southernwood in it to mark the spot. 'Even in those days,' she reflected.

15

Anne and Susan were both up very early, desiring to complete certain last preparations before Aunt Mary Maria should be about. Anne always liked to get up early and catch that mystical half-hour before sunrise when the world belongs to the fairies and the old gods. She liked to see the morning sky of pale rose and gold behind the church spire, the thin, translucent glow of sunrise spreading over the dunes, the first violet spirals of smoke floating up from the village roofs.

'It's as if we had had a day made to order, Mrs Doctor dear,' said Susan complacently, as she feathered an orange-frosted cake with coconut. 'I will try my hand at them new-fangled butter balls after breakfast, and I will phone Carter Flagg every half-hour to make sure that he will not forget the ice cream. And there will be time to scrub the veranda steps.'

'Is that necessary, Susan?'

'Mrs Doctor dear, you have invited Mrs Marshall Elliott have you not? *She* shall not see *our* veranda steps otherwise than spotless. But you will see to the decorations, Mrs Doctor dear? I was not born with the gift of arranging flowers.'

'Four cakes! Gee!' said Jem.

'When we give a party,' said Susan grandly, 'we *give* a party.'

The guests came in due time, and were received by Aunt Mary Maria in garnet taffeta, and by Anne in biscuit-coloured voile. Anne thought of putting on her white muslin for the day was summer warm, but decided otherwise.

'Very sensible of you, Annie,' commented Aunt Mary Maria. 'White, I always say, is only for the young.'

Everything went according to schedule. The table looked beautiful, with Anne's prettiest dishes and the exotic beauty of white and purple iris. Susan's butter balls made a sensation, nothing like them having been seen in the Glen before; her cream soup was the last word in soups: the chicken salad had been made of Ingleside 'chickens that *are* chickens'; the badgered Carter Flagg sent up the ice cream on the tick of the dot. Finally, Susan, bearing the birthday cake with its fifty-five lighted candles as if it were the Baptist's head on a charger, marched in and set it down before Aunt Mary Maria.

Anne, outwardly the smiling, serene hostess, had been feeling very uncomfortable for some time. In spite of all outward smoothness she had an ever-deepening conviction that something had gone terribly wrong. On the guests' arrival she had been too much occupied to notice the change that came over Aunt Mary Maria's face when Mrs Marshall Elliott cordially wished her many happy returns of the day. But when they were all finally seated around the table Anne wakened up to the fact that Aunt Mary Maria was looking anything but pleased. She was actually white . . . it *couldn't* be with fury! . . . and not one word did she say as the meal progressed, save curt replies to remarks addressed to her. She took only two teaspoonfuls of soup and three mouthfuls of salad; as for the ice cream, she behaved to it as if it wasn't there.

When Susan set the birthday cake, with its flickering candles, down before her Aunt Mary Maria gave a fearful gulp, which was not quite successful in swallowing a sob and consequently issued as a strangled whoop.

'Auntie, aren't you feeling well?' cried Anne.

Aunt Mary Maria stared at her icily.

'*Quite* well, Annie. Remarkably well, indeed, for *such an aged person* as myself.'

At this auspicious moment the twins popped in, carrying between them the basketful of fifty-five yellow roses, and, amid a suddenly frozen silence, presented it to Aunt Mary Maria, with lisped congratulations and good wishes. A chorus of admiration went up from the table, but Aunt Mary Maria did not join in it.

'The . . . the twins will blow out the candles for you,

Auntie,' faltered Anne nervously, 'and then . . . will you cut the birthday cake?'

'Not being quite senile . . . yet . . . Annie, I can blow the candles out myself.'

Aunt Mary Maria proceeded to blow them out, painstakingly and deliberately. With equal painstaking and deliberation she cut the cake. Then she laid the knife down.

'And now perhaps I may be excused, Annie. *Such an old woman* as I am needs rest after so much excitement.'

Swish, went Aunt Mary Maria's taffeta skirt. Crash, went the basket of roses as she swept past it. Click, went Aunt Mary Maria's high heels up the stairs. Bang, went Aunt Mary Maria's door in the distance.

The dumbfounded guests ate their slices of birthday cake with such appetite as they could muster, in a strained silence, broken only by a story Mrs Amos Martin told desperately of a doctor in Nova Scotia who had poisoned several patients by injecting diphtheria germs into them. The others, feeling that this might not be in the best of taste, did not back up her laudable effort to 'liven things up', and all went away as soon as they decently could.

A distracted Anne rushed to Aunt Mary Maria's room.

'Auntie, *what* is the matter?'

'Was it necessary to advertise my age in public, Annie? And to ask Adella Carey here . . . to have her find out how old I am . . . she's been dying to know for years!'

123

'Auntie, we meant . . . we meant . . .'

'I don't know what your purpose was, Annie. That there is something back of all this I know very well . . . oh, I can read your mind, dear Annie, but I shall not try to ferret it out, I shall leave it between you and your conscience.'

'Aunt Mary Maria, my only intention was to give you a happy birthday . . . I'm dreadfully sorry.'

Aunt Mary Maria put her handkerchief to her eyes and smiled bravely.

'Of course I forgive you, Annie. But you must realize that after such a deliberate attempt to injure my feelings I cannot stay here any longer.'

'Auntie, won't you believe . . .'

Aunt Mary Maria lifted a long, thin, knobbly hand.

'Don't let us discuss it, Annie. I want peace . . . just peace. "A wounded spirit who can bear?"'

Anne went to the concert with Gilbert that night, but it could not be said she enjoyed it. Gilbert took the whole matter 'just like a man', as Miss Cornelia might have said.

'I remember she was always a little touchy about her age. Dad used to rag her. I should have warned you . . . but it had slipped my memory. If she goes, don't try to stop her' . . . and refrained through clannishness from adding, 'Good riddance!'

'She will not go. No such good luck, Mrs Doctor dear,' said Susan incredulously.

But for once Susan was wrong. Aunt Mary Maria went away the very next day, forgiving everybody with her parting breath.

'Don't blame Annie, Gilbert,' she said magnanimously. 'I acquit her of all intentional insult. I never minded her having secrets from me, though to a sensitive mind like mine . . . but in spite of everything I've always liked poor Annie . . .' this with the air of one confessing a weakness. 'But Susan Baker is a cat of another colour. My last word to you, Gilbert, is . . . put Susan Baker in her place and keep her there.'

Nobody could believe in their good luck at first. Then they woke up to the fact that Aunt Mary Maria had really gone . . . that it was possible to laugh again without hurting anyone's feelings . . . open all the windows without anyone complaining of draughts . . . eat a meal without anyone telling you that something you specially liked was liable to produce cancer of the stomach.

'I've never sped a parting guest so willingly,' thought Anne, half guiltily. 'It *is* nice to call your soul your own again.'

The Shrimp groomed himself meticulously . . . the first peony burst into bloom in the garden.

'The world is just full of poetry, isn't it, Mummy?' said Walter.

'It is going to be a real nice June,' foretold Susan. 'The almanac says so. There are going to be a few brides, and most likely at least two funerals. Does it not seem strange to be able to draw a free breath again? When I think that I did all that lay in me to prevent you giving that party, Mrs Doctor dear, I realize afresh that there is an overruling Providence. And don't you think, Mrs Doctor dear, that the doctor would relish some onions with his fried steak today?'

16

'I felt I had to come up, dearie,' said Miss Cornelia, 'and explain about that telephone. It was all a mistake . . . I'm so sorry . . . Cousin Sarah isn't dead after all.'

Anne, smothering a smile, offered Miss Cornelia a chair on the veranda, and Susan, looking up from the collar of Irish crochet lace she was making for her niece Gladys, uttered a scrupulously polite, 'Good evening, *Mrs* Marshall Elliott.'

'The word came out from the hospital this morning that she had passed away in the night and I felt I ought to inform you, since she was the Doctor's patient. But it was another Sarah Chase, and Cousin Sarah is living and likely to live, I'm thankful to say. It's real nice and cool here, Anne. I always say, if there's a breeze to be had anywhere it's at Ingleside.'

'Susan and I have been enjoying the charm of this starlit evening,' said Anne, laying aside the dress of pink, smocked muslin she was making for Nan and clasping her hands over her knees. An excuse to be idle for a little while was not unwelcome. Neither she nor Susan had many idle moments nowadays.

There was going to be a moonrise, and the prophecy of it was even lovelier than the moonrise itself would be. Tiger lilies were 'burning bright' along the walk and whiffs of honeysuckle went and came on the wings of the dreaming wind.

'Look at that wave of poppies breaking against the garden wall, Miss Cornelia. Susan and I are very proud of our poppies this year, though we hadn't a single thing to do with them. Walter spilt a packet of seed there by accident in the spring and this is the result. Every year we have some delightful surprise like that.'

'I'm partial to poppies,' admitted Miss Cornelia, 'though they don't last long.'

'They have only a day to live,' admitted Anne, 'but how imperially, how gorgeously they live it! Isn't that better than being a stiff, horrible zinnia, that lasts practically for ever? We have no zinnias at Ingleside. They're the only flowers we are not friends with. Susan won't even speak to them.'

'Anybody being murdered in the Hollow?' asked Miss Cornelia. Indeed, the sounds that came drifting up would seem to indicate that someone was being burned at the stake. But Anne and Susan were too accustomed to that to be disturbed.

'Persis and Kenneth have been there all day and they

wound up by a banquet in the Hollow. As for Mrs Chase, Gilbert went to town this morning, so he would know the truth about her. I am glad for everyone's sake she is doing so well . . . the other doctors did not agree with Gilbert's diagnosis and he was a little worried.'

'Sarah warned us when she went to the hospital that we were not to bury her unless we were sure she was dead,' said Miss Cornelia, fanning herself majestically and wondering how the doctor's wife always managed to look so cool. 'You see, we were always a little afraid her husband was buried alive . . . he looked so lifelike. But nobody thought of it until it was too late. He was a brother of this Richard Chase who bought the old Moorside farm and moved there from Lowbridge in the spring. *He's* a card. Said he came to the country to get some peace . . . he had to spend all his time in Lowbridge dodging widows' . . . 'and old maids,' Miss Cornelia might have added, but did not, out of regard for Susan's feelings.

'I've met his daughter Stella . . . she comes to choir practice. We've taken quite a fancy to each other.'

'Stella *is* a sweet girl, one of the few girls left that can blush. I've always loved her. Her mother and I used to be great cronies. Poor Lisette!'

'She died young?'

'Yes, when Stella was only eight. Richard brought Stella up himself. And him an infidel if he's anything! He says women are only important biologically . . . whatever that may mean. He's always shooting off some big talk like that.'

'He doesn't seem to have made such a bad job of bringing her up,' said Anne, who thought Stella Chase one of the most charming girls she had ever met.

'Oh, you couldn't spoil Stella. And I'm not denying Richard has got a good deal in his head-piece. But he's a crank about young men . . . he has never let poor Stella have a single beau in her life. All the young men who tried to go with her he simply terrified out of their senses with sarcasm. He is the most sarcastic creature you ever heard of. Stella can't manage him . . . her mother before her couldn't manage him. They didn't know how. He goes by contraries, but neither of them ever seemed to catch on to that.'

'I thought Stella seemed very devoted to her father.'

'Oh, she is. She adores him. He is a most agreeable man when he gets his own way about everything. But he should have more sense about Stella's marrying. He must know he can't live for ever, though to hear him talk you'd think he meant to. He isn't an old man, of course . . . he was very young when he was married. But strokes run in that family. And what is Stella to do after he's gone? Just shrivel up, I suppose.'

Susan looked up from the intricate rose of her Irish crochet long enough to say decidedly, 'I do not hold with old folks spoiling young ones' lives in that fashion.'

'Perhaps if Stella really cared for anyone her father's objections might not weigh much with her.'

'That's where you're mistaken, Anne, dearie. Stella would never marry anyone her father didn't like. And I can tell you another whose life is going to be spoiled and that's Marshall's nephew, Alden Churchill. Mary is *determined* he shan't marry as long as she can keep him from it. She's even more contrary than Richard . . . if she was a weathervane she'd point north when the wind was south. The property is hers till Alden marries and then it goes to him, you know. Every time he's gone about with a girl she has contrived to put a stop to it somehow.'

'Indeed, is it *all* her doings, *Mrs* Marshall Elliott?' queried Susan drily. 'Some folks think that Alden is very changeable. I have heard him called a flirt.'

'Alden is handsome and the girls chase him,' retorted Miss Cornelia. '*I* don't blame him for stringing them along a bit and dropping them when he's taught them a lesson. But there's been one or two nice girls he really liked and Mary just blocked it every time. She told me so herself, told me she went to the Bible . . . she's always "going to the Bible" . . . and turned up a verse and every time it was a warning against Alden getting married. I've no patience with her and her odd ways. Why can't she go to church and be a decent creature like the rest of us around Four Winds? But no, she must set up a religion for herself, consisting of "going to the Bible". Last fall, when that valuable horse took sick . . . worth four hundred if a dollar . . . instead of sending for the Lowbridge vet she "went to the Bible" and turned up a verse: "The Lord giveth and the Lord taketh away. Blessed be the name of the Lord." So send for the vet she would not and the horse died. Fancy applying that verse in such a way, Anne, dearie. I call it irreverent. I told her so flat, but all the answer I got was a dirty look. And she won't have the phone put in. "Do you think I'm going to talk into a box on the wall?" she says when anyone broaches it.'

Miss Cornelia paused, rather out of breath. Her sister-in-law's vagaries always made her impatient.

'Alden isn't at all like his mother,' said Anne.

'Alden's like his father . . . a finer man never stepped . . . as men go. Why he ever married Mary was something the Elliotts could never fathom. Though they were more than glad to get her married off so well . . . she always had a screw loose and such a bean-pole of a girl. Of course, she had lots of money, her Aunt Mary left her every-thing . . . but that wasn't the reason. George Churchill was really in love with her. I don't know how Alden stands his mother's whims; but he's been a good son.'

'Do you know what has just occurred to me, Miss Cornelia?' said Anne with an impish smile. 'Wouldn't it be a nice thing if Alden and Stella should fall in love with each other?'

'There isn't much chance of that, and they wouldn't get

anywhere if they did. Mary would tear up the turf and Richard would show a plain farmer the door in a minute, even if he is a farmer himself now. But Stella isn't the kind of girl Alden fancies . . . he likes the high-coloured laughing ones. And Stella wouldn't care for *his* type. I did hear the new minister at Lowbridge was making sheep's eyes at her.'

'Isn't he rather anaemic and short-sighted?' asked Anne.

'And his eyes bulge,' said Susan. 'They must be dreadful when he tries to look sentimental.'

'At least he's a Presbyterian,' said Miss Cornelia, as if that atoned for much. 'Well, I must be going. I find if I'm out in the dew much my neuralgia troubles me.'

'I'll walk down to the gate with you.'

'You always looked like a queen in that dress, Anne, dearie,' said Miss Cornelia, admiringly and irrelevantly.

Anne met Owen and Leslie Ford at the gate and brought them back to the veranda. Susan had vanished to get lemonade for the doctor, who had just arrived home, and the children came swarming up from the Hollow, sleepy and happy.

'You were making a dreadful noise as I drove in,' said Gilbert. 'The whole countryside must have heard you.'

Persis Ford, shaking back her thick, honey-tinted curls, stuck out her tongue at him. Persis was a great favourite with 'Uncle Gil'.

'We were just imitating howling dervishes, so of course we had to howl,' explained Kenneth.

'Look at the state your blouse is in,' said Leslie rather severely.

'I fell in Di's mudpie,' said Kenneth, with decided satisfaction in his tone. He loathed those starched, spotless blouses Mother made him wear when he came up to the Glen.

'Mother dearwums,' said Jem, 'can I have those old ostrich feathers in the garret to sew in the back of my pants for a tail? We're going to have a circus tomorrow and I'm to be the ostrich. And we're going to get an elephant.'

'Do you know that it costs six hundred dollars a year to feed an elephant?' said Gilbert solemnly.

'An imaginary elephant doesn't cost anything,' explained Jem patiently.

Anne laughed. 'We never need to be economical in our imaginations, thank heaven.'

Walter said nothing. He was a little tired and quite content to sit down beside Mother on the steps and lean his black head against her shoulder. Leslie Ford, looking at him, thought that he had the face of a genius . . . the remote, detached look of a soul from another star. Earth was not his habitat.

Everybody was very happy in this golden hour of a golden day. A bell in a church across the harbour rang faintly and sweetly. The moon was making patterns on the water. The dunes shimmered in hazy silver. There was a tang of mint in the air and some unseen roses were unbearably sweet. And Anne, looking dreamily over the lawn with eyes that, in spite of six children, were still very young, thought there was nothing in the world so slim and elfin as a very young Lombardy poplar by moonlight.

Then she began to think about Stella Chase and Alden Churchill until Gilbert broke in and offered her a penny for her thoughts.

'I'm thinking seriously of trying my hand at match-making,' retorted Anne.

Gilbert looked at the others in mock despair.

'I was afraid it would break out again some day. I've done my best, but you can't reform a born matchmaker. She has a positive passion for it. The number of matches she has made is incredible. I couldn't sleep o' nights if I had such responsibilities on my conscience.'

'But they're all happy,' protested Anne. 'I'm really an adept. Think of all the matches I've made, or been accused of making . . . Theodora Dix and Ludovic Speed . . . Stephen Clark and Prissie Gardner . . . Janet Sweet and John Douglas . . . Professor Carter and Esme Taylor . . . Nora and Jim . . . Dovie and Jarvis . . .'

'Oh, I admit it. This wife of mine, Owen, has never lost her sense of expectation. Thistles may, for her, bear figs at any time. I suppose she'll keep on trying to marry people off until she grows up.'

'I think she had something to do with another match yet,' said Owen, smiling at his wife.

'Not I,' said Anne promptly. 'Blame Gilbert for that. I did my best to persuade him not to have that operation performed on George Moore. Talk about sleeping o' nights . . . there are nights when *I* wake up in a cold perspiration dreaming that I succeeded.'

'Well, they say it is only happy women who matchmake, so that is one up for me,' said Gilbert complacently. 'What new victims have you in mind now, Anne?'

Anne only grinned at him. Matchmaking is something requiring subtlety and discretion, and there are things you do not tell even to your husband.

17

Anne lay awake for hours that night and several nights thereafter, thinking about Alden and Stella. She had a feeling that Stella thought longingly about marriage . . . a home . . . babies. She had begged one night to be allowed to give Rilla her bath. 'It's so delightful to bathe her plump, dimpled little body' . . . and again, shyly, 'It's so lovely, Mrs Blythe, to have little darling velvet arms stretched out to you. Babies are so *right*, aren't they?' It would be a shame if a grouchy father should prevent the blossoming of those secret hopes.

It would be an ideal marriage. But how could it be brought about, with everybody concerned a bit stubborn and contrary? For the stubbornness and contrariness were not all on the old folks' side. Anne suspected that both Alden and Stella had a streak of it. This required an entirely different technique from any previous affairs. In the nick of time Anne remembered Dovie's father.

Anne tilted her chin and went at it. Alden and Stella, she considered, were as good as married from that hour.

There was no time to be lost. Alden, who lived at the Harbour Head and went to the Anglican church over the harbour, had not even met Stella Chase as yet . . . perhaps had not even seen her. He had not been dangling after any girl for some months, but he might begin at any moment. Mrs Janet Swift, of the Upper Glen, had a very handsome niece visiting her, and Alden was always after the new girls. The first thing to do, then, was to have Alden and Stella meet. How was this to be managed? It must be brought about in some way absolutely innocent in appearance. Anne racked her brains but could think of nothing more original than giving a party and inviting them both. She did not altogether like the idea. It was hot weather for a party . . . and the Four Winds young people were such romps. Anne knew Susan would never consent to a party without practically house-cleaning Ingleside from attic to cellar . . . and Susan was feeling the heat this summer. But a good cause demands sacrifices. Jen Pringle, B.A., had written that she was coming for a long-promised visit to Ingleside, and that would be the very excuse for a party. Luck seemed to be on her side. Jen came . . . the invitations were sent out . . . Susan gave Ingleside its over-hauling . . . she and Anne did all the cooking for the party themselves in the heart of a heat wave.

Anne was woefully tired the night before the party. The heat had been terrible . . . Jem was sick in bed with an attack of what Anne secretly feared was appendicitis, though Gilbert lightly dismissed it as only green apples . . . and the Shrimp had been nearly scalded to death when Jen Pringle, trying to help Susan, knocked a pan of hot water off the stove on him. Every bone in Anne's body ached, her head ached, her feet ached, her eyes ached. Jen had gone with a group of young fry to see the lighthouse, telling Anne to go right to bed; but instead of going to bed she sat out on the veranda in the dampness that followed the afternoon's thunderstorm and talked to Alden Churchill, who had called to get some medicine for his mother's bronchitis, but would not go into the house. Anne thought it was a heaven-sent opportunity, for she wanted very much to have a talk with him. They were quite good friends, since Alden often called on a similar errand.

Alden sat on the veranda step with his bare head thrown back against the post. He was, as Anne always thought, a very handsome fellow . . . tall and broad-shouldered, with a marble-white face that never tanned, vivid blue eyes, and a stiff upstanding brush of inky black hair. He had a laughing voice and a nice, deferential way which women of all ages liked. He had gone to Queen's for three years and had thought of going to Redmond, but his mother refused to let him go, alleging Biblical reasons, and Alden had settled down contentedly enough on the farm. He liked farming, he had told Anne; it was free, out-of-doors, independent work: he had his mother's knack of making money and his father's attractive personality. It was no wonder he was considered something of a matrimonial prize.

'Alden, I want to ask a favour of you,' said Anne winningly. 'Will you do it for me?'

'Sure, Mrs Blythe,' he answered heartily. 'Just name it. You know I'd do anything for you.'

Alden was really very fond of Mrs Blythe and would really have done a good deal for her.

'I'm afraid it will bore you,' said Anne anxiously. 'But it's just this . . . I want you to see that Stella Chase has a good time at my party tomorrow night. I'm so afraid she won't. She doesn't know many young people around here yet . . . most of them are younger than she is . . . at least the boys are. Ask her to dance and see that she isn't left alone and out of things. She's so shy with strangers. I do want her to have a good time.'

'Oh, I'll do my best,' said Alden readily.

'But you mustn't fall in love with her, you know,' warned Anne, laughing carefully.

'Have a heart, Mrs Blythe. Why not?'

'Well,' confidentially, 'I think Mr Paxton of Lowbridge has taken quite a fancy to her.'

'That conceited young coxcomb,' exploded Alden, with unexpected warmth.

Anne looked mild rebuke.

'Why, Alden, I'm told he is a very nice young man. It's

only that kind of a man who would have any chance with Stella's father, you know.'

'That so?' said Alden, relapsing into his indifference.

'Yes . . . and I don't know if even he would. I understand Mr Chase thinks there is nobody good enough for Stella. I'm afraid a plain farmer wouldn't have a look in. So I don't want to make trouble for yourself falling in love with a girl you could never get. I'm just dropping a friendly warning. I'm sure your mother would think as I do.'

'Oh, thanks . . . thanks. What sort of a girl is she, anyhow? Looks good?'

'Well, I admit she isn't a beauty. I like Stella very much . . . but she's a little pale and retiring. Not overly strong . . . but I'm told Mr Paxton has money of his own. To my thinking it should be an ideal match and I don't want anyone to spoil it.'

'Why didn't you invite Mr Paxton to your spree and tell *him* to give your Stella a good time?' demanded Alden rather truculently.

'You know a minister wouldn't come to a dance, Alden. Now, don't be cranky . . . and do see that Stella has a nice time.'

'Oh, I'll see that she has a rip-roaring time. Good night, Mrs Blythe.'

Alden swung off abruptly. Left alone, Anne laughed.

'Now, if I know anything of human nature that boy will sail right in to show the world he can get Stella if he wants her, in spite of anybody. He rose right to my bait about the minister. Now I suppose I'm in for a bad night with this headache.'

She had a bad night, complicated by what Susan called 'a crick in the neck', and felt about as brilliant as grey flannel in the morning: but in the evening she was a gay and gallant hostess. The party was a success. Everybody seemed to have a good time. Stella certainly had. Alden saw to that almost too zealously for good form, Anne thought. It was going a bit strong for a first meeting that Alden should whisk Stella off to a dim corner of the veranda after supper and keep her there for an hour. But on the whole Anne was satisfied when she thought things over the next morning. To be sure, the dining-room carpet had been practically ruined by two spilled saucerfuls of ice cream and a plateful of cake being ground into it; Gilbert's grandmother's Bristol glass candlesticks had been smashed to smithereens; somebody had upset a pitcherful of rainwater in the spare room which had soaked down and discoloured the library ceiling in a tragic fashion; the tassels were half torn off the chesterfield; Susan's big Boston fern, the pride of her heart, had apparently been sat upon by some large and heavy person. But on the credit side of the ledger was the fact that, unless all signs failed, Alden had fallen for Stella. Anne thought the balance was in her favour.

Local gossip within the next few weeks confirmed this view. It became increasingly evident that Alden was hooked.

But what about Stella? Anne did not think Stella was the sort of girl to fall too ripely into any man's outstretched hand. She had a spice of her father's 'contrariness', which in her worked out as a charming independence.

Again luck befriended a worried matchmaker. Stella came to see the Ingleside delphiniums one evening, and afterwards they sat on the veranda and talked. Stella Chase was a pale, slender thing, rather shy but intensely sweet. She had a soft cloud of pale gold hair and wood-brown eyes. Anne thought it was her eyelashes did the trick, for she was not really pretty. They were unbelievably long, and when she lifted them and dropped them it did things to masculine hearts. She had a certain distinction of manner which made her seem a little older than her twenty-four years and a nose that might be decidedly aquiline in later life.

'I've been hearing things about you, Stella,' said Anne, shaking a finger at her. 'And . . . I . . . don't . . . know if . . . I . . . liked . . . them. Will you forgive me for saying that I wonder if Alden Churchill is just the right beau for you?'

Stella turned a startled face.

'Why . . . I thought you liked Alden, Mrs Blythe.'

'I do like him. But . . . well, you see, he has the reputation of being very, very fickle. I'm told no girl can hold him long. A good many have tried, and failed. I'd hate to see you left like that if his fancy veered.'

'I think you are mistaken about Alden, Mrs Blythe,' said Stella slowly.

'I hope so, Stella. If you were a different type now, bouncing and jolly, like Eileen Swift . . .'

'Oh, well . . . I must be going home,' said Stella vaguely. 'Father will be lonely.'

When she had gone Anne laughed again.

'I rather think Stella has gone away secretly vowing that she will show meddlesome friends that she can hold Alden and that no Eileen Swift shall ever get her claws on him. That little toss of her head and that sudden flush on her cheeks told me that. So much for the young folks. I'm afraid the older ones will be tougher nuts to crack.'

18

Anne's luck held. The Women's Missionary Auxiliary asked her if she would call on Mrs George Churchill for her yearly contribution to the society. Mrs Churchill seldom went to church and was not a member of the Auxiliary, but she 'believed in missions' and always gave a generous sum if anyone called and asked for it. People enjoyed doing this so little that the members had to take their turn at it, and this year the turn was Anne's.

She walked down one evening, taking a daisied trail across lots which led over the sweet, cool loveliness of a hilltop to the road where the Churchill farm lay, a mile from the Glen. It was rather a dull road, with grey snake fences, running up steep little slopes . . . yet it had home-lights . . . a brook . . . the smell of hayfields that ran down to the sea . . . gardens. Anne stopped to look at every garden she passed. Her interest in gardens was perennial. Gilbert was wont to say that Anne *had* to buy a book if the word 'garden' were in the title.

A lazy boat idled down the harbour and far out a vessel

was becalmed. Anne always watched an outward-bound ship with a little quickening of her pulses. She understood Captain Franklin Drew when she heard him say once, as he went on board his vessel at the wharf, 'God, how sorry I am for the folks we leave on shore!'

The big Churchill house, with the grim iron lacework around its flat mansard roof, looked down on the harbour and the dunes. Mrs Churchill greeted her politely, if none too effusively, and ushered her into a gloomy and splendid parlour, the dark, brown-papered walls of which were hung with innumerable crayons of departed Churchills and Elliotts. Mrs Churchill sat down on a green plush sofa, folded her long thin hands, and gazed steadily at her caller.

Mary Churchill was tall and gaunt and austere. She had a prominent chin, deep-set blue eyes like Alden's, and a wide, compressed mouth. She never wasted words and she never gossiped. So Anne found it rather difficult to work up to her objective naturally, but she managed it through the medium of the new minister in the Anglican church across the harbour, whom Mrs Churchill did not like.

'He is not a spiritual man,' said Mrs Churchill coldly.

'I have heard that his sermons are remarkable,' said Anne.

'I heard one and do not wish to hear more. My soul sought food and was given a lecture. He believes the kingdom of heaven can be taken by brains. It cannot.'

'Speaking of ministers . . . they have a very clever one at Lowbridge now. I think he is interested in my young friend, Stella Chase. Gossip says it will be a match.'

'Do you mean a marriage?' said Mrs Churchill.

Anne felt snubbed but reflected that you had to swallow things like that when you were interfering in what didn't concern you.

'I think it would be a very suitable one, Mrs Churchill. Stella is especially fitted for a minister's wife. I've been telling Alden he mustn't try to spoil it.'

'Why?' asked Mrs Churchill, without the flicker of an eyelid.

'Well . . . really . . . you know, I'm afraid Alden would stand no chance whatever. Mr Chase doesn't think anyone good enough for Stella. All Alden's friends would hate to see him dropped suddenly like an old glove. He's too nice a boy for that.'

'No girl ever dropped my son,' said Mrs Churchill, compressing her thin lips. 'It was always the other way about. He found them out, for all their curls and giggles, their wrigglings and mincings. My son can marry any woman he chooses, Mrs Blythe . . . *any* woman.'

'Oh?' said Anne's tongue. Her tone said, 'Of course I am too polite to contradict you, but you have not changed my opinion.' Mary Churchill understood, and her white, shrivelled face warmed a little as she went out of the room to get her missionary contribution.

'You have the most wonderful view here,' said Anne, when Mrs Churchill ushered her to the door.

Mrs Churchill gave the gulf a glance of disapproval.

'If you felt the bite of the east wind in winter, Mrs Blythe, you might not think so much of the view. It's cool enough tonight. I should think you'd be afraid of catching cold in that thin dress. Not but what it's a pretty one. You are young enough still to care for gauds and vanities. I have ceased to feel any interest in such transitory things.'

Anne felt fairly well satisfied with the interview as she went home through the dim green twilight.

'Of course one can't count on Mrs Churchill,' she told a flock of starlings who were holding a parliament in a little field scooped out of the woods, 'but I think I worried her a little. I could see she didn't like having people think Alden *could* be jilted. Well, I've done what in me lies with all concerned except Mr Chase, and I don't see what I can do with him when I don't even know him. I wonder if he has the slightest notion that Alden and Stella are sweethearting. Not likely. Stella would never dare take Alden to the house, of course. Now, what *am* I to do about Mr Chase?'

It was really uncanny . . . the way things helped her out. One evening Miss Cornelia came along and asked Anne to accompany her to the Chase home.

'I'm going down to ask Richard Chase for a contribution to the new church kitchen stove. Will you come with me, dearie, just as a moral support? I hate to tackle him alone.'

They found Mr Chase standing on his front steps, looking, with his long legs and his long nose, rather like a meditative crane. He had a few shining strands of hair brushed over the top of his bald head and his little grey eyes twinkled at them. He happened to be thinking that if that was the doctor's wife with old Cornelia she had a mighty good figure. As for Cousin Cornelia, twice removed, she was a bit too solidly built and had about as much intellect as a grasshopper, but she wasn't a bad old cat at all if you always rubbed her the right way.

He invited them courteously into his small library, where Miss Cornelia settled into a chair with a little grunt.

'It's dreadful hot tonight. I'm afraid we'll have a thunderstorm. Mercy on us, Richard, that cat is bigger than ever.'

Richard Chase had a familiar in the shape of a yellow cat of abnormal size which now climbed up on his knee. He stroked it tenderly. 'Thomas the Rhymer gives the world assurance of a cat,' he said. 'Don't you, Thomas? Look at your Aunt Cornelia, Rhymer. Observe the baleful glances she is casting at you out of orbs created to express only kindness and affection.'

'Don't you call me that beast's Aunt Cornelia,' protested Mrs Elliott sharply. 'A joke is a joke, but that is carrying things too far.'

'Wouldn't you rather be the Rhymer's aunt than Neddy Churchill's aunt?' queried Richard Chase plaintively. 'Neddy is a glutton and a wine-bibber, isn't he? I've heard you giving a catalogue of his sins. Wouldn't you rather be aunt to a fine upstanding cat like Thomas with a blameless record where whisky and tabbies are concerned?'

'Poor Ned is a human being,' retorted Miss Cornelia. 'I don't like cats. That is the only fault I have to find with Alden Churchill. He has got the strangest liking for cats, too. Lord knows where he got it . . . both his father and mother loathed them.'

'What a sensible young man he must be!'

'Sensible! Well, he's sensible enough, except in the matter of cats and his hankering after evolution . . . another thing he didn't inherit from his mother.'

'Do you know, Mrs Elliott,' said Richard Chase solemnly, 'I have a secret leaning towards evolution myself.'

'So you've told me before. Well, believe what you want to, Dick Chase . . . just like a man. Thank God, nobody could ever make *me* believe that I descended from a monkey.'

'You don't look it, I confess, you comely woman. I see no simian resemblances in your rosy, comfortable, eminently gracious physiognomy. Still, your great-grandmother a million times removed swung herself from branch to branch by her tail. Science proves that, Cornelia . . . take it or leave it.'

'I'll leave it, then. I'm not going to argue with you on

that or any point. I've got my own religion, and no ape-ancestors figure in it. By the way, Richard, Stella doesn't look so well this summer as I'd like to see her.'

'She always feels the hot weather a good deal. She'll pick up when it's cooler.'

'I hope so. Lisette picked up every summer but the last, Richard . . . don't forget that. Stella has her mother's constitution. It's just as well she isn't likely to marry.'

'Why isn't she likely to marry? I ask from curiosity, Cornelia . . . rank curiosity. The processes of feminine thought are intensely interesting to me. From what premises or data do you draw the conclusion, in your own delightful offhand way, that Stella is not likely to marry?'

'Well, Richard, to put it plainly, she isn't the kind of girl that is very popular with men. She's a sweet, good girl but she doesn't take with men.'

'She has had admirers. I have spent much of my substance in the purchase and maintenance of shotguns and bulldogs.'

'They admired your moneybags, I fancy. They were easily discouraged, weren't they? Just one broadside of sarcasm from you and off they went. If they had really wanted Stella they wouldn't have wilted for that any more than for your imaginary bulldogs. No, Richard, you might as well admit the fact that Stella isn't the girl to win desirable beaux. Lisette wasn't, you know. She never had a beau till you came along.'

'But wasn't I worth waiting for? Surely Lisette was a wise young woman. You would not have me give my daughter to any Tom, Dick or Harry, would you? My Star, who, in spite of your disparaging remarks, is fit to shine in the palaces of kings?'

'We have no kings in Canada,' retorted Miss Cornelia. 'I'm not saying Stella isn't a lovely girl. I'm only saying the men don't seem to see it, and, considering her constitution, I think it is just as well. A good thing for you, too. You could never get on without her . . . you'd be as helpless as a baby. Well, promise us a contribution to the church stove range and we'll be off. I know you're dying to pick up that book of yours.'

'Admirable, clear-sighted woman! What a treasure you are for a cousin-in-law! I admit it . . . I *am* dying. But no other than yourself would have been perspicacious enough to see it or amiable enough to save my life by acting upon it. How much are you holding me up for?'

'You can afford five dollars.'

'I never argue with a lady. Five dollars it is. Ah, going? She never loses time, this unique woman! Once her object is attained she straightway leaves you in peace. They don't hatch her breed of cats nowadays. Good evening, pearl of in-laws.'

During the whole call Anne had not uttered one word. Why should she when Mrs Elliott was doing her work for her so cleverly and unconsciously? But as Richard Chase bowed them out he suddenly bent forward confidentially.

'You've got the finest pair of ankles I've ever seen, Mrs Blythe, and I've been about a bit in my time.'

'Isn't he dreadful?' gasped Miss Cornelia as they went down the lane. 'He's always saying outrageous things like that to women. You mustn't mind him, Anne, dearie.'

Anne didn't. She rather liked Richard Chase.

'I don't think,' she reflected, 'that he quite liked the idea of Stella not being popular with the men, in spite of the fact that their grandfathers were monkeys. I think he'd like to "show folks", too. Well, I have done all I can do. I have interested Alden and Stella in each other; and, between us, Miss Cornelia and I have, I think, made Mrs Churchill and Mr Chase rather for the match than against it. Now I must just sit tight and see how it turns out.'

A month later Stella Chase came to Ingleside and again sat down by Anne on the veranda steps . . . thinking, as she did so, that she hoped she would look like Mrs Blythe some day . . . with that *ripened* look . . . the look of a woman who has lived fully and graciously.

The cool, smoky evening had followed a cool, yellowish-grey day in early September. It was threaded with the gentle moan of the sea.

'The sea is unhappy tonight,' Walter would say when he heard that sound.

Stella seemed absent-minded and quiet. Presently she said abruptly, looking up at a sorcery of stars that was being woven in the purple night, 'Mrs Blythe, I want to tell you something.'

'Yes, dear?'

'I'm engaged to Alden Churchill,' said Stella desperately. 'We've been engaged ever since last Christmas. We told Father and Mrs Churchill right away but we've kept it a secret from everyone else just because it was so sweet to have such a secret. We hated to share it with the world. But we are going to be married next month.'

Anne gave an excellent imitation of a woman who had been turned to stone.

Stella was still staring at the stars so that she did not see the expression on Mrs Blythe's face. She went on, a little more easily:

'Alden and I met at a party in Lowbridge last November. We . . . we loved each other from the very first moment. He said he had always dreamed of me, had always been looking for me. He said to himself, "There is my wife," when he saw me come in at the door. And I . . . I felt just the same. Oh, we are so happy, Mrs Blythe.'

Still Anne said nothing, several times over.

'The only cloud on my happiness is your attitude about the matter, Mrs Blythe. Won't you try to approve? You've been such a dear friend to me since I came to Glen St Mary . . . I've felt as if you were an older sister. And I'll feel so badly if I think my marriage is against your wish.'

There was a sound of tears in Stella's voice. Anne recovered her power of speech.

'Dearest, your happiness is all I've wanted. I like Alden . . . he's a splendid fellow . . . only he *had* the reputation of being a flirt . . .'

'But he isn't. He was just looking for the right one, don't you see, Mrs Blythe? And he couldn't find her.'

'How does your father regard it?'

'Oh, Father is greatly pleased. He took to Alden from the start. They used to argue for hours about evolution. Father said he always meant to let me marry when the right man came along. I feel dreadfully about leaving him, but he says young birds have a right to their own nest. Cousin Delia Chase is coming to keep house for him and Father likes her very much.'

'And Alden's mother?'

'She is quite willing, too. When Alden told her last Christmas that we were engaged she went to the Bible and the very first verse she turned up was, "A man shall leave father and mother and cleave unto his wife." She said it was perfectly clear then what she ought to do and she consented at once. She is going to go to that little house of hers in Lowbridge.'

'I am glad you won't have to live with that green plush sofa,' said Anne.

'The sofa? Oh, yes, the furniture is very old-fashioned, isn't it? But she is taking it with her and Alden is going to refurnish completely. So you see everyone is pleased, Mrs Blythe, and won't you give us your good wishes, too?'

Anne leaned quickly forward and kissed Stella's cool satin cheek.

'I am *very* glad for you. God bless the days that are coming for you, my dear.'

When Stella had gone Anne flew up to her own room to avoid seeing anyone for a few moments. A cynical, lopsided old moon was coming out from behind some shaggy clouds in the east and the fields beyond seemed to wink slyly and impishly at her.

She took stock of all the preceding weeks. She had ruined her dining-room carpet, destroyed two treasured heirlooms, and spoiled her library ceiling; she had been trying to use Mrs Churchill as a cat's paw, and Mrs Churchill must have been laughing in her sleeve all the time.

'Who,' asked Anne of the moon, 'has been made the biggest fool of in this affair? I know what Gilbert's opinion will be. All the trouble I've gone to, to bring about a marriage between two people who were already engaged! I'm cured of matchmaking . . . absolutely cured. Never will I lift a finger to promote a marriage if nobody in the world ever gets married again. Well, there is one consolation . . . Jen Pringle's letter today saying she is going to marry Lewis Stedman, whom she met at my party. The Bristol candlesticks were not sacrificed entirely in vain.

Boys . . . boys! *Must* you make such unearthly noises down there?'

'We're owls . . . we *have* to hoot,' Jem's injured voice proclaimed from the dark shrubbery. He knew he was making a very good job of hooting. Jem could mimic the voice of any little wild thing out in the woods. Walter was not so good at it and he presently ceased being an owl and became a rather disillusioned little boy, creeping to Mother for comfort.

'Mummy, I thought crickets *sang* . . . and Mr Carter Flagg said today they don't . . . they just make that noise scraping their hindlegs. *Do* they, Mummy?'

'Something like that . . . I'm not quite sure of the process. But *that* is their way of singing, you know.'

'I don't like it. I'll never like to hear them singing again.'

'Oh, yes, you will. You'll forget about the hindlegs in time and just think of their fairy chorus all over the harvest meadows and the autumn hills. Isn't it bedtime, small son?'

'Mummy, will you tell me a bedtime story that will send a cold chill down my spine? And sit beside me afterwards till I go to sleep?'

'What else are mothers for, darling?'

19

'"The time has come the Walrus said to talk of" . . . having a dog,' said Gilbert.

They had not had a dog at Ingleside since old Rex had been poisoned, but boys should have a dog, and the doctor decided he would get them one. But he was so busy that fall that he kept putting it off; and finally one November day Jem arrived home from an afternoon spent with a school pal carrying a dog . . . a little 'yaller' dog with two black ears sticking cockily up.

'Joe Reese gave it to me, Mother. His name is Gyp. Hasn't he got the cutest tail? I can keep him, can't I, Mother?'

'What kind of a dog is he, darling?' asked Anne dubiously.

'I . . . I think he's a lot of kinds,' said Jem. 'That makes him more int'resting, don't you think, Mother? More exciting than if he was just one kind. *Please*, Mother.'

'Oh, if your father says yes . . .'

Gilbert said 'Yes' and Jem entered into his heritage. Everybody at Ingleside welcomed Gyp into the family except the Shrimp, who expressed his opinion without circumlocution. Even Susan took a liking to him, and when she spun in the garret on rainy days Gyp, in his master's absence at school, stayed with her, gloriously hunting imaginary rats in dark corners and uttering a yelp of terror whenever his eagerness brought him too close to the little spinning wheel. It was never used . . . the Morgans had left it there when they moved out . . . and sat in its dark corner like a little bent old woman. Nobody could understand Gyp's fear of it: he did not mind the big wheel at all, but sat quite close to it while Susan sent it whirling around with her wheel-pin, and raced back and forward beside her as she paced the length of the garret, twirling the long thread of wool. Susan admitted that a dog could be real company and thought his trick of lying on his back, waving his forepaws in the air, when he wanted a bone, the cleverest ever. She was as angry as Jem when Bertie Shakespeare sneeringly remarked:

'Call that a dog?'

'We *do* call it a dog,' said Susan with ominous calm. 'Perhaps *you* would call it a hippopotamus.' And Bertie had to go home that day without getting a piece of a wonderful concoction Susan called 'apple crunch pie' and made regularly for the two boys and their pals. She was not around when Mac Reese asked, 'Did the tide bring that in?' but Jem was able to stand up for his own dog, and when Nat Flagg said that Gypsy's legs were too long for his size Jem retorted that a dog's legs had to be long enough to reach the ground. Natty was not over bright and that floored him.

November was stingy of its sunshine that year: raw winds blew through the bare, silver-branched maple grove and the Hollow was almost constantly filled with mist ... not a gracious, eerie thing like a fog but what Dad called 'dank, dark, depressing, dripping, drizzly mist'. The Ingleside fry had to spend most of their playtime in the garret, but they made delightful friends of two partridges that came every evening to a certain huge old appletree and five gorgeous jays who came to the backyard, chuckling impishly as they ate the food the children put out for them. Only they were greedy and selfish and kept all the other birds away.

Winter set in with December and it snowed ceaselessly for three weeks. The fields beyond Ingleside were unbroken silver pastures, fence and gateposts wore tall white caps, windows whitened with fairy patterns and Ingleside lights bloomed out through the dim, snowy twilights, welcoming all wanderers home. It seemed to Susan that there had never been so many winter babies as there were that year; and when she left 'the doctor's bite' in the pantry for him night after night she darkly opined that it would be a miracle if he toughed it out till spring.

'The ninth Drew baby! As if there weren't enough Drews in the world already!'

'I suppose Mrs Drew will think it just the wonder we think Rilla, Susan.'

'You *will* have your joke, Mrs Doctor dear.'

But in the library or the big kitchen the children planned out their summer playhouse in the Hollow while storms howled outside, or fluffy white clouds were blown over frosty stars. For blow it high or blow it low there was always at Ingleside laughter and firelight and the odours of good cheer.

Christmas came and went undarkened this year by any shadow of Aunt Mary Maria. There were rabbit trails in the snow to follow, and great crusted fields over which you raced with your shadows, and glistening hills for coasting, and new skates to be tried out on the pond in the chill, rosy world of winter sunset. And always a yellow dog with black ears to run with you or meet you with ecstatic yelps of welcome when you came home, to sleep at the foot of your bed when you slept, and lie at your feet while you learned your spellings, to sit close to you at meals and give you occasional reminding nudges with his little paw.

'Mother dearwums, I don't know how I lived before Gyp came. He can talk, Mother . . . he can really . . . with his eyes, you know.'

Then . . . tragedy! One day Gyp seemed a little dull. He would not eat, though Susan tempted him with the spare rib bone he loved; the next day the Lowbridge vet was sent for and shook his head. It was hard to say . . . the dog might have found something poisonous in the woods . . . he might recover and he might not. The little dog lay very quietly, taking no notice of anyone except Jem; almost to the last he tried to wag his tail when Jem touched him.

'Mother dearwums, would it be wrong to pray for Gyp?'

'Of course not, dear. We can pray always for anything we love. But I am afraid . . . Gyppy is a very sick little dog.'

'Mother, you don't think Gyppy is going to die!'

Gyp died the next morning. It was the first time death had entered into Jem's world. No one of us ever forgets the experience of watching something we love die, even if it is 'only a little dog'. Nobody at weeping Ingleside used that expression, not even Susan, who wiped a very red nose and muttered:

'I never took up with a dog before . . . and I never will again. It hurts too much.'

Susan was not acquainted with Kipling's poem on the folly of giving your heart to a dog to tear; but if she had been she would, in spite of her contempt for poetry, have thought that for once a poet had uttered sense.

Night was hard for poor Jem. Mother and Father had to be away. Walter had cried himself to sleep, and he was alone . . . with not even a dog to talk to. The dear brown eyes that had always been lifted to him so trustingly were glazed in death.

'Dear God,' prayed Jem, 'please look after my little dog who died today. You'll know him by the two black ears. Don't let him be lonesome for me . . .'

Jem buried his face in the bedspread to smother a sob. When he put out the light the dark night would be looking through the window at him and there would be no Gyp. The cold winter morning would come and there would be no Gyp. Day would follow day for years and years and there would be no Gyp. He just couldn't bear it.

Then a tender arm was slipped around him and he was held close in a warm embrace. Oh, there was love left yet in the world, even if Gyppy had gone.

'Mother, will it always be like this?'

'Not always.' Anne did not tell him he would soon forget . . . that before long Gyppy would only be a dear memory. 'Not always, Little Jem. This will heal some time . . . as your burned hand healed, though it hurt so much at first.'

'Dad said he would get me another dog. I don't have to have it, do I? I don't want another dog, Mother . . . not ever.'

'I know, darling.'

Mother knew everything. Nobody had a mother like his. He wanted to do something for her, and all at once it came to him what he would do. He would get her one of those pearl necklaces in Mr Flagg's store. He had heard her say once that she really would like to have a pearl necklace, and Dad had said, 'When our ship comes in I'll get you one, Anne-girl.'

Ways and means must be considered. He had an allowance, but it was all needed for necessary things and pearl necklaces were not among the items budgeted for. Besides, he wanted to earn the money for it himself. It would be really his gift then. Mother's birthday was in March, only six weeks away. And the necklace would cost fifty cents!

20

It was not easy to earn money in the Glen, but Jem went at it determinedly. He made tops out of old reels for the boys in school for two cents apiece. He sold three treasured milk teeth for three cents. He sold his slice of apple crunch pie every Saturday afternoon to Bertie Shakespeare Drew. Every night he put what he had earned into the little brass pig Nan had given him for Christmas. Such a nice, shiny brass pig with a slit in his back wherein to drop coins. When you had put in fifty coppers the pig would open neatly of his own accord if you twisted his tail and yield you back your wealth. Finally, to make up the last eight cents he sold his string of birds' eggs to Mac Reese. It was the finest string in the Glen and it hurt a little to let it go. But the birthday was drawing nearer and the money must be come by. Jem dropped the eight cents into the pig as soon as Mac had paid him and gloated over it.

'Twist his tail and see if he will really open up,' said

Mac, who didn't believe he would. But Jem refused; he was not going to open it until he was ready to go for the necklace.

The Missionary Auxiliary met at Ingleside the next afternoon and never forgot it. Right in the middle of Mrs Norman Taylor's prayer . . . and Mrs Norman Taylor was credited with being very proud of her prayers . . . a frantic small boy burst into the living room.

'My brass pig's gone, Mother . . . my brass pig's gone!'

Anne hustled him out, but Mrs Norman always considered that her prayer was spoiled and, as she had especially wanted to impress a visiting minister's wife, it was long years before she forgave Jem or would have his father as a doctor again. After the ladies had gone home Ingleside was ransacked from top to bottom for the pig, without result. Jem, between the scolding he had got for his behaviour and his anguish over his loss, couldn't remember just when he had seen it last or where. Mac Reese, telephoned to, responded that the last he had seen of the pig it was standing on Jem's bureau.

'You don't suppose, Susan, that Mac Reese . . .'

'No, Mrs Doctor dear, I feel quite sure he didn't. The Reeses have their faults . . . terrible keen after money they are, but it has to be honestly come by. *Where* can that blessed pig be?'

'Maybe the rats et it?' said Di.

Jem scoffed at the idea, but it worried him. Of course

rats couldn't eat a brass pig with fifty coppers inside of him. But *could* they?

'No, no, dear. Your pig will turn up,' assured Mother.

It hadn't turned up when Jem went to school the next day. News of his loss had reached school before him and many things were said to him, not exactly comforting. But at recess Sissy Flagg sidled up to him ingratiatingly. Sissy Flagg liked Jem and Jem did not like her, in spite of . . . or perhaps because of . . . her thick yellow curls and huge brown eyes.

Even at eight one may have problems concerning the opposite sex.

'I can tell you who's got your pig.'

'Who?'

'You've got to pick me for Clap-in and Clap-out and I'll tell you.'

It was a bitter pill, but Jem swallowed it. Anything to find that pig. He sat in an agony of blushes beside the triumphant Sissy while they clapped in and clapped out, and when the bell rang he demanded his reward.

'Alice Palmer says Willy Drew told her Bob Russell told him Fred Elliot said he knew where your pig was. Go and ask Fred.'

'Cheat!' cried Jem, glaring at her. '*Cheat!*'

Sissy laughed arrogantly. *She* didn't care. Jem Blythe had had to sit with her for once anyhow.

Jem went to Fred Elliott, who at first declared he knew

nothing about the old pig and didn't want to. Jem was in despair. Fred Elliot was three years older than he was and a noted bully. Suddenly he had an inspiration. He pointed a grimy forefinger sternly at big, red-faced Fred Elliott.

'You are a transubstantiationalist,' he said distinctly.

'Here you, don't you call me names, young Blythe.'

'That is more than a name,' said Jem. 'That is a hoodoo word. If I say it again and point my finger at you . . . so . . . you may have bad luck for a week. Maybe your toes will drop off. I'll count ten, and if you haven't told me before I get to ten I'll hoodoo you.'

Fred didn't believe it. But the skating race came off that night and he wasn't taking chances. Besides, toes were toes. At six he surrendered.

'All right . . . all right. Don't bust your jaws saying that a second time. Mac knows where your pig is . . . he said he did.'

Mac was not in school, but when Anne heard Jem's story she telephoned his mother. Mrs Reese came up a little later, flushed and apologetic.

'Mac didn't take the pig, Mrs Blythe. He just wanted to see if it would open, so when Jem was out of the room he twisted the tail. It fell apart in two pieces and he couldn't get it together again. So he put the two halves of the pig and the money in one of Jem's Sunday boots in the closet. He hadn't ought to have touched it . . . and his father has whaled the stuffing out of him . . . but he didn't *steal* it, Mrs Blythe.'

'What was that word you said to Fred Elliot, Little Jem, dear?' asked Susan, when the dismembered pig had been found and the money counted.

'Transubstantiationalist,' said Jem proudly. 'Walter found it in the dictionary last week . . . you know he likes great big *full* words, Susan . . . and we both learned how to pronounce it. We said it over to each other twenty-one times in bed before we went to sleep so that we'd remember it.'

Now that the necklace was bought and stowed away in the third box from the top in the middle drawer of Susan's bureau, Susan having been privy to the plan all along, Jem thought the birthday would never come. He gloated over his unconscious mother. Little *she* knew what was hidden in Susan's bureau drawer . . . little *she* knew what her birthday would bring her . . . little *she* knew when she sang the twins to sleep with,

'*I saw a ship a-sailing on the sea,*
And oh, it was all laden with pretty things for me,'

what the ship would bring her.

Gilbert had an attack of influenza in early March which almost ran to pneumonia. There were a few anxious days at Ingleside.

Anne went about as usual, smoothing out tangles, administering consolation, bending over moonlit beds to see if dear little bodies were warm; but the children missed her laughter.

'What will the world do if Father dies?' whispered Walter, white-lipped.

'He isn't going to die, darling. He is out of danger now.'

Anne wondered herself what their small world of Four Winds and the Glens and the Harbour Head would do if . . . if . . . anything had happened to Gilbert. They were all coming to depend on him so. The Upper Glen people especially seemed really to believe that he could raise the dead, and only refrained because it would be crossing the purposes of the Almighty. He *had* done it once, they averred . . . old Uncle Archibald MacGregor had solemnly assured Susan that Samuel Hewett was dead as a doornail when Dr Blythe brought him to. However that might be, when living people saw Gilbert's lean, brown face and friendly hazel eyes by their bedside and heard his cheery, 'Why, there's nothing the matter with *you*' . . . well, they believed it until it came true. As for namesakes, he had more than he could count. The whole Four Winds district was peppered with young Gilberts. There was even a tiny Gilbertine.

So Dad was about again and Mother was laughing again, and . . . at last, it was the night before the birthday.

'If you go to bed early, Little Jem, tomorrow will come quicker,' assured Susan.

Jem tried it, but it didn't seem to work. Walter fell asleep promptly, but Jem squirmed about. He was afraid to go to sleep. Suppose he didn't waken in time and everybody else had given their presents to Mother? He wanted to be the very first. Why hadn't he asked Susan to be sure and call him? She had gone out to make a visit somewhere, but he would ask her when she came in. If he were sure of hearing her! Well, he'd just go down and lie on the living-room sofa and then he couldn't miss her.

Jem crept down and curled up on the chesterfield. He could see over the Glen. The moon was filling the hollows among the white, snowy dunes with magic. The great trees that were so mysterious at night held out their arms about Ingleside. He heard all the night sounds of a house . . . a floor creaking . . . someone turning in bed . . . the crumble and fall of coals in the fireplace . . . the scurrying of a little mouse in the china closet. Was that an avalanche? No, only snow sliding off the roof. It was a little lonesome . . . why didn't Susan come? . . . if he only had Gyp now . . . dear Gyppy. Had he forgotten Gyp? No, not forgotten exactly. But it didn't hurt so much now to think of him, one *did* think of other things a good deal of the time. Sleep well, dearest of dogs. Perhaps sometime he *would* have another dog after all. It would be nice if he had one right now in . . . or the Shrimp. But Shrimp wasn't round. Selfish old cat! Thinking of nothing but his own affairs!

No sign of Susan yet, coming along the long road that wound endlessly on through the strange white moonlit distance that was his own familiar Glen in daytime. Well, he would just have to imagine things to pass the time. Some day he would go to Baffin Land and live with Eskimos. Some day he would sail to far seas and cook a shark for Christmas dinner like Captain Jim. He would go on an expedition to the Congo in search of gorillas. He would be a diver and wander through radiant crystal halls under the sea. He would get Uncle Davy to teach him how to milk into the cat's mouth the next time he went up to Avonlea. Uncle Davy did that so expertly. Perhaps he would be a pirate. Susan wanted him to be a minister. The minister could do the most good, but wouldn't a pirate have the most fun? Suppose the little wooden soldier hopped off the mantelpiece and shot off his gun! Suppose the chairs began walking about the room! Suppose the tiger rug came alive! Suppose the 'quack bears', which he and Walter 'pretended' all over the house when they were very young, really were about! Jem was suddenly frightened. In daytime he did not often forget the difference between romance and reality, but it was different in the endless night. Tick-tack went the clock . . . tick-tack . . . and for every tick there was a quack bear sitting on a step of the stairs. The stairs were just *black* with quack bears. They would sit there till daylight . . . *gibbering*.

Suppose God forgot to let the sun rise! The thought was so terrible that Jem buried his face in the afghan to shut it out, and there Susan found him sound asleep when she came home in the fiery orange of a winter sunrise.

'Little Jem!'

Jem uncoiled himself and sat up, yawning. It had been a busy night for Silversmith Frost and the woods were fairyland. A far-off hill was touched with a crimson spear. All the white fields beyond the Glen were a lovely rose-colour. It was Mother's birthday morning.

'I was waiting for you, Susan . . . to tell you to call me . . . and you never came . . .'

'I went down to see the John Warrens, because their aunt had died, and they asked me to stay the night and sit up with the corpse,' explained Susan cheerfully. 'I didn't suppose you'd be trying to catch pneumonia, too, the minute my back was turned. Scamper off to your bed and I'll call you when I hear your Mother stirring.'

'Susan, how do you stab sharks?' Jem wanted to know before he went upstairs.

'I do not stab them,' answered Susan.

Mother was up when he went into her room, brushing her long, shining hair before the glass. Her eyes when she saw the necklace!

'Jem, darling! For me!'

'*Now* you won't have to wait till Dad's ship comes in,' said Jem with a fine nonchalance. What was that gleaming greenly on Mother's hand? A ring . . . Dad's present. All very well, but rings were common things . . . even Sissy Flagg had one. But a pearl necklace!

'A necklace is such a nice birthdayish thing,' said Mother.

21

When Gilbert and Anne went to dinner with friends in Charlottetown one evening in late March Anne put on a new dress of ice-green encrusted with silver around neck and arms: and she wore Gilbert's emerald ring and Jem's necklace.

'Haven't I got a handsome wife, Jem?' asked Dad proudly.

Jem thought Mother was very handsome and her dress very lovely. How pretty the pearls looked on her white throat! He always liked to see Mother dressed up, but he liked it still better when she took off a splendid dress. It had transformed her into an alien. She was not really Mother in it.

After supper Jem went to the village to do an errand for Susan and it was while he was waiting in Mr Flagg's store . . . rather afraid that Sissy might come in as she sometimes did and be entirely too friendly . . . that the blow fell . . . the shattering blow of disillusionment which is so terrible to a child because so unexpected and so seemingly inescapable.

Two girls were standing before the glass showcase where Mr Carter Flagg kept necklaces and chain bracelets and hair barettes.

'Aren't those pearl strings pretty?' said Abbie Russell.

'You'd almost think they were real,' said Leona Reese.

They passed on then, quite unwitting of what they had done to the small boy sitting on the nail keg. Jem continued to sit there for some time longer. He was incapable of movement.

'What's the matter, sonny?' inquired Mr Flagg. 'You seem kind of low in your mind.'

Jem looked at Mr Flagg with tragic eyes. His mouth was strangely dry.

'Please, Mr Flagg . . . are those . . . those necklaces . . . they *are* real pearls, aren't they?'

Mr Flagg laughed.

'No, Jem, I'm afraid you can't get real pearls for fifty cents, you know. A real pearl necklace like that would cost hundreds of dollars. They're just pearl beads, very good ones for the price, too. I got 'em at a bankrupt sale, that's why I can sell 'em so cheap. Ordinarily they run up to a dollar. Only one left . . . they went like hot cakes.'

Jem slid off the keg and went out, totally forgetting what Susan had sent him for. He walked blindly up the frozen road home. Overhead was a hard, dark, wintry sky; there was what Susan called 'a feel' of snow in the air, and a skim of ice over the puddles. The harbour lay black and sullen between its bare banks. Before Jem reached home a snow squall was whitening over them. He wished it would snow . . . and snow . . . and snow . . . till he was buried and everybody was buried . . . fathoms deep. There was no justice anywhere in the world.

Jem was heartbroken. And let no one scoff at his heartbreak for scorn of its cause. His humiliation was utter and complete. He had given Mother what he and she had supposed was a pearl necklace . . . and it was only an old imitation. What would she say, what would she feel like, when she knew? For, of course, she must be told. It never occurred to Jem to think for a moment that she need not be told. Mother must not be 'fooled' any longer. She must know that her pearls weren't real. Poor Mother! She had been so proud of them . . . had he not seen the pride shining in her eyes when she had kissed him and thanked him for them?

Jem slipped in by the side door and went straight to bed, where Walter was already sound asleep. But Jem could not sleep; he was awake when Mother came home and slipped in to see that Walter and he were warm.

'Jem, dear, are you awake at this hour? You're not sick?'

'No, but I'm very unhappy *here,* Mother dearwums,' said Jem, putting his hand on his stomach, fondly believing it to be his heart.

'What is the matter, dear?'

'I . . . I . . . there is something I must tell you, Mother . . . you'll be awful disappointed, Mother . . . but I didn't mean to deceive you, Mother, truly I didn't.'

'I'm sure you didn't, dear. What is it? Don't be afraid.'

'Oh, Mother dearwums, those pearls aren't real pearls . . . I thought they were . . . I *did* think they were, I *did* . .'

Jem's eyes were full of tears. He couldn't go on.

If Anne wanted to smile there was no sign of it on her face. Shirley had bumped his head that day, Nan had sprained her ankle, Di had lost her voice with a cold. Anne had kissed and bandaged and soothed; but *this* was different . . . this needed all the secret wisdom of mothers.

'Jem, I never thought you supposed they were real pearls. I knew they weren't . . . at least in one sense of real. In another, they are the most real things I've ever had given me. Because there was love and work and self-sacrifice in them . . . and *that* makes them more precious to me than all the gems that divers have fished up from the sea for queens to wear. Darling, I wouldn't exchange my pretty beads for the necklace I read of last night which some millionaire gave his bride and which cost half a million. So *that* shows you what your gift is worth to me, dearest of dear little sons. Do you feel better now?'

Jem was so happy he was ashamed of it. He was afraid it was babyish to be so happy. 'Oh, life is *bearable* again,' he said cautiously.

The tears had vanished from his sparkling eyes. All was well. Mother's arms were about him . . . Mother *did* like her necklace . . . nothing else mattered. Some day he would give her one that would cost no mere half, but a whole million. Meanwhile, he was tired . . . his bed was very warm and cosy . . . Mother's hands smelled like roses . . . and he didn't hate Leona Reese any more.

'Mother dearwums, you do look so sweet in that dress,' he said sleepily. 'Sweet and pure . . . pure as Epps cocoa.'

Anne smiled as she hugged him, and thought of a ridiculous thing she had read in a medical journal that day, signed Dr V. Z. Tomachowsky. 'You must never kiss your little son lest you set up a Jocasta complex.' She had laughed over it at the time and been a little angry as well. Now she only felt pity for the writer of it. Poor, poor man! For of course V. Z. Tomachowsky was a man. No woman would ever write anything so silly and wicked.

22

April came tiptoeing in beautifully that year with sunshine and soft winds for a few days; and then a driving north-east snowstorm dropped a white blanket over the world again. 'Snow in April is abominable,' said Anne. 'Like a slap in the face when you expected a kiss.' Ingleside was fringed with icicles and for two long weeks the days were raw and the nights hard-bitten. Then the snow grudgingly disappeared, and when the news went round that the first robin had been seen in the Hollow Ingleside plucked up heart and ventured to believe that the miracle of spring was really going to happen again.

'Oh, Mummy, it *smells* like spring today,' cried Nan, delightedly snuffing the fresh moist air. 'Mummy, isn't spring an exciting time!'

Spring was trying out her paces that day . . . like an adorable baby just learning to walk. The winter pattern of trees and fields was beginning to be overlaid with hints of green, and Jem had again brought in the first mayflowers. But an enormously fat lady, sinking puffingly into one of the Ingleside easy-chairs, sighed, and said sadly that the springs weren't so nice as they were when she was young.

'Don't you think perhaps the change is in us . . . not in the springs, Mrs Mitchell?' smiled Anne.

'Mebbe so. I know *I* am changed all too well. I don't suppose to look at me now you'd think I was once the prettiest girl in these parts?'

Anne reflected that she certainly wouldn't. The thin, stringy, mouse-coloured hair under Mrs Mitchell's crêpe bonnet and long sweeping 'widow's veil' was streaked with grey; her blue, expressionless eyes were faded and hollow; and to call her double chinned erred on the side of charity. But Mrs Anthony Mitchell was feeling quite contented with herself just then, for nobody in Four Winds had finer weeds. Her voluminous black dress was crêpe to the knees. One wore mourning in those days with a vengeance.

Anne was spared the necessity of saying anything, for Mrs Mitchell gave her no chance.

'My soft water system went dry this week . . . there's a leak in it . . . so I kem down to the village this morning to get Raymond Russell to come and fix it. And thinks I to myself, "Now that I'm here I'll just run up to Ingleside and ask Mrs Doctor Blythe to write an obitchery for Anthony."'

'An obituary?' said Anne blankly.

'Yes . . . them things they put in the papers about dead people, you know,' explained Mrs Anthony. 'I want

Anthony should have a real good one . . . something out of the common. You write things, don't you?'

'Occasionally I do write a little story,' admitted Anne. 'But a busy mother hasn't much time for that. I had wonderful dreams once, but now I'm afraid I'll never be in *Who's Who*, Mrs Mitchell. And I never wrote an obituary in my life.'

'Oh, they can't be hard to write. Old Uncle Charlie Bates over our way writes most of them for the Lower Glen, but he ain't a bit poetical, and I've set my heart on a piece of poetry for Anthony. My, but he was always so fond of poetry. I was up to hear you give that talk on bandages to the Glen Institute last week and thinks I to myself, "Anyone who can talk as glib as that can likely write a real poetical obitchery." You will do it for me, won't you, Mrs Blythe? Anthony would have liked it. He always admired you. He said once that when you come into a room you made all the other women look "common and undistinguished". He sometimes talked real poetical, but he meant well. I've been reading a lot of obitcheries . . . I have a big scrapbook full of them, but it didn't seem to me he'd have liked any of them. He used to laugh at them so much. And it's time it was done. He's been dead two months. He died lingering, but painless. Coming on spring's an inconvenient time for anyone to die, Mrs Blythe, but I've made the best of it. I s'pose Uncle Charlie will be hopping mad if I get anyone else to write Anthony's obitchery, but I don't care. Uncle Charlie has a wonderful flow of language, but him and Anthony never hit it off any too well, and the long and short of it is I'm *not* going to have him write Anthony's obitchery. I've been Anthony's wife . . . his faithful and loving wife for thirty-five years . . . thirty-five years, Mrs Blythe' . . . as if she were afraid Anne might think it only thirty-four . . . 'and I'm going to have an obitchery he'd like, if it takes a leg. That was what my daughter Seraphine said to me; she's married at Lowbridge, you know . . . nice name, Seraphine, isn't it? . . . I got it off a gravestone. Anthony didn't like it, he wanted to call her Judith, after his mother. But I said it was too solemn a name, and he gave in real kindly. He weren't no hand at arguing . . . though he always called her Seraph . . . where was I?'

'Your daughter was saying?'

'Oh, yes. Seraphine said to me, "Mother, whatever else you have or don't have, have a real, nice obitchery for father." Her and her father were always real thick, though he poked a bit of fun at her now and then, just as he did at me. Now, won't you, Mrs Blythe?'

'I really don't know a great deal about your husband, Mrs Mitchell.'

'Oh, I can tell you all about him . . . if you don't want to know the colour of his eyes. Do you know, Mrs Blythe, when Seraphine and me was talking things over after the funeral I couldn't tell the colour of his eyes, after living with him thirty-five years. They was kind of soft and dreamy anyhow. He used to look so pleading with them when he was courting me. He had a real hard time to get me, Mrs Blythe. He was mad about me for years. I was full of bounce then and meant to pick and choose. My life story would be real thrilling if you ever get short of material, Mrs Blythe. Ah, well, them days are gone. I had more beaux than you could shake a stick at. But they kept coming and going . . . and Anthony just kept coming. He was kind of good-looking, too . . . such a nice, lean man. I never could abide pudgy men . . . and he was a cut or two above me . . . I'd be the last one to deny that. "It'll be a step up for a Plummer if you marry a Mitchell," Ma said . . . I was a Plummer, Mrs Blythe . . . John A. Plummer's daughter. And he paid me such nice romantic compliments, Mrs Blythe. Once he told me I had the ethereal charm of moonlight. I knew it meant something else, though I don't know yet what "ethereal" means. I've always been meaning to look it up in the dictionary, but I never get around to it. Well, anyway, in the end I passed my word of honour that I would be his bride. That is . . . I mean . . . I said I'd take him. My, but I wish you could have seen me in my wedding-dress, Mrs Blythe. They all said I was a picture. Slim as a trout, with hair yaller as gold, and such a complexion. Ah, time makes turrible changes in us. *You* haven't come to that yet, Mrs Blythe. You're real pretty still . . . and a highly eddicated woman into the bargain. Ah, well, we can't all be clever, some of us have to do the cooking. That dress you've got on is real handsome, Mrs Blythe. You never wear black I notice . . . you're right . . . you'll have to wear it soon enough. Put it off till you have to, I say. Well, where was I?'

'You were . . . trying to tell me something about Mr Mitchell.'

'Oh, yes. Well, we were married. There was a big comet that night . . . I remember seeing it as we drove home. It's a real pity you couldn't have seen that comet, Mrs Blythe. It was simply pretty. I don't suppose you could work it into the obitchery, could you?'

'It . . . might be rather difficult . . .'

'Well,' Mrs Mitchell surrendered the comet with a sigh, 'you'll have to do the best you can. He hadn't a very exciting life. He got drunk once, he said he just wanted to see what it was like for once . . . he was always of an inquiring turn of mind. But, of course, you couldn't put that in an obitchery. Nothing much else ever happened to him. Not to complain, but just to state facts, he was a bit shiftless and easy-going. He would sit for an hour looking into a hollyhock. My, but he was fond of flowers . . . hated to mow down the buttercups. No matter if the wheat crop failed as long as there was farewell-summers and goldenrod. And trees . . . that orchard of his . . . I always told him, joking like, that he cared far more for his trees than for me. And his farm . . . my, but he loved his bit of land. He seemed to think it was a human being. Many's the time I've heard him say, "I think I'll go out and have a little talk to my farm."

'When we got old I wanted him to sell, seeing as we had no boys, and retire to Lowbridge, but he would say, "I can't sell my farm . . . I can't sell my heart." Ain't men funny? Not long before he died he took a notion to have a boiled hen for dinner, "Cooked in that way you have," sez he. He was always partial to my cooking, if I do say it. The only thing he couldn't abide was my lettuce salad with nuts in it. He said the nuts were so durned unexpected. But there wasn't a hen to spare . . . they was all laying good . . . and there was only one rooster left, and of course I couldn't kill him. My, but I like to see the roosters strutting round. Ain't anything much handsomer than a fine rooster, do you think, Mrs Blythe? Well, where was I?'

'You were saying your husband wanted you to cook a hen for him.'

'Oh, yes. And I've been so sorry ever since I didn't. I wake up in the night and think of it. But I didn't know he was going to die, Mrs Blythe. He never complained much, and always said he was better. And interested in things to the last. If I'd-a-known he was going to die, Mrs Blythe, I'd have cooked a hen for him, eggs or no eggs.'

Mrs Mitchell removed her rusty black lace mitts and wiped her eyes with a handkerchief, black-bordered a full two inches.

'He'd have enjoyed it,' she sobbed. 'He had his own teeth to the last, poor dear. Well, anyway' – folding the handkerchief and putting on the mitts – 'he was sixty-five so he weren't far from the allotted span. And I've got another coffin plate. Mary Martha Plummer and me started collecting coffin plates at the same time, but she soon got ahead of me . . . so many of her relations died, not to speak of her three children. She's got more coffin plates than anyone in these parts. I didn't seem to have much luck, but I've got a full mantelpiece at last. My cousin, Thomas Bates, was buried last week, and I wanted his wife to give me the coffin plate, but she had it buried with him. Said collecting coffin plates was a relic of barbarism. She was a Hampson, and the Hampsons were always odd. Well, where was I?'

Anne really could not tell Mrs Mitchell where she was this time. The coffin plates had dazed her.

'Oh, well, anyway, poor Anthony died. "I go gladly and in quietness," was all that he said, but he smiled just at the last . . . at the ceiling, not at me nor Seraphine. I'm so glad he was so happy just afore he died. There were times I used to think perhaps he wasn't quite happy, Mrs Blythe . . . he was so terrible high-strung and sensitive. But he looked real noble and sublime in his coffin. We had a grand funeral. It was just a lovely day. He was buried with loads of flowers. I took a sinking spell at the last, but otherwise everything went off very well. We buried him in the Upper Glen graveyard, though all his family were buried in Lowbridge. But he picked out his graveyard long ago . . . said he wanted to be buried near his farm and where he could hear the sea and the wind in the trees . . . there's trees around three sides of that graveyard, you know. I was glad, too, I always thought it was such a cosy little graveyard, and we can keep geraniums growing on his grave. He was a good man . . . he's likely in heaven now, so that needn't trouble you. I always think it must be some chore to write an obitchery when you *don't* know where the departed is. I can depend on you then, Mrs Blythe?'

Anne consented, feeling that Mrs Mitchell would stay there and talk until she did consent. Mrs Mitchell, with another sigh of relief, heaved herself out of her chair.

'I must be stepping. I'm expecting a hatching of turkey poults today. I've enjoyed my conversation with you and I wish I could have stayed longer. It's lonesome being a widow woman. A man mayn't amount to an awful lot, but you sort of miss him when he goes.'

Anne politely saw her down the walk. The children were stalking robins on the lawn and daffodil tips were poking up everywhere.

'You've got a nice proud house here . . . a real, nice, proud house, Mrs Blythe. I've always felt I'd like a big house. But with only us and Seraphine . . . and where was the money to come from? And, anyway, Anthony'd never hear of it. He had an awful affection for that old house. I'm meaning to sell if I get a fair offer and live either in Lowbridge or Mowbray Narrows. Whichever I decide would be the best place to be a widow in. Anthony's insurance will come in handy. Say what you like, it's easier to bear a full sorrow than an empty one. You'll find that out when you're a widow yourself . . . though I hope that'll be a good few years yet. How is the doctor getting on? It's been a real sickly winter so he ought to have done pretty well. My, what a nice little family you've got! Three girls! Nice now, but wait you till they come to the boy-crazy age. Not that I'd much trouble with Seraphine. She was quiet . . . like her father . . . and stubborn like him. When she fell in love with John Whitaker, have him she would in spite of all I could say. A rowan tree? Whyn't you have it planted by the front door? It would keep the fairies out.'

'But who would want to keep the fairies out, Mrs Mitchell?'

'Now you're talking like Anthony. I was only joking. O' course I don't believe in fairies . . . but if they did happen to exist I've heard they were pesky mischievous. Well, goodbye, Mrs Blythe. I'll call round next week for the obitchery.'

23

'You've let yourself in for it, Mrs Doctor dear,' said Susan, who had overheard most of the conversation as she polished her silver in the pantry.

'Haven't I? But, Susan, I really do want to write that "obituary". I liked Anthony Mitchell . . . what little I've seen of him . . . and I feel sure that he'd turn over in his grave if his obituary was like the run of the mill in the *Daily Enterprise*. Anthony had an inconvenient sense of humour.'

'Anthony Mitchell was a real nice fellow when he was young, Mrs Doctor dear. Though a bit dreamy; they said. He didn't hustle enough to suit Bessy Plummer, but he made a decent living and paid his debts. Of course he married the last girl he should have. But although Bessy Plummer looks like a comic valentine now, she was pretty as a picture then. Some of us, Mrs Doctor dear,' concluded Susan with a sigh, 'haven't even that much to remember.'

'Mummy,' said Walter, 'the snack-dragons are coming up thick all around the back porch. And a pair of robins are beginning to build a nest on the pantry windowsill.

You'll let them, won't you, Mummy. You won't open the window and scare them away?'

Anne had met Anthony Mitchell once or twice, though the little grey house between the spruce woods and the sea, with the great big willow tree over it like a huge umbrella, where he lived, was in the lower Glen, and the doctor from Mowbray Narrows attended most of the people there. But Gilbert had bought hay from him now and then, and once when he had brought a load Anne had taken him all over her garden and they found out that they talked the same language. She had liked him . . . his lean, lined, friendly face, his brave, shrewd, yellowish-hazel eyes that had never faltered or been hood-winked . . . save once, perhaps, when Bessy Plummer's shallow and fleeting beauty had tricked him into a foolish marriage. Yet he never seemed unhappy or unsatisfied. As long as he could plough and garden and reap he was as contented as a sunny old pasture. His black hair was but lightly frosted with silver, and a ripe, serene spirit revealed itself in his rare but sweet smiles. His old fields had given him bread and delight, joy of conquest and comfort in sorrow. Anne was satisfied because he was buried near them. He might have 'gone gladly', but he had lived gladly, too. The Mowbray Narrows doctor had said that when he told Anthony Mitchell he could hold out to him no hope of recovery Anthony had smiled and replied, 'Well, life is a trifle monotonous at times now I'm getting old. Death will be something of a change. I'm real curious about it, doctor.' Even Mrs Anthony, among all her rambling absurdities, had dropped a few things that revealed the real Anthony. Anne wrote 'The Old Man's Grave' a few evenings later by her room window, and read it over with a sense of satisfaction.

> Make it where the winds may sweep
> Through the pine boughs soft and deep,
> And the murmur of the sea
> Come across the orient lea,
> And the falling raindrops sing
> Gently to his slumbering.
>
> Make it where the meadows wide
> Greenly lie on every side,
> Harvest fields he reaped and trod,
> Westering slopes of clover sod,
> Orchard lands where bloom and blow
> Trees he planted long ago.
>
> Make it where the starshine dim
> May be alway close to him,
> And the sunrise glory spread
> Lavishly around his bed,
> And the dewy grasses creep
> Tenderly above his sleep.

> *Since these things to him were dear*
> *Through full many a well-spent year,*
> *It is surely meet their grace*
> *Should be on his resting place,*
> *And the murmur of the sea*
> *Be his dirge eternally.*

'I think Anthony Mitchell would have liked that,' said Anne, flinging her window open to lean out to the spring. Already there were crooked little rows of young lettuce in the children's garden; the sunset was soft and pink behind the maple grove; the Hollow rang with the faint, sweet laughter of children.

'Spring is so lovely, I hate to go to sleep and miss any of it,' said Anne.

Mrs Anthony Mitchell came up to get her 'obitchery' one afternoon the next week. Anne read it to her with a secret bit of pride; but Mrs Anthony's face did not express unmixed satisfaction.

'My, I call that real sprightly. You do put things so well. But . . . but . . . you didn't say a word about him being in heaven. Weren't you *sure* he is there?'

'So sure that it wasn't necessary to mention it, Mrs Mitchell.'

'Well, *some* people might doubt. He . . . he didn't go to church as often as he might . . . though he was a member in good standing. And it doesn't tell his age . . . nor mention the flowers. Why, you just couldn't count the wreaths on the coffin. Flowers are poetical enough I should think!'

'I'm sorry . . .'

'Oh, I don't blame you . . . not a mite do I blame you. You've done your best and it sounds beautiful. What do I owe you?'

'Why . . . why . . . *nothing*, Mrs Mitchell. I couldn't think of such a thing.'

'Well, I thought likely you'd say that so I brung you up a bottle of my dandelion wine. It sweetens the stomach if you're ever bothered with gas. I'd have brung a bottle of my yarb tea, too, only I was afraid the Doctor mightn't approve. But if you'd like some and think you can smuggle it in unbeknownst to him you've only to say the word.'

'No, no, thank you,' said Anne rather flatly. She had not yet quite recovered from 'sprightly'.

'Just as you like. You'd be welcome to it. I'll not be needing any more medicine myself this spring. When my second cousin, Malachi Plummer, died in the winter I asked his widow to give me the three bottles of medicine there was left over . . . they got it by the dozen. She was going to throw them out, but I was always one that could never bear to waste anything. I couldn't take more than one bottle myself but I made our hired man take the other two. "If it doesn't do you any good it won't do you any harm," I told him. I won't say I'm not rather relieved you didn't want any cash for the obitchery, for I'm rather short of ready money just now. A funeral is so expensive, though D. B. Martin is about the cheapest undertaker in these parts. I haven't even got my black paid for yet. I won't feel I'm really in mourning till it is. Luckily I hadn't to get a new bunnit. This was the bunnit I had made for Mother's funeral ten years ago. It's kind of fortunate black becomes me, ain't it? If you'd see Malachi Plummer's widow now, with her saller face! Well, I must be stepping. And I'm much obliged to you, Mrs Blythe, even if . . . but I feel sure you did your best and it's lovely poetry.'

'Won't you stay and have supper with us?' asked Anne. 'Susan and I are all alone . . . the doctor is away and the children are having their first picnic supper in the Hollow.'

'I don't mind,' said Mrs Anthony, slipping willingly back into her chair. 'I'll be glad to set a spell longer. Somehow it takes so long to get rested when you get old. And,' she added, with a smile of dreamy beatitude on her pink face, 'didn't I smell fried parsnips?'

Anne almost grudged the fried parsnips when the *Daily Enterprise* came out the next week. There, in the obituary column, was 'The Old Man's Grave' . . . with five verses instead of the original four! And the fifth verse was:

> *A wonderful husband, companion and aid,*
> *One who was better the Lord never made.*
> *A wonderful husband, tender and true,*
> *One in a million, dear Anthony, was you.*

'!!!' said Ingleside.

'I hope you didn't mind me tacking on another verse,' said Mrs Mitchell to Anne, the next Institute meeting. 'I just wanted to praise Anthony, a little more . . . and my nephew, Johnny Plummer, writ it. He just sat down and scribbled it off quick as a wink. He's like you . . . he doesn't look clever but he can poetize. He got it through his mother . . . she was a Wickford. The Plummers haven't a speck of poetry in them, not a speck.'

'What a pity you didn't think of getting him to write Mr Mitchell's "obitchery" in the first place,' said Anne coldly.

'Yes, isn't it? But I didn't know he could write poetry and I'd set my heart on it for Anthony's send-off. Then his mother showed me a poem he'd writ on a squirrel drowned in a pail of maple syrup . . . a really touching thing. But yours was real nice, too, Mrs Blythe. I think the two combined together made something out of the common, don't you?'

'I do,' said Anne.

24

The Ingleside children were having bad luck with pets. The wriggly curly little black pup Dad brought home from Charlottetown one day just walked out the next week and disappeared into the blue. Nothing was ever seen or heard of him again, and, though there were whispers of a sailor from the Harbour Head having been seen taking a small black pup on board his ship the night she sailed, his fate remained one of the deep and dark unsolved mysteries of the Ingleside chronicles. Walter took it harder than Jem, who had not yet quite forgotten his anguish over Gyp's death and was not ever again going to let himself love a dog not wisely but too well. Then Tiger Tom, who lived in the barn and was never allowed in the house because of his thieving propensities but got a good deal of petting for all that, was found stark and stiff on the barn floor and had to be buried with pomp and circumstance in the Hollow. Finally Jem's rabbit, Bun, which he had bought from Joe Russell for a quarter, sickened and died. Perhaps its death was hastened by a dose of patent medicine Jem gave him, perhaps not. Joe had advised it and Joe ought to know. But Jem felt as if he had murdered Bun.

'*Is* there a curse on Ingleside?' he demanded gloomily, when Bun had been laid to rest beside Tiger Tom. Walter wrote an epitaph for him, and he and Jem and the twins wore black ribbons tied round their arms for a week, to the horror of Susan, who deemed it sacrilege. Susan was not inconsolable for the loss of Bun, who had got out once and worked havoc in her garden. Still less did she approve of two toads Walter brought in and put in the cellar. She put one of them out when evening came but could not find the other, and Walter lay awake and worried.

'Maybe they were husband and wife,' he thought. 'Maybe they're awful lonely and unhappy now they're separated. It was the little one Susan put out, so I guess she was the lady toad and maybe she's frightened to death all alone in that big yard without anyone to protect her . . . just like a widow.'

Walter couldn't endure thinking about the widow's woes so he slipped down to the cellar to hunt for the gentleman toad, but only succeeded in knocking down a pile of Susan's discarded tinware with a resulting racket that might have wakened the dead. It woke only Susan, however, who came marching down with a candle, the fluttering flame of which cast the weirdest shadows on her gaunt face.

'Walter Blythe, whatever are you doing?'

'Susan, I've got to find that toad,' said Walter desperately. 'Susan, just think how you would feel without your husband if you had one.'

'What on earth are you talking about?' demanded the justifiably mystified Susan.

At this point the gentleman toad, who had evidently given himself up for lost when Susan appeared on the scene, hopped out into the open from behind Susan's crock of dill pickles. Walter pounced on him and slipped him out through the window, where it is to be hoped he rejoined his supposed love and lived happily ever afterwards.

'You know you shouldn't have brought these creatures into the cellar,' said Susan sternly. 'What would they live on?'

'Of course I meant to catch insects for them,' said Walter, aggrieved. 'I wanted to *study* them.'

'There is simply no being up to them,' moaned Susan, as she followed an indignant young Blythe up the stairs. And she did not mean the toads.

They had better luck with their robin. They had found him, little more than a baby, on the doorstep after a June night storm of wind and rain. He had a grey back and a mottled breast and bright eyes, and from the first he seemed to have complete confidence in all the Ingleside people, not even excepting the Shrimp, who never attempted to molest him, not even when Cock Robin hopped saucily up to his plate and helped himself. They fed him on worms at first, and he had such an appetite that Shirley spent most of his time digging them. He stored the worms in cans and left them around the house, much to Susan's disgust, but she would have endured more than that for Cock Robin, who lighted so fearlessly on her work-worn finger and chirruped in her very face. Susan had taken a great fancy to Cock Robin and thought it worth mentioning in a letter to Rebecca Dew that his breast was beginning to change to a beautiful rusty red.

'Do not think that my intellect is weakening, I beg of you, Miss Dew, dear,' she wrote. 'I suppose it is very silly to be so fond of a bird, but the human heart has its weaknesses. He is not imprisoned like a canary . . . something I could never abide, Miss Dew, dear . . . but ranges at will through house and garden and sleeps on a bough by Walter's study platform up in the big apple tree looking into Rilla's window. Once when they took him to the Hollow he flew away but returned at eventide to their great joy, and, I must in all candour add, to my own.'

The Hollow was 'the Hollow' no longer. Walter had begun to feel that such a delightful spot deserved a name more in keeping with its romantic possibilities. One rainy afternoon they had to play in the garret, but the sun broke out in the early evening and flooded the Glen with splendour.

'Oh, look at the nithe wainbow,' cried Rilla, who always talked with a charming little lisp.

It was the most magnificent rainbow they had ever seen. One end seemed to rest on the very spire of the Presbyterian church, while the other dropped down into the reedy corner of the pond that ran into the upper end of the valley. And Walter then and there named it Rainbow Valley.

Rainbow Valley had become a world in itself to the children of Ingleside. Little winds played there ceaselessly and bird songs re-echoed from dawn to dark. White birches glimmered all over it and from one of them . . . the White Lady . . . Walter pretended that a little dryad came out every night to talk to them. A maple tree and a spruce tree, growing so closely together that their boughs intertwined, he named 'The Tree Lovers' and an old string of sleigh bells he had hung upon them made elfin and aerial when the wind shook them. A dragon guarded the stone bridge they had built across the brook. The trees that met over it could be swart Paynims at need and the rich green mosses along the banks were carpets, none finer, from Samarcand. Robin Hood and his merry men lurked on all sides; three water sprites dwelt in the spring; the deserted old Barclay house at the Glen end, with its grass-grown dyke and its garden overgrown with caraway, was easily transformed into a beleaguered castle. The Crusader's sword has long been rust, but the Ingleside butcher knife was a blade forged in fairyland, and whenever Susan missed the cover of her roasting pan she knew that it was serving as a shield for a plumed and glittering knight on high adventure bent in Rainbow Valley. Sometimes they played pirates, to please Jem, who at ten years was beginning to like a tang of gore in his amusements, but Walter always balked at walking the plank, which Jem thought the best of the performance. Sometimes he wondered if Walter really was enough of a stalwart to be a buccaneer, though he smothered the thought loyally and had more than one pitched and successful battle with boys in school who called Walter 'Sissy Blythe' . . . or had called him that until they found out it meant a set-to with Jem, who had a most disconcerting knack with his fists.

Jem was sometimes allowed now to go down to the Harbour Mouth of an evening to buy fish. It was an errand he delighted in, for it meant that he could sit in Captain Malachi Russell's cabin at the foot of a bent-covered field close to the harbour, and listen to Captain Malachi and his cronies, who had once been daredevil young sea captains, spinning yarns. Every one of them had something to tell when tales were going round. Old Oliver Reese . . . who was actually suspected of being a pirate in his youth . . . had been taken captive by a cannibal king . . . Sam Elliott had been through the San Francisco earthquake . . . 'Bold William' MacDougall had had a lurid fight with a shark . . . Andy Baker had been caught in a waterspout. Moreover, Andy could spit straighter, as he averred, than any man in Four Winds. Hook-nosed, lean-jawed Captain Malachi, with his bristly grey moustache, was Jem's favourite. He had been captain of a brigantine when he was only seventeen, sailing to Buenos Aires with cargoes of lumber. He had an anchor tattooed on each cheek and he had a wonderful old watch you wound with a key. When he was in good humour he let Jem wind it, and when he was in very good humour he would take Jem out cod fishing or digging clams at low tide, and when he was in his best humour he would show Jem the many ship models he had carved. Jem thought they were romance itself. Among them was a Viking boat, with a striped square sail and a fearsome dragon in front . . . a caravel of Columbus . . . the *Mayflower* . . . a rakish craft called *The Flying Dutchman* . . . and no end of beautiful brigantines and schooners and barques and clipper ships and timber droghers.

'Will you teach me how to carve ships like that, Captain Malachi?' pleaded Jem.

Captain Malachi shook his head and spat reflectively into the gulf.

'It doesn't come by teaching, son. Ye'd have to sail the seas for thirty or forty years and then maybe ye'd have enough understanding of ships to do it . . . understanding *and* love. Ships are like weemen, son . . . they've got to be understood and loved or they'll never give up their secrets. And even at that ye may think ye know a ship from stem to stern, inside *and* out, and ye'll find she's still hanging out on ye and keeping her soul shut on you. She'd fly from you like a bird if ye let go your grip on her. There's one ship I sailed on that I've never been able to whittle a model of, times out of mind as I've tried. A dour, stubborn vessel she was! And there was one woman . . . but it's time I took in the slack of my jaw. I've got a ship all ready to go into a bottle and I'll let ye into the secret of that, son.'

So Jem never heard anything more of the 'woman' and didn't care, for he was not interested in the sex, apart from Mother and Susan. *They* were not 'weemen'. They were just Mother and Susan.

When Gyp had died Jem had felt he never wanted another dog; but time heals amazingly, and Jem was beginning to feel doggish again. The puppy wasn't really a dog . . . he was only an accident.

Jem had a procession of dogs marching around the walls of his attic den where he kept Captain Jim's collection of curios . . . dogs clipped from magazines . . . a lordly mastiff, a nice jowly bulldog . . . a dachshund that looked as if somebody had taken a dog by his head and heels and pulled him out like elastic . . . a shaven poodle with a tassel on the end of his tail . . . a fox terrier . . . a Russian wolfhound . . . Jem wondered if Russian wolfhounds ever got anything to eat . . . a saucy Pom . . . a spotted Dalmatian . . . a spaniel with appealing eyes. All dogs of high degree but all lacking something in Jem's eyes . . . he didn't just know what.

Then the advertisement came out in the *Daily Enterprise*. 'For sale, a dog. Apply Roddy Crawford, Harbour Head.' Nothing more. Jem could not have told why the advertisement stuck in his mind or why he felt there was a sadness in its very brevity. He found out from Craig Russell who Roddy Crawford was.

'Roddy's father died a month ago and he has to go to live with his aunt in town. His mother died years ago. And Jake Millison has bought the farm. But the house is going to be torn down. Maybe his aunt won't let him keep the dog. It's no great shakes of a dog, but Roddy has always had an awful notion of it.'

'I wonder how much he wants for it. I've only got a dollar,' said Jem.

'I guess what he wants most is a good home for it,' said Craig. 'But your Dad would give you the money for it, wouldn't he?'

'Yes. But I want to buy a dog with my own money,' said Jem. 'It would feel more like *my* dog then.'

Craig shrugged. Those Ingleside kids *were* funny. What did it matter who put up the cash for an old dog?

That evening Dad drove Jem down to the old, thin, run-down Crawford farm where they found Roddy Crawford and his dog. Roddy was a boy of about Jem's age . . . a pale lad, with straight, reddish-brown hair and a crop of freckles; his dog had silky brown ears, brown nose and tail, and the most beautiful soft brown eyes ever seen in a dog's head. The moment Jem saw that darling dog, with the white stripe down his forehead that parted in two between his eyes and framed his nose, he knew he must have him.

'You want to sell your dog?' he asked eagerly.

'I *don't* want to sell him,' said Roddy dully. 'But Jake says I'll have to or he'll drown him. He says Aunt Vinnie won't have a dog about.'

'What do you want for him?' asked Jem, scared that some prohibitive price would be named.

Roddy gave a great gulp. He held out his dog.

'Here, take him,' he said hoarsely. 'I ain't going to sell him . . . I ain't. Money would never pay for Bruno. If you'll give him a good home . . . and be kind to him . . .'

'Oh, I'll be kind to him,' said Jem eagerly. 'But you must take my dollar. I wouldn't feel he was *my* dog if you didn't. I won't *take* him if you don't.'

He forced the dollar into Roddy's reluctant hand, he took Bruno and held him close to his breast. The little dog looked back at his master. Jem could not see his eyes but he could see Roddy's.

'If you want him so much . . .'

'I want him but I can't have him,' snapped Roddy. 'There's been five people here after him and I wouldn't let one of them have him . . . Jake was awful mad, but I don't care. They weren't *right*. But you . . . I want *you* to have him since *I* can't, and take him out of my sight quick!'

Jem obeyed. The little dog was trembling in his arms, but he made no protest. Jem held him lovingly all the way back to Ingleside.

'Dad, how did Adam know that a dog was a *dog*?'

'Because a dog couldn't be anything but a dog,' grinned Dad. 'Could he now?'

Jem was too excited to sleep for ever so long that night. He had never seen a dog he liked so much as Bruno. No wonder Roddy hated parting with him. But Bruno would soon forget Roddy and love *him*. They would be pals. He must remember to ask Mother to make sure the butcher sent up the bones.

'I love everybody and everything in the world,' said Jem. 'Dear God, bless every cat and dog in the world but specially Bruno.'

Jem fell asleep at last. Perhaps a little dog lying at the foot of the bed with his chin upon his outstretched paws slept, too: and perhaps he did not.

25

Cock Robin had ceased to subsist on worms and ate rice, corn, lettuce and nasturtium seeds. He had grown to be a huge size . . . the 'big robin' at Ingleside was becoming locally famous . . . and his breast had turned to a beautiful red. He would perch on Susan's shoulder and watch her knit. He would fly to meet Anne when she returned after an absence and hop before her into the house: he came to Walter's windowsill every morning for crumbs.

He took his daily bath in a basin in the backyard, in the corner of the sweet-briar hedge, and would raise the most unholy fuss if he found no water in it. The doctor complained that his pens and matches were always strewn all over the library, but found nobody to sympathize with him, and even he surrendered when Cock Robin lit fearlessly on his hand one day to pick up a flower seed. Everybody was bewitched by Cock Robin, except perhaps Jem, who had set his heart on Bruno and was slowly but all too surely learning a bitter lesson . . . that you can buy a dog's body but you cannot buy his love.

At first Jem never suspected this. Of course Bruno would be a bit homesick and lonesome to begin with, but that would soon wear off. Jem found it did not. Bruno was the most obedient little dog in the world; he did exactly what he was told, and even Susan admitted that a better behaved animal couldn't be found. But there was no life in him. When Jem took him out Bruno's eyes would gleam alertly at first, his tail would wag, and he would start off cockily. But after a little while the glow would leave his eyes and he would trot meekly beside Jem with drooping crest. Kindness was showered upon him by all, the juiciest and meatiest of bones were at his disposal, not the slightest objection was made to his sleeping at the foot of Jem's bed every night. But Bruno remained remote . . . inaccessible . . . a stranger. Sometimes in the night Jem woke and reached down to pat the sturdy little body; but there was never any answering lick of tongue or thump of tail. Bruno permitted caresses but he would not respond to them.

Jem set his teeth. There was a good bit of determination in James Matthew Blythe and he was not going to be beaten by a dog . . . *his* dog, whom he had bought fairly and squarely with money hardly saved from his allowance. Bruno would just *have* to get over being homesick for Roddy . . . *have* to give up looking at you with the pathetic eyes of a lost creature . . . *have* to learn to love him.

Jem had to stand up for Bruno, for the other boys in

school, suspecting how he loved the dog, were always trying to 'pick on' him.

'Your dog has fleas . . . Great Big Fleas,' taunted Perry Reese.

Jem had to trounce him before Perry would take it back and say Bruno hadn't a single flea, not one.

'*My* pup takes fits once a week,' boasted Bob Russell. 'I'll bet your old pup never had a fit in his life. If I had a dog like that I'd run him through the meat-grinder.'

'We *had* a dog like that once,' said Mike Drew. 'But we drowned him.'

'My dog's an *awful* dog,' said Sam Warren proudly. 'He kills the chickens and chews up all the clothes on washday. Bet your dog hasn't spunk enough for that.'

Jem sorrowfully admitted to himself, if not to Sam, that Bruno hadn't. He almost wished it had. And it stung him when Watty Flagg shouted: 'Your dog's a *good* dog . . . he never barks on Sunday,' because Bruno didn't bark any day.

But with it all he was such a dear, adorable little dog.

'Bruno, *why* don't you love me?' almost sobbed Jem. 'There's nothing I wouldn't do for you . . . we could have *such* fun together.' But he would not admit defeat to anyone.

Jem hurried home one evening from a mussel-bake at the Harbour Mouth because he knew a storm was coming. The sea moaned so. Things had a sinister, lonely look.

There was a long rip and tear of thunder as Jem dashed into Ingleside.

'Where's Bruno?' he shouted.

It was the first time he had gone anywhere without Bruno. He had thought the long walk to the Harbour Mouth would be too much for a little dog. Jem would not admit to himself that such a long walk with a dog whose heart was not in it would be a little too much for him as well.

It developed that nobody knew where Bruno was. He had not been seen since Jem left after supper. Jem hunted everywhere, but he was not to be found. The rain was coming down in floods, the world was drowned in lightning. Was Bruno out in that black night . . . *lost*? Bruno was afraid of thunderstorms. The only times he had ever seemed to come near Jem in spirit was when he crept close to him while the sky was riven asunder.

Jem worried so that when the storm was spent Gilbert said, 'I ought to go up to the Head anyway to see how Roy Westcott is getting on. You can come, too, Jem, and we'll drive round by the old Crawford place on our way home. I've an idea Bruno has gone back there.'

'Six miles? He'd never!' said Jem.

But he had. When they got to the old deserted, lightless Crawford house a shivering, bedraggled little creature was huddled forlornly on the wet doorstep, looking at them with tired, unsatisfied eyes. He made no objection when

Jem gathered him up in his arms and carried him out to the buggy through the knee-high, tangled grass.

Jem was happy. How the moon was rushing through the sky as the clouds tore past her! How delicious were the smells of the rain-wet woods as they drove along! What a world it was!

'I guess Bruno will be contented at Ingleside after this, Dad.'

'Perhaps,' was all Dad said. He hated to throw cold water, but he suspected that a little dog's heart, losing its last hope, was finally broken.

Bruno had never eaten very much, but after that night he ate less and less. Came a day when he would not eat at all. The vet was sent for but could find nothing wrong.

'I knew one dog in my experience who died of grief and I think this is another,' he told the doctor aside.

He left a 'tonic' which Bruno took obediently and then lay down again, his head on his paws, staring into vacancy. Jem stood looking at him for a long while, his hands in his pockets; then he went into the library to have a talk with Dad.

Gilbert went to town the next day, made some inquiries, and brought Roddy Crawford out to Ingleside. When Roddy came up the veranda steps Bruno, hearing his footfall from the living room, lifted his head and cocked his ears. The next moment his emaciated little body hurled itself across the rug towards the pale, brown-eyed lad.

'Mrs Doctor dear,' said Susan in an awed tone that night, 'the dog was *crying* . . . he *was*. The tears actually rolled down his nose. I do not blame you if you do not believe it. Never would I have believed it if I had not seen it with my own eyes.'

Roddy held Bruno against his heart and looked half defiantly, half pleadingly at Jem.

'You bought him, I know . . . but he belongs to me. Jake told me a lie. Aunt Vinnie says she wouldn't mind a dog a bit . . . but I thought I mustn't ask for him back. Here's your dollar . . . I never spent a cent of it . . . I couldn't.'

For just a moment Jem hesitated. Then he saw Bruno's eyes.

'What a little pig I am!' he thought in disgust with himself. He took the dollar.

Roddy suddenly smiled. The smile changed his sulky face completely, but all he could say was a gruff 'Thanks'.

Roddy slept with Jem that night, a replete Bruno stretched between them. But before he went to bed Roddy knelt to say his prayers and Bruno squatted on his haunches beside him, laying his forepaws on the bed. If ever a dog prayed Bruno prayed then . . . a prayer of thanksgiving and renewed joy in life.

When Roddy brought him food Bruno ate it eagerly, keeping an eye on Roddy all the time. He pranced friskily after Jem and Roddy when they went down to the Glen. 'Such a perked-up dog you never saw,' declared Susan.

But the next evening, after Roddy and Bruno had gone back, Jem sat on the side doorstep in the owl light for a long time. He refused to go digging for pirate hoards in Rainbow Valley with Walter . . . Jem felt no longer splendidly bold and buccaneering. He wouldn't even look at the Shrimp, who was humped in the mint, lashing his tail like a fierce mountain lion crouching to spring. What business had cats to go on being happy at Ingleside when dogs broke their hearts!

He was even grumpy with Rilla when she brought him her blue velvet elephant. Velvet elephant, when Bruno had gone! Nan got as short shrift when she came and suggested they should say what they thought of God in a whisper.

'You don't s'pose I'm blaming God for *this*?' said Jem sternly. 'You haven't any sense of proportion, Nan Blythe.'

Nan went away quite crushed, though she hadn't the least glimmering what Jem meant, and Jem scowled at the embers of the smouldering sunset. Dogs were barking all over the Glen. The Jenkins down the road were out calling theirs . . . all of them took turns at it . . . everyone, even the Jenkins tribe could have a dog . . . everyone but him. Life stretched before him like a desert where there would be no dogs.

Anne came and sat down on a lower step, carefully not looking at him. Jem *felt* her sympathy.

'Motherest,' he said in a choked voice, '*why* wouldn't

Bruno love me when I loved him so much? Am I . . . do you think I am the kind of boy dogs don't like?'

'No, darling. Remember how Gyp loved you. It was just that Bruno had only so much love to give . . . and he had given it all. There are dogs like that . . . one-man dogs.'

'Anyhow, Bruno and Roddy are happy,' said Jem with grim satisfaction, as he bent over and kissed the top of Mother's smooth, ripply head. 'But I'll never have another dog.'

Anne thought this would pass; he had felt the same when Gyppy died. But it did not. The iron had bitten deeply into Jem's soul. Dogs were to come and go at Ingleside . . . dogs that belonged just to the family, and were nice dogs, whom Jem petted and played with as the others did. But there was to be no 'Jem's dog' until a certain 'Little Dog Monday' was to take possession of his heart and love him with a devotion passing Bruno's love, a devotion that was to make history in the Glen. But that was still many a long year away; and a very lonely boy climbed into Jem's bed that night.

'I wish I was a girl,' he thought fiercely, 'so's I could cry *and* cry!'

26

Nan and Di were going to school. They started the last week in August. 'Will we know *everything* by night, Mummy?' asked Di solemnly the first morning. Now, in early September, Anne and Susan had got used to it, and even took pleasure in seeing the two mites trip off every morning, so tiny and carefree and neat, thinking going to school quite an adventure. They always took an apple in their basket for teacher and they wore frocks of pink and blue ruffled gingham. Since they did not look in the least alike, they were never dressed alike. Diana, with her red hair, could not wear pink, but it suited Nan, who was much the prettier of the Ingleside twins. She had brown eyes, brown hair, and a lovely complexion, of which she was quite aware even at seven. A certain starriness had gone to the fashioning of her. She held her head proudly, with her little saucy chin a wee bit in evidence, and so was already thought rather 'stuck-up'.

'She'll imitate all her mother's tricks and poses,' said

Mrs Alice Davies. 'She has all her airs and graces already, if you ask me.'

The twins were dissimilar in more than looks. Di, in spite of her physical resemblance to her mother, was very much her father's child, so far as disposition and qualities went. She had the beginnings of his practical bent, his plain common sense, his twinkling sense of humour. Nan had inherited in full her mother's gift of imagination and was already making life interesting for herself in her own way. For example, she had had no end of excitement this summer making bargains with God, the gist of the matter being, 'If you'll do such-and-such a thing I'll do such-and-such a thing.'

All the Ingleside children had been started in life with the old classic, 'Now I lay me' . . . then promoted to 'Our Father' . . . then encouraged to make their own small petitions also in whatever language they chose. What gave Nan the idea that God might be induced to grant her petitions by promises of good behaviour or displays of fortitude would be hard to say. Perhaps a certain rather young and pretty Sunday School teacher was indirectly responsible for it by her frequent admonitions that if they were not good girls God would not do this or that for them. It was easy to turn this idea inside out and come to the conclusion that if you *were* this or that, *did* this or that, you had a right to expect that God would do the things you wanted. Nan's first 'bargain' in the spring had been so successful that it outweighed some failures and she had gone on all summer. Nobody knew of it, not even Di. Nan hugged her secret and took to praying at sundry times and in divers places, instead of only at night. Di did not approve of this and said so.

'Don't mix God up with *everything*,' she told Nan severely. 'You make Him too *common*.'

Anne, overhearing this, said, 'God *is* in everything, dear. He is the friend who is always near us to give strength and courage. And Nan is quite right in praying to Him when and where she wants to.' Though, if Anne had known the truth about her small daughter's devotions, she would have been rather horrified.

Nan had said one night in May, 'If You'll make my tooth grow in before Amy Taylor's party next week, dear God, I'll take every dose of castor oil Susan gives me without a bit of fuss.'

The very next day the tooth, whose absence had made such an unsightly and too prolonged gap in Nan's pretty mouth, had appeared and by the day of the party was fully through. What more certain sign could you want than that?

Nan kept her side of the compact faithfully, and Susan was amazed and delighted whenever she administered castor oil after that. Nan took it without a grimace or protest, though she sometimes wished she had set a time limit . . . say three months.

God did not always respond. But when she asked Him to send her a special button for her button-string . . . collecting buttons had broken out everywhere among the Glen small girls like the measles . . . assuring Him that if He did she would never make a fuss when Susan set the chipped plate for her, the button came the very next day, Susan having found one on an old dress in the attic. A beautiful red button set with tiny diamonds, or what Nan believed to be diamonds. She was the envy of all because of that elegant button, and when Di refused the chipped plate that night Nan said virtuously, 'Give it to me, Susan. I'll *always* take it after this,' Susan thought she was angelically unselfish and said so. Whereupon Nan both looked and felt smug. She got a fine day for the Sunday School picnic, when everyone predicted rain the night before, by promising to brush her teeth every morning without being told. Her lost ring was restored on the condition that she kept her fingernails scrupulously clean; and when Walter handed over his picture of a flying angel which Nan had long coveted she ate the fat with the lean uncomplainingly at dinner thereafter. When, however, she asked God to make her battered and patched Teddy Bear young again, promising to keep her bureau drawer tidy, something struck a snag. Teddy did not grow young, though Nan looked for the miracle anxiously every morning and wished God would hurry. Finally, she resigned herself to Teddy's age. After all, he was a nice old bear and it would be awfully hard to keep that bureau drawer tidy. When Dad brought her home a new Teddy Bear she didn't really like it, and, though with sundry misgivings of her small conscience, decided she need not take any special pains with the bureau drawer. Her faith returned when, having prayed that the missing eye of her china cat would be restored, the eye was in its place next morning, though somewhat askew, giving the cat a rather cross-eyed aspect. Susan had found it when sweeping and stuck it in with glue, but Nan did not know this and cheerfully carried out her promise of walking fourteen times around the barn on all fours.

What good walking fourteen times around the barn on all fours could do God or anybody else Nan did not stop to consider. But she hated doing it . . . the boys were always wanting her and Di to pretend they were some kind of animals in Rainbow Valley . . . and perhaps there was some vague thought in her budding mind that penance might be pleasing to the mysterious Being who gave or withheld at pleasure. At any rate, she thought out several weird stunts that summer, causing Susan to wonder frequently where on earth children got the notions they did.

'Why do you suppose, Mrs Doctor dear, that Nan must go twice around the living room every day without walking on the floor?'

'Without walking on the floor! How does she manage it, Susan?'

'By jumping from one piece of furniture to the other, including the fender. She slipped on that yesterday, and pitched head-first into the coal-scuttle. Mrs Doctor dear, do you suppose she needs a dose of worm medicine?'

That year was always referred to in the Ingleside chronicles as the one in which Dad *almost* had pneumonia and Mother *had* it. One night, Anne, who already had a nasty cold, went with Gilbert to a party in Charlottetown . . . wearing a new and very becoming dress and Jem's string of pearls. She looked so well in it that all the children who had come in to see her before she left thought it was wonderful to have a mother you could be proud of.

'Such a nice swishy petticoat,' sighed Nan. 'When I grow up will I have tafty petticoats like that, Mummy?'

'I doubt if girls will be wearing petticoats at all by that time,' said Dad. 'I'll backwater, Anne, and admit that dress is a stunner even if I didn't approve of the sequins. Now, don't try to vamp me, woman. I've paid you all the compliments I'm going to tonight. Remember what we read in the *Medical Journal* today, "Life is nothing more than delicately balanced organic chemistry", and let it make you humble and modest. Sequins, indeed! Taffeta petticoat, forsooth. We're nothing but a "fortuitous concatenation of atoms". The great Dr Von Bemburg says so.'

'Don't quote that horrible Von Bemburg to me. He must have had a bad case of chronic indigestion. *He* may be a concatenation of atoms, but *I* am not.'

In a few days thereafter Anne was a very sick 'concatenation of atoms' and Gilbert a very anxious one. Susan went about looking harassed and tired, the trained nurse came and went with an anxious face, and a nameless shadow suddenly swooped and spread and darkened at Ingleside. The children were not told of the seriousness of their mother's illness, and even Jem did not realize it fully. But they all felt the chill and the fear and went softly and unhappily. For once there was no laughter in the maple grove and no games in Rainbow Valley. But the worst of all was that they were not allowed to see Mother. No Mother meeting them with smiles when they came home . . . no Mother slipping in to kiss them goodnight, no Mother to soothe and sympathize and understand, no Mother to laugh over jokes with . . . nobody ever laughed like Mother. It was far worse than when she was away, because then you knew she was coming back, and now you knew . . . just *nothing*. Nobody would tell you anything, they just put you off.

Nan came home from school very pale over something Amy Taylor had told her.

'Susan, is Mother . . . Mother isn't . . . she isn't going to *die*, Susan?'

'Of course not,' said Susan, too sharply and quickly. Her hands trembled as she poured out Nan's glass of milk. 'Who has been talking to you?'

'Amy. She said . . . oh, Susan, she said she thought Mother would make a sweet-looking corpse!'

'Never you mind what she said, my pet. The Taylors have all waggling tongues. Your blessed mother is sick enough, but she is going to pull through and that you may tie to. Do you not know that your father is at the helm?'

'God wouldn't let Mother die, would He, Susan?' asked a white-lipped Walter, looking at her with the grave intentness that made it very hard for Susan to utter her comforting lies. Susan was a badly frightened woman. The nurse had shaken her head that afternoon. The doctor had refused to come down to supper.

'I suppose the Almighty knows what He's about,' muttered Susan as she washed the supper dishes . . . and broke three of them . . . but for the first time in her honest, simple life she doubted it.

Nan wandered unhappily around. Dad was sitting by the library table with his head in his hands. The nurse went in and Nan heard her say she thought the crisis would come that night.

'What is a crisis?' she asked Di.

'I think it is what a butterfly hatches out of,' said Di cautiously. 'Let's ask Jem.'

Jem knew, and told them before he went upstairs to shut himself in his room. Walter had disappeared . . . he was lying face downward under the White Lady in Rainbow Valley . . . and Susan had taken Shirley and Rilla off to bed.

Nan went out alone and sat down on the steps. Behind her in the house was a terrible, unaccustomed quiet. Before her the Glen was brimming with evening sunshine, but the long red road was misty with dust and the bent grasses in the harbour fields were burned white in the drought. It had not rained for weeks and the flowers drooped in the garden . . . the flowers Mother had loved.

Nan was thinking deeply. Now, if ever, was the time to bargain with God. What would she promise to do if He made Mother well? It must be something tremendous . . . something that would make it worth His while. Nan remembered what Dicky Drew had said to Stanley Reese in school one day: 'I dare you to walk through the graveyard after night.' Nan had shuddered at the time. How could *anybody* walk through the graveyard after night . . . how could anyone even *think* of it? Nan had a horror of the graveyard not a soul in Ingleside suspected. Amy Taylor had once told her it was full of dead people . . . 'and they don't always *stay* dead,' said Amy darkly and mysteriously. Nan could hardly bring herself to walk past it alone in broad daylight.

Far away the trees on a misty golden hill were touching the sky. Nan had often thought if she could get to that hill she could touch the sky, too. God lived just on the other side of it . . . He might hear you better there. But she could not get to that hill . . . she must just do the best she could here at Ingleside.

She clasped her little sunburned paws and lifted her tearstained face to the sky.

'Dear God,' she whispered, 'if you make Mother well I'll *walk through the graveyard after night*. Oh, dear God, *please, please*. And if You do this I won't bother You for ever so long again.'

27

It was life, not death, that came at the ghostliest hour of the night to Ingleside. The children, sleeping at last, must have felt even in their sleep that the Shadow had withdrawn as silently and swiftly as it had come. For when they woke, to a day dark with welcome rain, there was sunshine in their eyes. They hardly needed to be told the good news by a Susan who had grown ten years younger. The crisis was past and Mother was going to live.

It was Saturday, so there was no school. They could not stir outside . . . even though they loved to be out in the rain. This downpour was too much for them . . . and they had to be very quiet inside. But they had never felt happier. Dad, almost sleepless for a week, had flung himself on the spare-room bed for a long deep slumber . . . but not before he had sent a long-distance message to a green-gabled house in Avonlea where two old ladies had been trembling every time the telephone rang.

Susan, whose heart of late had not been in her desserts,

concocted a glorious 'orange shuffle' for dinner, promised a jam roly-poly for supper, and baked a double batch of butterscotch cookies. Cock Robin chirped all over the place. The very chairs looked as if they wanted to dance. The flowers in the garden lifted up their faces bravely again as the dry earth welcomed the rain. And Nan, amid all her happiness, was trying to face the consequences of her bargain with God.

She had no thought of trying to back out of it, but she kept putting it off, hoping she would get a little more courage for it. The very thought of it 'made her blood curdle', as Amy Taylor was so fond of saying. Susan saw there was something the matter with the child and administered castor oil, with no visible improvement. Nan took the dose quietly, though she could not help thinking that Susan gave her castor oil much oftener since that earlier bargain. But what was castor oil compared to walking through the graveyard after dark? Nan simply did not see how she could ever do it. But she must.

Mother was still so weak that nobody was allowed to see her save for a brief peep. And then she looked so white and thin. Was it because she, Nan, was not keeping her bargain?

'We must give her time,' said Susan.

How could you give anyone time, Nan wondered. But *she* knew why Mother was not getting well faster. Nan set her little pearly teeth. Tomorrow was Saturday again, and tomorrow night she would do what she had promised to do.

It rained again all the next forenoon, and Nan could not help a feeling of relief. If it was going to be a rainy night, nobody, not even God, could expect her to go prowling about graveyards. By noon the rain had stopped, but there came a fog creeping up the harbour and over the Glen, surrounding Ingleside with its eerie magic. So still Nan hoped. If it was foggy she couldn't go either. But at supper time a wind sprang up and the dreamlike landscape of the fog vanished.

'There'll be no moon tonight,' said Susan.

'Oh, Susan, can't you *make* a moon,' cried Nan despairingly. If she had to walk through the graveyard there *must* be a moon.

'Bless the child, nobody can make moons,' said Susan. 'I only meant it was going to be cloudy and you could not see the moon. And what difference can it make to you whether there is a moon or not?'

That was just what Nan could not explain, and Susan was more worried than ever. *Something* must ail the child . . . she had been acting so strangely all the week. She did not eat half enough and she moped. Was she worrying about her mother. She needn't . . . Mrs Doctor dear was coming on nicely.

Yes, but Nan knew that Mother would soon stop coming on nicely if she didn't keep her bargain. At sunset the clouds rolled away and the moon rose. But such a strange moon . . . such a huge, blood-red moon. Nan had never seen such a moon. It terrified her. Almost would she have preferred the dark.

The twins went to bed at eight, and Nan had to wait until Di had gone to sleep. Di took her time about it. She was feeling too sad and disillusioned to sleep readily. Her chum, Elsie Palmer, had walked home from school with another girl and Di believed that life was practically ended for her. It was nine o'clock before Nan felt it safe to slip out of bed and dress with fingers that trembled so she could hardly cope with her buttons. Then she crept down and out of the side door while Susan set the bread in the kitchen and reflected comfortably that all under her charge were safe in bed except the poor Doctor, who had been summoned post-haste to a Harbour Mouth household where a baby had swallowed a tack.

Nan went out and down to Rainbow Valley. She must take the short cut through it and up the hill pasture. She knew that the sight of an Ingleside twin prowling along the road and through the village would cause wonderment and somebody would likely insist on bringing her home. How cold the early October night was! She had not thought about that and had not put on her jacket. Rainbow Valley by night was not the friendly haunt of daytime. The moon had shrunk to a reasonable size and was no longer red, but it cast sinister black shadows. Nan had always been rather frightened of shadows. Was that paddy feet in the darkness of the withered bracken by the brook?

Nan held up her head and stuck out her chin. 'I'm not frightened,' she said aloud valiantly. 'It's only my stomach feels a little queer. I'm being a *heroine*.'

The pleasant idea of being a heroine carried her halfway up the hill. Then a strange shadow fell over the world . . . a cloud was crossing the moon . . . and Nan thought of the Bird. Amy Taylor had once told her such a terrifying tale of a Great Black Bird that swooped down on you in the night and carried you off. Was it the Bird's shadow that had crossed over her? But Mother had said there was no Big Black Bird. 'I don't believe Mother could tell me a lie . . . not *Mother*,' said Nan . . . and went on until she reached the fence. Beyond was the road, and across it the graveyard. Nan stopped to get her breath.

Another cloud was over the moon. All around her lay a strange, dim, unknown land. 'Oh, the world is too big!' shivered Nan, crowding against the fence. If she were only back in Ingleside! But . . . 'God is watching me,' said the seven-year-old scrap . . . and climbed the fence.

She fell off on the other side, skinning her knee and tearing her dress. As she got to her feet a sharp weed stub pierced completely through her slipper and cut her foot. But she limped across the road to the graveyard gate.

The old graveyard lay in the shadow of the firs at its eastern end. On one side was the Methodist church, on the other the Presbyterian manse, now dark and silent during the minister's absence. The moon broke out suddenly from the cloud and the graveyard was full of shadows, shadows that shifted and danced, shadows that would grasp at you if you trusted yourself among them. A newspaper someone had discarded blew along the road, like a dancing old witch, and though Nan knew it for what it was, it was all part and parcel of the uncanniness of the night. Swish, swish, went the night wind in the firs. A long leaf on the willow by the gate suddenly flicked her cheek like the touch of an elfin hand. For a moment her heart stood still . . . yet she put her hand on the hook of the gate.

Suppose a long arm reached out of a grave and dragged you down!

Nan turned. She knew now that, bargain or no bargain, she could *never* walk through that graveyard by night. The grisliest groan suddenly sounded quite close to her. It was only Mrs Ben Baker's old cow, which she pastured on the road, getting up from behind a clump of spruces. But Nan did not wait to see what it was. In a spasm of uncontrollable panic she tore down the hill, through the village and up the road to Ingleside. Outside of the gate she dashed headlong through what Rilla called a 'pud-muddle'. But there was home, with the soft, glowing lights in the windows, and a moment later she stumbled into Susan's kitchen, mud-spattered, with wet, bleeding feet.

'Good grief!' said Susan blankly.

'I couldn't walk through the graveyard, Susan . . . I couldn't,' gasped Nan.

Susan asked no questions at first. She picked the chilled, distraught Nan up and peeled her wet, pink feet. She undressed her and put on her nightgown and carried her to bed. Then she went down to get a 'bite' for her. No matter what the child had been up to she couldn't be let go to bed on an empty stomach.

Nan ate her supper and sipped her glass of hot milk. How lovely it was to be back in the warm, lighted room, safe in her nice warm bed! But she would not tell Susan one thing about it. 'It's a secret between me and God, Susan.' Susan went to bed, vowing she would be a happy woman when Mrs Doctor dear was up and about again.

'They're getting beyond *me*,' sighed Susan helplessly.

Mother would certainly die now. Nan woke up with that terrible conviction in her mind. She had not kept her bargain and she could not expect God would. Life was very dreadful for Nan that following week. She could take no pleasure in anything, not even in watching Susan spin in the garret . . . something she had always found so fascinating. She would never be able to laugh again. It wouldn't matter what she did. She gave her sawdust dog, off which Ken Ford had pulled the ears and which she loved even better than old Teddy . . . Nan always loved old things . . . to Shirley because Shirley had always wanted it, and she gave her prized house made of shells, which Captain Malachi had brought her all the way from the West Indies, to Rilla, hoping that it would satisfy God; but she feared it would not. And when her grey kitten, which she had given to Amy Taylor because Amy wanted it, came back home and persisted in coming back home, Nan knew God was not satisfied. Nothing could do for Him but walking through the graveyard; and poor haunted Nan knew now she could never do *that*. She was a coward and a sneak. Only sneaks, Jem had said once, tried to get out of bargains.

28

Anne was allowed to sit up in bed. She was nearly well again after being ill. She would soon be able to keep her house again . . . read her books . . . lie easily on her pillows . . . eat everything she wanted . . . sit by her fireplace . . . look to her garden . . . see her friends . . . listen to the juicy bits of gossip . . . welcome the days shining like jewels on the necklace of the year . . . be again a part of the colourful pageantry of life.

She had had such a nice dinner . . . Susan's stuffed leg of lamb had been done to a turn. It was delightful to feel hungry again. She looked about her room at all the things she loved. She must get new curtains for it, something between spring green and pale gold; and certainly those new cupboards for towels must be put in the bathroom. Then she looked out of the window. There was some magic in the air. She could catch a blue glimpse of the harbour through the maples: the weeping birch on the lawn was a soft rain of falling gold; vast sky-gardens arched over an opulent land holding autumn in fee, a land of unbelievable colours, mellow light and lengthening shadows. Cock Robin was tilting crazily on a fir top; the children were laughing in the orchard as they picked apples. Laughter had come back to Ingleside. Life *is* something more than 'delicately balanced organic chemistry', she thought happily.

Into the room crept Nan, eyes and nose crimson from crying.

'Mummy, I *have* to tell you . . . I can't wait any longer. Mummy, *I've cheated God*.'

Anne thrilled again to the soft touch of a child's little clinging hand . . . a child seeking help and comfort in its bitter little problems. She listened while Nan sobbed out the whole story and managed to keep a straight face. Anne always had contrived to keep a straight face when a straight face was indicated, no matter how crazily she might laugh it over with Gilbert afterwards. She knew Nan's worry was real and dreadful to her; and she also realized that this small daughter's theology needed attention.

'Darling, you're terribly mistaken about it all. God doesn't make bargains. He *gives* . . . gives without asking from us in return, except love. When you ask Father or me for something you want *we* don't make bargains with you . . . and God is ever and ever so much kinder than we are. And He knows so much better than we do what is good to give.'

'And He won't . . . He won't make you die, Mummy, because I didn't keep my promise?'

'Certainly not, darling.'

'Mummy, even if I was mistooken about God . . . oughtn't I to keep my bargain when I made it? I *said* I would, you know. Daddy says we should always keep our promises. Won't I be *disgraced for ever* if I don't?'

'When I get quite well, dear, I'll go with you some night . . . and stay outside the gate . . . and I don't think you'll be a bit afraid to go through the graveyard then. That will relieve your poor little conscience, and you won't make any more foolish bargains with God?'

'No,' promised Nan, with a rather regretful feeling that she was giving up something that, with all its drawbacks, had been pleasantly exciting. But the sparkle had come back to her eyes and a bit of the old ginger to her voice.

'I'll go and wash my face and then I'll come back and kiss you, Mummy. And I'll pick you all the snack-dragons I can find. It's been *dreadful* without you, Mummy.'

'Oh, Susan,' said Anne, when Susan brought in her supper, 'what a world it is! What a beautiful, interesting, wonderful world! Isn't it, Susan?'

'I will go so far,' admitted Susan, recalling the beautiful row of pies she had just left in the pantry, 'as to say that it is a very tolerable world.'

29

October was a very happy month at Ingleside that year, full of days when you just *had* to run and sing and whistle. Mother was about again, refusing to be treated as a convalescent any longer, making garden plans, laughing again . . . Jem always thought Mother had such a beautiful joyous laugh . . . answering innumerable questions. 'Mummy, how far is it from here to the sunset?' . . . 'Mummy, why can't we gather up the spilled moonlight?' . . . 'Mummy, do the souls of dead people *really* come back on Hallowe'en?' . . . 'Mother, what causes the cause?' . . . 'Mummy, wouldn't you rather be killed by a rattlesnake than a tiger, because the tiger would mess you up and eat you?' . . . 'Mummy, what is a cubby?' . . . 'Mother, is a widow really a woman whose dreams have come true? . . . Wally Taylor said she was' . . . 'Mummy, what do little birds do when it rains *hard*?' . . . 'Mummy, are we *really* a too romantic family?'

The last from Jem, who had heard in school that Mrs Alec Davies had said so. Jem did not like Mrs Alec Davies because whenever she met him with Mother or Father she invariably dabbed her long forefinger at him and demanded, 'Is Jemmy a good boy in school?' Jemmy! Perhaps they *were* a bit romantic . . . I'm sure Susan thought so when she discovered the boardwalk to the barn lavishly decorated with splotches of crimson paint. 'We *had* to have them for our sham battle, Susan,' explained Jem. 'They represent gobs of gore.'

At night there might be a line of wild geese flying across a low red moon and Jem, when he saw them, ached mysteriously to fly away with them too, to unknown shores and bring back monkeys . . . leopards . . . parrots . . . things like that . . . to explore the Spanish Main . . . some phrases like 'the Spanish Main' always sounded irresistibly alluring to Jem . . . 'secrets of the sea' was another. To be caught in the deadly coils of a python, and have a combat with a wounded rhinoceros was all in the day's work with Jem. And the very word 'dragon' gave him a tremendous thrill. His favourite picture, tacked on the wall at the foot of his bed, was a knight in armour on a beautiful plump white horse, standing on its hind legs while its rider speared a dragon who had a lovely tail flowing behind him in kinks and loops, ending with a fork. A lady in a pink robe knelt peacefully and composedly in the background with clasped hands. There was no doubt in the world that the said lady looked a good deal like Maybelle Reese for whose nine-year-old favour lances were already being shattered in the Glen school. Even Susan noticed the resemblance and teased the furiously blushing Jem about it. But the dragon was really a little disappointing, it looked so small and insignificant under the huge horse. There didn't seem to be any special valour about spearing it. The dragons from which Jem rescued Maybelle in secret dreams were much more dragonish. He *had* rescued her last Monday from old Sarah Palmer's gander. Peradventure . . . ah, 'peradventure' had a good smack! . . . she had noticed the lordly air with which he had caught the hissing creature by its snaky neck and flung it over the fence. But a gander was, somehow, not nearly so romantic as a dragon.

It was an October of winds, small winds that purred in the valley and big ones that lashed the maple tops, winds that howled along the sand shore, but crouched when they came to the rocks . . . crouched and sprang. The nights, with their sleepy red hunter's moon, were cool enough to make the thought of a warm bed pleasant, the blueberry bushes turned scarlet, the dead ferns were a rich red-brown, sumacs burned behind the barn, green pastures lay here and there like patches on the sere harvest fields of the upper Glen and there were gold and russet chrysanthemums in the spruce corner of the lawn. There were squirrels chattering joyfully everywhere and cricket fiddlers for fairy dances on a thousand hills. There were apples to be picked, carrots to be dug. Sometimes the boys went digging 'cow-hawks' with Captain Malachi when the mysterious 'tides' permitted . . . tides that came in to caress the land, but slipped back to their own deep sea. There was a reek of leaf fires all through the Glen, a heap of big yellow pumpkins in the barn, and Susan made the first cranberry pies.

Ingleside rang with laughter from dawn to sunset. Even when the older children were in school Shirley and Rilla were big enough now to keep up the tradition of laughter. Even Gilbert laughed more than usual this autumn. 'I like a dad who can laugh,' Jem reflected. Dr Bronson of Mowbray Narrows never laughed. He was said to have built up his practice entirely on his owlish look of wisdom; but Dad had a better practice still, and people were pretty far gone when they couldn't laugh over one of his jokes.

Anne was busy in her garden every warm day, drinking in colour like wine, where the late sunshine fell on crimson maples, revelling in the exquisite sadness of fleeting beauty. One gold-grey, smoky afternoon she and Jem planted all the tulip bulbs, that would have a resurrection of rose and scarlet and purple and gold in June. 'Isn't it nice to be preparing for spring when you know you've got to face the winter, Jem?' 'And it's nice to be making the garden beautiful,' said Jem. 'Susan says it is God who makes everything beautiful, but we can help Him out a bit, can't we, Mums?'

'Always . . . always, Jem. He shares that privilege with us.'

Still, nothing is ever quite perfect. The Ingleside folks were worried over Cock Robin. They had been told that when the robins went away he would want to go too.

'Keep him shut up till all the rest are gone and the snow comes,' advised Captain Malachi. 'Then he'll kind of forget about it and be all right till spring.'

So Cock Robin was a sort of prisoner. He grew very restless. He flew aimlessly about the house or sat on the windowsill and looked wistfully out at his fellows who were preparing to follow who knew what mysterious call. His appetite failed, and even worms and Susan's nuttiest nuts would not tempt him. The children pointed out to him all the dangers he might encounter . . . cold, hunger, friendlessness, storms, black nights, cats. But Cock Robin had felt or heard the summons and all his being yearned to answer.

Susan was the last to give in. She was very grim for several days. But finally . . .

'Let him go,' she said. 'It is against nature to hold him.'

They set him free the last day of October, after he had been mewed up for a month. The children kissed him goodbye with tears. He flew joyfully off, returning next morning to Susan's sill for crumbs, and then spreading his wings for the long flight. 'He may come back to us in the spring, darling,' Anne said to the sobbing Rilla. But Rilla was not to be comforted.

'That ith too far away,' she sobbed.

Anne smiled and sighed. The seasons that seemed so long to Baby Rilla were beginning to pass all too swiftly for her. Another summer was ended, lighted out of life by the ageless gold of Lombardy torches. Soon . . . all too soon . . . the children of Ingleside would be children no longer. But they were still hers . . . hers to welcome when they came home at night . . . hers to fill life with tender wonder and delight . . . hers to love and cheer and scold . . . a little. For sometimes they were very naughty, even though they hardly deserved to be called by Mrs Alec Davies 'that pack of Ingleside demons' when she heard that Bertie Shakespeare Drew had been slightly scorched while playing the part of a Red Indian burned at the stake in Rainbow Valley. It had taken Jem and Walter a little longer to untie him than they had bargained for. They got slightly singed too, but nobody pitied *them*.

November was a dismal month that year, a month of east wind and fog. Some days there was nothing but cold mist driving past or drifting over the grey sea beyond the bar. The shivering poplar trees dropped their last leaves. The garden was dead and all its colour and personality had gone from it, except the asparagus bed, which was still a fascinating golden jungle. Walter had to desert his study roost in the maple tree and learn his lessons in the house. It rained . . . and rained . . . and rained. 'Will the world *ever* be dry again?' moaned Di despairingly. Then there was a week steeped in the magic of Indian summer sunshine, and in the cold sharp evenings Mother would touch a match to the kindling in the grate, and Susan would have baked potatoes with supper.

The big fireplace was the centre of the home those evenings. It was the high spot of the day when they gathered around it after supper. Anne sewed and planned little winter wardrobes . . . 'Nan must have a red dress, since she is so set on it' . . . and sometimes thought of Hannah, weaving her little coat every year for the small Samuel. Mothers were the same all through the centuries . . . a great sisterhood of love and service . . . the remembered and the unremembered alike.

Susan heard the children's spellings and then they amused themselves as they liked. Walter, living in his world of imagination and beautiful dreams, was absorbed in writing a series of letters from the chipmunk who lived in Rainbow Valley to the chipmunk who lived behind the barn. Susan pretended to scoff at them when he read them to her, but she secretly made copies of them and sent them to Rebecca Dew.

'I found these readable, Miss Dew, dear, though you may consider them too trivial to peruse. In that case I know you will pardon a *doting old woman* for troubling you with them. He is considered very clever in school, and at least these compositions are not poetry. I might also add that Little Jem made *ninety-nine* in his arithmetic examination last week and nobody can understand why the other mark was cut off. Perhaps I should not say so, Miss Dew, dear, but it is my conviction that that child is *born for greatness*. We may not live to see it, but he may yet be the Premier of Canada.'

The Shrimp basked in the glow, and Nan's kitten, Pussy-willow, which always suggested some dainty exquisite little lady in black and silver, climbed everybody's legs impartially. 'Two cats, and mouse tracks everywhere in the pantry,' was Susan's disapproving parenthesis; the children talked over their little adventures together, and the wail of the distant ocean came through the cold autumn night.

Sometimes Miss Cornelia dropped in for a short call while her husband exchanged opinions in Carter Flagg's store. Little pitchers pricked up their long ears then for Miss Cornelia always had the latest gossip and they always heard the most interesting things about people. It would be such fun next Sunday to sit in church and look at the said people, savouring what you knew about them, prim and proper as they looked.

'My, but you're cosy here, Anne, dearie. It's a real keen night and starting to snow. Is the Doctor out?'

'Yes. I hated to see him go . . . but they telephoned from the Harbour Head that Mrs Brooker Shaw insisted on seeing him,' said Anne, while Susan swiftly and stealthily removed from the hearthrug a huge fishbone the Shrimp had brought in, praying that Miss Cornelia had not noticed it.

'She's no more sick than I am,' said Susan bitterly. 'But I hear she had got a *new lace nightgown* and no doubt she wants her doctor to see her in it. Lace nightgowns!'

'Her daughter Leona brought it home from Boston for her. She came Friday evening, with *four trunks*,' said Miss Cornelia. 'I can remember her starting off to the States nine years ago, lugging a broken old Gladstone bag with things oozing out of it. That was when she was feeling pretty blue over Phil Turner's jilting her. She tried to hide it, but everyone *knew*. Now she's back to "nurse her mother", so she says. She'll be trying to flirt with the Doctor. I warn you, Anne, dearie. But I don't suppose it will matter to him even if he is a man. And you're not like Mrs Doctor Bronson at Mowbray Narrows. She is very jealous of her husband's female patients, I am told.'

'*And* of the trained nurses,' said Susan.

'Well, some of those trained nurses *are* far too pretty for their job,' said Miss Cornelia. 'There's Janie Arthur now, she's taking a rest between cases and trying to keep her two young men from finding out about each other.'

'Pretty as she is, she is no spring chicken now,' said Susan firmly, 'and it would be far better for her to make a choice and settle down. Look at her Aunt Eudora . . . *she* said she didn't intend to marry till she got through flirting, and behold the result. Even yet she tries to flirt with every man in sight, though she is forty-five if she is a day. That is what comes of forming a habit. Did you ever hear, Mrs Doctor dear, what she said to her cousin Fanny when *she* got married? "You're taking my leavings," she said. I am informed there was a shower of sparks and they have never spoken since.'

'Life and death are in the power of the tongue,' murmured Anne absently.

'A true word, dearie. Speaking of that, I wish Mr Stanley would be a little more judicious in his sermons. He has offended Wallace Young, and Wallace is going to leave the church. Everyone says the sermon last Sunday was preached at him.'

'If a minister preaches a sermon that hits home to some particular individual people always suppose he meant it for that very person,' said Anne. 'A hand-me-down cap is bound to fit somebody's head, but it doesn't follow that it was made for him.'

'Sound sense,' approved Susan. 'And I have no use for Wallace Young. He let a firm paint ads. on his cows three years ago. That is *too* economical in my opinion.'

'His brother David is going to be married at last,' said Miss Cornelia. 'He's been a long time making up his mind which was cheaper, marrying or hiring. "Ye *can* keep a house without a woman, but it's hard sledding, Cornelia," he said to me once after his mother died. I had an idea that he was feeling his way, but he got no encouragement from *me*. And at last he's going to marry Jessie King.'

'Jessie King! But I thought he was supposed to be courting Mary North.'

'*He* says he wasn't going to marry any woman who eats cabbage. But there's a story going round that he proposed to her and she boxed his ears. And Jessie King is reported to have said that she would have liked a better-looking man, but that he'd have to do. Well, of course, it is any port in a storm for some folks.'

'I do not think, Mrs Marshall Elliott, that people in these parts say half the things they are reported to have said,' rebuked Susan. 'It is my opinion that Jessie King will make David Young a far better wife than he deserves . . . though as far as outward seeming goes, I will admit he looks like something that washed in with the tide.'

'Do you know that Alden and Stella have a little daughter?' asked Anne.

'So I understand. I hope Stella will be a little more sensible over it than Lisette was over *her*. Would you believe, Anne, dearie, Lisette positively cried because her cousin Dora's baby walked before Stella did?'

'We mothers are a foolish race,' smiled Anne. 'I remember that I felt perfectly murderous when little Bob Taylor, who was the same age as Jem to a day, cut three teeth before Jem cut one.'

'Bob Taylor's got to have an operation on his tonsils,' said Miss Cornelia.

'Why don't *we* ever have operations, Mother?' demanded Walter and Di together in injured tones. They so often said the same thing together. Then they linked their fingers and made a wish. 'We think and feel the same about *everything*,' Di was wont to explain earnestly.

'Shall I ever forget Elsie Taylor's marriage?' said Miss Cornelia reminiscently. 'Her best friend, Maisie Millison, was to play the Wedding March. She played the Dead March in *Saul* in place of it. Of course she always said she made a mistake because she was so flustered, but people had their own opinion. *She* wanted Mac Moorside for herself. A good-looking rogue with a silver tongue . . . always saying to women just what he thought they'd like to hear. He made Elsie's life miserable. Ah, well, Anne, dearie, they've both passed long since into the Silent Land, and Maisie's been married to Harley Russell for years, and everybody has forgotten that he proposed to her, expecting her to say "No" and she said "Yes" instead. Harley has forgotten it himself . . . just like a man. He thinks he has got the best wife in the world and congratulates himself on being clever enough to get her.'

'Why did he propose to her if he wanted her to say "No"? It seems to me a very strange proceeding,' said Susan, immediately adding with crushing humility, 'but of course *I* would not be expected to know anything about *that*.'

'His father ordered him to. He didn't want to, but he thought it was quite safe. There's the Doctor now.'

As Gilbert came in a little flurry of snow blew in with him. He threw off his coat and sat gladly down to his own fireside.

'I'm later than I expected to be.'

'No doubt the new lace nightgown was very attractive,' said Anne, with an impish grin at Miss Cornelia.

'What are you talking about? Some feminine joke beyond my coarse masculine perception, I suppose. I went on to the Upper Glen to see Walter Cooper.'

'It's a mystery how that man does hang on,' said Miss Cornelia.

'I've no patience with him,' smiled Gilbert. 'He ought to have been dead long ago. A year ago I gave him two months, and here he is ruining my reputation by keeping on living.'

'If you knew the Coopers as well as I do you wouldn't risk predictions on them. Don't you know his grandfather came back to life after they'd dug the grave and got the coffin? The undertaker wouldn't take it back either. However, I understand Walter Cooper is having lots of fun rehearsing his own funeral . . . just like a man. Well, there's Marshall's bells . . . and this jar of pickled pears is for you, Anne, dearie.'

They all went to the door to see Miss Cornelia off. Walter's dark grey eyes peered out into the stormy night.

'I wonder where Cock Robin is tonight, and if he misses us,' he said wistfully. Perhaps Cock Robin had gone to that mysterious place Mrs Elliott was always referring to as the Silent Land.

'Cock Robin is in a land of sunshine,' said Anne. 'He'll be back in the spring, I feel quite sure, and that's only five months away. Chickabids, you should all have been in bed long ago.'

'Susan,' Di was saying in the pantry, 'would you like to have a baby? I know where you could get one, brand new.'

'Ah, now, where?'

'They have a new one at Amy's. Amy says the angels brought it and she thinks they might have had more sense. They've eight children now, not counting it. I heard you say yesterday that it made you lonesome to see Rilla getting so big . . . you'd no baby now. I'm sure Mrs Taylor would give you hers.'

'The things children think of! It runs in the Taylors to have big families. Andrew Taylor's father never could tell off-hand how many children he had . . . always had to stop and reckon them up. But I do not think I will take any outside babies on just yet.'

'Susan, Amy Taylor says you are an old maid. Are you, Susan?'

'Such has been the lot an all-wise Providence has ordained for me,' said Susan unflinchingly.

'Do you *like* being an old maid, Susan?'

'I cannot truthfully say I do, my pet. But,' added Susan, remembering the lot of some wives she knew, 'I have learned that there are compensations. Now take your father's apple pie to him and I'll bring his tea. The poor man must be faint from hunger.'

'Mother, we've got the loveliest home in the world, haven't we?' said Walter as he went sleepily upstairs. 'Only . . . don't you think it would improve it if we had a few ghosts?'

'Ghosts?'

'Yes. Jerry Palmer's house is full of ghosts. He saw one . . . a tall lady in white with a skeleton hand. I told Susan about it and she said he was either fibbing or there was something the matter with his stomach.'

'Susan was right. As for Ingleside, nobody but happy people have ever lived here . . . so you see, we're not ghostable. Now say your prayers and go to sleep.'

'Mother, I guess I was naughty last night. I said, "Give us *tomorrow* our daily bread," instead of *today*. It seemed more *logical*. Do you think God minded, Mother?'

30

Cock Robin did come back when Ingleside and Rainbow Valley burned again with the green, evasive flames of spring and brought a bride with him. The two built a nest in Walter's apple tree and Cock Robin resumed all his old habits, but his bride was shyer or less venturesome and would never let anyone come very near her. Susan thought Cock Robin's return a positive miracle, and wrote Rebecca Dew about it that very night.

The spotlight in the little drama of life at Ingleside shifted from time to time, now falling on this one, now on that. They had got through the winter without anything very much out of the way happening to anyone, and in June it was Di's turn to have an adventure.

A new girl had begun coming to the Glen school . . . a girl who said, when the teacher asked her name, 'I am Jenny Penny,' as one might say, 'I am Queen Elizabeth,' or, 'I am Helen of Troy.' You felt the minute she said it that not to know Jenny Penny argued yourself unknown, and not to be condescended to by Jenny Penny meant you didn't exist at all. At least, that was how Diana Blythe felt about it, even if she couldn't have put it into those exact words.

Jenny Penny had nine years to Di's eight, but from the first she took rank with the 'big girls' of ten and eleven. They found they could not snub or ignore her. She was not pretty, but her appearance was striking . . . everybody looked at her twice. She had a round, creamy face, with a soft glossless cloud of soot-black hair about it and enormous dusky blue eyes with long tangled black lashes. When she slowly raised those lashes and looked at you with those scornful eyes you felt that you were a worm honoured in not being stepped on. You liked better to be snubbed by her than courted by any other: and to be selected as a temporary confidant of Jenny Penny's was an honour almost too great to be borne. For Jenny Penny's confidences were exciting. Evidently the Pennys were no common people. Jenny's Aunt Lina, it appeared, possessed a wonderful gold and garnet necklace which had been given her by an uncle who was a millionaire. One of her cousins had a diamond ring that cost a thousand dollars, and another cousin had won a prize in elocution over seventeen hundred competitors. She had an aunt who was a missionary and worked among the leopards in India. In short, the Glen schoolgirls, for a time at least, accepted Jenny Penny at her own valuation, looked up to her with mingled admiration and envy, and talked so much about her at their supper tables that their elders were finally constrained to take notice.

'*Who* is this little girl Di seems so taken up with, Susan?' asked Anne one evening, after Di had been telling of 'the mansion' Jenny lived in, with white wooden lace around its roof, five bay windows, a wonderful birch grove behind it, and a red marble mantelpiece in the parlour. 'Penny is a name I've never heard in Four Winds. Do you know anything about them?'

'They are a new family that have moved to the old Conway farm on the Base Line, Mrs Doctor dear. Mr Penny is said to be a carpenter who couldn't make a living carpentering . . . being too busy, as I understand, trying to prove there is no God . . . and has decided to try farming. From all I can make out, they are a queer lot. The young ones do just as they like. He says he was bossed to death when he was a kid and his children are not going to be. That is why this Jenny one is coming to the Glen school. They are nearer the Mowbray Narrows school and the other children go there, but Jenny made up her mind to come to the Glen. Half the Conway farm is in this district, so Mr Penny pays rates to both schools, and of course he can send his children to both if he likes. Though it seems this Jenny is his niece, not his daughter. Her father and mother are dead. They say it was George Andrew Penny who put the sheep in the basement of the Baptist church at Mowbray Narrows. I do not say they are not respectable, but they are all so *unkempt*, Mrs Doctor dear . . . and the house is topsy-turvy . . . and, if I may presume to advise, you do not want Diana mixed up with a monkey tribe like that.'

'I can't exactly prevent her from associating with Jenny in school, Susan. I don't really know anything against the child, though I feel sure she draws a long bow in telling of her relatives and adventures. However, Di will probably soon get over this "crush" and we'll hear no more of Jenny Penny.'

They continued to hear of her, however. Jenny told Di she liked her best of all the girls in the Glen school, and Di, feeling that a queen had stooped to her, responded adoringly. They became inseparable at recesses; they wrote notes to each other over the weekends: they gave and received 'chews' of gum: they traded buttons and co-operated in dust piles; and finally, Jenny asked Di to go home with her from school and stay all night with her.

Mother said 'No' very decidedly, and Di wept copiously.

'You've let me stay all night with Persis Ford,' she sobbed.

'That was different,' said Anne, a little vaguely. She did not want to make a snob of Di, but all she had heard about the Penny family had made her realize that as friends for the Ingleside children they were quite out of the question and she had been considerably worried of late over the fascination Jenny so evidently possessed for Diana.

'I don't see any difference,' wailed Di. 'Jenny is just as much of a lady as Persis, so there. She *never* chews bought gum. She has a cousin who knows all the rules of etiquette, and Jenny has learned them all from her. Jenny says *we* don't know what etiquette is. And she has had the most exciting adventures.'

'Who says she has?' demanded Susan.

'She told me herself. Her folks aren't rich, but they have got very rich and respectable relatives. Jenny has an uncle who is a judge, and a cousin of her mother's is captain of the biggest vessel in the world. Jenny christened the ship for him when it was launched. *We* haven't got an aunt who is a missionary to leopards either.'

'Lepers, dear, not leopards.'

'Jenny *said* leopards. I guess she ought to know, since it is her aunt. And there are so many things at her house I want to see . . . her room is papered with *parrots* . . . and their parlour is *full* of stuffed owls . . . and they have a hooked rug with a house on it in the hall . . . and window blinds just covered with roses . . . and a *real house* to play in . . . her uncle built it for them . . . and her Granny lives with them and is the oldest person in the world. Jenny says she lived before the flood. I may never have another chance to see a person who lived before the flood.'

'The grandmother is close on a hundred, I am told,' said Susan, 'but if your Jenny said she lived before the flood she is fibbing. You would be likely to catch goodness knows what if you went to a place like that.'

'They've had everything they could have long ago,' protested Di. 'Jenny says they've had mumps and measles and whooping cough and scarlet fever all in one year.'

'I wouldn't put it past them having the smallpox,' muttered Susan. 'Talk of people being bewitched!'

'Jenny has to have her tonsils out,' sobbed Di. 'But *that* isn't catching, is it? Jenny had a cousin who died when she had her tonsils out . . . she bled to death without gaining conscious. So it is likely Jenny will too, if it runs in the family. She is delicate . . . she fainted three times last week. But she is *quite prepared*. And that is partly why she is so anxious to have me spend a night with her . . . so that I'd have it to remember after she passed away. *Please*, Mother. I'll go without the new hat with ribbon streamers you promised if you'll let me.'

But Mother was adamant and Di betook herself to a tearful pillow. Nan had no sympathy for her . . . Nan 'had no use' for Jenny Penny.

'I don't know what has got into the child,' said Anne worriedly. 'She has never behaved like this before. As you say, that Penny girl seems to have bewitched her.'

'You were quite right in refusing to let her go to a place so far beneath her, Mrs Doctor dear.'

'Oh, Susan, I don't want her to feel that anyone is "beneath" her. But we must draw the line somewhere. It's not Jenny so much . . . I think she is harmless enough apart from her habit of exaggeration . . . but I'm told the boys are really dreadful. The Mowbray Narrows teacher is at her wits' end with them.'

'Do they *tryanize* over you like that?' asked Jenny loftily when Di told her she was not allowed to go. '*I* wouldn't let anyone use me like that. I have too much spirit. Why, I sleep out of doors all night whenever I take the notion. I s'pose you'd never dream of doing that?'

Di looked wistfully at this mysterious girl who had 'often slept out all night'. How wonderful!

'You don't blame me for not going, Jenny? You know I want to go?'

'Of course I don't blame you. *Some* girls wouldn't put up with it, of course, but I s'pose you just can't help it. We could have had fun. I'd planned we'd go fishing by moonlight in our back brook. We often do. I've caught trout *that* long. And we have the dearest little pigs and a new foal that's just sweet and a litter of puppies. Well, I guess I must ask Sadie Taylor. *Her* father and mother let her call her soul her own.'

'My father and mother are very good to me,' protested Di loyally. 'And my father is the best doctor in P.E. Island. Everyone says so.'

'Putting on airs because you have a father and mother and I have none,' said Jenny disdainfully. 'Why, *my* father has wings and always wears a golden crown. But I don't go about with my head in the air on that account, do I? Now, Di, I don't want to quarrel with you, but I hate to hear anyone bragging about their folks. It's not etiket. And I have made up my mind to be a lady. When that Persis Ford you're always talking of comes to Four Winds this summer I am not going to 'sociate with her. There's something queer about her ma, Aunt Lina says. She was married to a dead man and he come alive.'

'Oh, it wasn't like that at all, Jenny, I know . . . Mother told me . . . Aunt Leslie . . .'

'*I* don't want to hear about her. Whatever it is, it's something that'd better not be talked of, Di. There's the bell.'

'Are you really going to ask Sadie?' choked Di, her eyes widening with hurt.

'Well, not right at once. I'll wait and see. Maybe I'll give you one more chance. But if I do it will be the last.'

A few days later Jenny Penny came to Di at recess.

'I heard Jem saying your pa and ma went away yesterday and wouldn't be back till tomorrow night?'

'Yes, they went up to Avonlea to see Aunt Marilla.'

'Then it's *your chance*.'

'My chance?'

'To stay all night with me.'

'Oh, Jenny . . . but I couldn't.'

'Of course you can. Don't be a ninny. They'll never know.'

'But Susan wouldn't let me . . .'

'You don't have to ask her. Just come home with me from school. Nan can tell her where you've gone, so she won't be worried. And she won't tell on you when your pa and ma come back. She'll be scared they'd blame her.'

Di stood in an agony of indecision. She knew perfectly well she should not go with Jenny, but the temptation was irresistible. Jenny turned the full battery of her extraordinary eyes full upon Di.

'This is your *last chance*,' she said dramatically. 'I can't go on 'sociating with anyone who thinks herself too good to visit me. If you don't come we *part for ever*.'

That settled it. Di, still in the thrall of Jenny Penny's fascination, couldn't face the thought of parting for ever. Nan went home alone that afternoon to tell Susan that Di had gone to stay all night with that Jenny Penny.

Had Susan been her usual active self she would have gone straight to the Pennys' and brought Di home. But Susan had strained her ankle that morning, and while she could make shift to hobble around and get the children's meals she knew she could never walk a mile down the Base Line road. The Pennys had no telephone, and Jem and Walter flatly refused to go. They were invited to a mussel-bake at the lighthouse and nobody would eat Di at the Pennys'. Susan had to resign herself to the inevitable.

Di and Jenny went home across the fields, which made it little more than a quarter of a mile. Di, in spite of her prodding conscience was happy. They went through so much beauty . . . little bays of bracken, elfin haunted, in the edges of deep-green woods, a rustling windy hollow where you waded knee-deep in buttercups, a winding lane under young maples, a brook that was a rainbow scarf of blossom, a sunny pasture field full of strawberries. Di, just wakening to a perception of the loveliness of the world, was enraptured and almost wished Jenny wouldn't talk so much. That was all right at school, but here Di wasn't sure she wanted to hear about the time Jenny poisoned herself . . . 'zackzidentally' of course . . . by taking the wrong kind of medicine. Jenny painted her dying agonies finely but was somewhat vague as to the reason she hadn't died after all. She had 'lost conscious' but the doctor had managed to pull her back from the brink of the grave.

'Though I've never been the same since. Di Blythe, what *are* you staring at? I don't believe you've been listening at all.'

'Oh, yes, I have,' said Di guiltily. 'I do think you've had the most wonderful life, Jenny. But look at the view.'

'The view? What's a view?'

'Why . . . why . . . something you're looking at. *That* . . .' waving her hand at the panorama of meadow and woodland and cloud-smitten hill before them, with that sapphire dent of sea between the hills.

Jenny sniffed.

'Just a lot of old trees and cows. I've seen it a hundred

times. You're awfully funny by spells, Di Blythe. I don't want to hurt your feelings, but sometimes I think you're not all there, I really do. But I s'pose you can't help it. They say your ma is always raving like that. Well, there's our place.'

Di gazed at the Penny house and lived through her first shock of disillusionment. Was *this* the 'mansion' Jenny had talked of? It was big enough certainly and had the five bay windows; but it was woefully in need of painting and much of the 'wooden lace' was missing. The veranda had sagged badly and the once lovely old fanlight over the front door was broken. The blinds were crooked, there were several brown-paper panes, and the 'beautiful birch grove' behind the house was represented by a few lean sinewy old trees. The barns were in a very tumbledown condition, the yard was full of old rusty machinery, and the garden was a perfect jungle of weeds. Di had never seen such a shabby-looking place in her life, and for the first time it occurred to her to wonder if *all* Jenny's tales were true. *Could* anyone have so many narrow escapes of her life, even in nine years, as she had claimed to have?

Inside it was not much better. The parlour into which Jenny ushered her was musty and dusty. The ceiling was discoloured and covered with cracks. The famous marble mantelpiece was only painted . . . even Di could see that . . . and draped with a hideous Japanese scarf, held in place by a row of 'moustache' cups. The stringy lace curtains were a bad colour and full of holes. The blinds were of blue paper, much cracked and torn, with a huge basketful of roses depicted on them. As for the parlour being full of stuffed owls there was a small glass case in one corner containing three rather dishevelled birds, one with its eyes missing entirely. To Di, accustomed to the beauty and dignity of Ingleside, the room looked like something you had seen in a bad dream. The odd thing, however, was that Jenny seemed quite unconscious of any discrepancy between her descriptions and reality. Di wondered if she had just dreamed that Jenny had told her such and such.

It was not so bad outside. The little playhouse Mr Penny had built in the spruce corner, looking like a real house in miniature, *was* a very interesting place and the little pigs and the new foal were 'just sweet'. As for the litter of mongrel puppies, they were as woolly and delightful as if they had belonged to the dog caste of Vere de Vere. One was especially adorable, with long brown ears and a white spot on its forehead, a wee pink tongue, and white paws. Di was bitterly disappointed to learn that they had all been promised.

'Though I don't know as we could give you one even if they weren't,' said Jenny. 'Uncle's awful particular where he puts his dogs. We've heard you can't get a dog to stay at Ingleside *at all*. There must be something queer about you. Uncle says dogs *know* things people don't.'

'I'm sure they can't know anything nasty about *us*,' cried Di.

'Well, I *hope* not. Is your pa cruel to your ma?'

'No, of course he isn't.'

'Well, I heard that he beat her . . . beat her till she *screamed*. But of course I didn't believe *that*. Ain't it awful the lies people tell? Anyway, I've always liked you, Di, and I'll always stand up for you.'

Di felt she ought to be very grateful for this, but somehow she was not. She was beginning to feel very much out of place, and the glamour with which Jenny had been invested in her eyes was suddenly and irrevocably gone. She did not feel the old thrill when Jenny told her about the time she had been almost drowned falling in a mill pond. She *did not believe it* – Jenny just *imagined* those things. And likely the millionaire uncle and the thousand-dollar diamond ring and the missionary to the leopards had just been imagined too. Di felt as flat as a pricked balloon.

But there was Gammy yet. Surely Gammy was real. When Di and Jenny returned to the house Aunt Lina, a full-breasted, red-cheeked lady in a none-too-fresh cotton print, told them Gammy wanted to see the visitor.

'Gammy's bed-rid,' explained Jenny. 'We always takes everybody who comes in to see her. She gets mad if we don't.'

'Mind you don't forget to ask her how her backache is,'

cautioned Aunt Lina. 'She doesn't like it if folks don't remember her back.'

'And Uncle John,' said Jenny. 'Don't forget to ask her how Uncle John is.'

'Who is Uncle John?' asked Di.

'A son of hers who died fifty years ago,' explained Aunt Lina. 'He was sick for years afore he died and Gammy kind of got accustomed to hearing folks ask how he was. She misses it.'

At the door of Gammy's room Di suddenly hung back. All at once she was terribly frightened of this incredibly old woman.

'What's the matter?' demanded Jenny. 'Nobody's going to bite you.'

'Is she . . . she did really live before the flood, Jenny?'

'Of course not. Whoever said she did? She'll be a hundred, though, if she lives till her next birthday. Come on.'

Di went, gingerly. In a small, badly cluttered bedroom Gammy lay in a huge bed. Her face, unbelievably wrinkled and shrunken, looked like an old monkey's. She peered at Di with sunken, red-rimmed eyes and said testily:

'Stop staring. Who are you?'

'This is Diana Blythe, Gammy,' said Jenny . . . a rather subdued Jenny.

'Humph! A nice high-sounding name! They tell me you've got a proud sister.'

'Nan isn't proud,' cried Di, with a flash of spirit. Had Jenny been running down Nan?

'A little saucy, ain't you? *I* wasn't brought up to speak like that to my betters. She *is* proud. Anyone who walks with her head in the air like young Jenny tells me she does, is proud. One of your hoity-toitys! Don't contradict *me*.'

Gammy looked so angry that Di hastily inquired how her back was.

'Who says I've got a back. Such presumption! My back's my own business. Come here . . . come close to my bed.'

Di went, wishing herself a thousand miles away. What was this dreadful old woman going to do to her?

Gammy hitched herself alertly to the edge of the bed and put a claw-like hand on Di's hair.

'Sort of carroty but real slick. That's a pretty dress. Turn it up and show me your petticoat.'

Di obeyed, thankful that she had on her white petticoat with its trimming of Susan's crocheted lace. But what sort of a family was it where you were made to show your petticoat?

'I always judge a girl by her petticoats,' said Gammy. 'Yours'll pass. Now your drawers.'

Di dared not refuse. She lifted her petticoat.

'Humph! Lace on them too! That's extravagance. And you've never asked after John!'

'How is he?' gasped Di.

'"How is he," says she, bold as brass. He might be dead for all you know. Tell me this. Is it true your mother has a gold thimble . . . a solid gold thimble?'

'Yes. Daddy gave it to her her last birthday.'

'Well, I'd never have believed it. Young Jenny told me she had, but you can't ever believe a word young Jenny says. A solid gold thimble! I never heard the beat of that. Well, you'd better go out and get your suppers. Eating never goes out of fashion. Jenny, pull up your pants. One leg's hanging below your dress. Let us have decency at least.'

'My pant . . . drawer leg isn't hanging down,' said Jenny indignantly.

'Pants for Pennys and drawers for Blythes. That's the distinction between you and always will be. Don't contradict *me*.'

The whole Penny family were assembled around the supper table in the big kitchen. Di had not seen any of them before except Aunt Lina, but as she shot a glance around the board she understood why Mother and Susan had not wanted her to come here. The tablecloth was ragged and daubed with ancient gravy stains. The dishes were a nondescript assortment. Flies swarmed over everything. As for the Pennys . . . Di had never sat at table with such company before and she wished herself safely back at Ingleside. But she must go through with it now.

Uncle Ben, as Jenny called him, sat at the head of the

table; he had a flaming red beard and a bald, grey-fringed head. His bachelor brother, Parker, lank and unshaven, had arranged himself at an angle convenient for spitting in the wood-box, which he did at frequent intervals. The boys, Curt, twelve, and George Andrew, thirteen, had pale-blue, fishy eyes, with a bold stare and bare skin showing through the holes in their ragged shirts. Curt had his hand, which he had cut on a broken bottle, tied up with a blood-stained rag. Annabel Penny, eleven, and 'Gert' Penny, ten, were two rather pretty girls with round brown eyes. 'Tuppy', aged two, had delightful curls and rosy cheeks, and the baby, with roguish black eyes, on Aunt Lina's lap, would have been adorable if it had been *clean*.

'Curt, why didn't you clean your nails when you knew company was coming,' demanded Jenny. 'Annabel, don't speak with your mouth full. I'm the only one who ever tries to teach this family any manners,' she explained aside to Di.

'Shut up,' said Uncle Ben in a great booming voice.

'I won't shut up . . . you can't make me shut up,' cried Jenny.

'Don't sass your uncle,' said Aunt Lina placidly. 'Come now, girls, behave like ladies. Curt, pass the potatoes to Miss Blythe.'

'Oh, ho, *Miss* Blythe,' sniggered Curt.

But Diana had got at least one thrill. For the first time in her life she had been called Miss Blythe.

For a wonder the food was good and abundant. Di, who was hungry, would have enjoyed the meal . . . though she hated drinking out of a chipped cup . . . if she had only been sure it was clean . . . and if everybody hadn't quarrelled so. Private fights were going on all the time . . . between George Andrew and Curt . . . between Curt and Annabel . . . between Gert and Jen . . . even between Uncle Ben and Aunt Lina. *They* had a terrible fight and hurled the bitterest accusations at each other. Aunt Lina cast up to Ben all the fine men she might have married, and Uncle Ben said he only wished she had married anybody but him.

'Wouldn't it be dreadful if my father and mother fought like that?' thought Di. 'Oh, if I were only back home.'

'Don't suck your thumb, Tuppy.'

She said that before she thought. They had had *such* a time breaking Rilla of sucking her thumb.

Instantly Curt was red with rage.

'Let him alone,' he shouted. 'He can suck his thumb if he likes. *We* ain't bossed to death like you Ingleside kids are. Who do you think you are?'

'Curt, Curt! Miss Blythe will think you haven't any manners,' said Aunt Lina. She was quite calm and smiling again and put two teaspoons of sugar in Uncle Ben's tea. 'Don't mind him, dear. Have another piece of pie.'

Di did not want another piece of pie. She only wanted to go home . . . and she did not see how it could be brought about.

'Well,' boomed Uncle Ben, as he drained the last of his tea noisily from the saucer. 'That's so much over. Get up in the morning, work all day, eat three meals and go to bed. What a life!'

'Pa loves his little joke,' smiled Aunt Lina.

'Talking of jokes . . . I saw the Methodist minister in Flagg's store today. He tried to contradict me when I said there was no God. "You talk on Sunday," I told him. "It's my turn now. Prove to me there's a God," I told him. "It's you that's doing the talking," sez he. They all laughed like ninnies. Thought he was smart.'

No God! The bottom seemed falling out of Di's world. She wanted to cry.

31

It was worse after supper. Before that she and Jenny had been alone at least. Now there was a mob. George Andrew grabbed her hand and galloped her through a mud-puddle before she could escape him. Di had never been treated like this in her life. Jem and Walter teased her, as did Ken Ford, but she did not know anything about boys like these.

Curt offered her a chew of gum, fresh from his mouth, and was mad when she refused it.

'I'll put a live mouse on you,' he yelled. 'Smarty cat! Stuckupitty! Got a sissy for a brother!'

'Walter isn't a sissy,' said Di. She was half sick from fright, but she would not hear Walter called names.

'He is. He writes poetry. Do you know what I'd do if I'd a brother that writ po'try? I'd drown him . . . like they do kittens.'

'Talking of kittens, there's a lot of wild ones in the barn,' said Jen. 'Let's go and hunt them out.'

Di simply would not go hunting kittens with those boys and said so.

'We've got plenty of kittens at home. We've got eleven,' she said proudly.

'I don't believe it,' cried Jen. 'You haven't! Nobody ever had eleven kittens! . . . it wouldn't be *right* to have eleven kittens.'

'One cat has five and the other six. And I'm not going to the barn anyhow. I fell off the loft in Amy Taylor's barn last winter. I'd have been killed if I hadn't lit on a pile of chaff.'

'Well, I'd have fell off our loft once if Curt hadn't caught me,' said Jen sulkily. Nobody had any right to be falling off lofts but her. Di Blythe having adventures! The impudence of her!

'You should say "I'd *have fallen*",' said Di; and from that moment everything was over between her and Jenny.

But the night had to be got through somehow. They did not go to bed till late because none of the Pennys ever went to bed early. The big bedroom where Jenny took her at half-past ten had two beds in it. Annabel and Gert were getting ready for theirs. Di looked at the other. The pillows were very frowsy. The quilt needed washing very badly, the paper . . . the famous 'parrot' paper . . . had been leaked on and even the parrots did not look very parrotty. On the stand by the bed were a granite pitcher and a tin wash-basin half full of dirty water. She could never wash her face in *that*. Well, for once she must go to bed without washing her face. At least the nightgown Aunt Lina had left for her was clean.

When Di got up from saying her prayers Jenny laughed.

'My, but you're old-fashioned. You looked so funny and holy saying your prayers. I didn't know anybody said prayers now. Prayers ain't any good. What do you say them for?'

'I've got to save my soul,' said Di, quoting Susan.

'I haven't any soul,' mocked Jenny.

'Perhaps not, but *I* have,' said Di, drawing herself up.

Jenny looked at her. But the spell of Jenny's eyes was broken. Never again would Di succumb to its magic.

'You're not the girl I thought you were, Diana Blythe,' said Jenny sadly, as one much deceived.

Before Di could reply George Andrew and Curt rushed into the room. George Andrew wore a mask, a hideous thing with an enormous nose. Di screamed.

'Stop squealing like a pig under a gate,' ordered George Andrew. 'You've got to kiss us goodnight.'

'If you don't we'll lock you up in that closet . . . and it's full of rats,' said Curt.

George Andrew advanced towards Di, who shrieked again and retreated before him. The mask paralysed her with terror. She knew quite well it was only George Andrew behind it and she was not afraid of *him;* but she would die if that awful mask came near her . . . she knew she would. Just as it seemed that the dreadful nose was touching her face she tripped over a stool and fell backward on the floor, striking her head on the sharp edge of Annabel's bed as she fell. For a moment she was dazed and lay with her eyes shut.

'She's gone dead . . . she's gone dead,' sniffled Gert, beginning to cry.

'Oh, won't you get a licking if you've killed her, George Andrew!' said Annabel.

'Maybe she's only pretending,' said Curt. 'Put a worm on her. I've some in this can. If she's only foxing that will bring her to.'

Di heard this, but was too frightened to open her eyes. (*Perhaps they would go away and leave her alone if they thought her dead. But if they put a worm on her . . .*)

'Prick her with a pin. If she bleeds she ain't dead,' said Gert. (*She could stand a pin but not a worm.*)

'She ain't dead . . . she *can't* be dead,' whimpered Jenny. 'You've just scared her into a fit. But if she comes to she'll be screeching all over the place, and Uncle Ben'll come in and lambast the daylights out of us. I wish I'd never asked her here, the fraid-cat!'

'Do you s'pose we could carry her home before she comes to?' suggested George Andrew.

(*Oh, if they only would!*)

'We couldn't . . . not that far,' said Jenny.

'It's only a quarter of a mile 'cross lots. We'll each take

an arm or a leg, you and Curt and me and Annabel.'

Nobody but the Pennys could have conceived such an idea or carried it out if they had. But they were used to doing anything they took it into their heads to do, and a 'lambasting' from the head of the household was something to be avoided if possible. Dad didn't bother about them up to a certain point, but beyond that . . . good*night*!

'If she comes to while we're carrying her we'll just cut and run,' said George Andrew.

There wasn't the least danger of Di coming to. She trembled with thankfulness when she felt herself being hoisted up between the four of them. They crept downstairs and out of the house, across the yard and over the long clover field . . . past the woods . . . down the hill. Twice they had to lay her down while they rested. They were quite sure now she was dead and all they wanted was to get her home without being seen. If Jenny Penny never prayed in her life before she was praying now . . . that nobody in the village would be up. If they could get Di Blythe home they would all swear she had got so homesick at bedtime that she had insisted on going home. What happened after that would be no concern of theirs.

Di ventured to open her eyes once as they plotted this. The sleeping world around them looked very strange to her. The fir trees were dark and alien. The stars were laughing at her. (*I don't like such a big sky. But if I can just hold on a little spell longer I'll be home. If they find*

275

out that I'm not dead they'll just leave me here and I'll
never get home in the dark alone.)

When the Pennys dropped Di on the veranda of Ingleside they ran like mad. Di did not dare come back to life too soon, but at last she ventured to open her eyes. Yes, she was home. It seemed almost too good to be true. She had been a very, very naughty girl, but she was quite sure she would never be naughty again. She sat up, and the Shrimp came stealthily up the steps and rubbed against her, purring. She hugged him to her. How nice and warm and friendly he was! She did not think she would be able to get in . . . she knew Susan would have all the doors locked when Dad was away and she dared not wake Susan up at this hour. But she did not mind. The June night was cold enough, but she would get into the hammock and cuddle down with the Shrimp, knowing that near to her, behind those locked doors, were Susan and the boys and Nan . . . and *home.*

How strange the world was after dark! Was every one in it asleep but her? The large white roses on the bush by the steps looked like small human faces in the night. The smell of the mint was like a friend. There was a glint of firefly in the orchard. After all, she would be able to brag that she had 'slept out all night'.

But it was not to be. Two dark figures came through the gate and up the driveway. Gilbert went around by the back way to force open a kitchen window, but Anne came up the steps and stood looking in amazement at the poor mite who sat there, with her armful of cat.

'Mummy . . . oh, Mummy!' She was safe in Mother's arms.

'Di, darling! What does this mean?'

'Oh, Mummy, I was bad . . . but I'm so sorry . . . and you were right . . . but I thought you wouldn't be back till tomorrow?'

'Daddy got a telephone from Lowbridge . . . they have to operate on Mrs Parker tomorrow and Dr Parker wanted him to be there. So we caught the evening train and walked up from the station. Now, tell me . . .'

The whole story was sobbed out by the time Gilbert had got in and opened the front door. He thought he had effected a very silent entrance, but Susan had ears that could hear a bat squeak when the safety of Ingleside was concerned, and she came limping downstairs with a wrapper over her nightgown.

There were exclamations and explanations, but Anne cut them short.

'Nobody is blaming you, Susan, dear. Di has been very naughty, but she knows it and I think she has had her punishment. I'm sorry we disturbed you . . . you must go straight back to bed, and the doctor will see to your ankle.'

'I was not asleep, Mrs Doctor dear. Do you think I could sleep, knowing where that blessed child was? And ankle or no ankle I am going to get you both a cup of tea.'

'Mummy,' said Di, from her own white pillow. 'Is Daddy ever cruel to you?'

'Cruel? To me? Why, Di . . .'

'The Pennys said he was . . . said he beat you . . .'

'Dear, you know what the Pennys are now, so you know better than to worry your small head over anything they said. There is always a bit of malicious gossip floating round in any place . . . people like that *invent* it. You must never bother about it.'

'Are you going to scold me in the morning, Mummy?'

'No. I think you've learned your lesson. Now go to sleep, precious.'

'Mummy is so *sensible*,' was Di's last conscious thought. But Susan, as she stretched out peacefully in bed, with her ankle expertly and comfortably bandaged, was saying to herself, 'I must hunt up the fine-tooth comb in the morning . . . and when I see my fine Miss Jenny Penny I shall give her a ticking-off she will not forget.'

Jenny Penny never got the promised ticking-off, for she came no more to the Glen school. Instead she went with the other Pennys to Mowbray Narrows school, whence rumours drifted back of her yarns, among them being one of how Di Blythe, who lived in the 'big house' at Glen St Mary but was always coming down to sleep with her, had fainted one night and had been carried home at midnight, pick-a-back, by her, Jenny Penny, alone and unassisted. The Ingleside people had knelt and kissed her hands out of gratitude, and the doctor himself had got out his fringed-top buggy and his famous dappled grey span and driven her home. 'And if there is ever *anything* I can do for you, Miss Penny, for your kindness to my beloved child you have only to name it. My best heart's blood would not be enough to repay you. I would go to Equatorial Africa to reward you for what you have done,' the doctor had vowed.

32

'I know something you don't know . . . something *you* don't know . . . something *you* don't know,' chanted Dovie Johnson, as she teetered back and forth on the very edge of the wharf.

It was Nan's turn for the spotlight . . . Nan's turn to add a tale to the do-you-remembers of after-Ingleside years. Though Nan to the day of her death would blush to be reminded of it. She *had* been so silly.

Nan shuddered to see Dovie teetering . . . and yet it had a fascination. She was so sure Dovie would fall off some time, and then what? But Dovie never fell. Her luck always held.

Everything Dovie did, or said she did . . . which were, perhaps, two very different things, although Nan, brought up at Ingleside, where nobody ever told anything but the truth, even as a joke, was too innocent and credulous to know that . . . had a fascination for Nan. Dovie, who was eleven and had lived in Charlottetown all her life, knew so much more than Nan, who was only eight. Charlottetown,

Dovie said, was the only place where people knew anything. What could you know, shut off in a one-horse place like Glen St Mary?

Dovie was spending part of her vacation with her Aunt Ella in the Glen and she and Nan had struck up a very intimate friendship, in spite of the difference in their ages. Perhaps because Nan looked up to Dovie, who seemed to her to be almost grown up, with the adoration we needs must give the highest when we see it . . . or think we see it, Dovie liked her humble and adoring little satellite.

'There's no harm in Nan Blythe . . . she's only a bit soft,' she told Aunt Ella.

The watchful folks at Ingleside could not see anything out of the way about Dovie . . . even if, as Anne reflected, her mother was a cousin of the Avonlea Pyes . . . and made no objection to Nan's chumming with her, though Susan from the first mistrusted those gooseberry-green eyes with their pale golden lashes. But what would you? Dovie was 'nice-mannered', well-dressed, ladylike, and did not talk too much. Susan could not give any reason for her mistrust and held her peace. Dovie would be going home when school opened, and in the meantime there was certainly no need of fine-tooth combs in this case.

So Nan and Dovie spent most of their spare time together at the wharf, where there was generally a ship or two with their folded wings, and Rainbow Valley hardly knew Nan that August. The other Ingleside children did not care greatly for Dovie and no love was lost. She had played a practical joke on Walter and Di had been furious and 'said things'. Dovie was, it seemed, fond of playing practical jokes. Perhaps that was why none of the Glen girls ever tried to lure her from Nan.

'Oh, please tell me,' pleaded Nan. But Dovie only winked a wicked eye and said that Nan was far too young to be told such a thing. This was just maddening.

'*Please* tell me, Dovie.'

'Can't. It was told me as a secret by Aunt Kate and she's dead. I'm the only person in the world that knows it now. I promised when I heard it that I'd never tell a soul. You'd tell somebody . . . you couldn't help it.'

'I wouldn't . . . I could so,' cried Nan.

'People say you folks at Ingleside tell each other everything. Susan'd pick it out of you in no time.'

'She wouldn't. I know lots of things I've never told Susan. Secrets. I'll tell mine to you if you'll tell me yours.'

'Oh, I'm not int'rested in the secrets of a little girl like you,' said Dovie.

A nice insult that! Nan thought her little secrets were lovely . . . that one wild cherry tree she had found blooming in the spruce wood away back behind Mr Taylor's hay-barn . . . her dream of a tiny white fairy lying on a lily pad in the marsh . . . her fancy of a boat coming up the harbour drawn by swans attached to silver chains . . . the romance she was beginning to weave about the beautiful lady at the old MacAllister place. They were all very wonderful and magical to Nan and she felt glad, when she thought it over, that she did not have to tell them to Dovie after all.

But what *did* Dovie know about *her* that *she* didn't know? The query haunted Nan like a mosquito.

The next day Dovie again referred to her secret knowledge.

'I've been thinking it over, Nan, perhaps you *ought* to know it since it's about you. Of course, what Aunt Kate meant was that I mustn't tell anyone but the person concerned. Look here. If you'll give me that china stag of yours I'll tell you now what I know about you.'

'Oh, I couldn't give you *that*, Dovie. Susan gave it to me my last birthday. It would hurt her feelings dreadfully.'

'*All* right then. If you'd rather have your old stag than know an important thing about yourself you can keep him. *I* don't care. I'd rather keep it. I always like to know things other girls don't. It makes you *important*. I'll look at you next Sunday in church and I'll think to myself, "If *you* just knew what *I* know about you, Nan Blythe." It'll be fun.'

'Is what you know about me *nice*?' queried Nan.

'Oh, it's *very* romantic . . . just like something you'd read in a story book. But never mind. *You* ain't interested and *I* know what I know.'

By this time Nan was crazy with curiosity. Life wouldn't be worth living if she couldn't find out what Dovie's mysterious knowledge was. She had a sudden inspiration.

'Dovie, I can't give you my stag, but if you'll tell me what you know about me I'll give you my red parasol.'

Dovie's gooseberry eyes gleamed. She had been eaten up by envy of that parasol.

'The new red parasol your mother brought you from town last week?' she bargained.

Nan nodded. Her breath came quickly. Was it . . . Oh, was it possible that Dovie would really tell her?

'Will your mother let you?' demanded Dovie.

Nan nodded again, but a little uncertainly. She was none too sure of it. Dovie scented the uncertainty.

'You'll have to have that parasol right here,' she said firmly, 'before I can tell you. No parasol, no secret.'

'I'll bring it tomorrow,' promised Nan hastily. She just *had* to know what Dovie knew about her, that was all there was to it.

'Well, I'll think it over,' said Dovie doubtfully. 'Don't get your hopes up. I don't expect I'll tell you after all. You're too young . . . I've told you so often enough.'

'I'm older than I was yesterday,' pleaded Nan. 'Oh, come, Dovie, don't be mean.'

'I guess I've got a right to my own knowledge,' said Dovie crushingly. 'You'd tell Anne . . . that's your mother . . .'

'Of course I know my own mother's name,' said Nan,

a trifle on her dignity. Secrets or no secrets, there were limits. 'I told you I wouldn't tell *anybody* at Ingleside.'

'Will you swear it?'

'*Swear* it!'

'Don't be a poll parrot. Of course I mean just promising solemnly.'

'I promise solemnly.'

'Solemner than that.'

Nan didn't see how she could be any solemner. Her face would set if she was.

> 'Clasp your hands, look at the sky,
> Cross your heart and hope to die,'

said Dovie.

Nan went through the ritual.

'You'll bring the parasol tomorrow and we'll see,' said Dovie.

'What did your mother do before she was married, Nan?'

'She taught school . . . and taught it well,' said Nan.

'Well, I was just wondering. Mother thinks it was a mistake for your Dad to marry her. Nobody knew anything about her *family*. And the girls he might have had, Mother says. I must be going now. O revor.'

Nan knew that meant 'till tomorrow'. She was very proud of having a chum who could talk French. She continued to sit on the wharf long after Dovie had gone home. She liked to sit on the wharf and watch the fishing boats going out and coming in, and sometimes a ship drifting down the harbour bound to fair lands far away . . . 'far, far away'; Nan repeated the words to herself with a relish. They savoured of magic. Like Jem, she often wished she could sail away in a ship . . . down the blue harbour, past the bar of shadowy dunes, past the light-house point where at night the revolving Four Winds Light became an outpost of mystery, out, out to the blue mist that was the summer gulf, on, on to enchanted islands in golden morning seas. Nan flew on the wings of her imagination all over the world as she squatted there on the old sagging wharf.

But this afternoon she was all keyed up over Dovie's secret. Would Dovie really tell her? What would it be . . . what *could* it be? And what about those girls Father might have married? Nan liked to speculate about those girls. One of them might have been her mother. But that was horrible. Nobody could be her mother except Mother. The thing was simply unthinkable.

'I *think* Dovie Johnson is going to tell me a secret,' Nan confided to Mother that night when she was being kissed bye-bye. 'Of course I won't be able to tell even you, Mummy, because I've promised I wouldn't. You won't mind, will you, Mummy?'

'Not at all,' said Anne, much amused.

When Nan went down to the wharf the next day she took the parasol. It was her parasol, she told herself. It had been given to her, so she had a perfect right to do what she liked with it. Having quieted her conscience with this sophistry, she slipped away when nobody could see her. It gave her a pang to think of giving her her dear, gay little parasol, but by this time the craze to find out what Dovie knew had become too strong to be resisted.

'Here's the parasol, Dovie,' she said breathlessly. 'And now tell me the secret.'

Dovie was really taken aback. She had never meant matters to go as far as this . . . she had never believed Nan Blythe's mother would *let* her give away her red parasol. She pursed her lips.

'I don't know as that shade of red will suit my complexion after all. It's rather *gaudy*. I guess I won't tell.'

Nan had a spirit of her own and Dovie had not yet quite charmed it into blind submission. Nothing roused it more quickly than injustice.

'A bargain is a bargain, Dovie Johnson. You *said* the parasol for the secret. Here is the parasol and you've *got* to keep your promise.'

'Oh, very well,' said Dovie in a bored way.

Everything grew very still. The gusts of wind had died away. The water stopped glug-glugging round the piles of the wharf. Nan shivered with delicious ecstasy. She was going to find out at last what Dovie knew.

'You know the Jimmy Thomases down at the Harbour Mouth,' said Dovie. 'Six-toed Jimmy Thomas?'

Nan nodded. Of course she knew the Thomases . . . at least, knew of them. Six-toed Jimmy sometimes called at Ingleside selling fish. Susan said you never could be sure of getting good ones from him. Nan did not like the look of him. He had a bald head, with a fluff of curly white hair on either side of it, and a red, hooked nose. But what could the Thomases possibly have to do with the matter?

'And you know Cassie Thomas?' went on Dovie.

Nan had seen Cassie Thomas once when Six-toed Jimmy had brought her round with him in his fish-wagon. Cassie was just about her own age, with a mop of red curls and bold, greenish-grey eyes. She had stuck her tongue out at Nan.

'Well . . .' Dovie drew a long breath . . . 'this is the *truth* about you. *You* are Cassie Thomas and *she* is Nan Blythe.'

Nan stared at Dovie. She hadn't the faintest glimmer of Dovie's meaning. What she had said made no sense.

'I . . . I . . . what do you mean?'

'It's plain enough, I should think,' said Dovie with a pitying smile. Since she had been *forced* to tell this she was going to make it worth the telling. 'You and her were born the same night. It was when the Thomases lived in the Glen. The nurse took her down to Thomases and put her in your cradle and took you back to her ma. She didn't dare take Di too, or she would have. She hated your ma and she took that way of getting even. And that is why you are really Cassie Thomas and you ought to be living down there at the Harbour Mouth and poor Cass ought to be up at Ingleside instead of being banged about by that old stepmother of hers. I feel so sorry for her many's the time.'

Nan believed every word of this preposterous yarn. She had never been lied to in her life, and not for the moment did she doubt the truth of Dovie's tale. It never occurred to her that anyone, much less her beloved Dovie, would or could make up such a story. She gazed at Dovie with anguished, disillusioned eyes.

'How . . . how did your Aunt Kate find it out?' she gasped through dry lips.

'The nurse told her on her deathbed,' said Dovie solemnly. 'I s'pose her conscience troubled her. Aunt Kate never told anyone but me. When I came to the Glen and saw Cassie Thomas . . . Nan Blythe, I mean . . . I took a good look at her. She's got red hair and eyes the same colour as your mother's. You've got brown eyes and brown hair. That's why you don't look like Di . . . twins *always* look exactly alike. And Cass has just the same kind of ears as your father . . . lying so nice and flat against her head. I don't s'pose anything can be done about it now. But I've often thought it wasn't fair, you having such an easy time and being kept like a doll and poor Cass . . . Nan . . . in rags, and not even getting enough to eat, many's the time. And old Six-toed beating her when he comes home drunk! Why, what are you looking at me like that for?'

Nan's pain was greater than she could bear. All was horribly clear to her now. Folks had always thought it funny she and Di didn't look one bit alike. *This* was why.

'I *hate* you for telling me this, Dovie Johnson!'

Dovie shrugged her fat shoulders.

'I didn't tell you you'd like it, did I? You *made* me tell. Where are you going?'

For Nan, white and dizzy, had risen to her feet.

'Home . . . to tell Mother,' she said miserably.

'You mustn't . . . you dassn't. Remember you swore you wouldn't tell,' cried Dovie.

Nan stared at her. It was true she had promised not to tell. And Mother always said you mustn't break a promise.

'I guess I'll be getting home myself,' said Dovie, not altogether liking the look of Nan.

She snatched up the parasol and ran off, her plump bare legs twinkling along the old wharf. Behind her she left a broken-hearted child, sitting amid the ruins of her small universe. Dovie didn't care. Soft was no name for Nan. It really wasn't much fun to fool her. Of course, she would tell her mother as soon as she got home and find out she had been hoaxed.

'Just as well I'm going home Sunday,' reflected Dovie.

Nan sat on the wharf for what seemed hours . . . blind,

crushed, despairing. She wasn't Mother's child! She was Six-toed Jimmy's child . . . Six-toed Jimmy, of whom she had always had a secret dread simply because of his six toes. She had no business to be living at Ingleside, loved by Mother and Dad. 'Oh!' Nan gave a piteous little moan. Mother and Dad wouldn't love her any more if they knew. All their love would go to Cassie Thomas.

Nan put her hand to her head. 'It makes me dizzy,' she said.

33

'What is the reason you are not eating anything, pet?' asked Susan at the supper table.

'Were you out in the sun too long, dear?' asked Mother anxiously. 'Does your head ache?'

'Ye-e-s,' said Nan. But it wasn't her head that ached. Was she telling a lie to Mother? And if so, how many more would she have to tell? For Nan knew she would never be able to eat again . . . never so long as this horrible knowledge was hers. And she knew she could never tell Mother. Not so much because of the promise . . . hadn't Susan said once that a bad promise was better broken than kept? . . . but because it would hurt Mother. Somehow, Nan knew beyond any doubt that it would hurt Mother horribly. And Mother mustn't . . . shouldn't . . . be hurt. Nor Dad.

And yet . . . there was Cassie Thomas. She *wouldn't* call her Nan Blythe. It made Nan feel awful beyond description to think of Cassie Thomas as being Nan Blythe. She felt as if it blotted *her* out altogether. If she wasn't Nan

Blythe she wasn't anybody. She would *not* be Cassie Thomas.

But Cassie Thomas haunted her. For a week Nan was beset by her, a wretched week during which Anne and Susan were really worried over the child, who wouldn't eat and wouldn't play and, as Susan said, 'just moped around'. Was it because Dovie Johnson had gone home? Nan said it wasn't. Nan said it wasn't *anything*. She just felt tired. Dad looked her over and prescribed a dose which Nan took meekly. It was not so bad as castor oil, but even castor oil meant nothing now. Nothing meant anything except Cassie Thomas . . . and the awful question which had emerged from her confusion of mind and taken possession of her.

Shouldn't Cassie Thomas have her rights?

Was it fair that she, Nan Blythe . . . Nan clung to her identity frantically . . . should have all the things Cassie Thomas was denied and which were hers by rights? No, it wasn't fair. Nan was despairingly sure it wasn't fair. Somewhere in Nan there was a very strong sense of justice and fair play. And it became increasingly borne in upon her that it was only fair that Cassie Thomas should be told.

After all, perhaps nobody would care very much. Mother and Dad would be a little upset at first, of course, but as soon as they knew that Cassie Thomas was their own child all their love would go to Cassie, and she, Nan,

would be of no account to them. Mother would kiss Cassie
Thomas and sing to her in the summer twilights . . . sing
the song Nan liked best . . .

I saw a ship a-sailing, a-sailing on the sea,
And oh, it was all laden with pretty things for me.

Nan and Di had often talked about the day their ship
would come in. But now the pretty things, her share of
them anyhow, would belong to Cassie Thomas. Cassie
Thomas would take her part as fairy queen in the forth-
coming Sunday School concert and wear *her* dazzling
band of tinsel. How Nan had looked forward to that!
Susan would make fruit puffs for Cassie Thomas and
Pussy-willow would purr for her. She would play with
Nan's dolls in Nan's moss-carpeted playhouse in the maple
grove, and sleep in her bed. Would Di like that? Would
Di like Cassie Thomas for a sister?

There came a day when Nan knew she could bear it no
longer. She must do what was fair. She would go down to
the Harbour Mouth and tell the Thomases the truth. *They*
could tell Mother and Dad. Nan felt that she simply could
not do *that*.

Nan felt a little better when she had come to this deci-
sion, but very, very sad. She tried to eat a little supper
because it would be the last meal she would ever eat at
Ingleside.

'I'll always call Mother "Mother",' thought Nan desperately. 'And I *won't* call Six-toed Jimmy "Father". I'll just say "Mr Thomas" very respectfully. Surely he won't mind *that*.'

But something choked her. Looking up, she read castor oil in Susan's eye. Little Susan thought she wouldn't be here at bedtime to take it. Cassie Thomas would have to swallow it. That was the one thing Nan didn't envy Cassie Thomas.

Nan went off immediately after supper. She must go before it was dark or her courage would fail her. She went in her checked gingham play-dress, not daring to change it, lest Susan or Mother ask why. Besides, all her nice dresses really belonged to Cassie Thomas. But she did put on the new apron Susan had made for her . . . such a smart little scalloped apron, the scallops bound in turkey red. Nan loved that apron. Surely Cassie Thomas wouldn't grudge her that much.

She walked down to the village, through the village, past the wharf road, and down the harbour road, a gallant, indomitable little figure. Nan had no idea that she was a heroine. On the contrary, she felt very much ashamed of herself because it was so hard to do what was right and fair, so hard to keep from hating Cassie Thomas, so hard to keep from fearing Six-toed Jimmy, so hard to keep from turning round and running back to Ingleside.

It was a lowering evening. Out to sea hung a heavy

black cloud, like a great dark bat. Fitful lightning played over the harbour and the wooded hills beyond. The cluster of fishermen's houses at the Harbour Mouth lay flooded in a red light that escaped from under the cloud. Pools of water here and there glowed like great rubies. A ship, silent, white-sailed, was drifting past the dim, misty dunes to the mysterious calling ocean, the gulls were crying strongly.

Nan did not like the smell of the fishing house or the groups of dirty children who were playing and fighting and yelling on the sands. They looked curiously at Nan when she stopped to ask them which was Six-toed Jimmy's house.

'That one over there,' said a boy pointing. 'What's your business with him?'

'Thank you,' said Nan, turning away.

'Have ye got no more manners than that?' yelled a girl. 'Too stuck-up to answer a civil question!'

The boy got in front of her.

'See that house back of Thomases?' he said. 'I've got a sea-serpent in it, and I'll lock you up in it if you don't tell me what you want with Six-toed Jimmy.'

'Come now, Miss Proudy,' taunted a big girl. 'You're from the Glen, and the Glenners all think they're the cheese. Answer Bill's question.'

'If you don't, look out,' said another boy. 'I'm going to drown some kittens and I'll quite likely pop you in, too.'

'If you've got a dime about you I'll sell you a tooth,' said a black-browed girl, grinning. 'I had one pulled yesterday.'

'I haven't got a dime and your tooth wouldn't be of any use to me,' said Nan, plucking up a little spirit. 'You let me alone.'

'None of your lip,' said the black-browed.

Nan started to run. The sea-serpent boy stuck out a foot and tripped her up. She fell her length on the tide-rippled sand.

The others screamed with laughter.

'You won't hold your head so high now, I reckon,' said the black-browed. 'Strutting about here with your red scallops!'

Then someone exclaimed, 'There's Blue Jack's boat coming in,' and away they all ran.

The black cloud had dropped lower and every ruby pool was grey.

Nan picked herself up. Her dress was plastered with sand and her stockings were soiled. But she was free from her tormentors. Would these be her playmates in the future?

She must not cry . . . she must not! She climbed the rickety board steps that led up to Six-toed Jimmy's door. Like all the Harbour Mouth houses, Six-toed Jimmy's was raised on blocks of wood to be out of the reach of any unusually high tide, and the space underneath it was filled with a medley of broken dishes, empty cans, old lobster traps, and all kinds of rubbish. The door was open, and Nan looked into a kitchen the like of which she had never seen in her life. The bare floor was dirty, the ceiling was stained and smoked, the sink was full of dirty dishes. The remains of a meal were on the rickety old wooden table, and horrid big black flies were swarming over it. A woman with an untidy mop of greyish hair was sitting on a rocker nursing a fat lump of a baby . . . a baby grey with dirt.

'*My sister*,' thought Nan.

There was no sign of Cassie or Six-toed Jimmy, for which latter fact Nan felt grateful.

'Who are you and what do you want?' said the woman rather ungraciously.

She did not ask Nan in but Nan walked in. It was beginning to rain outside and a peal of thunder made the house shake. Nan knew she must say what she had come to say before her courage failed her, or she would turn and run from that dreadful house and from that dreadful baby and those dreadful flies.

'I want to see Cassie, please,' she said. 'I have *something important* to tell her.'

'Indeed, now!' said the woman. 'It must be important from the size of you. Well, Cass isn't home. Her dad took her to the Upper Glen for a ride, and with this storm coming up there's no telling when they'll be back. Sit down.'

Nan sat down on a broken chair. She had known the

Harbour Mouth folks were poor, but she had not known any of them were like this. Mrs Tom Fitch in the Glen was poor, but Mrs Tom Fitch's house was as neat and tidy as Ingleside. Of course, everyone knew that Six-toed Jimmy drank up everything he made. And this was to be her home henceforth!

'Anyhow, I'll try to clean it up,' thought Nan forlornly. But her heart was like lead. The flame of high self-sacrifice which had lured her on had gone out.

'What are you wanting to see Cass for?' asked Mrs Six-toed curiously, as she wiped the baby's dirty face with a still dirtier apron. 'If it's about that Sunday School concert she can't go and that's flat. She hasn't a decent rag. How can I get her any? I ask you.'

'No, it's not about the concert,' said Nan drearily. She might as well tell Mrs Thomas the whole story. She would have to know it anyhow. 'I came to tell her . . . to tell her that . . . that she is me and I'm her!'

Perhaps Mrs Six-toed might be forgiven for not thinking this very lucid.

'You must be cracked,' she said. 'Whatever on earth do you mean?'

Nan lifted her head. The worst was now over.

'I mean that Cassie and I were born the same night and . . . and . . . the nurse changed us because she had a spite at Mother, and . . . and . . . Cassie ought to be living at Ingleside . . . and having advantages.'

The last phrase was one she had heard her Sunday School teacher use, but Nan thought it made a dignified ending to a very lame speech.

Mrs Six-toed stared at her.

'Am I crazy or are you? What you've been saying doesn't make any sense. Whoever told you such a rigmarole?'

'Dovie Johnson.'

Mrs Six-toed threw back her tousled head and laughed. She might be dirty and draggled, but she had an attractive laugh. 'I might have knowed it. I've been washing for her aunt all summer and that kid is a pill. My, doesn't she think it smart to fool people! Well, littie Miss What's-your-name, you'd better not be believing all Dovie's yarns or she'll lead you a merry dance.'

'Do you mean it isn't true?' gasped Nan.

'Not very likely. Good glory, you must be pretty green to fall for anything like that. Cass must be a good year older than you. Who on earth are you, anyhow?'

'I'm Nan Blythe.' Oh, beautiful thought! She *was* Nan Blythe!

'Nan Blythe! One of the Ingleside twins! Why, I remember the night you were born. I happened to call at Ingleside on an errand. I wasn't married to Six-toed then . . . more's the pity I ever was . . . and Cass's mother was living and healthy, with Cass beginning to walk. You look like your Dad's mother . . . she was there that night, too, proud as Punch over her twin granddaughters. And to think you'd no more sense than to believe a crazy yarn like that.'

'I'm in the habit of believing people,' said Nan, rising with a slight stateliness of manner, but too deliriously happy to want to snub Mrs Six-toed very sharply.

'Well, it's a habit you'd better get out of in this kind of a world,' said Mrs Six-toed cynically, 'and quit running round with kids who like to fool people. Sit down, child. You can't go home till this shower's over. It's pouring rain and dark as a stack of black cats. Why, she's gone . . . the child's gone.'

Nan was already blotted out in the downpour. Nothing but the wild exultation born of Mrs Six-toed's assurances could have carried her home through that storm. The wind buffeted her, the rain streamed upon her, the appalling thunderclaps made her think the world had burst open. Only the incessant icy-blue glare of the lightning showed her the road. Again and again she slipped and fell. But at last she reeled, dripping and mud-plastered, into the hall at Ingleside.

Mother ran and caught her in her arms.

'Darling, what a fright you have given us! Oh, where have you been?'

'I only hope Jem and Walter won't catch their deaths out in that rain searching for you,' said Susan, the sharpness of strain in her voice.

Nan had almost had the breath battered out of her. She could only gasp as she felt Mother's arm enfolding her:

'Oh, Mother, I'm me . . . really me. I'm not Cassie Thomas and I'll never be anybody but me again.'

'The poor pet is delirious,' said Susan. 'She must have et something that disagreed with her.'

Anne bathed Nan and put her to bed before she would let her talk.

Then she heard the whole story.

'Oh, Mummy, am I really your child?'

'Of course, darling. How could you think anything else?'

'I didn't ever think Dovie would tell me a story . . . not *Dovie*. Mummy, can you believe *anybody*? Jen Penny told Di awful stories . . .'

'They are only two girls out of all the little girls you know, dear. None of your other playmates has ever told you what wasn't true. There *are* people in the world like that, grown-ups as well as children. When you are a little older you will be better able to "tell the gold from the tinsel".'

'Mummy, I wish Walter and Jem and Di needn't know what a silly I was.'

'They needn't. Di went to Lowbridge with Daddy, and the boys need only know you went too far down the Harbour Road and were caught in the storm. You were foolish to believe Dovie, but you were a very fine, brave little girl to go and offer what you thought her rightful place to poor little Cassie Thomas. Mother is proud of you.'

The storm was over. The moon was looking down on a cool, happy world.

'Oh, I'm so glad I'm *me*!' was Nan's last thought as she fell asleep.

Gilbert and Anne came in later to look on the little sleeping faces that were so sweetly close to each other. Diana slept with the corners of her firm little mouth tucked in, but Nan had gone to sleep smiling. Gilbert had heard the story and was so angry that it was well for Dovie Johnson that she was a good thirty miles away from him. But Anne was feeling conscience-stricken.

'I should have found out what was troubling her, but I've been too much taken up with other things this week . . . things that really mattered nothing compared to a child's unhappiness. Think of what the poor darling has suffered.'

She stooped repentantly, gloatingly, over them. They were still hers . . . wholly hers, to mother and love and protect. They still came to her with every love and grief of their little hearts. For a few years longer they would be hers . . . and then? Anne shivered. Motherhood was very sweet . . . but very terrible.

'I wonder what life holds for them,' she whispered.

'At least, let's hope and trust they'll each get as good a husband as their mother got,' said Gilbert teasingly.

34

'So the Ladies' Aid is going to have their quilting at Ingleside?' said the Doctor. 'Bring out all your lordly dishes, Susan, and provide several brooms to sweep up the fragments of reputations afterwards.'

Susan smiled wanly, as tolerant of a man's lack of all understanding of vital things, but she did not feel like smiling . . . at least, until everything concerning the Aid supper had been settled.

'Hot chicken pie,' she went about murmuring, 'mashed potatoes and creamed peas for the main course. And it will be such a good chance to use your new lace tablecloth, Mrs Doctor dear. Such a thing has never been seen in the Glen and I am confident it will make a sensation. I am looking forward to Annabel Clow's face when she sees it. And will you be using your blue and silver basket for the flowers?'

'Yes, full of pansies and yellow-green ferns from the maple grove. And I want you to put those three magnificent pink geraniums of yours somewhere around . . . in the living room if we quilt there, or on the balustrade of the veranda if it's warm enough to work out there. I'm glad we have so many flowers left. The garden has never been so beautiful as it has been this summer, Susan. But then I say that every autumn, don't I?'

There were many things to be settled. Who should sit by whom? It was essential that Mrs Simon Millison should not be asked to sit beside Mrs William McCreery, for they never spoke to each other because of some obscure old feud dating back to school days. Then there was the question of whom to invite, for it was the hostess's privilege to ask a few guests apart from the members of the Aid.

'I'm going to have Mrs Best and Mrs Campbell,' said Anne.

Susan looked doubtful.

'They are newcomers, Mrs Doctor dear' . . . much as she might have said, 'They are crocodiles.'

'The Doctor and I were newcomers once, Susan.'

'But the Doctor's uncle was here for years before that. Nobody knows anything about these Bests and Campbells. But it is your house, Mrs Doctor dear, and who am I to object to anyone you wish to have? I remember one quilting at Mrs Carter Flagg's many years ago when Mrs Flagg invited a strange woman. She came in *wincey*, Mrs Doctor dear . . . said she didn't think a Ladies' Aid worth dressing up for! At least there will be no fear of that with Mrs Campbell. She is very dressy . . . though I could never see myself wearing hydrangea blue to church.'

Anne could not either, but she dared not smile.

'I thought that dress was lovely with Mrs Campbell's silver hair, Susan. And by the way, she wants your recipe for spiced gooseberry relish, Susan. She says she had some of it at the Harvest Home supper and it was delicious.'

'Oh, well, Mrs Doctor dear, it is not everyone who can make spiced gooseberry' . . . and no more disapproval was expressed of hydrangea blue dresses. Mrs Campbell might henceforth appear out in the costume of a Fiji Islander if she chose and Susan would find excuses for it.

The young months had grown old, but autumn was still remembering summer and the quilting day was more like June than October. Every member of the Ladies' Aid who could possibly come came, looking forward pleasurably to a good dish of gossip and an Ingleside supper, besides seeing some sweet new thing in fashions, since the Doctor's wife had recently been to town.

Susan, unbowed by the culinary cares that were heaped upon her, stalked about, showing the ladies to the guest room, serene in the knowledge that not one of them possessed an apron trimmed with crochet lace five inches deep made from Number One Hundred thread. Susan had captured first prize at the Charlottetown Exhibition the week before with that lace. She and Rebecca Dew had trysted there and made a day of it, and Susan had come home that night the proudest woman in Prince Edward Island.

Susan's face was perfectly controlled, but her thoughts were her own, sometimes spiced with a trifle of mild malice.

Celia Reese is here, looking for something to laugh at as usual. Well, she will not find it at our supper table and that you may tie to. Myra Murray in red velvet . . . a little too sumptuous for a quilting in my opinion, but I am not denying she looks well in it. At least it is not wincey. Agatha Drew . . . and her glasses tied on with a string as usual . . . Sarah Taylor . . . it may be her last quilting . . . she has got a terrible heart, the doctor says, but the spirit of her! Mrs Donald Reese . . . thank the Good Lord she didn't bring Mary Anna with her, but no doubt we will hear plenty. Jane Burr from the Upper Glen. She isn't a member of the Aid. Well, I shall count the spoons after supper and that you may tie to. That family were all light-fingered. Candace Crawford . . . she doesn't often trouble an Aid meeting, but a quilting is a good place to show off her pretty hands and her diamond ring. Emma Pollock, with her petticoat showing below her dress of course. A pretty woman, but flimsy minded like all that tribe. Tillie MacAllister, don't you go and upset the jelly on the tablecloth like you did at Mrs Palmer's quilting. Martha Crothers, you will have a decent meal for once. It is too bad your husband could not have come too . . . I hear he has to live on nuts or something like that. Mrs Elder Baxter . . . I hear the elder has scared Harold Reese away from Mina at last.

Harold always had a wishbone in place of a backbone, and faint heart never won fair lady, as the Good Book says. Well, we have enough for two quilts and some over to thread needles.

The quilts were set up on the broad veranda and everyone was busy with fingers and tongues. Anne and Susan were deep in preparations for supper in the kitchen, and Walter, who had been kept home from school that morning because of a slight sore throat, was squatted on the veranda steps, screened from view of the quilters by a curtain of vines. He always liked to listen to older people talking. They said such surprising, mysterious things . . . things you could think over afterwards and weave into the very stuff of drama, things that reflected the colours and shadows, the comedies and tragedies, the jests and the sorrows, of every Four Winds clan.

Of all the women present Walter liked Mrs Myra Murray best, with her easy, infectious laugh and the jolly little wrinkles round her eyes. She could tell the simplest story and make it seem dramatic and vital; she gladdened life wherever she went; and she did look so pretty in her cherry-red velvet, with the smooth ripples in her black hair, and the little red drops in her ears. Mrs Tom Chubb, who was thin as a needle, he liked least . . . perhaps because he had once heard her calling him 'a sickly child'. He thought Mrs Allan Milgrave looked just like a sleek grey hen, and that Mrs Grant Clow was like nothing so much as a barrel on legs. Young Mrs David Ransome, with her taffy-coloured hair, was very handsome . . . 'too handsome for a farm', Susan had said when Dave married her. The young bride, Mrs Morton MacDougall, looked like a sleepy white poppy. Edith Bailey, the Glen dressmaker, with her misty silvery curls and humorous black eyes, didn't look as if she could be 'an old maid'. He liked Mrs Meade, the oldest woman there, who had gentle, tolerant eyes and listened far more than she talked, and he did not like Celia Reese, with her sly, amused look, as if she were laughing at everybody.

The quilters had not really started talking yet . . . they were discussing the weather and deciding whether to quilt in fans or diamonds, so Walter was thinking of the beauty of the ripened day, the big lawn with its magnificent trees, and the world that looked as if some great kind Being had put golden arms about it. The tinted leaves were drifting slowly down, but the knightly hollyhocks were still gay against the brick wall and the poplars wove sorcery of aspen along the path to the barn. Walter was so absorbed in the loveliness around him that the quilting conversation was in full swing before he was recalled to consciousness of it by Mrs Simon Millison's pronouncement.

'That clan were noted for their sensational funerals. Will any of you who were there ever forget what happened at Peter Kirk's funeral?'

Walter pricked up his ears. This sounded interesting.

But much to his disappointment, Mrs Simon did not go on to tell what had happened. Everybody must have been at the funeral or heard the story.

(*But why are they all looking so uncomfortable about it?*)

'There is no doubt that everything Clara Wilson said about Peter was true, but he is in his grave, poor man, so let us leave him there,' said Mrs Tom Chubb self-righteously . . . as if somebody had proposed exhuming him.

'Mary Anna is always saying such clever things,' said Mrs Reese. 'Do you know what she said the other day when we were starting to Margaret Hollister's funeral? "Ma," she said, "will there be any ice cream at the funeral?"'

A few women exchanged furtive amused smiles. The most of them ignored Mrs Donald. It was really the only thing to do when she began dragging Mary Anna into the conversation as she invariably did, in season and out of season. If you gave her the least encouragement she was maddening. 'Do you know what Mary Anna said?' was a standing catchword in the Glen.

'Talking of funerals,' said Celia Reese, 'there was a queer one in Mowbray Narrows when I was a girl. Stanton Lane had gone out west and word came back that he had died. His folks wired to have the body sent home, so it was, but Wallace MacAllister, the undertaker, advised them against opening the casket. The funeral had just got off to a good start when in walked Stanton Lane himself, hale and hearty. It was never found out who the corpse really was.'

'What did they do with him?' queried Agatha Drew.

'Oh, they buried him. Wallace said it couldn't be put off. But you couldn't rightly call it a funeral, with everyone so happy over Stanton's return. Mr Dawson changed the last hymn from "Take Comfort, Christians", to "Sometimes a Light Surprises", but most people thought he'd better have left well enough alone.'

'Do you know what Mary Anna said to me the other day? She said, "Ma, do the ministers know *everything*?"'

'Mr Dawson always lost his head in a crisis,' said Jane Burr. 'The Upper Glen was part of his charge then and I remember one Sunday he dismissed the congregation and then remembered that the collection hadn't been taken up. So what does he do but grab a collection plate and run round the yard with it. To be sure,' added Jane, 'people gave that day who never gave before or after. They didn't like to refuse the minister. But it was hardly dignified of him.'

'What I had against Mr Dawson,' said Miss Cornelia, 'was the unmerciful length of his prayers at a funeral. It actually came to such a pass that people said they envied the corpse. He surpassed himself at Letty Grant's funeral. I saw her mother was on the point of fainting, so I gave him a nudge and told him he'd prayed long enough.'

'He buried my poor Jarvis,' said Mrs George Carr, tears dropping down. She always cried when she spoke of her husband, although he had been dead for twenty years.

'His brother was a minister, too,' said Christine Marsh. 'He was in the Glen when I was a girl. We had a concert in the hall one night and as he was one of the speakers he was sitting on the platform. He was as nervous as his brother and he kept fidgeting his chair farther and farther back and all at once he went, chair and all, clean over the edge on the bank of flowers and house plants we had arranged around the base. All that could be seen of him was his feet sticking up above the platform. Somehow, it always spoiled his preaching for me after that. His feet were *so* big.'

'The Lane funeral might have been a disappointment,' said Emma Pollock, 'but at least it was better than not having any funeral at all. You remember the Cromwell mix-up?'

There was a chorus of reminiscent laughter. 'Let us hear the story,' said Mrs Campbell. 'Remember, Mrs Pollock, I'm a stranger here, and all the family sagas are quite unknown to me.'

Emma didn't know what 'sagas' meant, but she loved to tell a story.

'Abner Cromwell lived over near Lowbridge on one of the biggest farms in that district and he was an M.P.P. in those days. He was one of the biggest frogs in the Tory puddle and acquainted with everybody of any importance on the Island. He was married to Julia Flagg, whose mother was a Reese and her grandmother was a Clow, so they were connected with almost every family in Four Winds as well. One day a notice came out in the *Daily Enterprise* . . . Mr Abner Cromwell had died suddenly at Lowbridge and his funeral would be held at two o'clock the next afternoon. Somehow the Abner Cromwells missed seeing the notice . . . and of course there were no rural telephones in those days. The next morning Abner left for Kingsport to attend a Liberal convention. At two o'clock people began arriving for the funeral, coming early to get a good seat, thinking there'd be such a crowd on account of Abner being such a prominent man. And a crowd there was, believe you me. For miles around the roads were just a string of buggies, and people kept pouring in till about three. Mrs Abner was just about crazy trying to make them believe her husband wasn't dead. Some wouldn't believe her at first . . . she said to me in tears that they seemed to think she'd made away with the corpse . . . and when they were convinced they acted as if they thought Abner ought to be dead. And they tramped all over the lawn flower beds she was so proud of. Any number of distant relations arrived too, expecting supper and beds for the night, and she hadn't much cooked . . . Julie was never very forehanded, that has to be admitted. When Abner arrived home two days afterwards he found her in bed with nervous prostration, and she was months getting over it. She didn't eat a thing for six weeks . . . well, hardly anything. I heard she said if there really had been a funeral she couldn't have been more upset. But I never believed she really did say it.'

'You can't be sure,' said Mrs William McCreery. 'People do say such awful things. When they're upset the truth pops out. Julie's sister Clarice actually went and sang in the choir as usual the first Sunday after her husband was buried.'

'Not even a husband's funeral could damp Clarice down long,' said Agatha Drew. 'There was nothing *solid* about her. Always dancing and singing.'

'*I* used to dance and sing . . . on the shore, where nobody heard me,' said Myra Murray.

'Ah, but you've grown wiser since then,' said Agatha.

'No-o-o, foolisher,' said Myra Murray slowly. 'Too foolish now to dance along the shore.'

'At first,' said Emma, not to be cheated out of a complete story, 'they thought the notice had been put in for a joke . . . because Abner had lost his election a few days before . . . but it turned out it was for an Amasa Cromwell, living away in the backwoods the other side of Lowbridge, no relation at all. He had really died. But it was a long time before people forgave Abner the disappointment, if they ever did.'

'Well, it *was* a little inconvenient, driving all that distance, right in planting time, too, and finding you had your journey for your pains,' said Mrs Tom Chubb defensively.

'And people like funerals as a rule,' said Mrs Donald

Reese with spirit. 'We're all like children, I guess. I took Mary Anna to her Uncle Gordon's funeral and she enjoyed it so. "Ma, couldn't we dig him up and have the fun of burying him over again?" she said.'

They *did* laugh at this . . . everybody except Mrs Elder Baxter, who primmed up her long, thin face and jabbed the quilt mercilessly. Nothing was sacred nowadays. Everyone laughed at everything. But she, an elder's wife, was not going to countenance any laughter connected with a funeral.

'Speaking of Abner, do you remember the obituary his brother John wrote for *his* wife?' asked Mrs Allan Milgrave. 'It started out with, "God, for reasons best known to Himself, has been pleased to take my beautiful bride and leave my Cousin William's ugly wife alive." Shall I ever forget the fuss it made!'

'How did such a thing ever come to be printed at all?' asked Mrs Best.

'Why, he was managing editor of the *Enterprise* then. He worshipped his wife . . . Bertha Morris, she was . . . and he hated Mrs William Cromwell because she hadn't wanted him to marry Bertha. She thought Bertha too flighty.'

'But she was pretty,' said Elizabeth Kirk.

'The prettiest thing I ever saw in my life,' agreed Mrs Milgrave. 'Good looks ran in the Morrises. But fickle . . . fickle as a breeze. Nobody ever knew how she came to stay in one mind long enough to marry John. They say her mother kept her up to the notch. Bertha was in love with Fred Reese, but he was notorious for flirting. "A bird in the hand is worth two in the bush," Mrs Morris told her.'

'I've heard that proverb all my life,' said Myra Murray, 'and I wonder if it's true. Perhaps the birds in the bush could *sing* and the one in the hand couldn't.'

Nobody knew just what to say, but Mrs Tom Chubb said it, anyhow.

'You're always so whimsical, Myra.'

'Do you know what Mary Anna said to me the other day?' said Mrs Donald. 'She said, "Ma, what will I do if nobody ever asks me to marry him?"'

'*Us* old maids could answer that, couldn't we?' asked Celia Reese, giving Edith Bailey a nudge with her elbow. Celia disliked Edith because Edith was still rather pretty and not entirely out of the running.

'Gertrude Cromwell *was* ugly,' said Mrs Grant Clow. 'She had a figure like a slat. But a great housekeeper. She washed every curtain she owned every month, and if Bertha washed hers once a year it was as much as ever. And her window shades were *always* crooked. Gertrude said it just gave her the shivers to drive past John Cromwell's house. And yet John Cromwell worshipped Bertha, and William just put up with Gertrude. Men *are* strange. They say William overslept on his wedding morning and dressed in such a tearing hurry he got to the church with old shoes and odd socks on.'

'Well, that was better than Oliver Random,' giggled Mrs George Carr. '*He* forgot to have a wedding suit made, and his old Sunday suit was simply impossible. It had been *patched*. So he borrowed his brother's best suit. It only fitted him here and there.'

'And at least William and Gertrude did get married,' said Mrs Simon. 'Her sister Caroline *didn't*. She and Ronny Drew quarrelled over what minister they'd have marry them and never got married at all. Ronny was so mad he went and married Edna Stone before he'd time to cool off. Caroline went to the wedding. She held her head high, but her face was like death.'

'But she held her tongue, at least,' said Sarah Taylor. 'Philippa Abbey didn't. When Jim Mowbray jilted her she went to his wedding and said the bitterest things out loud all through the ceremony. They were all Anglicans, of course,' concluded Sarah Taylor, as if that accounted for any vagaries.

'Did she really go to the reception afterwards wearing all the jewellery Jim had given her while they were engaged?' asked Celia Reese.

'No, she didn't! I don't know how such stories get around, I'm sure. You'd think some people never did anything but repeat gossip. I dare say Jim Mowbray lived to wish he'd stuck to Philippa. His wife kept him down good and solid . . . though he always had a riotous time in her absence.'

317

'The only time I ever saw Jim Mowbray was the night the June bugs nearly stampeded the congregation at the anniversary service in Lowbridge,' said Christine Crawford. 'And what the June bugs left undone Jim Mowbray contributed. It was a hot night and they had all got the windows open. The June bugs poured in and blundered about in hundreds. They picked up eighty-seven dead bugs on the choir platform the next morning. Some of the women got hysterical when the bugs flew too near their faces. Just across the aisle from me the new minister's wife was sitting . . . Mrs Peter Loring. She had on a big lace hat with willow plumes . . .'

'She was always considered far too dressy and extravagant for a minister's wife,' interpolated Mrs Elder Baxter.

'"Watch me flick that bug off Mrs Preacher's hat," I heard Jim Mowbray whisper . . . he was sitting right behind her. He leaned forrard and aimed a blow at the bug . . . missed it, but side-swiped the hat and sent it skittering down the aisle clean to the communion railing. Jim almost had a conniption. When the minister saw his wife's hat come sailing through the air he lost his place in his sermon, couldn't find it again, and gave up in despair. The choir sang the last hymn, dabbing at June bugs all the time. Jim went down and brought the hat back to Mrs Loring. He expected a calling down, for she was said to be high-spirited. But she just stuck it on her pretty yellow head again and laughed at him. "If you hadn't done that," she said, "Peter would have gone on for another twenty minutes and we'd all have been stark staring mad." Of course it was nice of her not to be angry, but people thought it wasn't just the thing for her to say of her husband.'

'But you must remember how she was born,' said Martha Crothers.

'Why, *how*?'

'She was Bessy Talbot from up west. Her father's house caught fire one night and in all the fuss and upheaval Bessy was born . . . *out in the garden* . . . under the stars.'

'How romantic,' said Myra Murray.

'Romantic! I call it barely *respectable*.'

'But think of being born under the stars,' said Myra dreamily. 'Why, she ought to have been a child of the stars . . . sparkling . . . beautiful . . . brave . . . true . . . with a twinkle in her eyes.'

'She was all that,' said Martha, 'whether the stars were accountable for it or not. And a hard time she had in Lowbridge, where they thought a minister's wife should be all prunes and prisms. Why, one of the elders caught her dancing around her baby's cradle one day and he told her she ought not to rejoice over her son until she found out if he was *elected* or not.'

'Talking of babies do you know what Mary Anna said the other day, "Ma," she said, "do *queens* have babies?"'

'That must have been Alexander Wilson,' said Mrs Allan. 'A born crab if ever there was one. He wouldn't allow his family to speak a word at mealtime, I've heard. As for laughing . . . there never was any done in *his* house.'

'Think of a house without laughter!' said Myra. 'Why, it's . . . sacrilegious.'

'Alexander used to take spells, when he wouldn't speak to his wife for three days at a time,' continued Mrs Allan. 'It was such a relief to her,' she added.

'Alexander Wilson was a good, honest business man at least,' said Mrs Grant Clow stiffly. The said Alexander was her fourth cousin and the Wilsons were clannish. 'He left her forty thousand dollars when he died.'

'Such a pity he had to *leave* it,' said Celia Reese.

'His brother Jeffry didn't leave a cent,' said Mrs Clow. 'He was the ne'er-do-well of that family I must admit. Goodness knows *he* did enough laughing. Spent everything he earned . . . hail-fellow-well-met with everyone . . . and died penniless. What did *he* get out of life with all his flinging about and laughing?'

'Not much perhaps,' said Myra, 'but think of all he put into it. He was always *giving* . . . cheer, sympathy, friendliness, even money. He was rich in friends at least . . . and Alexander never had a friend in his life.'

'Jeff's friends didn't bury him,' retorted Mrs Allan. 'Alexander had to do that . . . and put up a real fine tombstone too. It cost a hundred dollars.'

'But when Jeff asked him for a loan of one hundred to

pay for an operation that might have saved his life, didn't Alexander refuse it?' asked Celia Drew.

'Come, come, we're getting too uncharitable,' protested Mrs Carr. 'After all, we don't live in a world of forget-me-nots and daisies, and everyone has some faults.'

'Lem Anderson is marrying Dorothy Clark today,' said Mrs Millison, thinking it was high time the conversation took on a more cheerful line. 'And it isn't a year since he swore he would blow out his brains if Jane Elliott wouldn't marry him.'

'Young men do say such odd things,' said Mrs Chubb. 'They've kept it very close . . . it never leaked out till three weeks ago that they were engaged. I was talking to his mother last week and she never hinted at a wedding so soon. I am not sure that I care much for a woman who can be such a Sphinx.'

'*I* am surprised at Dorothy Clark taking him,' said Agatha Drew. 'I thought last spring that she and Frank Clow were going to make a match of it.'

'*I* heard Dorothy said that Frank was the best match, but she really couldn't abide the thought of seeing that nose sticking out over the sheet every morning when she woke up.'

Mrs Elder Baxter gave a spinsterish shudder and refused to join in the laughter.

'You shouldn't say such things before a young girl like Edith,' said Celia, winking around the quilt.

'Is Ada Clark engaged yet?' asked Emma Pollock.

'No, not exactly,' said Mrs Millison. 'Just hopeful. But she'll land him yet. Those girls all have a knack of picking husbands. Her sister Pauline married the best farm over the harbour.'

'Pauline is pretty, but she is as full of silly notions as ever,' said Mrs Milgrave. 'Sometimes I think she'll never learn any sense.'

'Oh, yes, she will,' said Myra Murray. 'Some day she will have children of her own and she will learn wisdom from them . . . as you and I did.'

'Where are Lem and Dorothy going to live?' asked Mrs Meade.

'Oh, Lem has bought a farm at the Upper Glen. The old Carey place, you know, where poor Mrs Roger Carey murdered her husband.'

'Murdered her husband!'

'Oh, I'm not saying he didn't deserve it, but everybody thought she went a little too far. Yes, weed-killer in his teacup . . . or was it his soup? Everybody knew it, but nothing was ever done about it. The spool, please, Celia.'

'But do you mean to say, Mrs Millison, that she was never tried . . . or punished?' gasped Mrs Campbell.

'Well, nobody wanted to get a neighbour into a scrape like that. The Careys were well connected in the Upper Glen. Besides, she was driven to desperation. Of course, nobody approves of murder as a habit, but if ever a man deserved to be murdered Roger Carey did. She went to the States and married again. She's been dead for years. Her second outlived her. It all happened when I was a girl. They used to say Roger Carey's ghost *walked*.'

'Surely nobody believes in ghosts in this enlightened age,' said Mrs Baxter.

'Why aren't we to believe in ghosts?' demanded Tillie MacAllister. 'Ghosts are interesting. I *know* a man who was haunted by a ghost that always laughed at him . . . sneering like. It used to make him so mad. The scissors please, Mrs MacDougall.'

The little bride had to be asked for the scissors twice, and handed them over blushing deeply. She was not yet used to being called Mrs MacDougall.

'The old Truax house over the harbour was haunted for years . . . raps and knocks all over the place . . . a most mysterious thing,' said Christine Marsh.

'All the Truaxes had bad stomachs,' said Mrs Baxter.

'Of course if you don't believe in ghosts they can't happen,' said Mrs MacAllister sulkily. 'But my sister worked in a house in Nova Scotia that was haunted by chuckles of laughter.'

'What a jolly ghost!' said Myra. 'I shouldn't mind that.'

'Likely it was owls,' said the determinedly sceptical Mrs Baxter.

'*My* mother seen angels around her deathbed,' said Agatha Drew with an air of plaintive triumph.

'Angels ain't ghosts,' said Mrs Baxter.

'Speaking of mothers, how is your Uncle Parker, Tillie?' asked Mrs Chubb.

'Very poorly by spells. We don't know what is going to come of it. It's holding us all up . . . about our winter clothes, I mean. But I said to my sister the other day when we were talking it over, "We'd better get black dresses, anyhow," I said, "and then it's no matter what happens."'

'Do you know what Mary Anna said the other day? She said, "Ma, I'm going to stop asking God to make my hair curly. I've asked Him every night for a week and He hasn't done a thing."'

'I've been asking Him something for twenty years,' bitterly said Mrs Bruce Duncan, who had not spoken before or lifted her dark eyes from the quilt. She was noted for her beautiful quilting . . . perhaps because she was never diverted by gossip from setting each stitch precisely where it should be.

A brief hush fell over the circle. They could all guess what she had asked for, but it was not a thing to be discussed at a quilting. Mrs Duncan did not speak again.

'Is it true that May Flagg and Billy Carter have broken up and that he is going with one of the over-harbour MacDougalls?' asked Martha Crothers, after a decent interval.

'Yes. Nobody knows what happened though.'

'It's sad . . . what little things break off matches some-times,' said Candace Crawford. 'Take Dick Pratt and Lillian MacAllister . . . he was just starting to propose to her at a picnic when his nose began to bleed. He had to go to the brook, and he met a strange girl there who lent him her handkerchief. He fell in love, and they were married in two weeks' time.'

'Did you hear what happened to Big Jim MacAllister last Saturday night in Milt Cooper's store at the Harbour Head?' asked Mrs Simon, thinking it time somebody introduced a more cheerful topic than ghosts and jiltings. 'He had got into the habit of setting on the stove all summer. But Saturday night was cold and Milt had lit a fire. So when poor Big Jim sat down . . . well, he scorched his . . .'

Mrs Simon would not say what he had scorched, but she patted a portion of her anatomy silently.

'His bottom,' said Walter gravely, poking his head through the creeper screen. He honestly thought that Mrs Simon could not remember the right word.

An appalled silence descended on the quilters. Had Walter Blythe been there all the time? Everyone was raking her recollection of the tales told to recall if any of them had been too terribly unfit for the ears of youth. Mrs Doctor Blythe was said to be so fussy about what her children heard. Before their paralysed tongues recovered Anne had come out and asked them to come to supper.

'Just ten minutes more, Mrs Blythe. We'll have both quilts finished then,' said Elizabeth Kirk.

The quilts were finished, taken out, shaken, held up, and admired.

'I wonder who'll sleep under them,' said Myra Murray.

'Perhaps a new mother will hold her first baby under one of them,' said Anne.

'Or little children cuddle under them on a cold prairie night,' said Miss Cornelia unexpectedly.

'Or some poor old rheumatic body be cosier for them,' said Mrs Meade.

'I hope nobody *dies* under them,' said Mrs Baxter sadly.

'Do you know what Mary Anna said before I came?' said Mrs Donald as they filed into the dining room. 'She said, "Ma, don't forget you must eat *everything* on your plate."'

Whereupon they all sat down and ate and drank to the glory of God, for they had done a good afternoon's work and there was very little malice in most of them after all.

After supper they went home. Jane Burr walked as far as the village with Mrs Simon Millison.

'I must remember all the fixings to tell Ma,' said Jane wistfully, not knowing that Susan was counting the spoons. 'She never gets out since she's bed-rid, but she loves to hear about things. That table will be a real treat to her.'

'It was just like a picture you'd see in a magazine,' agreed Mrs Simon with a sigh. 'I can cook as good a supper as anyone, if I do say it, but I can't fix up a table with a single *prestige* of style. As for that young Walter, I could spank *his* bottom with a relish. Such a turn as he gave me!'

'And I suppose Ingleside is strewn with dead characters?' the Doctor was saying.

'I wasn't quilting,' said Anne, 'so I didn't hear any gossip.'

'You never do, dearie,' said Miss Cornelia, who had lingered to help Susan bind the quilts. 'When *you* are at the quilt they never let themselves go. They think you don't approve of gossip.'

'It all depends on the kind,' said Anne.

'Well, nobody really said anything too terrible today. Most of the people they talked about were dead . . . or ought to be,' said Miss Cornelia, recalling the story of Abner Cromwell's abortive funeral with a grin. 'Only Mrs Millison had to drag in that gruesome old murder story again about Madge Carey and her husband. I remember it all. There wasn't a vestige of proof that Madge did it . . . except that a cat died after eating some of the soup. The animal had been sick for a week. If you ask me, Roger Carey died of appendicitis, though, of course, nobody knew they had appendixes then.'

'And, indeed, I think it is a great pity they ever found out,' said Susan. 'The spoons are all intact, Mrs Doctor dear, and nothing happened to the tablecloth.'

'Well, I must be getting home,' said Miss Cornelia. 'I'll send you up some spare ribs next week when Marshall kills the pig.'

Walter was again sitting on the steps with eyes full of dreams. Dusk had fallen. Where, he wondered, had it fallen from? Did some great spirit with bat-like wings pour it all over the world from a purple jar? The moon was rising and three wind-twisted old spruces looked like three lean, humpbacked old witches hobbling up a hill against it. Was that a little faun with furry ears crouching in the shadows? Suppose he opened the door in the brick wall *now* wouldn't he step, not into the well-known garden, but into some strange land of faery, where princesses were waking from enchanted sleeps, where perhaps he might find and follow Echo as he so often longed to do? One dared not speak. Something would vanish if one did.

'Darling,' said Mother, coming out, 'you mustn't sit here any longer. It is getting cold. Remember your throat.'

The spoken word *had* broken the spell. Some magic light had gone. The lawn was still a beautiful place, but it was no longer fairyland. Walter got up.

'Mother, will you tell me what happened at Peter Kirk's funeral?'

Anne thought for a moment . . . then shivered.

'Not now, dear. Perhaps . . . some time . . .'

35

Anne, alone in her room . . . for Gilbert had been called out . . . sat down at her window for a few minutes of communion with the tenderness of the night and of enjoyment of the eerie charm of her moonlit room. 'Say what you will,' thought Anne, 'there is always something a little strange about a moonlit room. Its whole personality is changed. It is not so friendly . . . so human. It is remote and aloof and wrapped up in itself. Almost it regards you as an intruder.'

She was a little tired after her busy day and everything was so beautifully quiet now . . . the children asleep, Ingleside restored to order. There was no sound in the house except a faint rhythmic thumping from the kitchen where Susan was setting her bread.

But through the open window came the sounds of the night, every one of which Anne knew and loved. Low laughter drifted up from the harbour on the still air. Someone was singing down in the Glen and it sounded like the haunting notes of some song heard long ago. There were silvery moonlight paths over the water, but Ingleside was hooded in shadow. The trees were whispering 'dark sayings of old' and an owl was hooting in Rainbow Valley.

'What a happy summer this has been,' thought Anne . . . and then recalled with a little pang something she had heard Aunt Highland Kitty of the Upper Glen say once . . . 'the same summer will never be coming twice.'

Never quite the same. Another summer would come . . . but the children would be a little older and Rilla would be going to school . . . 'and I'll have no baby left,' thought Anne sadly. Jem was twelve now and there was already talk of 'the Entrance' . . . Jem, who but yesterday had been a wee baby in the old House of Dreams. Walter was shooting up and that very morning she had heard Nan teasing Di about some 'boy' in school; and Di had actually blushed and tossed her red head. Well, that was life. Gladness and pain . . . hope and fear . . . and change. Always change! You could not help it. You had to let the old go and take the new to your heart, learn to love *it* and then let *it* go in turn. Spring, lovely as it was, must yield to summer and summer lose itself in autumn. The birth . . . the bridal . . . the death . . .

Anne suddenly thought of Walter asking to be told what had happened at Peter Kirk's funeral. She had not thought of it for years, but she had not forgotten it.

Nobody who had been there, she felt sure, had forgotten it or ever would. Sitting there in the moonlight dusk she recalled it all.

It had been in November . . . the first November they had spent at Ingleside . . . following a week of Indian summer days. The Kirks lived at Mowbray Narrows but came to the Glen church and Gilbert was their doctor; so he and Anne both went to the funeral.

It had been, she remembered, a mild, calm, pearl-grey day. All around them had been the lonely brown-and-purple landscape of November, with patches of sunlight here and there on upland and slope where the sun shone through a rift in the clouds. 'Kirkwynd' was so near the shore that a breath of salt wind blew through the grim firs behind it. It was a big, prosperous-looking house, but Anne always thought that the gable of the L looked exactly like a long, narrow, spiteful face.

Anne paused to speak to a little knot of women on the stiff flowerless lawn. They were all good hardworking souls to whom a funeral was a not unpleasant excitement.

'I forgot to bring a handkerchief,' Mrs Bryan Blake was saying plaintively. 'Whatever will I do when I cry?'

'Why will you have to cry?' bluntly asked her sister-in-law, Camilla Blake. Camilla had no use for women who cried too easily. 'Peter Kirk is no relation to you and you never liked him.'

'I think it is *proper* to cry at a funeral,' said Mrs Blake stiffly. 'It shows *feeling* when a neighbour has been summoned to his long home.'

'If nobody cries at Peter's funeral except those who liked him there won't be many wet eyes,' said Mrs Curtis Rodd drily. 'That is the truth and why mince it? He was a pious old humbug and I know it if nobody else does. *Who* is that coming in at the little gate? Don't . . . *don't* tell me it's Clara Wilson.'

'It *is*,' whispered Mrs Bryan incredulously.

'Well, you know after Peter's first wife died she told him she would never enter his house again until she came to his funeral and she's kept her word,' said Camilla Blake. 'She's a sister of Peter's first wife' . . . in an explanatory aside to Anne, who looked curiously at Clara Wilson as she swept past them, unseeing, her smouldering topaz eyes staring straight ahead. She was a thin slip of a woman with a dark-browed, tragical face and black hair under one of the absurd bonnets elderly women still wore, a thing of feathers and 'bugles' with a skimpy nose veil. She looked at and spoke to no one, as her long black taffeta skirt swished over the grass and up the veranda steps.

'There's Jed Clinton at the door, putting on his funeral face,' said Camilla sarcastically. 'He's evidently thinking it is time we went in. It's always been his boast that at *his* funerals everything goes according to schedule. He's never forgiven Winnie Clow for fainting *before* the sermon. It wouldn't have been so bad afterwards. Well, nobody is likely to faint at *this* funeral. Olivia isn't the fainting kind.'

'Jed Clinton . . . the Lowbridge undertaker,' said Mrs Reese. 'Why didn't they have the Glen man?'

'Who? Carter Flagg? Why, woman dear, Peter and him have been at daggers drawn all their lives. Carter wanted Amy Wilson, you know.'

'A good many wanted her,' said Camilla. 'She was a very pretty girl, with her coppery red hair and inky black eyes. Though people thought Clara the handsomer of the two then. It's odd she never married. There's the minister at last . . . and the Reverend Mr Owen of Lowbridge with him. Of course, he is Olivia's cousin. All right, except that he puts too many "Oh's" in his prayers. We'd better go in or Jeds will have a conniption.'

Anne paused to look at Peter Kirk on her way to a chair. She had never liked him. 'He has a cruel face,' she thought, the first time she had ever seen him. Handsome, yes . . . but with cold steely eyes even then becoming pouchy, and the thin, pinched, merciless mouth of a miser. He was known to be selfish and arrogant in his dealings with his fellow-men in spite of his profession of piety and his unctuous prayers. 'Always feels his importance,' she had heard someone say once. Yet, on the whole, he had been respected and looked up to.

He was as arrogant in his death as in his life, and there was something about the too-long fingers clasped over his still breast that made Anne shudder. She thought of a woman's heart being held in them and glanced at Olivia Kirk, sitting opposite to her in her mourning. Olivia was a tall, fair, handsome woman with large blue eyes . . . 'no ugly women for me,' Peter Kirk had said once . . . and her face was composed and expressionless. There was no apparent trace of tears . . . but then Olivia had been a Random and the Randoms were not emotional. At least she sat decorously and the most heart-broken widow in the world could not have worn heavier weeds.

The air was cloyed with the perfume of the flowers that banked the coffin . . . for Peter Kirk who had never known flowers existed. His lodge had sent a wreath, the Church had sent one, the Conservative Association had sent one, the School Trustees had sent one, the Cheese Board had sent one. His one, long-alienated son had sent nothing, but the Kirk clan at large had sent a huge anchor of white roses with 'Harbour at Last' in red rosebuds across it, and there was one from Olivia herself . . . a pillow of calla lilies. Camilla Blake's face twitched as she looked at it, and Anne remembered that she had once heard Camilla say that she had been at Kirkwynd soon after Peter's second marriage when Peter had fired out of the window a potted calla lily which the bride had brought with her. He wasn't, so he said, going to have his house cluttered up with weeds.

Olivia had apparently taken it very coolly and there had been no more calla lilies at Kirkwynd. Could it be possible that Olivia . . . but Anne looked at Mrs Kirk's placid face and dismissed the suspicion. After all, it was generally the florist who suggested the flowers.

The choir sang, 'Death like a narrow sea divides that heavenly land from ours', and Anne caught Camilla's eye and knew they were both wondering just how Peter Kirk would fit into that heavenly land. Anne could almost hear Camilla saying, 'Fancy Peter Kirk with a harp and halo if you dare.'

The Reverend Mr Owen read a chapter and prayed, with many 'Oh's' and many entreaties that sorrowing hearts might be comforted. The Glen minister gave an address which many privately considered entirely too fulsome, even allowing for the fact that you had to say something good of the dead. To hear Peter Kirk called an affectionate father and a tender husband, a kind neighbour and an earnest Christian was, they felt, a misuse of language. Camilla took refuge behind her handkerchief, *not* to shed tears, and Stephen MacDonald cleared his throat once or twice. Mrs Bryan must have borrowed a handkerchief from someone, for she was weeping into it, but Olivia's down-dropped blue eyes remained tearless.

Jed Clinton drew a breath of relief. All had gone beautifully. Another hymn . . . the customary parade for a last look at 'the remains' . . . and another successful funeral would be added to his long list.

There was a slight disturbance in a corner of the large

room, and Clara Wilson made her way through the maze of chairs to the tables beside the casket. She turned there and faced the assembly. Her absurd bonnet had slipped a trifle to one side and a loose end of her heavy black hair had escaped from its coil and hung down on her shoulder. But nobody thought Clara Wilson looked absurd. Her long sallow face was flushed, her haunted, tragic eyes were flaming. She was a woman possessed. Bitterness, like some gnawing incurable disease, seemed to pervade her being.

'You have listened to a pack of lies . . . you people who have come here "to pay your respects" . . . or glut your curiosity, which ever it was. Now I shall tell you the truth about Peter Kirk. *I* am no hypocrite . . . I never feared him living and I do not fear him now that he is dead. Nobody has ever dared to tell the truth about him to his face, but it is going to be told now . . . here at his funeral, where he has been called a good husband and a kind neighbour. A good husband! He married my sister Amy . . . my beautiful sister, Amy. You all know how sweet and lovely she was. He made her life a misery to her. He tortured and humiliated her . . . he liked to do it. Oh, he went to church regularly . . . and made long prayers . . . and paid his debts. But he was a bully . . . his very dog ran when he heard him coming.

'I told Amy she would repent marrying him. I helped her make her wedding dress . . . I'd rather have made her shroud. She was wild about him then, poor thing, but she hadn't been his wife a week before she knew what he was. His mother had been a slave and he expected his wife to be one. "There will be no arguments in *my* household," he told her. She hadn't the spirit to argue . . . her heart was broken. Oh, I know what she went through, my poor pretty darling. He crossed her in everything. She couldn't have a flower garden . . . she couldn't even have a kitten . . . I gave her one and he drowned it. She had to account to him for every cent she spent. Did ever any of you see her in a decent stitch of clothes? He would fault her for wearing her best hat if it looked like rain. Rain couldn't hurt any hat *she* had, poor soul. Her that loved pretty clothes! He was always sneering at her people. He never laughed in his life . . . did any of you ever hear him really laugh? He smiled . . . oh, yes he always smiled, calmly and sweetly, when he was doing the most maddening things. He smiled when he told her after her little baby was born dead that she might as well have died, too, if she couldn't have anything but dead brats. She died after ten years of it . . . and I was glad she had escaped him. I told him then I'd never enter his house again till I came to his funeral. Some of you heard me. I've kept my word and now I've come and told the truth about him. It *is* the truth . . . *you* know it' . . . she pointed fiercely at Stephen MacDonald . . . '*you* know it' . . . the long finger darted at Camilla Blake . . . '*you* know it' . . . Olivia Kirk did not move a muscle . . . '*you* know it' . . . the poor minister himself felt as if that finger stabbed completely through him. 'I cried at Peter Kirk's wedding, but I told him I'd laugh at his funeral. And I'm going to do it.'

She swished furiously about and bent over the casket. Wrongs that had festered for years had been avenged. She had wreaked her hatred at last. Her whole body vibrated with triumph and satisfaction as she looked down at the cold quiet face of the dead man. Everybody listened for the burst of vindictive laughter. It did not come. Clara Wilson's angry face suddenly changed . . . twisted . . . crumpled up like a child's. Clara Wilson was . . . crying.

She turned, with the tears streaming down her ravaged cheeks, to leave the room. But Olivia Kirk rose before her and laid a hand on her arm. For a moment the two women looked at each other.

The room was engulfed in a silence that seemed like a personal presence.

'Thank you, Clara Wilson,' said Olivia Kirk. Her face was as inscrutable as ever, but there was an undertone in her calm, even voice that made Anne shudder. She felt as if a pit had suddenly opened before her eyes. Clara Wilson might hate Peter Kirk, alive and dead, but Anne felt that her hatred was a pale thing compared to Olivia Kirk's.

Clara went out, weeping, passing an infuriated Jed with a spoiled funeral on his hands. The minister, who had intended to announce for a last hymn, 'Asleep in Jesus', thought better of it and simply pronounced a tremulous benediction.

Jed did not make the usual announcement that friends and relatives might now take a parting look at 'the remains'. The only decent thing to do, he felt, was to shut down the cover of the casket at once and bury Peter Kirk out of sight as soon as possible.

Anne drew a long breath as she went down the veranda steps. How lovely the cold fresh air was after that stifling, perfumed room where two women's bitterness had been as their torment.

The afternoon had grown colder and greyer. Little groups here and there on the lawn were discussing the affair with muted voices. Clara Wilson could still be seen crossing a sere pasture field on her way home.

'Well, didn't that beat all?' said Nelson Craig dazedly.

'Shocking . . . shocking!' said Elder Baxter.

'Why didn't some of us stop her?' demanded Henry Reese.

'Because you all wanted to hear what she had to say,' retorted Camilla.

'It wasn't . . . decorous,' said Uncle Sandy MacDougall. He had got hold of a word that pleased him and rolled it under his tongue. 'Not decorous. A funeral should be decorous whatever else it may be . . . decorous.'

'Gosh, ain't life funny?' said Augustus Palmer.

'I mind when Peter and Amy began keeping company,'

mused old James Porter. 'I was courting my woman that same winter. Clara was a fine-looking bit of goods then. And what a cherry pie she could make!'

'She was always a bitter-tongued girl,' said Boyce Warren. 'I suspected there'd be dynamite of some kind when I saw her coming, but I didn't dream it would take that form. And Olivia! Would you have thought it? Weemen *are* a queer lot.'

'It will make quite a story for the rest of our lives,' said Camilla. 'After all, I suppose if things like this never happened history would be dull stuff.'

A demoralized Jed had got his pall-bearers rounded up and the casket carried out. As the hearse drove down the lane, followed by the slow-moving procession of buggies, a dog was heard howling heartbrokenly in the barn. Perhaps, after all, one living creature mourned Peter Kirk.

Stephen MacDonald joined Anne as she waited for Gilbert. He was a tall Upper Glen man with the head of an old Roman emperor. Anne had always liked him.

'Smells like snow,' he said. 'It always seems to me that November is a *homesick* time. Does it ever strike you that way, Mrs Blythe?'

'Yes. The year is looking back sadly to her lost spring.'

'Spring . . . spring! Mrs Blythe, I'm getting old. I find myself imagining that the seasons are changing. Winter isn't what it was . . . I don't recognize summer . . . and spring . . . there are *no* springs now. At least, that's how we feel when folks we used to know don't come back to share them with us. Poor Clara Wilson now . . . what did you think of it all?'

'Oh, it was heart-breaking. Such hatred . . .'

'Ye-e-e-s. You see, she was in love with Peter herself long ago . . . terribly in love. Clara was the handsomest girl in Mowbray Narrows then . . . little dark curls all round her cream-white face . . . but Amy was a laughing, lilting thing. Peter dropped Clara and took up with Amy. It's strange the way we're made, Mrs Blythe.'

There was an eerie stir in the wind-torn firs behind Kirkwynd: far away a snow squall whitened over a hill where a row of Lombardies stabbed the grey sky. Everybody was hurrying to get away before it reached Mowbray Narrows.

'Have I any right to be so happy when other women are so miserable?' Anne wondered to herself as they drove home, remembering Olivia Kirk's eyes as she thanked Clara Wilson.

Anne got up from her window. It was nearly twelve years ago now. Clara Wilson was dead and Olivia Kirk had gone to the coast, where she had married again. She had been much younger than Peter.

'Time is kinder than we think,' thought Anne. 'It's a dreadful mistake to cherish bitterness for years . . . hugging it to our hearts like a treasure. But I think the story of what happened at Peter Kirk's funeral is one which Walter must never know. It was certainly no story for children.'

36

Rilla sat on the veranda steps at Ingleside with one knee crossed over the other . . . such adorable little fat brown knees! . . . very busy being unhappy. And if anyone asks why a petted little puss should be unhappy that inquirer must have forgotten her own childhood, when things that were the merest trifles to grown-ups were dark and dreadful tragedies to her. Rilla was lost in deeps of despair because Susan had told her she was going to bake one of her silver-and-gold cakes for the Orphanage social that evening and she, Rilla, must carry it to the church in the afternoon.

Don't ask me why Rilla felt she would rather die than carry a cake through the village to the Glen St Mary Presbyterian Church. Tots get odd notions into their little pates at times, and somehow Rilla had got it into hers that it was a shameful and humiliating thing to be seen carrying a cake *anywhere*. Perhaps it was because, one day when she was only five, she had met old Tillie Pake carrying a cake down the street with all the little village

boys yelping at her heels and making fun of her. Old Tillie
lived down at the Harbour Mouth and was a very dirty,
ragged old woman.

> 'Old Tillie Pake
> Up and stole a cake,
> And it gave her stomach ache,'

chanted the boys.

To be classed with Tillie Pake was something Rilla just
could not bear. The idea had become lodged in her mind
that you just 'couldn't be a lady' and carry cakes about.
So this was why she sat disconsolately on the steps and
the dear little mouth, with one front tooth missing, was
without its usual smile. Instead of looking as if she understood what daffodils were thinking about or as if she
shared with the golden rose a secret they alone knew, she
looked like one crushed for ever. Even her big hazel eyes
that almost shut up when she laughed were mournful
and tormented, instead of being the usual pools of allure-
ment. 'It's the fairies that have touched your eyes,' Aunt
Kitty MacAllister told her once. Her father vowed she
was a born charmer and had smiled at Dr Parker half an
hour after she was born. Rilla could, as yet, talk better
with her eyes than her tongue, for she had a decided lisp.
But she would grow out of that, she was growing fast.
Last year Daddy had measured her by a rose bush; this

year it was the phlox; soon it would be the hollyhocks and she would be going to school. Rilla had been very happy and well contented with herself until this terrible announcement of Susan's. Really, Rilla told the sky indignantly, Susan had no sense of shame. To be sure, Rilla pronounced it 'thenth of thame', but the lovely, soft-blue sky looked as if it understood.

Mummy and Daddy had gone to Charlottetown that morning and all the other children were in school, so Rilla and Susan were alone at Ingleside. Ordinarily Rilla would have been delighted under such circumstances. She was never lonely; she would have been glad to sit there on the steps or on her own particular mossy green stone in Rainbow Valley, with a fairy kitten or two for company, and spin fancies about everything she saw . . . the corner of the lawn that looked like a merry little band of butterflies . . . the poppies floating over the garden . . . that great fluffy cloud all alone in the sky . . . the big bumble bees booming over the nasturtiums . . . the honeysuckle that hung down to touch her red-brown curls with a yellow finger . . . the wind that blew . . . where did it blow to? . . . Cock Robin, who was back again and strutting importantly along the railing of the veranda, wondering why Rilla would not play with him . . . Rilla, who could think of nothing but the terrible fact that she must carry a cake, a *cake*, through the village to the church for the old social they were getting up for the orphans. Rilla was dimly aware that the Orphanage was at Lowbridge and that poor children lived there who had no fathers or mothers. She felt terribly sorry for them. But not even for the orphanest of orphans was small Rilla Blythe willing to be seen in public *carrying a cake*.

Perhaps if it rained she wouldn't have to go. It didn't *look* like rain, but Rilla clasped her hands together . . . there was a dimple at the root of every finger . . . and said earnestly:

'Plethe, dear God, make it rain hard. Make it rain pitchforkth. Or elth . . .' Rilla thought of another saving possibility . . . 'make Thusanth cake burn . . . burn to a crithp.'

Alas, when dinner time came the cake, done to a turn, filled and iced, was sitting triumphantly on the kitchen table. It was a favourite cake of Rilla's . . . 'gold-and-silver cake' did sound so *luxuriant* . . . but she felt that never again would she be able to eat a mouthful of it.

Still . . . wasn't that thunder rolling over the low hills across the harbour? Perhaps God had heard her prayer, perhaps there would be an earthquake before it was time to go. Couldn't she take a pain in her stomach if worst came to worst? No. Rilla shuddered. That would mean castor oil. Better the earthquake!

The rest of the children did not notice that Rilla, sitting in her own dear chair, with the saucy white duck worked in crewels on the back, was very quiet. Thelfith pigth! If Mummy had been home *she* would have noticed it.

Mummy had seen right away how troubled she was that dreadful day when Dad's picture had come out in the *Enterprise*. Rilla was crying bitterly in bed when Mummy came in and found out that Rilla thought it was only murderers that had their pictures in the papers. It had not taken Mummy long to put *that* to rights. Would Mummy like to see *her* daughter carrying a cake through the Glen like old Tillie Pake?

Rilla found it hard to eat any dinner, though Susan had put down her own lovely blue plate with the wreath of rosebuds on it that Aunt Rachel Lynde had sent her on her last birthday and which she was generally allowed to have only on Sundays. Blue plateth and rothbudth! When you had to do such a shameful thing! Still, the fruit puffs Susan had made for dessert *were* nice.

'Thuthan, can't Nan and Di take the cake after thcool?' she pleaded.

'Di is going home from school with Jessie Reese and Nan has a bone in her leg,' said Susan, under the impression that she was being joky. 'Besides, it would be too late. The committee wants all the cakes in by three so they can cut them up and arrange the tables before they go home to have their suppers. Why in the world don't you want to go, Roly-poly? You always think it is such fun to go for the mail.'

Rilla *was* a bit of a roly-poly but she hated to be called that.

'I don't want to hurt my feelingth,' she explained stiffly.

Susan laughed. Rilla was beginning to say things that made the family laugh. She never could understand why they laughed, because she was always in earnest. Only Mummy never laughed; she hadn't laughed even when she found out that Rilla thought Daddy was a murderer.

'The social is to make money for poor little boys and girls who haven't any kind father or mother,' explained Susan . . . as if she was a baby who didn't understand!

'*I'm* next thing to a norphan,' said Rilla. 'I've only got one father and mother.'

Susan just laughed again. *Nobody* understood.

'You know your mother *promised* the committee that cake, pet. I have not time to take it myself and it *must* go. So put on your blue gingham and toddle off.'

'My doll hath been tooken ill,' said Rilla desperately. 'I mutht put her to bed and thtay with her. Maybe itth ammonia.'

'Your doll will do very well till you get back. You can go and come in half an hour,' was Susan's heartless response.

There was no hope. Even God had failed her . . . there wasn't a sign of rain. Rilla, too near tears to protest any further, went up and put on her new smocked organdy and her Sunday hat, trimmed with daisies. Perhaps if she looked *respectable* people wouldn't think she was like old Tillie Pake.

'I think my fathe itth clean if you will kindly look behind my earth,' she told Susan with great stateliness.

She was afraid Susan might scold her for putting on her best dress and hat. But Susan merely inspected her ears, handed her a basket containing the cake, told her to mind her pretty manners and for goodness' sake not to stop to talk to every cat she met.

Rilla made a rebellious 'face' at Gog and Magog and marched away. Susan looked after her tenderly.

'Fancy our baby being old enough to carry a cake all alone to the church,' she thought, half proudly, half sorrowfully, as she went back to work, blissfully unaware of the torture she was inflicting on a small mite she would have given her life for.

Rilla had not felt so mortified since the time she had fallen asleep in church and tumbled off the seat. Ordinarily she loved going down to the village: there were so many interesting things to see; but today Mrs Carter Flagg's fascinating clothes line, with all those lovely quilts on it, did not win a glance from Rilla, and the new cast-iron deer Mr Augustus Palmer had set up in his yard left her cold. She had never passed it before without wishing they could have one like it on the lawn at Ingleside. But what were cast-iron deer now? Hot sunshine poured along the street like a river and *everybody* was out. Two girls went by, whispering to each other. Was it about *her*? She imagined what they might be saying. A man driving along the road stared at her. He was really wondering if that could be the Blythe baby and, by George, what a little beauty she was! But Rilla felt that his eyes pierced the basket and saw the cake. And when Annie Drew drove by with her father, Rilla was sure she was laughing at her. Annie Drew was ten and a very big girl in Rilla's eyes.

Then there was a whole crowd of boys and girls on Russell's corner. *She had to walk past them*. It was dreadful to feel that their eyes were all looking at her and then at each other. She marched by, so proudly desperate that they all thought she was stuck-up and had to be brought down a peg or two. *They'd* show that kitten-faced thing! A regular hoity-toity like all those Ingleside girls! Just because they lived up at the big house!

Millie Flagg strutted along behind her, imitating her walk and scuffing up clouds of dust over them both.

'Where's the basket going with the child?' shouted 'Slicky' Drew.

'There's a smudge on your nose, jam-face,' jeered Bill Palmer.

'Cat got your tongue?' said Sarah Warren.

'Snippet!' sneered Beenie Bentley.

'Keep on your side of the road or I'll make you eat a June bug,' big Sam Flagg stopped gnawing a raw carrot long enough to say.

'Look at her blushing,' giggled Mamie Taylor.

'Bet you're taking a cake to the Presbyterian Church,'

said Charlie Warren. 'Half dough like all Susan Baker's cakes.'

Pride would not let Rilla cry but there was a limit to what one could bear. After all, an Ingleside cake . . .

'The next time any of you are thick I'll tell my father not to give you any medithine,' she said defiantly.

Then she stared in dismay. That couldn't be Kenneth Ford coming around the corner of the Harbour road! It couldn't be! It was!

It was not to be borne. Ken and Walter were pals and Rilla thought in her small heart that Ken was the nicest, handsomest boy in the whole world. He seldom took much notice of her . . . though once he had given her a chocolate duck. And one unforgettable day he had sat down beside her on a mossy stone in Rainbow Valley and told her the story of the Three Bears and the Little House in the Wood. But she was content to worship afar. And now this wonderful being had caught her *carrying a cake*!

'Lo, Roly-poly! Heat's something fierce, isn't it? Hope I'll get a slice of that cake tonight.'

So he knew it was a cake! Everybody knew it!

Rilla was through the village and thought the worst was over when the worst happened. She looked down a side road and saw her Sunday School teacher, Miss Emmy Parker, coming along it. Miss Emmy Parker was still quite a distance away, but Rilla knew her by her dress . . . that frilled organdy dress of pale green with clusters of little white flowers all over it . . . the 'cherry blossom dress', Rilla secretly called it. Miss Emmy had it on in Sunday School last Sunday and Rilla had thought it the sweetest dress she had ever seen. But then Miss Emmy always wore such pretty dresses, sometimes lacy and frilly, sometimes with the whisper of silk about them.

Rilla worshipped Miss Emmy. She was so pretty and dainty, with her white, white skin and her brown, brown eyes and her sad, sweet smile . . . sad, another small girl had whispered to Rilla one day, because the man she was going to marry had died. She was so glad she was in Miss Emmy's class. She would have hated to be in Miss Florrie Flagg's class . . . Florrie Flagg was *ugly* and Rilla couldn't bear an ugly teacher.

When Rilla met Miss Emmy away from Sunday School and Miss Emmy smiled and spoke to her it was one of the high moments of life for Rilla. Only to be nodded to on the street by Miss Emmy gave a strange, sudden lift of the heart, and when Miss Emmy had invited all her class to a soap-bubble party, where they made the bubbles red with strawberry juice, Rilla had all but died of sheer bliss.

But to meet Miss Emmy, carrying a cake, was just not to be endured and Rilla was not going to endure it. Besides, Miss Emmy was going to get up a dialogue for the next Sunday School concert, and Rilla was cherishing secret hopes of being asked to take the fairy's part in it . . . a fairy in scarlet with a little peaked green hat. But there would be no use in hoping for that if Miss Emmy saw her *carrying a cake*.

Miss Emmy was not going to see her! Rilla was standing on the little bridge crossing the brook, which was quite deep and creek-like there. She snatched the cake out of the basket and hurled it into the brook where the alders met over a dark pool. The cake hurtled through the branches and sank with a plop and a gurgle. Rilla felt a wild spasm of relief and freedom and *escape,* as she turned to meet Miss Emmy, who, she now saw, was carrying a big, bulgy, brown paper parcel.

Miss Emmy smiled down at her, from beneath a little green hat with a tiny orange feather in it.

'Oh, you're beautiful, teacher . . . beautiful,' gasped Rilla adoringly. Miss Emmy smiled again. Even when your heart is broken . . . and Miss Emmy truly believed hers was . . . it is not unpleasant to be given such a sincere compliment.

'It's the new hat, I expect, dear. Fine feathers, you know. I suppose' . . . glancing at the empty basket . . . 'you've been taking your cake up for the social. What a pity you're not going instead of coming. I'm taking mine . . . such a big, gooey chocolate cake.'

Rilla gazed up piteously, unable to utter a word. Miss Emmy was *carrying a cake*. Therefore, it could not be a disgraceful thing to carry a cake. And she . . . oh, what had she done? She had thrown Susan's lovely gold-and-silver cake into the brook . . . and she had lost the chance of walking up to the church with Miss Emmy, *both* carrying cakes!

After Miss Emmy had gone on Rilla went home with her dreadful secret. She buried herself in Rainbow Valley until suppertime, when again nobody noticed that she was very quiet. She was terribly afraid Susan would ask to whom she had given the cake, but there were no awkward questions. After supper the others went to play in Rainbow Valley, but Rilla sat alone on the steps until the sun went down and the sky was all a windy gold behind Ingleside and the lights sprang up in the village below. Always Rilla liked to watch them blooming out, here and there, all over the Glen, but tonight she was interested in nothing. She had never been so unhappy in her life. She just didn't see how she could live. The evening deepened to purple and she was still more unhappy. A most delectable odour of maple sugar buns drifted out to her . . . Susan had waited for the evening coolness to do the family baking . . . but maple sugar buns, like all else, were just vanity. Miserably she climbed the stairs and went to bed under the new, pink-flowered spread she had once been so proud of. But she could not sleep. She was haunted by the ghost of the cake she had drowned. Mother had promised the committee the cake . . . what would they think of Mother for not sending it? And it would have been the prettiest cake there! The wind had such a lonely sound tonight. It was reproaching her. It was saying, 'Silly . . . silly . . . silly', over and over again.

'What is keeping you awake, pet?' said Susan, coming in with a maple sugar bun.

'Oh, Thuthan, I'm . . . I'm jutht tired of being *me*.'

Susan looked troubled. Come to think of it, the child had looked tired at supper.

'And of course the doctor's away. Doctors' families die and shoemakers' wives go barefoot,' she thought. Then, aloud:

'I am going to see if you have a temperature, my pet.'

'No, no, Thuthan. It'th jutht . . . I've done thomething dreadful, Thuthan . . . Thatan made me do it . . . no, no, he didn't, Thuthan . . . I did it mythelf. I . . . threw the cake into the creek.'

'Land of hope and glory!' said Susan blankly. 'Whatever made you do that?'

'Do what?' It was Mother, home from town. Susan retreated gladly, thankful that Mrs Doctor had the situation in hand. Rilla sobbed out the whole story.

'Darling, I don't understand. *Why* did you think it was such a dreadful thing to take a cake to the church?'

'I thought it wath jutht like old Tillie Pake, Mummy. And I've dithgrathed you . . . oh, Mummy, if you'll forgive me I'll never be tho naughty again . . . and I'll tell the committee you *did* thend a cake . . .'

'Never mind the committee, darling. They would have more than enough cakes . . . they always do. It's not likely anyone would notice we didn't send one. We just won't talk of this to anybody. But always after this, Bertha Marilla Blythe, remember the fact that neither Susan nor Mother would ever ask you to do anything disgraceful.'

Life was sweet again. Daddy came to the door to say 'Goodnight, Kittenkin,' and Susan slipped in to say they were going to have a chicken pie for dinner tomorrow.

'With lotth of gravy, Thuthan?'

'Lashings of it.'

'And may I have a *brown* egg for breakfath, Thuthan. I don't detherve it . . .'

'You shall have two brown eggs if you want them. And now you *must* eat your bun and go to sleep, little pet.'

Rilla ate her bun, but before she went to sleep she slipped out of bed and knelt down. Very earnestly she said:

'Dear God, pleathe make me a good and obedient child alwayth, no matter what I'm told to do. And bleth dear Mith Emmy and all the poor orphanth.'

37

The Ingleside children played together and walked together and had all kinds of adventures together; and each of them, in addition to this, had his and her own inner life of dream and fancy. Especially Nan, who from the very first had fashioned secret drama for herself out of everything she heard or saw or read, and sojourned in realms of wonder and romance quite unsuspected in her household circle. At first she wove patterns of pixy dances and elves in haunted valleys and dryads in birch trees. She and the great willow at the gate had secrets only they knew, and the old empty Bailey house at the upper end of Rainbow Valley was the ruin of a haunted tower. For weeks she might be a king's daughter imprisoned in a lonely castle by the sea . . . for months she was a nurse in a leper colony in India or some land 'far, far away'. 'Far, far away' were still words of magic to Nan . . . like faint music over a windy hill.

As she grew older she built up her dramas about the real people she saw in her little life. Especially the people in church. Nan liked to look at the people in church because everyone was so nicely dressed. It was almost miraculous. They looked so different from what they did on weekdays.

The quiet, respectable occupants of the various family pews would have been amazed and perhaps a little horrified if they had known the romances the demure, brown-eyed maiden in the Ingleside pew was concocting about them. Black-browed, kind-hearted Annetta Millison would have been thunderstruck to know that Nan Blythe pictured her as a kidnapper of children, boiling them alive to make potions that would keep her young for ever. Nan pictured this so vividly that she was half frightened to death when she met Annetta Millison once, in a twilight lane astir with the golden whisper of buttercups. She was positively unable to reply to Annetta's friendly greeting, and Annetta reflected that Nan Blythe was really getting to be a proud and saucy little puss and needed a bit of training in good manners. Pale Mrs Rod Palmer never dreamed that she had poisoned someone and was dying of remorse. Elder Gordon MacAllister of the solemn face, had no notion that a curse had been put on him at birth by a witch, the result being that he could never smile. Dark-moustached Fraser Palmer, of a blameless life, little knew that when Nan Blythe looked at him she was thinking, 'I believe that man has committed a dark and desperate deed. He looks as if he had some dreadful secret on his conscience.' And Archibald Fyfe had no suspicion that when Nan Blythe saw him coming she was busy making up a rhyme as a reply to any remark he might make because he was never to be spoken to except in rhyme. He never did speak to her, being exceedingly afraid of children, but Nan got no end of fun out of desperately and quickly inventing a rhyme.

> *I'm very well, thank you, Mr Fyfe.*
> *How are you yourself and your wife?*

or

> *Yes, it is a very fine day,*
> *Just the right kind for making hay.*

There is no knowing what Mrs Morton Kirk would have said if she had been told that Nan Blythe would never come to her house . . . supposing she had ever been invited . . . because there was a *red footprint* on her doorstep, and her sister-in-law, placid, kind, unsought Elizabeth Kirk, did not dream she was an old maid because her lover had dropped dead at the altar just before the wedding ceremony.

It was all very amusing and interesting, and Nan never lost her way between fact and fiction until she became possessed with the Lady of the Mysterious Eyes.

It is no use asking how dreams grow. Nan herself could never have told you how it came about. It started with the GLOOMY HOUSE . . . Nan saw it always just like that, spelled in capitals. She liked to spin her romances about places as well as people, and the GLOOMY HOUSE was the only place around, except the old Bailey house, which lent itself to romance. Nan had never seen the HOUSE itself . . . she only knew that it was there, behind a thick, dark spruce wood on the Lowbridge side road, and had been vacant from time immemorial. So Susan said. Nan didn't know what time immemorial was, but it was a most fascinating phrase, just suited to gloomy houses.

Nan always ran madly past the lane that led up to the GLOOMY HOUSE when she went along the side road to visit her chum, Dora Clow. It was a long, dark, tree-arched lane with thick grass growing between its ruts and ferns waist-high under the spruces. There was a long grey maple bough near the tumble-down gate that looked exactly like a crooked old arm reaching down to encircle her. Nan never knew when it might reach a wee bit farther and grab her. It gave her such a thrill to escape it.

One day Nan, to her astonishment, heard Susan saying that Thomasine Fair had come to live in the GLOOMY HOUSE . . . or, as Susan unromantically phrased it, the old MacAllister place.

'She will find it rather lonely I should imagine,' Mother had said. 'It's so out-of-the-way.'

'She will not mind that,' said Susan. 'She never goes anywhere, not even to church. Hasn't gone anywhere for years . . . though they say she walks in her garden at night. Well, well, to think what she has come to . . . her that was so handsome and such a terrible flirt. The hearts she broke in her day! And look at her now! Well, it is a warning and that you may tie to.'

Just to whom it was a warning Susan did not explain and nothing more was said for nobody at Ingleside was very much interested in Thomasine Fair. But Nan, who had grown a little tired of all her old dream lives and was agog for something new, seized on Thomasine Fair in the GLOOMY HOUSE. Bit by bit, day after day, night after night . . . one could believe *anything* at night . . . she built up a legend about her until the whole thing flowered out unrecognizably and became a dearer dream to Nan than any she had hitherto known. Nothing before had ever seemed so entrancing, so *real*, as this vision of the Lady with the Mysterious Eyes. Great black velvet eyes . . . *hollow* eyes . . . *haunted* eyes . . . filled with remorse for the heart she had broken. *Wicked* eyes . . . anyone who broke hearts and never went to church must be wicked. Wicked people were so interesting. The Lady was burying herself from the world as a penance for her crimes. Could she be a princess? No, princesses were too scarce in P.E. Island. But she was tall, slim, remote, icily beautiful like a princess, with long jet-black hair in two thick braids over her shoulders, right to her feet. She would have a clear-cut ivory face, a beautiful Grecian nose, like the nose of Mother's Artemis of the Silver Bow, and white lovely hands which she would wring as she walked in the garden at night, waiting for the one true lover she had disdained and learned too late to love . . . you perceive how the legend was growing? . . . while her long black velvet skirts trailed over the grass. She would wear a golden girdle and great pearl earrings in her ears and she must live her life of shadow and mystery until the lover came to set her free. Then she would repent of her old wickedness and heartlessness and hold out her beautiful hands to him and bend her proud head in submission at last. They would sit by the fountain . . . there was a fountain by this time . . . and pledge their vows anew and she would follow him, 'over the hills and far away, beyond their utmost purple rim', just as the Sleeping Princess did in the poem Mother read to her one night from the old volume of Tennyson Father had given her long, long ago. But the lover of the Mysterious Eyed gave her jewels beyond all compare.

The GLOOMY HOUSE would be beautifully furnished, of course, and there would be secret rooms and staircases, and the Lady with the Mysterious Eyes would sleep on a bed made of mother-of-pearl under a canopy of purple velvet. She would be attended by a greyhound . . . a brace of them . . . a whole retinue of them . . . and she would always be listening . . . listening . . . listening . . . for the music of a very far-off harp. But she could not hear it as long as she was wicked . . . not until she repented and her lover came and forgave her . . . and there you were.

Of course it sounds very foolish. Dreams do sound so foolish when they are put into cold, brutal words. Ten-year-old Nan never put hers into words, she only lived them. This dream of the wicked Lady with the Mysterious Eyes became as real to her as the life that went on around her. It took possession of her. For two years now it had been part of her . . . she had somehow come, in some strange way, to believe it. Not for worlds would she have told anyone, not even Mother, about it. It was her own peculiar treasure, her inalienable secret, without which she could no longer imagine life going on. She would rather steal off by herself to dream of the Lady with the Mysterious Eyes than play in Rainbow Valley. Anne noticed this tendency and worried a little over it. Nan was getting too much that way. Gilbert wanted to send her up to Avonlea for a visit, but Nan, for the first time, pleaded passionately not to be sent. She didn't want to leave home, she said piteously. To herself she said she would just die if she had to go so far away from the strange, sad, lovely Lady with the Mysterious Eyes. True, the Mysterious Eyed never went out anywhere. But she *might* go out some day, and if she, Nan, were away she would miss seeing her.

How wonderful it would be to get just a glimpse of her. Why, the very road along which she passed would be for ever romantic. The day on which it happened would be different from all other days. She would make a ring around it in the calendar. Nan had got to the point when she greatly desired to see her just once. She knew quite well that much she had imagined about her was nothing but imagination. But she hadn't the slightest doubt that Thomasine Fair was young and lovely and wicked and alluring . . . Nan was by this time absolutely certain she had heard Susan say so, and as long as she was that Nan could go on imagining things about her for ever.

Nan could hardly believe her ears when Susan said to her one morning, 'There is a parcel I want to send up to Thomasine Fair at the old MacAllister place. Your father brought it out from town last night. Will you run up with it this afternoon, pet?'

Just like that! Nan caught her breath. *Would* she? Did dreams really come true in such fashion? She would see the GLOOMY HOUSE . . . she would see her beautiful, wicked Lady with the Mysterious Eyes. Actually see her . . . perhaps hear her speak . . . perhaps . . . oh, bliss! . . . touch her slender white hand. As for the greyhounds and the fountain and so forth, Nan knew she had only imagined them, but surely the reality would be equally wonderful.

Nan watched the clock all the forenoon, seeing the time

draw slowly, oh, so slowly, nearer and nearer. When a thundercloud rolled up ominously and rain began to fall she could hardly keep the tears back.

'I don't see *how* God could let it rain today,' she whispered rebelliously.

But the shower was soon over and the sun shone again. Nan could eat hardly any dinner for excitement.

'Mummy, may I wear my yellow dress?'

'Why do you want to dress up like that to call on a neighbour, child?'

A neighbour! But of course Mother didn't understand . . . couldn't understand.

'*Please*, Mummy.'

'Very well,' said Anne. The yellow dress would be outgrown very soon. May as well let Nan get the good of it.

Nan's legs were fairly trembling as she set off, the precious small parcel in her hand. She took a short cut through Rainbow Valley, up the hill, to the side road. The raindrops were still lying on the nasturtium leaves like great pearls; there was a delicious freshness in the air; the bees were buzzing in the white clover that edged the brook: slim blue dragonflies were glittering over the water . . . devil's darning needles, Susan called them; in the hill pasture the daisies nodded to her . . . swayed to her . . . waved to her . . . laughed to her, with the cool gold-and-silver laughter. Everything was so lovely and she was going to see the WICKED LADY WITH THE MYSTERIOUS EYES. What would the Lady say to her? And was it *quite* safe to go to see her? Suppose you stayed a few minutes with her and found that a hundred years had gone by, as in the story she and Walter had read last week?

38

Nan felt a queer tickly sensation in her spine as she turned into the lane. Did the dead maple bough move? No, she had escaped it . . . she was past. Aha, old witch, you didn't catch *me*! She was walking up the lane of which the mud and the ruts had no power to blight her anticipation. Just a few steps more . . . the GLOOMY HOUSE was before her, amid and behind those dark dripping trees. She was going to see it at last. She shivered a little . . . and did not know that it was because of a secret unadmitted fear of losing her dream. Which is always, for youth or maturity or age, a catastrophe.

She pushed her way through a gap in the wild growth of young spruces that was choking up the end of the lane: her eyes were shut; could she dare to open them? For a moment sheer terror possessed her and for two pins she would have turned and run. After all . . . the Lady *was* wicked. Who knew what she might do to you? She might even be a witch. How was it that it had never occurred to her before that the wicked Lady might be a witch?

Then she resolutely opened her eyes and stared piteously.

Was *this* the GLOOMY HOUSE . . . the dark, stately, towered and turreted mansion of her dream. This!

It was a big house, once white, now a muddy grey. Here and there, broken shutters, once green, were swinging loose. The front steps were broken. A forlorn glassed-in porch had most of its panes shattered. The scrolled trimming around the veranda was broken. Why, it was only a tired old house worn out with living.

Nan looked about desperately. There was no fountain . . . no garden . . . well, nothing you could really call a garden. The space in front of the house, surrounded by a ragged paling, was full of weeds and twitch grass. A lank pig rooted beyond the paling. Burdocks grew along the mid-walk. Straggly clumps of golden glow were in the corners, but there *was* one splendid clump of militant tiger lilies and, just by the worn steps, a gay bed of marigolds.

Nan went slowly up the walk to the marigold bed. The GLOOMY HOUSE was gone for ever. But the Lady with the Mysterious Eyes remained. Surely *she* was real . . . she must be? *What* had Susan really said about her so long ago?

'Laws-a-mercy, ye nearly scared the liver out of me!' said a rather mumbly though friendly voice.

Nan looked at the figure that had suddenly risen up

from beside the marigold bed. *Who was it?* It could *not* be . . . Nan refused to believe that this was Thomasine Fair. It would be just too terrible.

'Why,' thought Nan, heartsick with disappointment, 'she . . . she's *old*!'

Thomasine Fair, if Thomasine Fair it was . . . and she knew now it was Thomasine Fair . . . was certainly old. And fat! She looked like the feather bed with the string tied round its middle to which angular Susan was always comparing stout ladies. She was barefooted, wore a green dress that had faded yellowish, and a man's old felt hat on her sparse, sandy-grey hair. Her face was round as an O, ruddy and wrinkled, with a snub nose. Her eyes were a faded blue, surrounded by great, jolly-looking crow's feet.

Oh, my Lady . . . my charming, wicked Lady of the Mysterious Eyes, where are you? What has become of you? You *did* exist!

'Well, now, and what nice little girl are you?' asked Thomasine Fair.

Nan clutched after her manners.

'I'm . . . I'm Nan Blythe. I came up to bring you this.'

Thomasine pounced on the parcel joyfully.

'Well, if I ain't glad to get my specs back,' she said. 'I've missed 'em turrible for reading that almanac on Sundays. And you're one of the Blythe girls? What pretty hair you've got! I've always wanted to see some of you.

I've heered your ma was bringing you up scientific. Do you like it?'

'Like . . . what?' Oh, wicked, charming Lady, *you* did not read the almanac on Sundays. Nor did you talk of 'ma's'.

'Why, bein' brought up scientific.'

'I like the way I'm being brought up,' said Nan, trying to smile and barely succeeding.

'Well, your ma is a real, fine woman. She's holding her own. I declare the first time I saw her at Libby Taylor's funeral I thought she was a bride, she looked so happy. I always think when I see your ma come into a room that everyone perks up as if they expected something to happen. The new fashions set her, too. Most of us just ain't made to wear 'em. But come in and set awhile . . . I'm glad to see someone . . . it gets kinder lonesome by spells. I can't afford a telephone. Flowers is company . . . did ye ever see finer merry-golds? . . . and I've got a cat.'

Nan wanted to flee to the uttermost parts of the earth, but she felt it would never do to hurt the old lady's feelings by refusing to go in. Thomasine, her petticoat showing below her skirt, led the way up the sagging steps into a room which was evidently kitchen and living room combined. It was scrupulously clean and gay with thrifty house plants. The air was full of the pleasant fragrance of newly cooked bread.

'Set here,' said Thomasine kindly, pushing forward a

rocker with a gay patched cushion. 'I'll move that callow lily out of your way. Wait till I get my lower plate in. I look funny with it out, don't I? But it hurts me a mite. There, I'll talk clearer now.'

A spotted cat, uttering all kinds of fancy meows, came forward to greet them. Oh, for the greyhounds of a vanished dream!

'That cat's a fine ratter,' said Thomasine. 'This place is overrun with rats. But it keeps the rain out, and I got sick of living round with relations. Couldn't call my soul my own. Ordered round as if I was dirt. Jim's wife was the worst. Complained because I was making faces at the moon one night. Well, what if I was? Did it hurt the moon? Sez I, "I ain't going to be a pincushion any longer." So I come here on my own, and here I'll stay as long as I have the use of my legs. Now, what'll you have? Can I make you an onion sandwich?'

'No . . . no, thank you.'

'They're fine when you have a cold. I've been having one . . . notice how hoarse I am? But I just tie a piece of red flannel with turpentine and goose-grease on it round my throat when I go to bed. Nothing better.'

Red flannel and goose-grease! Not to speak of turpentine!

'If you won't have a sandwich . . . sure you won't? . . . I'll see what's in the cookie box.'

The cookies, cut in the shape of roosters and ducks,

were surprisingly good and fairly melted in your mouth. Mrs Fair beamed at Nan out of her round, faded eyes.

'Now you'll like me, won't you? I like to have little girls like me.'

'I'll try,' gasped Nan, who at that moment was hating poor Thomasine Fair as we can hate only those who destroy our illusions.

'I've got some little grandchildren of my own out west, you know.'

Grandchildren!

'I'll show you their pictures. Pretty, ain't they? That's poor dear Poppa's picture up there. Twenty years since he died.'

Poor dear Poppa's picture was a large 'crayon' of a bearded man with a curly fringe of white hair surrounding a bald head.

Oh, lover disdained!

'He was a good husband though he was bald at thirty,' said Mrs Fair fondly. 'My, but I had the pick of the beaux when I was a girl. I'm old now, but I had a fine time when I was young. The beaux on Sunday nights! Trying to sit each other out! And me holding up my head as haughty as any queen! Poppa was among them from the start, but at first I hadn't nothing to say to him. I liked 'em a bit more dashing. There was Andrew Metcalf now . . . I was as near as no matter running away with him. But I knew 'twould be unlucky. Don't you ever run away. It *is* unlucky and don't let anyone ever tell you different.'

'I . . . I . . . indeed I won't.'

'In the end I married Poppa. His patience gave out finally and he gave me twenty-four hours to take him or leave him. My pa wanted me to settle down. He got nervous when Jim Hewitt drowned himself because I wouldn't have him. Poppa and I were real happy when we got used to each other. He said I suited him because I didn't do too much thinking. Poppa held women weren't made for thinking. He said it made 'em dried-up and unnatural. Baked beans disagreed with him turrible, and he had spells of lumbago, but my balmagilia balsam always straightened that out. There was a specialist in town said he could cure him permanent, but Poppa always said if you got into the hands of them specialists they'd never let you out again . . . never. I miss him to feed the pig. He was real fond of pork. I never eat a bit of bacon but I think of him. That picture opposite Poppa is Queen Victoria. Sometimes I say to her, "If they stripped all them lace and jewels off you, my dear, I doubt if you'd be any better looking than I am."'

Before she let Nan go she insisted on her taking a bag of peppermints, a pink glass slipper for holding flowers, and a glass of gooseberry jelly. 'That's for your ma. I've always had good luck with my gooseberry jelly. I'm coming down to Ingleside some day. I want to see them chiney dogs of yours. Tell Susan Baker I'm much obliged for that mess of turnip greens she sent me in the spring.'

Turnip greens!

'I meant to thank her at Jacob Warren's funeral, but she got away too quick. I like to take my time at funerals. There hasn't been one for a month. I always think it's a dull old time when there's no funerals going. There's always a fine lot of funerals over Lowbridge way. It don't seem fair. Come again and see me, won't you? You've got something about you . . . "loving favour is better than silver and gold", the Good Book says, and I guess it's right.'

She smiled very pleasantly at Nan . . . she *had* a sweet smile. In it you saw the pretty Thomasine of long ago. Nan managed another smile herself. Her eyes were stinging. She *must* get away before she cried outright.

'Nice, well-behaved leetle creetur,' mused old Thomasine Fair, looking out of her window after Nan. 'Hasn't got her ma's gift of the gab, but maybe none the worse of that. Most of the kids today think they're smart when they're just being sassy. That little thing's visit has kind of made me feel young again.'

Thomasine sighed and went out to finish cutting her marigolds and hoeing up some of the burdocks.

'Thank goodness I've kept limber,' she reflected.

Nan went back to Ingleside the poorer by a lost dream. A dell full of daisies could not lure her . . . singing water called to her in vain. She wanted to get home and shut herself away from human eyes. Two girls she met giggled after they passed her. Were they laughing at her? How everybody would laugh if they knew! Silly little Nan Blythe who had spun a romance of cobweb fancies about a pale queen of mystery and found instead poor Poppa's widow and peppermints.

Peppermints!

Nan would not cry. Big girls of ten must not cry. But she felt indescribably dreary. Something precious and beautiful was gone . . . lost . . . a secret store of joy which, so she believed, could never be hers again. She found Ingleside filled with the delicious smell of spice cookies, but she did not go into the kitchen to coax some out of Susan. At supper her appetite was noticeably to seek, even though she read castor oil in Susan's eye. Anne had noticed that Nan had been very quiet since her return from the old MacAllister place . . . Nan, who sang literally from daylight to dark and after. Had the long walk on a hot day been too much for the child?

'Why that anguished expression, daughter?' she asked casually, when she went into the twins' room at dusk with fresh towels and found Nan curled up on the window seat, instead of being down stalking tigers in equatorial jungles with the others in Rainbow Valley.

Nan hadn't meant to tell *anybody* that she had been so silly. But somehow things told themselves to Mother.

'Oh, Mother, is *everything* in life a disappointment?'

'Not everything, dear. Would you like to tell me what disappointed you today?'

'Oh, Mummy, Thomasine Fair is . . . is *good*! And her nose turns up!'

'But why,' asked Anne in honest bewilderment, 'should you care whether her nose turns up or down?'

It all came out then. Anne listened with her usual serious face, praying that she be not betrayed into a stifled shriek of laughter. She remembered the child she had been at old Green Gables. She remembered the Haunted Wood and two small girls who had been terribly frightened by their own pretendings thereof. And she knew the dreadful bitterness of losing a dream.

'You mustn't take the vanishing of your fancies so much to heart, dear.'

'I can't help it,' said Nan despairingly. 'If I had my life to live over again I'd never imagine *anything*. And I never will again.'

'My foolish dear . . . my *dear* foolish dear, don't say that. An imagination is a wonderful thing to have . . . but like every gift, we must possess it and not let it possess us. You take your imaginings a wee bit too seriously. Oh, it's delightful . . . I know that rapture. But you must learn to keep on this side of the borderline between the real and the unreal. *Then* the power to escape at will into a beautiful world of your own will help you amazingly through the hard places of life. I can always solve a problem more easily after I've had a voyage or two to the Island of Enchantment.'

Nan felt her self-respect coming back to her with these words of comfort and wisdom. Mother did not think it so silly after all. And no doubt there was somewhere in the world a Wicked, Beautiful Lady with Mysterious Eyes, even if she did not live in the GLOOMY HOUSE . . . which, now that Nan came to think of it, was not such a bad place after all, with its orange marigolds and its friendly spotted cat and its geraniums and poor dear Poppa's picture. It was really rather a jolly place and perhaps some day she would go and see Thomasine Fair again and get some more of those nice cookies. She did not hate Thomasine any longer.

'What a nice mother you are!' she sighed, in the shelter and sanctuary of those beloved arms.

A violet-grey dusk was coming over the hill. The summer night darkened about them . . . a night of velvet and whispers. A star came out over the big apple tree. When Mrs Marshall Elliott came and Mother had to go down, Nan was happy again. Mother had said she was going to repaper their room with a lovely buttercup yellow paper and get a new cedar chest for her and Di to keep things in. Only it would not be a cedar chest. It would be an enchanted treasure chest which could not be opened unless certain mystic words were pronounced. One word the Witch of the Snow might whisper to you, the cold and lovely white Witch of the Snow. A wind might tell you another as it passed you . . . a sad, grey wind that mourned. Sooner or later you would find all the words and open the chest, to find it filled with pearls and rubies and diamonds galore. Wasn't galore a nice word?

Oh, the old magic had not gone. The world was still full of it.

39

'Can I be your dearest friend this year?' asked Delilah Green, during the afternoon recess.

Delilah had very round, dark blue eyes, sleek sugar-brown curls, a small rosy mouth, and a thrilling voice with a little quaver in it. Diana Blythe responded to the charm of that voice instantly.

It was known in the Glen school that Diana Blythe was rather at loose ends for a chum. For two years she and Pauline Reese had been cronies, but Pauline's family had moved away and Diana felt very lonely. Pauline had been a good sort. To be sure, she was quite lacking in the mystic charm that the now almost forgotten Jenny Penny had possessed. She was practical, full of fun, *sensible*. That last was Susan's adjective and was the highest praise Susan could bestow. She had been entirely satisfied with Pauline as a friend for Diana.

Diana looked at Delilah doubtfully, then glanced across the playground at Laura Carr, who was also a new girl. Laura and she had spent the forenoon recess together and had found each other very agreeable. But Laura was rather plain, with freckles and unmanageable sandy hair. She had none of Delilah Green's beauty and not a spark of her allure.

Delilah understood Diana's look, and a hurt expression crept over her face; her blue eyes seemed ready to brim with tears.

'If you love *her* you can't love *me*. Choose between us,' said Delilah, holding out her hands dramatically. Her voice was more thrilling than ever . . . it positively sent a creep along Diana's spine. She put her hands in Delilah's and they looked at each other solemnly, feeling dedicated and sealed. At least, Diana felt that way.

'You'll love me *for ever,* won't you?' asked Delilah passionately.

'For ever,' vowed Diana with equal passion.

Delilah slipped her arm around Diana's waist and they walked down to the brook together. The rest of the Fourth Class understood that an alliance had been concluded. Laura Carr gave a tiny sigh. She had liked Diana Blythe very much. But she knew she could not compete with Delilah.

'I'm *so* glad you're going to let me love you,' Delilah was saying. 'I'm so very affectionate . . . I just can't help loving people. *Please* be kind to me, Diana. I am a child of sorrow. I was put under a curse at birth. Nobody . . . *nobody* loves me.'

Delilah somehow contrived to put ages of loneliness and loveliness into that 'nobody'. Diana tightened her clasp.

'You'll never have to say that after this, Delilah. *I* will always love you.'

'World without end?'

'World without end,' answered Diana. They kissed each other, as in a rite. Two boys on the fence whooped derisively, but who cared?

'You'll like me ever so much better than Laura Carr,' said Delilah. 'Now that we're dear friends I can tell you what I wouldn't have *dreamed* of telling you if you had picked her. *She is deceitful.* Dreadfully deceitful. Pretends to be your friend to your face, and behind your back she makes fun of you and says the *meanest* things. A girl I know went to school with her at Mowbray's Narrows and she told me. You've had a narrow escape. *I'*m so different from that . . . I am as true as gold, Diana.'

'I'm sure you are. But what did you mean by saying you were a child of sorrow, Delilah?'

Delilah's eyes seemed to expand until they were absolutely enormous.

'I have a *stepmother*,' she whispered.

'A stepmother?'

'When your mother dies and your father marries again *she* is a stepmother,' said Delilah, with still more thrills in her voice. 'Now you know it all, Diana. If you knew the way I am treated! But I never complain. I suffer in silence.'

If Delilah really suffered in silence it might be wondered where Diana got all the information she showered on the Ingleside folks during the next few weeks. She was in the throes of a wild passion of adoration and sympathy for and with sorrow-laden, persecuted Delilah, and she had to talk about her to anyone who would listen.

'I suppose this new infatuation will run its course in due time,' said Anne. 'Who is this Delilah, Susan? I don't want the children to be little snobs . . . but after our experience with Jenny Penny . . .'

'The Greens are very respectable, Mrs Doctor dear. They are well known at Lowbridge. They moved into the old Hunter place this summer. Mrs Green is the second wife and has two children of her own. I do not know much about her, but she seems to have a slow, kind, easy way with her. I can hardly believe she uses Delilah as Di says.'

'Don't put too much credence in everything Delilah tells you,' Anne warned Diana. 'She may be prone to exaggerate a little. Remember Jenny Penny.'

'Why, Mother, Delilah isn't a single bit like Jenny Penny,' said Di, indignantly. 'Not one bit. She is *scrupulously* truthful. If you only saw her, Mother, you'd know she couldn't tell a lie. They all pick on her at home because she is so *different*. And she has *such* an affectionate nature. She has been persecuted from her birth. Her stepmother *hates* her. It just breaks my heart to hear of her sufferings. Why, Mother, she doesn't get enough to eat, truly she doesn't. She never knows what it is not to be hungry. Mother, they send her to bed without any supper lots of times and she cries herself to sleep. Did *you* ever cry because you were hungry, Mother?'

'Often,' said Mother.

Diana stared at her mother, all the wind taken out of the sails of her rhetorical question.

'I was often very hungry before I came to Green Gables. At the orphanage . . . and before. I've never cared to talk of those days.'

'Well, you ought to be able to understand Delilah, then,' said Di, rallying her confused wits. 'When she is *so* hungry she just sits down and imagines things to eat. Just *think* of her imagining things to eat!'

'You and Nan do enough of that yourselves,' said Anne, but Di would not listen.

'Her sufferings are not only physical, but *spiritual*. Why, she wants to be a missionary, Mother . . . to consecrate her life . . . and they *all laugh at her*.'

'Very heartless of them,' agreed Anne. But something in her voice made Di suspicious.

'Mother, *why* will you be so sceptical?' she demanded reproachfully.

'For the second time,' smiled Mother, 'I must remind you of Jenny Penny. You believed in her too.'

'I was only a *child* then and it was easy to fool me,' said Diana in her stateliest manner. She felt that Mother was not her usual sympathetic and understanding self in regard to Delilah Green. After that Diana talked only to Susan about her, since Nan only hooted when Delilah's name was mentioned. 'Just jealousy,' thought Diana sadly.

Not that Susan was so markedly sympathetic either. But Diana had to talk to somebody about Delilah, and Susan's derision did not hurt like Mother's. You wouldn't expect Susan to understand fully. But Mother had been a girl . . . Mother had such a tender heart. How was it that the account of poor Delilah's ill-treatment left her so cold?

'Maybe she's a little jealous, too, because I love Delilah so much,' reflected Diana sagely. 'They say mothers do get like that. Kind of *possessive*.'

'It makes my blood boil to hear of the way her stepmother treats Delilah,' Di told Susan. 'She is a *martyr*, Susan. She never has anything but a little porridge for breakfast and supper . . . a very little bit of porridge. And she isn't allowed sugar on the porridge. Susan, I've given up taking sugar on mine because it made me feel *guilty*.'

'Oh, so that's why. Well, sugar had gone up a cent, so maybe it is just as well.'

Diana vowed she wouldn't tell Susan anything more about Delilah, but next evening she was so indignant she couldn't help herself.

'Susan, Delilah's mother chased her last night with a

red-hot tea-kettle. Think of it, Susan. Of course Delilah says she doesn't do that very often . . . only when she is *greatly exasperated*. Mostly she just locks Delilah in a dark garret . . . a *haunted* garret. The ghosts that poor child has seen, Susan! It can't be healthy for her. The last time they shut her in the garret she saw the *weirdest* little black creature sitting on the spinning-wheel, *humming*.'

'What kind of a creature?' asked Susan gravely. She was beginning to enjoy Delilah's tribulations and Di's italics, and she and Mrs Doctor laughed over them in secret.

'I don't know . . . it was just a *creature*. It almost drove her to suicide. I am really afraid she will be driven to it yet. You know, Susan, she had an uncle who committed suicide *twice*.'

'Was not once enough?' asked Susan heartlessly. Di went off in a huff, but next day she had to come back with another tale of woe.

'Delilah has never had a doll, Susan. She did so hope she would get one in her stocking last Christmas. And what do you think she found instead, Susan? A *switch*! They whip her almost every day, you know. Think of that poor child being whipped, Susan.'

'I was whipped several times when I was young and I am none the worse of it now,' said Susan, who would have done goodness knows what if anyone had ever tried to whip an Ingleside child.

'When I told Delilah about our Christmas tree she wept,

Susan. She never had a Christmas tree. But she is bound she is going to have one this year. She has found an old umbrella with nothing but the ribs and she is going to set it in a pail and decorate it for a Christmas tree. Isn't that *pathetic*, Susan?'

'Are there not plenty of young spruces handy? The back of the old Hunter place has practically gone spruce of late years,' said Susan. 'I do wish that girl was called anything but Delilah. Such a name for a Christian child!'

'Why, it is in the Bible, Susan. Delilah is very proud of her Bible name. Today in school, Susan, I told Delilah we were going to have chicken for dinner tomorrow, and she said . . . what do you think she said, Susan?'

'I am sure I could never guess,' said Susan emphatically. 'And you have no business to be talking in school.'

'Oh, we don't. Delilah says we must never break any of the rules. Her standards are very high. We write each other letters in our scribblers and exchange them. Well, Delilah said, "Could you bring me a bone, Diana?" It brought tears to my eyes. I'm going to take her a bone . . . with a lot of meat on it. Delilah *needs* good food. She has to work like a slave . . . a *slave*, Susan. She has to do all the housework . . . well, nearly all, anyway. And if it isn't done right she is *savagely shaken* . . . or made to eat in the kitchen *with the servants.*'

'The Greens have only one little French hired boy.'

'Well, she has to eat with him. And he sits in his sock

385

feet and eats in his shirtsleeves. Delilah says she doesn't mind those things now when she has me to love her. She has no one to love her but me, Susan.'

'Awful!' said Susan, with great gravity of countenance.

'Delilah says if she had a million dollars she'd give it all to me, Susan. Of course, I wouldn't take it, but it shows how good her heart is.'

'It is as easy to give away a million as a hundred if you have not got either,' was as far as Susan would go.

40

Diana was overjoyed. After all, Mother wasn't jealous . . . Mother wasn't possessive . . . Mother did understand.

Mother and Father were going up to Avonlea for the weekend and Mother had told her she could ask Delilah Green to spend Saturday and Saturday night at Ingleside.

'I saw Delilah at the Sunday School picnic,' Anne told Susan. 'She is a pretty, lady-like little thing . . . though of course she *must* exaggerate. Perhaps her stepmother *is* a little hard on her . . . and I've heard her father is rather dour and strict. She probably has some grievances and likes to dramatize them by way of getting sympathy.'

Susan was a bit dubious.

'But at least anyone living in Laura Green's house will be clean,' she reflected. Fine-tooth combs did not enter into this question.

Diana was full of plans for Delilah's entertainment.

'Can't we have a roast chicken, Susan . . . with lots of stuffing? And *pie*. You don't know how that poor child longs to taste pie. They never have pies . . . her stepmother is too mean.'

Susan was very nice about it. Jem and Nan had gone to Avonlea, and Walter was down at the House of Dreams with Kenneth Ford. There was nothing to cast a shadow on Delilah's visit and it certainly seemed to go off very well. Delilah arrived Saturday morning very nicely dressed in pink muslin . . . at least the stepmother seemed to do her well in the matter of clothes. And she had, as Susan saw at a glance, irreproachable ears and nails.

'This is *the* day of my life,' she said solemnly to Diana. 'My, what a grand house this is! And them's the china dogs! Oh, they're wonderful!'

Everything was wonderful. Delilah worked the poor word to death. She helped Diana set the table for dinner and picked the little glass basket full of pink sweet peas for a centrepiece.

'Oh, you don't know how I love to do something just because I *like* to do it,' she told Diana. 'Isn't there anything else I can do, *please*?'

'You can crack the nuts for the cake I'm going to make this afternoon,' said Susan, who was herself falling under the spell of Delilah's beauty and voice. After all, perhaps Laura Green was a Tartar. You couldn't always go by what people seemed like in public. Delilah's plate was heaped with chicken and stuffing and gravy and she got a second piece of pie without hinting for it.

'I've often wondered what it would be like to have all you could eat for once. It is a wonderful sensation,' she told Diana as they left the table.

They had a gay afternoon. Susan had given Diana a box of candy and Diana shared it with Delilah. Delilah admired one of Di's rings and Di gave it to her. They cleaned out the pansy bed and dug up a few stray dandelions that had invaded the lawn. They helped Susan polish the silver and assisted her to get supper. Delilah was so efficient and tidy that Susan capitulated completely. Only two things marred the afternoon . . . Delilah contrived to spatter her dress with ink and she lost her pearl bead necklace. But Susan took the ink out nicely . . . some of the colour coming out too . . . with salts of lemon, and Delilah said it didn't matter about the necklace.

Nothing mattered except that she was at Ingleside with her dearest Diana.

'Aren't we going to sleep in the spare-room bed?' asked Diana when bedtime came. 'We always put company in the spare room, Susan.'

'Your Aunt Diana is coming with your father and mother tomorrow night,' said Susan. 'The spare room has been made up for her. You can have the Shrimp on your own bed and you couldn't have him in the spare room.'

'My, but your sheets smell nice!' said Delilah as they snuggled down.

'Susan always boils them with orris root,' said Diana.

Delilah sighed.

'I wonder if you know what a lucky girl you are, Diana. If *I* had a home like you . . . but it's my lot in life. I just have to bear it.'

Susan, on her nightly round of the house before retiring, came in and told them to stop chattering and go to sleep. She gave them two maple sugar buns apiece.

'I can never forget your kindness, Miss Baker,' said Delilah, her voice quivering with emotion. Susan went to her bed reflecting that a nicer-mannered, more appealing little girl she had never seen. Certainly she had misjudged Delilah Green. Though at that moment it occurred to Susan that, for a child who never got enough to eat, the bones of the said Delilah Green were very well covered!

Delilah went home the next afternoon, and Mother and Father and Aunt Diana came at night. On Monday the bolt fell from the proverbial blue. Diana, returning to school at noon hour, caught her own name as she entered the school porch. Inside the schoolroom Delilah Green was the centre of a group of curious little girls.

'I was so disappointed in Ingleside. After the way Di has bragged about her house I expected a *mansion*. Of course it's big enough, but some of the furniture is shabby. The chairs want to be recovered the *worst* way.'

'Did you see the china dogs?' asked Bessy Palmer.

'They're nothing wonderful. They haven't even got hair. I told Diana right on the spot I was disappointed.'

Diana was standing 'rooted to the ground' . . . or at least to the porch floor. She did not think about eavesdropping . . . she was simply too dumbfounded to move.

'I'm sorry for Diana,' went on Delilah. 'The way her parents neglect their family is something scandalous. Her mother is an awful gadabout. The way she goes off and leaves them young ones is terrible with only that old Susan to look after them . . . and she's half cracked! She'll land them all in the poorhouse yet. The waste that goes on in her kitchen you wouldn't believe. The doctor's wife is too gay and lazy to cook even when she is home, so Susan has it all her own way. She was going to give us our meals *in the kitchen* but I just up and said to her, "Am I company or am I not?" Susan said if I gave her any sass she'd shut me up in the back closet. I said, "You don't dare to" and she didn't. "You can overcrow the Ingleside children, Susan Baker, but you can't overcrow *me*," I said to her. Oh, I tell you I stood up to Susan. I wouldn't let her give Rilla soothing syrup. "Don't you know it's poison to children?" I said. She took it out on me at meals though. The mean little helpings she gives you! There was chicken but I only got the Pope's nose and nobody even asked me to take the second piece of pie. But Susan would have let me sleep in the spare room though, and Di wouldn't hear to it . . . just out of pure meanness. She's so jealous. But still I'm sorry for her. She told me Nan pinches her *something scandalous*. Her arms are black and blue. We slept in her room and a mangy old tom cat was lying on the foot of the bed all night. It wasn't *haygeenic* and I told Di so. And my pearl necklace *disappeared*. Of course I'm not saying Susan took it. I believe she's *honest* . . . but it's funny. And Shirley threw an inkbottle at me. It ruined my dress but I don't care. Ma'll have to get me a new one. Well, anyhow, I dug all the dandelions out of their lawn for them and polished up the silver. You should have seen it. I don't know *when* it has been cleaned before. I tell you Susan takes it easy when the doctor's wife's away. I let her see I saw through her. "Why don't you ever wash the potato pot, Susan?" I asked her. You should of seen her face. Look at my new ring, girls. A boy I know at Lowbridge give it to me.'

'Why, I've seen Diana Blythe wearing that ring often,' said Peggy MacAllister contemptuously.

'And I don't believe one single word you've been saying about Ingleside, Delilah Green,' said Laura Carr.

Before Delilah could reply Diana, who had recovered her powers of locomotion and speech, dashed into the schoolroom.

'Judas!' she said. Afterwards she thought repentantly that it had not been a very ladylike thing to say. But she had been stung to the heart, and when your feelings are all stirred up you can't pick and choose your words.

'I ain't Judas,' muttered Delilah, flushing, probably for the first time in her life.

'You are! There isn't one spark of sincerity in you! Don't you ever speak to me again as long as you live.'

Diana rushed out of the schoolhouse and ran home. She couldn't stay in school that afternoon . . . she just couldn't! The Ingleside front door was banged as it had never been banged before.

'Darling, what is the matter?' asked Anne, interrupted in her kitchen conference with Susan by a weeping daughter who flung herself stormily against the maternal shoulder.

The whole story was sobbed out, somewhat disjointedly.

'I've been hurt in all my *finer feelings*, Mother. And I'll never believe in anyone again.'

'My dear, all your friends won't be like this. Pauline wasn't.'

'This is *twice*,' said Diana bitterly, still smarting under the sense of betrayal and loss. 'There isn't going to be any third time.'

'I'm sorry Di has lost her faith in humanity,' said Anne rather ruefully, when Di had gone upstairs. 'This is a real tragedy for her. She *has* been unlucky in some of her chums. Jenny Penny . . . and now Delilah Green. The trouble is Di always falls for the girls who can tell interesting stories. And Delilah's martyr pose was very alluring.'

'If you ask me, Mrs Doctor dear, that Green child is a perfect minx,' said Susan, all the more implacably because she had been so nearly fooled herself by Delilah's eyes and manners. 'The idea of her calling our cats mangy! I am not saying that there are not such things as torn cats, Mrs Doctor dear, but little girls should not talk of them. I am no lover of cats, but the Shrimp is seven years old and should at least be *respected*. And as for my potato pot . . .'

But Susan really couldn't express her feelings about the potato pot!

In her room Di was reflecting that perhaps it was not too late to be 'best friends' with Laura Carr after all. Laura was *true*, even if she wasn't very exciting. Di sighed. Some colour *had* gone out of life with her belief in Delilah's piteous lot.

41

A bitter east wind was snarling around Ingleside like a shrewish old woman. It was one of those chill, drizzly, late August days that take the heart out of you, one of those days when everything goes wrong . . . what in old Avonlea days had been called 'a Jonah day'. The new pup Gilbert had brought home for the boys had gnawed the enamel off the dining-table leg . . . Susan had found that the moths had been having a Roman holiday in the blanket closet . . . Nan's new kitten had ruined the choicest fern . . . Jem and Bertie Shakespeare had been making the most abominable racket in the garret all the afternoon with tin pails for drums . . . Anne herself had broken a painted glass lampshade. But somehow it had done her just good to hear it smash! Rilla had earache and Shirley had a mysterious rash on his neck which worried Anne but at which Gilbert only glanced casually and said in an absent-minded voice that he didn't think it meant anything. Of course it didn't mean anything to *him*! Shirley was only his own son. And it didn't matter to him either that he had invited the Trents to dinner one evening last week and forgotten to tell Anne until they arrived. She and Susan had had an extra busy day and had planned a pick-up supper. And Mrs Trent with the reputation of being Charlottetown's smartest hostess! *Where* were Walter's stockings with the black tops and the blue toes? 'Do you think, Walter, that you could, *just for once*, put a thing where it belongs? Nan, I *don't* know where the Seven Seas are. For mercy's sake stop asking questions! I don't wonder they poisoned Socrates. They *ought* to have.'

Walter and Nan stared. Never had they heard their mother speak in such a tone before. Walter's look annoyed Anne still more.

'Diana, is it necessary to be forever reminding you not to twist your legs around the piano stool? Shirley, if you haven't got that new magazine all sticky with jam! And perhaps *somebody* would be kind enough to tell me where the prisms of the hanging lamp have gone!'

Nobody could tell her . . . Susan having unhooked them and taken them out to wash them . . . and Anne whisked herself upstairs to escape from the grieved eyes of her children. In her own room she paced up and down feverishly. *What* was the matter with her? Was she turning into one of those peevish creatures who had no patience with anybody? Everything annoyed her these days. A little mannerism of Gilbert's she had never minded before got on her nerves. She was sick and tired of never-ending, monotonous duties . . . sick and tired of catering to her family's whims. Once everything she did for her house and household gave her delight. Now she did not seem to care what she did. She felt all the time like a creature in a nightmare, trying to overtake someone with fettered feet.

The worst of it all was that Gilbert never noticed that there was any change in her. He was busy night and day and seemed to care for nothing but his work. The only thing he had said at dinner that day had been, 'Pass the mustard, please.'

'*I* can talk to the chairs and tables, of course,' thought Anne bitterly. 'We're just getting to be a sort of *habit* with each other . . . nothing else. He never noticed that I had on a new dress last night. And it's so long since he called me "Anne-girl" that I've forgotten when. Well, I suppose all marriages come to this in the end. Probably most women go through this. He just takes me for granted. His work is the only thing that means anything to him now. *Where* is my handkerchief?'

Anne got her handkerchief and sat down in her chair to torture herself luxuriantly. Gilbert didn't love her any more. When he kissed her he kissed her absently . . . just 'habit'. All the glamour was gone. Old jokes they had laughed together over came up in recollection, charged with tragedy now. How could she ever have thought them funny? Monty Turner, who kissed his wife systematically once a week . . . made a memorandum to remind him. (*Would any wife want such kisses?*) Curtis Ames, who met his wife in a new bonnet and didn't know her. Mrs Clancy Dare, who had said, 'I don't care an awful lot about my husband, but I'd miss him if he wasn't around.' (*I suppose Gilbert would miss me if I weren't around! Has it come to that with us?*) Nat Elliott, who told his wife after ten years of marriage, 'If you must know I'm just tired of being married.' (*And we've been married fifteen years!*) Well, perhaps all men were like that. Probably Miss Cornelia would say that they were. After a time they were hard to hold. (*If my husband has to be 'held' I don't want to hold him.*) But there was Mrs Theodore Clow, who had said proudly at a Ladies' Aid, 'We've been married twenty years and my husband loves me as much as he did on our wedding day.' But perhaps she was deceiving herself or only 'keeping face' – and she looked every day of her age and more. (*I wonder if I am beginning to look old.*)

For the first time her years felt like a weight. She went to the mirror and looked at herself critically. There *were* some tiny crow's feet around her eyes, but they were only visible in a strong light. Her chin lines were yet unblurred. She had always been pale. Her hair was thick and wavy, without a grey thread. But did anybody *really* like red hair? Her nose was still definitely good. Anne patted it as a friend, recalling certain moments of life when her nose was all that carried her through. But Gilbert just took her nose for granted now. It might be crooked or pug for all it mattered to him. Likely he had forgotten that she *had* a nose. Like Mrs Dare, he might miss it if it wasn't there.

'Well, I must go and see to Rilla and Shirley,' thought Anne drearily. 'At least, *they* need me still, poor darlings. What made me so snappish with them? Oh, I suppose they're all saying behind my back, "How cranky poor Mother is getting!"'

It continued to rain and the wind continued to wail. The fantasia of tin pans in the garret had stopped, but the ceaseless chirping of a solitary cricket in the living room nearly drove her mad.

The noon mail brought her two letters. One was from Marilla . . . but Anne sighed as she folded it up. Marilla's handwriting was getting so frail and shaky. The other letter was from Mrs Barrett Fowler of Charlottetown, whom Anne knew very slightly. And Mrs Barrett Fowler wanted Dr and Mrs Blythe to dine with her next Tuesday night at seven o'clock 'to meet your old friend, Mrs Andrew Dawson of Winnipeg, *née* Christine Stuart'.

Anne dropped the letter. A flood of old memories poured over her . . . some of them decidedly unpleasant. Christine Stuart of Redmond . . . the girl to whom people had once said Gilbert was engaged . . . the girl of whom she had once been so bitterly jealous . . . yes, she admitted it now, twenty years after . . . she *had* been jealous . . . she had hated Christine Stuart. She had not thought of

Christine for years, but she remembered her distinctly. A tall, ivory-white girl with great dark-blue eyes and blue-black masses of hair. And a certain air of distinction. But with a long nose . . . yes, definitely a long nose. Handsome . . . oh, you couldn't deny that Christine had been very handsome. She remembered hearing many years ago that Christine had 'married well' and gone west.

Gilbert came in for a hurried bite of supper . . . there was an epidemic of measles in the Upper Glen . . . and Anne silently handed him Mrs Fowler's letter.

'Christine Stuart! Of course we'll go. I'd like to see her for old time's sake,' he said, with the first appearance of animation he had shown for weeks. 'Poor girl, she has had her own troubles. She lost her husband four years ago, you know.'

Anne didn't know. And how came Gilbert to know? Why had he never told her? And had he forgotten that next Tuesday was the anniversary of their own wedding day? A day on which they had never accepted any invitation, but went off on a little bat of their own. Well, *she* wouldn't remind him. He could see his Christine if he wanted to. What had a girl at Redmond once said to her darkly? 'There was a good deal more between Gilbert and Christine than you ever knew, Anne.' She had merely laughed at it at the time . . . Claire Hallett was a spiteful thing. But perhaps there had been something in it. Anne suddenly remembered, with a little chill of the spirit, that not long after her marriage she had found a small photograph of Christine in an old pocket-book of Gilbert's. Gilbert had seemed quite indifferent and said he'd wondered where that old snap had got to. But . . . was it one of those unimportant things that are significant of things tremendously important? Was it possible . . . had Gilbert ever loved Christine? Was she, Anne, only a second choice? The consolation prize?

'Surely I'm not . . . jealous,' thought Anne, trying to laugh. It was all very ridiculous. What more natural than that Gilbert should like the idea of meeting an old Redmond friend? What more natural than that a busy man, married for fifteen years, should forget times and seasons and days and months? Anne wrote to Mrs Fowler, accepting her invitation . . . and then put in the three days before Tuesday hoping desperately that somebody in the Upper Glen would start having a baby Tuesday afternoon about half-past five.

42

The hoped-for baby arrived too soon. Gilbert was sent for at nine Monday night. Anne wept herself to sleep and wakened at three. It used to be delicious to wake in the night . . . to lie and look out of her window at the night's enfolding loveliness . . . to hear Gilbert's regular breathing beside her . . . to think of the children across the hall and the beautiful new day that was coming. But now! Anne was still awake when the dawn, clear and green as fluorspar, was in the eastern sky and Gilbert came home at last. 'Twins,' he said hollowly as he flung himself into bed and was asleep in a minute. Twins, indeed! The dawn of the fifteenth anniversary of your wedding day and all your husband could say to you was 'Twins'. He didn't even remember it *was* an anniversary.

Gilbert apparently didn't remember it any better when he came down at eleven. For the first time he did not mention it; for the first time he had no gift for her. Very well, *he* shouldn't get his gift either. She had had it ready for weeks . . . a silver-handled pocketknife with the date on one side and his initials on the other. Of course, he must buy it from her with a cent, lest it cut their love. But since he had forgotten she would forget too, with a vengeance.

Gilbert seemed in a sort of daze all day. He hardly spoke to anyone and moped about the library. Was he lost in glamorous anticipation of seeing his Christine again? Probably he had been hankering after her all these years in the back of his mind. Anne knew quite well this idea was absolutely unreasonable, but when was jealousy ever reasonable? It was no use trying to be philosophical. Philosophy had no effect on her mood.

They were going to town on the five o'clock train. 'Can we come in and watch you dreth, Mummy?' asked Rilla.

'Oh, if you want to,' said Anne . . . then pulled herself up sharply. Why, her voice was getting querulous. 'Come along, darling,' she added repentantly.

Rilla had no greater delight than watching Mummy dress. But even Rilla thought Mummy was not getting much fun out of it that night.

Anne took some thought as to what dress she should wear. Not that it mattered, she told herself bitterly, what she put on. Gilbert never noticed now. The mirror was no longer her friend . . . she looked pale and tired . . . and *unwanted*. But she must not look too countrified and passé before Christine. (*I won't have her sorry for me.*) Was it to be her new apple-green net over a slip with rosebuds in it? Or her cream silk gauze with its Eton jacket of Cluny lace? She tried both of them on and decided on the net. She experimented with several hair-do's and concluded that the new drooping pompadour was very becoming.

'Oh, Mummy, you look beautiful!' gasped Rilla in round-eyed admiration. Well, children and fools were supposed to tell the truth. Had not Rebecca Dew once told her that she was 'comparatively beautiful'? As for Gilbert, he used to pay her compliments in the past, but when had he given utterance to one of late months? Anne could not recall a single one.

Gilbert passed through on his way to his dressing closet and said not a word about her new dress. Anne stood for a moment burning with resentment: then she petulantly tore off the dress and flung it on the bed. She would wear her old black . . . a thin affair that was considered extremely 'smart' in Four Winds circles, but which Gilbert had never liked. What should she wear on her neck? Jem's beads, though treasured for years, had long since crumbled. She really hadn't a decent necklace. Well . . . . she got out the little box containing the pink enamel heart Gilbert had given her at Redmond. She seldom wore it now . . . after all, pink didn't go well with her red hair . . . but she would put it on tonight. Would Gilbert notice it? There, she was ready. Why wasn't Gilbert? What was keeping him? Oh, no doubt he was shaving *very* carefully! She tapped sharply on the door.

'Gilbert, we're going to miss the train if you don't hurry.'

'You sound school-teacherish,' said Gilbert, coming out. 'Anything wrong with your metatarsals?'

Oh, he could make a joke of it, could he? She would not let herself think how well he looked in his tails. After all, the modern fashions of men's clothes were really ridiculous. Entirely lacking in glamour. How gorgeous it must have been in 'the spacious days of Great Elizabeth' when men could wear white satin doublets and cloaks of crimson velvet and lace ruffs. Yet they were not effeminate. They were the most wonderful and adventurous men the world had ever seen.

'Well, come along if you're in such a hurry,' said Gilbert absently. He was always absent now when he spoke to her. She was just a part of the furniture . . . yes, just a piece of furniture!

Jem drove them to the station. Susan and Miss Cornelia . . . who had come up to ask Susan if they could depend on her as usual for scalloped potatoes for the church supper . . . looked after them admiringly.

'Anne is holding her own,' said Miss Cornelia.

'She is,' agreed Susan, 'though I have sometimes thought these past few weeks that her liver needed stirring up a bit. But she keeps her looks. And the doctor has got the same nice flat stomach he always had.'

'An ideal couple,' said Miss Cornelia.

The ideal couple said nothing in particular very beautifully all the way to town. Of course Gilbert was too profoundly stirred over the prospect of seeing his old love to talk to his wife! Anne sneezed. She began to be afraid she was taking a cold in the head. How ghastly it would be to sniffle all through dinner under the eyes of Mrs Andrew Dawson, *née* Christine Stuart! A spot on her lip stung . . . probably a horrible cold sore was coming on it. Did Juliet ever sneeze? Fancy Portia with chilblains! Or Argive Helen hiccupping! Or Cleopatra with corns!

When Anne came downstairs in the Barrett Fowler residence she stumbled over the bear's head on the rug in the hall, staggered through the drawing-room door, across the wilderness of overstuffed furniture and gilt fandangoes Mrs Barrett Fowler called her drawing room, and fell on the chesterfield, fortunately landing right side up. She looked about in dismay for Christine, then thankfully realized that Christine had not yet put in an appearance. How awful it would have been had she been sitting there amusedly watching Gilbert Blythe's wife make such a drunken entrance! Gilbert hadn't even asked if she were hurt. He was already deep in conversation with Dr Fowler and some unknown Dr Murray, who hailed from New Brunswick and was the author of a notable monograph on tropical diseases which was making a stir in medical circles. But Anne noticed that when Christine came downstairs, heralded by a sniff of heliotrope, the monograph was promptly forgotten. Gilbert stood up with a very evident light of interest in his eyes.

Christine stood for an impressive moment in the doorway. No falling over bears' heads for her. Christine, Anne remembered, had of old that habit of pausing in the doorway to show herself off. And no doubt she regarded this as an excellent chance to show Gilbert what he had lost.

She wore a gown of purple velvet with long, flowing sleeves, lined with gold, and a fish-tail train lined with gold lace. A gold bandeau encircled the still dark wings of her hair. A long, thin gold chain, starred with diamonds, hung from her neck. Anne instantly felt frumpy, provincial, unfinished, dowdy, and six months behind the fashion. She wished she had not put on that silly enamel heart.

There was no question that Christine was as handsome as ever. A bit too sleek and well-preserved, perhaps . . . yes, considerably stouter. Her nose had assuredly not grown any shorter and her chin was definitely middle-aged. Standing in the doorway like that, you saw that her feet were . . . substantial. And wasn't her air of distinction getting a little shop-worn? But her cheeks were still like smooth ivory and her great dark-blue eyes still looked out brilliantly from under that intriguing parallel crease that had been considered so fascinating at Redmond. Yes, Mrs Andrew Dawson was a very handsome woman . . . and did not at all convey the impression that her heart had been wholly buried in the said Andrew Dawson's grave.

Christine took possession of the whole room the

moment she entered it. Anne felt as if she were not in the picture at all.

But she sat up erectly. Christine should not see any middle-aged sag. She would go into battle with all flags flying. Her grey eyes turned exceedingly green and a faint flush coloured her oval cheek. *Remember you have a nose!* Dr Murray, who had not noticed her particularly before, thought in some surprise that Blythe had a very uncommon-looking wife. That posturing Mrs Dawson looked positively commonplace beside her.

'Why, Gilbert Blythe, you're as handsome as ever,' Christine was saying archly . . . Christine *arch!* . . . 'It's so nice to find you haven't changed.'

(*She talks with the same old drawl. How I always hated that velvet voice of hers!*)

'When I look at you,' said Gilbert, 'time ceases to have any meaning at all. Where did you learn the secret of immortal youth?'

Christine laughed.

(*Isn't her laughter a little tinny?*)

'You could always pay a pretty compliment, Gilbert. You know' . . . with an arch glance around the circle . . . 'Dr Blythe was an old flame of mine in those days he is pretending to think were of yesterday. And Anne Shirley! You haven't changed as much as I've been told . . . though I don't think I'd have known you if we'd just happened to meet on the street. Your hair is a *little* darker than it used to be, isn't it? Isn't it *divine* to meet again like this? I was so afraid your lumbago wouldn't let you come.'

'*My* lumbago!'

'Why, yes, aren't you subject to it? I thought you were . . .'

'I must have got things twisted,' said Mrs Fowler apologetically. 'Somebody told me you were down with a very severe attack of lumbago . . .'

'That is Mrs Dr Parker of Lowbridge. I have never had lumbago in my life,' said Anne in a flat voice.

'How very nice that you haven't got it,' said Christine, with something faintly insolent in her tone. 'It's *such* a wretched thing. I have an aunt who is a perfect martyr to it.'

Her air seemed to relegate Anne to the generation of aunts. Anne managed a smile with her lips, not her eyes. If she could only think of something clever to say! She knew that at three o'clock that night she would probably think of a brilliant retort she might have made, but that did not help now.

'They tell me you have seven children,' said Christine, speaking to Anne but looking at Gilbert.

'Only six living,' said Anne, wincing. Even yet she could never think of little white Joyce without pain.

'*What* a family!' said Christine.

Instantly it seemed a disgraceful and absurd thing to have a large family.

'You, I think, have none,' said Anne.

'I never cared for children, you know.' Christine shrugged her remarkably fine shoulders, but her voice was a little hard. 'I'm afraid I'm not the maternal type. I really never thought that it was woman's sole mission to bring children into an already overcrowded world.'

They went in to dinner then. Gilbert took Christine, Dr Murray took Mrs Fowler, and Dr Fowler, a rotund little man, who could not talk to anybody except another doctor, took Anne.

Anne felt that the room was rather stifling. There was a mysterious sickly scent in it. Probably Mrs Fowler had been burning incense. The menu was good and Anne went through the motions of eating without any appetite and smiled until she felt she was beginning to look like a Cheshire cat. She could not keep her eyes off Christine, who was smiling at Gilbert continuously. Her teeth were beautiful . . . almost too beautiful. They looked like a toothpaste advertisement. Christine made very effective play with her hands as she talked. She had lovely hands . . . rather large, though.

She was talking to Gilbert about rhythmic speeds for living. What on earth did she mean? Did she know herself?

Then they switched to the Passion Play.

'Have you ever been to Oberammegau?' Christine asked Anne.

When she knew perfectly well Anne hadn't! Why did

the simplest question sound insolent when Christine asked it?

'Of course a family ties you down terribly,' said Christine. 'Oh, whom do you think I saw last month when I was in Kingsport? That little friend of yours . . . the one who married the ugly minister . . . what *was* her name?'

'Jonas Blake,' said Anne. 'Philippa Gordon married him. And I never thought he was ugly.'

'*Didn't* you? Of course, tastes differ. Well, anyway, I met them. *Poor* Philippa!'

Christine's use of 'poor' was very effective.

'Why poor?' asked Anne. 'I think she and Jonas have been very happy.'

'Happy! My dear, if you could see the place they live in! A wretched little fishing village where it was an excitement if the pigs broke into the garden! I was told that the Jonas-man had had a good church in Kingsport, and had given it up because he thought it his "duty" to go to the fishermen who "needed" him. I have no use for such fanatics. "How can you live in such an isolated, out-of-the-way place as this?" I asked Philippa. Do you know what she said?'

Christine threw out her beringed hands expressively.

'Perhaps what I would say of Glen St Mary,' said Anne. 'That it was the only place in the world to live in.'

'Fancy you being contented there,' smiled Christine. (*That terrible mouthful of teeth!*) 'Do you really never feel that you want a broader life? You used to be quite ambitious, if I remember aright. Didn't you write some rather clever little things when you were at Redmond? A bit fantastic and whimsical, of course, but still . . .'

'I wrote them for the people who still believe in fairyland. There is a surprising lot of them, you know, and they like to get news from that country.'

'And you've quite given it up?'

'Not altogether . . . but I'm writing living epistles now,' said Anne, thinking of Jem and Co.

Christine stared, not recognizing the quotation. What did Anne Shirley mean? But then, of course, she had been noted at Redmond for her mysterious speeches. She had kept her looks astonishingly, but probably she was one of those women who got married and stopped thinking. Poor Gilbert! She had hooked him before he came to Redmond. He had never had the least chance to escape her.

'Does anybody ever eat philopenas now?' asked Dr Murray, who had just cracked a twin almond. Christine turned to Gilbert.

'Do you remember that philopena *we* ate once?' she asked.

(*Did a significant look pass between them?*)

'Do you suppose I could forget it?' asked Gilbert.

They plunged into a spate of 'do-you-remembers', while Anne stared at the picture of fish and oranges hanging over the sideboard. She had never thought Gilbert and

Christine had had so many memories in common. Do you remember our picnic up the Arm? . . . do you remember the night we went to the negro church? . . . do you remember the night we went to the masquerade? . . . you were a Spanish lady in a black velvet dress, with a lace mantilla and fan.

Gilbert apparently remembered them all in detail. But he had forgotten his wedding anniversary!

When they went back to the drawing room Christine glanced out of the window at an eastern sky that was showing pale silver behind the dark poplars.

'Gilbert, let us take a stroll in the garden, I want to learn again the meaning of moonrise in September.'

(*Does moonrise mean anything in September that it doesn't mean in any other month? And what does she mean by 'again'. Did she ever learn it before . . . with him?*)

Out they went. Anne felt that she had been very neatly and sweetly brushed aside. She sat down on a chair that commanded a view of the garden . . . though she would not admit even to herself that she selected it for that reason. She could see Christine and Gilbert walking down the path. What were they saying to each other? Christine seemed to be doing most of the talking. Perhaps Gilbert was too dumb with emotion to speak. Was he smiling out there in the moonrise over memories in which she had no share? She recalled nights she and Gilbert had walked in moonlit gardens of Avonlea. Had *he* forgotten?

Christine was looking up at the sky. Of course she knew she was showing off that fine, full white throat of hers when she lifted her face like that. Did ever a moon take so long in rising?

Other guests were dropping in when they finally came back. There was talk, laughter, music. Christine sang . . . very well. She had always been 'musical' – She sang *at* Gilbert . . . 'the dear, dead days beyond recall'. Gilbert leaned back in an easy-chair and was uncommonly silent. Was he looking back wistfully to those dear, dead days? Was he picturing what his life would have been if he had married Christine? (*I've always known what Gilbert was thinking of before. If we don't get away soon I'll be throwing up my head and howling. Thank heaven our train leaves early.*)

When Anne came downstairs Christine was standing in the porch with Gilbert. She reached up and picked a leaf from his shoulder; the gesture was like a caress.

'Are you really well, Gilbert? You look frightfully tired. I *know* you're overdoing it.'

A wave of horror swept over Anne. Gilbert *did* look tired, frightfully tired . . . and she hadn't seen it until Christine pointed it out! Never would she forget the humiliation of that moment. (*I've been taking Gilbert too much for granted and blaming him for doing the same thing.*)

Christine turned to her.

'It's been so nice to meet you again, Anne. Quite like old times.'

'Quite,' said Anne.

'But I've just been telling Gilbert he looked a little tired. You ought to take better care of him, Anne. There was a time, you know, when I really had quite a fancy for this husband of yours. I believe he really was the nicest beau I ever had. But you must forgive me, since I didn't take him from you.'

Anne froze up again.

'Perhaps he is pitying himself that you didn't,' she said, with a certain 'queenishness' not unknown to Christine in Redmond days, as she stepped into Dr Fowler's carriage for the drive to the station.

'You dear, funny thing!' said Christine, with a shrug of beautiful shoulders. She was looking after them as if something amused her hugely.

43

'Had a nice evening?' asked Gilbert, more absently than ever as he helped her on the train.

'Oh, lovely,' said Anne . . . who felt that she had, in Jane Welsh Carlyle's splendid phrase, 'spent the evening under a harrow'.

'What made you do your hair that way?' said Gilbert, still absently.

'It's the new fashion.'

'Well, it doesn't suit you. It may be all right for some hair, but not for yours.'

'Oh, it is too bad my hair is red,' said Anne icily.

Gilbert thought he was wise in dropping a dangerous subject. Anne, he reflected, had always been a bit sensitive about her hair. He was too tired to talk, anyway. He leaned his head back on the car seat and shut his eyes. For the first time Anne noticed little glints of grey in the hair above his ears. But she hardened her heart.

They walked silently home from the Glen Station by the short cut to Ingleside. The air was filled with the breath of spruce and spice fern. The moon was shining over dew-wet fields. They passed an old, deserted house with sad, broken windows that had once danced with light. 'Just like my life,' thought Anne. Everything seemed to have for her some dreary meaning now. The dim white moth that fluttered past them on the lawn was, she thought sadly, like a ghost of faded love. Then she caught her foot in a croquet hoop and nearly fell headlong into a clump of phlox. What on earth did the children mean by leaving it there? She would tell them what she thought about it tomorrow!

Gilbert only said 'O-o-o-ps!' and steadied her with a hand. Would he have been so casual about it if it had been Christine who had tripped while they were puzzling out the meaning of moonrises?

Gilbert rushed off to his study the moment they were inside the house, and Anne went silently up to their room, where the moonlight was lying on the floor, still and silver and cold. She went to the open window and looked out. It was evidently the Carter Flaggs' dog's night to howl and he was putting his heart into it. The Lombardy leaves glistened like silver in the moonlight. The house about her seemed whispering tonight . . . whispering sinisterly, as if it were no longer her friend.

Anne felt sick and cold and empty. The gold of life had turned to withered leaves. Nothing had any meaning any longer. Everything seemed remote and unreal.

Far down the tide was keeping its world-old tryst with

the shore. She could . . . now that Norman Douglas had cut down his spruce bush . . . see her little House of Dreams. How happy they had been there, when it was enough just to be together in their own home, with their visions, their caresses, their silences! All the colour of the morning in their lives . . . Gilbert looking at her with that smile in his eyes he kept for her alone, finding every day a new way of saying 'I love you', sharing laughter as they shared sorrow.

And now . . . Gilbert had grown tired of her. Men had always been like that . . . always would be. She had thought Gilbert was an exception, but now she knew the truth. And how was she going to adjust her life to it? 'There are the children, of course,' she thought dully. 'I must go on living for them. And nobody must know . . . *nobody*. I will not be pitied.'

What was that? Somebody was coming up the stairs, three steps at a time, as Gilbert used to do long ago in the House of Dreams . . . as he had not done for a long time now. It couldn't be Gilbert . . . it was!

He burst into the room . . . he flung a little packet on the table . . . he caught Anne by the waist and waltzed her round and round the room like a crazy schoolboy, coming to rest at last breathlessly in a silver pool of moonlight.

'I was right, Anne . . . thank God I was right. Mrs Garrow is going to be all right . . . the specialist has said so.'

'Mrs Garrow? Gilbert, have you gone crazy?'

'Didn't I tell you? Surely I told you . . . well, I suppose

it's been such a sore subject I just couldn't talk of it. I've been worried to death about it for the past two weeks, couldn't think of anything else, waking or sleeping. Mrs Garrow lives in Lowbridge and was Parker's patient. He asked me in for a consultation . . . I diagnosed her case differently from him . . . we almost fought . . . I was sure I was right . . . I insisted there was a chance . . . we sent her to Montreal. Parker said she'd never come back alive, her husband was ready to shoot me on sight. When she was gone I went to bits . . . perhaps I *was* mistaken . . . perhaps I'd tortured her needlessly. I found the letter in my office when I went in . . . I was *right* . . . they've operated . . . she has an excellent chance of living. Anne-girl, I could jump over the moon! I've shed twenty years.'

Anne had either to laugh or cry . . . so she began to laugh. It was lovely to be able to laugh again, lovely to feel like laughing. Everything was suddenly all right.

'I suppose that is why you forgot this was our anniversary?' she taunted him.

Gilbert released her long enough to pounce on the little packet he had dropped on the table.

'I didn't forget it. Two weeks ago I sent to Toronto for this. And it didn't come till tonight. I felt so small this morning when I hadn't a thing to give you that I didn't mention the day . . . thought you'd forgotten it too . . . hoped you had. When I went into the office there was my present, along with Parker's letter. See how you like it.'

It was a little diamond pendant. Even in the moonlight it sparkled like a living thing.

'Gilbert . . . and I . . .'

'Try it on. I wish it had come this morning . . . then you'd have had something to wear to the dinner besides that old enamel heart. Though it *did* look rather nice snuggling in that pretty white hollow in your throat, darling. Why didn't you leave on that green dress, Anne? I liked it . . . it reminded me of that dress with the rosebuds on it you used to wear at Redmond.'

(*So he had noticed the dress! So he still remembered the old Redmond one he had admired so much!*)

Anne felt like a released bird . . . she was flying again. Gilbert's arms were around her . . . his eyes were looking into hers in the moonlight. 'You *do* love me, Gilbert? I'm not just a habit with you? You haven't *said* you loved me for so long.'

'My dear, dear love! I didn't think you needed words to know that. I couldn't live without you. Always you give me strength. There's a verse somewhere in the Bible that is meant for you . . . "She will do him good and not evil all the days of her life."'

Life which had seemed so grey and foolish a few moments before was golden and rose and splendidly rainbowed again. The diamond pendant slipped to the floor, unheeded for the moment. It was beautiful . . . but there were so many things lovelier . . . confidence and peace and delightful work . . . laughter and kindliness . . . that old, *safe* feeling of a sure love. 'Oh, if we could keep this moment for ever, Gilbert!'

'We're going to have some moments. It's time we had a second honeymoon. Anne, there's going to be a big medical congress in London next February. We're going to it . . . and after it we'll see a bit of the Old World. There's a holiday coming to us. We'll be nothing but lovers again . . . it will be just like being married over again. You haven't been like yourself for a long time.' (*So he had noticed.*) 'You're tired and overworked . . . you need a change.' (*You, too, dearest. I've been so horribly blind.*) 'I'm not going to have it cast up to me that doctors' wives never get a pill. We'll come back rested and fresh, with our sense of humour completely restored. Well, try your pendant on and let's get to bed. I'm half dead for sleep . . . haven't had a decent night's sleep for weeks what with twins and worry over Mrs Garrow.'

'What on earth were you and Christine talking about so long in the garden tonight?' asked Anne, peacocking before the mirror with her diamonds.

Gilbert yawned.

'Oh, I don't know, Christine just gabbled on. But here is one fact she presented me with. A flea can jump two hundred times its own length. Did you know that, Anne?'

(*They were talking of fleas when I was writhing with jealousy. What an idiot I've been!*)

'How on earth did you come to be talking of fleas?'

'I can't remember . . . perhaps it was Dobermann pinschers suggested it.'

'Dobermann pinschers! *What* are Dobermann pinschers?'

'A new kind of dog. Christine seems to be a dog connoisseur. I was so obsessed with Mrs Garrow that I didn't pay much attention to what she was saying. Now and then I caught a word about complexes and repressions . . . that new psychology that's coming up . . . and art . . . and gout and politics and frogs.'

'Frogs!'

'Some experiments a Winnipeg research man is making. Christine was never very entertaining, but she's a worse bore than ever. And malicious! She never used to be malicious.'

'What did she say that was so malicious?' asked Anne innocently.

'Didn't you notice? Oh, I suppose you wouldn't catch on . . . you're so free from that sort of thing yourself. Well, it doesn't matter. That laugh of hers got on my nerves a bit. And she's got fat. Thank goodness you haven't got fat, Anne-girl.'

'Oh, I don't think she is so very fat,' said Anne charitably. 'And she certainly is a very handsome woman.'

'So-so. But her face has got hard . . . she's the same age as you, but she looks ten years older.'

'And you talking to her about immortal youth!'

Gilbert grinned guiltily.

'One has to say something civil. Civilization can't exist

without a little hypocrisy. Oh, well, Christine isn't a bad old scout, even if she doesn't belong to the race of Joseph. It's not her fault that the pinch of salt was left out of her. What's this?'

'My anniversary remembrance for you. And I want a cent for it . . . I'm not taking any risks. Such tortures as I've endured this evening! I was eaten up with jealousy of Christine.'

Gilbert looked genuinely astonished. It had never occurred to him that Anne could be jealous of anybody.

'Why, Anne-girl, I never thought you had it in you.'

'Oh, but I have! Why, years ago I was madly jealous of your correspondence with Ruby Gillis.'

'*Did* I ever correspond with Ruby Gillis? I'd forgotten. Poor Ruby! But what about Roy Gardner? The pot mustn't call the kettle black.'

'Roy Gardner? Philippa wrote me not long ago that she'd seen him and he'd got positively corpulent. Gilbert, Dr Murray may be a very eminent man in his profession, but he looks just like a lath. Dr Fowler looked like a doughnut. You looked so handsome . . . and *finished* . . . beside them.'

'Oh, thanks . . . thanks. That's something like a wife should say. By way of returning the compliment, I thought you looked unusually well tonight, Annie, in spite of that dress. You had a little colour and your eyes were gorgeous. Ah-h-h, that's good! There's another verse in the Bible . . .

queer how those old verses you learn in Sunday School come back to you through life! . . . "I will lay me down in peace and sleep." In peace . . . and sleep . . . goo'-night.'

Gilbert was asleep almost before he finished the word. Dearest, tired Gilbert! Babies might come and babies might go, but none should disturb his rest that night. The telephone might ring its head off.

Anne was not sleepy. She was too happy to sleep just yet. She moved softly about the room, putting things away, braiding her hair, looking like a beloved woman. Finally she slipped on a *negligee* and went across the hall to the boys' room. Walter and Jem in their bed and Shirley in his cot were all sound asleep. The Shrimp, who had outlived generations of pert kittens and become a family habit, was curled up at Shirley's feet. Jem had fallen asleep while reading *The Life Book of Captain Jim* . . . it was open on the spread. Why, how *long* Jem looked lying under the bedclothes! He would soon be grown up. What a sturdy, reliable little chap he was! Walter was smiling in his sleep as someone who knew a charming secret. The moon was shining on his pillow through the bars of the leaded window . . . casting the shadow of a clearly defined cross on the wall above his head. In long after-years Anne was to remember that and wonder if it was an omen of Courcelette . . . of a cross-marked grave 'somewhere in France'. But tonight it was only a shadow . . . nothing more. The rash had quite gone from Shirley's neck. Gilbert had been right. He was always right.

Nan and Diana and Rilla were in the next room . . . Diana, with darling little damp red curls all over her head and one little sunburned hand under her cheek, and Nan with long fans of lashes brushing hers. The eyes behind those blue-veined lids were hazel, like her father's. And Rilla was sleeping on her stomach. Anne turned her right side up, but her buttoned eyes never opened.

They were all growing so fast. In just a few short years they would be all young men and women . . . youth tip-toe . . . expectant . . . astir with its sweet, wild dreams . . . little ships sailing out of safe harbour to unknown parts. The boys would go away to their life work, and the girls . . . ah, the mist-veiled forms of beautiful brides might be seen coming down the old stairs at Ingleside. But they would be still hers for a few years yet . . . hers to love and guide . . . to sing the songs that so many mothers had sung. Hers . . . and Gilbert's.

She went out and down the hall to the oriel window. All her suspicions and jealousies and resentments had gone where old moons go. She felt confident and gay and blithe.

'Blythe! I feel Blythe,' she said, laughing at the foolish little pun. 'I feel exactly as I did that morning Pacifique told me Gilbert had "got de turn".'

Below her was the mystery and loveliness of a garden at night. The faraway hills, dusted with moonlight, were a poem. Before many months she would be seeing moonlight on the far dim hills of Scotland . . . over Melrose . . . over ruined Kenilworth . . . over the church by the Avon where Shakespeare slept . . . perhaps even over the Colosseum . . . over the Acropolis . . . over sorrowful rivers flowing by dead empires.

The night was cool; soon the sharper, cooler nights of autumn would come; then the deep snow . . . the deep white snow . . . the deep cold snow of winter . . . nights wild with wind and storm. But who would care? There would be the magic of firelight in gracious rooms . . . hadn't Gilbert spoken not long ago of apple logs he was getting to burn in the fireplace? They would glorify the grey days that were bound to come. What would matter drifted snow and biting wind, when love burned clear and bright, with spring beyond? And all the little sweetnesses of life sprinkling the road.

She turned away from the window. In her white gown, with her hair in its two long braids, she looked like the Anne of Green Gables days . . . of Redmond days . . . of the House of Dreams days. That inward glow was still shining through her. Through the open doorway came the soft sound of children breathing. Gilbert, who seldom snored, was indubitably snoring now. Anne grinned. She thought of something Christine had said. Poor childless Christine, shooting her little arrows of mockery.

'What a family!' Anne repeated exultantly.

PUFFIN CLASSICS

Anne of Ingleside

With Puffin Classics, the adventure isn't
over when you reach the final page.
Want to discover more about your favourite
characters, their creators and their worlds?
Read on . . .

CONTENTS

NAME: Lucy Maud Montgomery, known by family and friends as Maud

BORN: 30 November 1874 in Clifton (now New London), Prince Edward Island, Canada

DIED: 24 April 1942 in Toronto, buried in Cavendish, Prince Edward Island

NATIONALITY: Canadian

LIVED: Halifax in Nova Scotia, Cavendish on Prince Edward Island and Leaskdale, Ontario

MARRIED: to the Reverend Ewan Macdonald

CHILDREN: three sons: Chester Cameron, Hugh Alexander (who died at birth) and Ewan Stuart

What was she like?

Lucy Maud Montgomery lived life to the full, travelled and defied many of the conventions laid down for women in that era. At the same time, she held strong, traditional, religious beliefs, was a devoted mother and home-keeper, and always returned to her family and her place of birth. All her experiences influenced her writing, but it was the years she spent on the beautiful Prince Edward Island that inspired her stories of the lovable, red-headed orphan, Anne Shirley.

Where did she grow up?

Maud – as she liked to be called – was born on Prince Edward Island. Her mother died when she was less than two years old, so she lived with her grandparents in their farmhouse in Cavendish, amongst a rural, close-knit community of farmers and fishermen. As much of her childhood was spent with elderly people, she often entertained herself by reading and using her imagination.

What did she do apart from writing books?

Writing was always a huge part of Maud's life. Apart from writing books, she kept journals and scrapbooks – where she often recorded ideas for her stories – and wrote for newspapers and magazines. She was also a keen photographer, creating her own darkroom and experimenting with special effects.

When she finished school, Maud went to college to train to be a teacher, then on to university, where she studied English Literature. This was very unusual at a time when few women received higher education. She put both her degrees to good use, working as a teacher and a newspaper reporter for several years.

Where did Maud get the idea for Anne of Green Gables?

She was inspired by her surroundings on Prince Edward Island, and by the friendly community in which she lived. Maud also drew from her own character when she was writing. In many ways, she and Anne are very similar, in their love of writing and nature, their years at college, and their time working as teachers.

What did people think of Anne of Green Gables when it was first published?

The book didn't get off to a very good start! It was rejected by four publishers and Maud packed it away in a hatbox for a year, in frustration. It was finally published in 1908 and was an immediate success. Maud received hundreds of fan letters, including one from Mark Twain, who called the book 'the sweetest creation of child life yet written'. *Anne of Green Gables* has now been serialized on television and made into a film, and is still a massive favourite worldwide.

What other books did she write?

L. M. Montgomery had around 500 short stories and poems, and twenty novels published. Nineteen of her novels are set on Prince Edward Island and six of them feature Anne as the main character. You can read more about her adventures in *Anne of Avonlea*, *Anne of the Island*, *Anne of Windy Willows*, *Anne's House of Dreams* and *Anne of Ingleside*. Although Anne is her most famous and best-loved character, Maud always said that Emily Starr, who first appears in *Emily of New Moon*, was her personal favourite.

Main Characters

Anne Blythe – Anne is married to her childhood sweetheart, Gilbert Blythe. At the start of the story she has five children and is about to give birth to a sixth child. Ingleside is a very happy home, and Anne is a gentle, caring mother. She is still full of laughter and romantic notions, but one day she begins to worry that Gilbert may not love her any more.

Dr Gilbert Blythe – Anne's husband. Gilbert is now a much respected doctor and in great demand. He is often called away to see to his many patients, but always tries to make time to be at home with his family.

Aunt Mary Maria – Gilbert's interfering elderly aunt who comes to stay at Ingleside and outstays her welcome. Aunt Mary Maria is highly critical of Anne and her children, and constantly complains about the housekeeper, Susan Baker.

Susan Baker – the Blythes' cook and housekeeper, Susan has been with the Blythes for many years. She loves the children dearly, especially Shirley, whom she cared for when he was first born.

Cornelia Bryant – Anne and Gilbert's neighbour and a dear old friend of Anne's. Cornelia always has the latest gossip.

Rebecca Dew – the housekeeper and cook from Windy Willows

who comes to visit Anne. Rebecca and Susan become 'kindred spirits', united in their dislike of Aunt Mary Maria.

THE BLYTHE CHILDREN
(and their age at the start of the story)

Jem (James), seven years old – the eldest, Jem is an easy-going boy who gets himself into all sorts of adventures. His best friend is Bertie Shakespeare Drew.

Walter, six years old – Anne and Gilbert's second son is the quiet one, with dark hair and dark eyes. He is a highly imaginative child, likes reading and writing, and is teased by the local children for being a bit of a 'sissy'.

Nan (Anne Meredith) and Di (Diana), four-year-old non-identical twins – Nan has inherited her father's dark looks and her mother's vivid imagination and naivety, whereas Di resembles her mother with her bright red hair but is more practical by nature like her father.

Shirley, two years old – the youngest boy in the family.

Bertha Marilla (Rilla) – Anne and Gilbert's chubby, gold-haired new baby daughter.

Who is your favourite Blythe child and why?

If you had the chance to play any of the characters in *Anne of Ingleside*, who would it be?

Who do you think changes most during *Anne of Ingleside*? How and why?

What do you think of the story of *Anne of Ingleside* compared to the rest of the books in the series?

Here are some quotes from *Anne of Ingleside*. Can you work out who said them?

1. *'Mother dearwums, I don't know how I lived before Gyp came. He can talk, Mother . . . he can really . . . with his eyes, you know.'*

2. *'I'm in the habit of believing people . . .'*

3. *'The garden has never been so beautiful as it has been this summer . . . but then I say that every autumn, don't I?'*

4. *'My doll hath been tooken ill . . . I mutht put her to bed and thtay with her. Maybe itth ammonia.'*

5. 'My dear dear love! I didn't think you needed words to know that. I couldn't live without you. Always you give me strength.'

The Green Gables stories are based around real places on Prince Edward Island, Canada, and the island has become a popular destination for Green Gables fans from all over the world. Research some interesting facts about Prince Edward Island to find out more about where the author (and Anne Shirley) lived.

Anne's favourite time of year is spring. What is your favourite time of year? Describe your neighbourhood in springtime.

How would you portray a modern adaptation of *Anne of Ingleside*?

* What would your costumes and sets look like?

* How would you go about turning the novel into a film script?

* Who would you cast as the main characters?

Why not include your friends in this task and put on a performance of the book, setting it in modern times?

In *Anne of Ingleside* little Rilla mistakenly believes that it is shameful to be seen carrying a cake, so instead of taking housekeeper Susan's lovely 'gold-and-silver' cake to the church social evening as she'd been told, she hastily tosses it into the brook before anyone sees her with it. But when she sees her beloved Sunday-school teacher carrying a cake, Rilla soon realizes that she's made a dreadful mistake . . . !

Try baking your own 'gold-and-silver' cake – only when you've made it, please don't throw it away!

This recipe has two mixtures that, when combined together in the cake tin, will produce a pretty gold and silver marbled sponge.

Ask an adult to help you with this recipe.

You will need
A 20cm round cake tin, 3 large mixing bowls, an electric mixer (or a wooden spoon if mixing by hand) and baking parchment.

Firstly, set the oven to 350°F /180°C, then grease and line the cake tin with the baking parchment.

Ingredients for the 'gold' mixture
90g butter
80g caster sugar
3 tablespoons warm water

3 egg yolks, lightly beaten
100g plain flour
1½ level teaspoons baking powder
2 tablespoons ground almonds
A few drops almond essence

INGREDIENTS FOR THE 'SILVER' MIXTURE
90g butter
80g caster sugar
1½ tablespoons warm water
3 egg whites
100g plain flour
¾ teaspoon baking powder
2 tablespoons ground almonds
A few drops almond essence

METHOD:
- *For the gold mixture*, using an electric mixer (or by hand with a wooden spoon), beat together the butter and *half* the sugar, then gradually beat in the rest of the sugar, and the warm water, until the mixture is pale and fluffy.
- Beat in the egg yolks. Sift the flour and baking powder together, and fold gently into the mixture. Then fold in the ground almonds and almond essence.
- Put spoonfuls of the mixture into the base of the prepared cake tin, leaving space in between each blob.
- *For the silver mixture*, beat the butter until it's soft. Gradually beat in the sugar and warm water until the mixture is pale and fluffy.

- Fold in the ground almonds and almond essence.
- In a separate bowl, whip the egg whites until they form soft peaks (not too stiff).
- Sift the flour with the baking powder and then fold the beaten egg whites and flour into the mixture alternately a spoonful at a time.
- Add spoonfuls of gold cake mixture between the spoonfuls of the silver mixture in the cake tin.
- Bake the cake in the middle of the preheated oven for 50 minutes or until the top of the cake is firm but springy when you press it gently. Leave the cake to cool in the tin and then then carefully turn it out on to a wire rack.
- When it is cold, dust the top of the cake with sifted icing sugar.
- Eat and enjoy!

GLOSSARY

asphodel – a plant belonging to the lily family

crimpers – waves or curls, especially in hair that has been crimped using curling tongs

demesnes – land, surrounding a house or manor, retained by the owner for his own use

disdained – looked down upon or treated with contempt

dory – a boat with a narrow, flat bottom, high bow, stern and sides

fantasia – a musical composition made up of all different styles

vagaries – erratic or outlandish ideas or actions; whims